I0716289

OPPORTUNITY FOR EVIL

D. H. COOP

ISBN 978-1-957943-35-0 (paperback)
ISBN 979-8-9913102-0-8 (digital)

Copyright © 2024 by D. H. Coop

All rights reserved. No part of this publication may be reproduced, distributed, or transmitted in any form or by any means, including photocopying, recording, or other electronic or mechanical methods without the prior written permission of the publisher.

Printed in the United States of America

THE PENNY BLACK

Messages have been sent by mail since the Mesopotamian empires used a system of mail more than 9,500 years ago for communications of records, taxes, and issuing decrees. These methods were always subject to abuse, so various methods were devised to ensure and protect the contents of the communication. The oldest surviving piece of mail is a piece of papyrus that was discovered in a papyri waste dump from the Egyptian empire around 255 BCE. By the time of the Chinese Han Dynasty and the Roman Empire, the Silk Road commercial traders communicated between the East and the West worlds. As the powers of Europe began to expand their political and economic influence, securing the mail became more important.

King Henry VIII appointed the first "Master of Post" in 1516 to expedite his official mail. At the same time officials and ordinary citizens were encouraged to use this mail system at a cost. The city of London had a 'Penny Post' that allowed a letter to be mailed within the city for one penny; however, outside the city, the mail was expensive and erratic.

A British educator named Rowland Hill proposed a method of sending mail at a set standard rate in 1837. He proposed a postage system that would be paid for by the sender buying what he called small "bits of paper with glutinous wash." This idea was accepted, and Queen Victoria issued the world's first postage stamp on May 6, 1840.

The Penny Black was the first adhesive postage stamp. It was issued for only one year because the black stamp made the canceled mark in red print difficult to read. Therefore, the stamp color was changed in 1841 to a red-brown color. The limited run of the early Penny Black stamps increased their value over time.

A single mint condition of the Penny Black stamp today can run close to eight million U.S. dollars or more. A consequence of the introduction of the Penny Black and the printing of government stamps opened a new area for Black Market forgeries in the marketplace as early as the 1860s. By then the first books were being printed on how to identify the counterfeit and forged stamps.

Stamp forgeries are copies of stamps and they may or may not have been created with the intent to defraud. Many forgeries were made as space fillers in collector's albums. However, with anything of value bad intentions will most likely follow.

On the other hand, counterfeit stamps are created with the intent to defraud the government or individuals. The forgeries and counterfeit stamps were so common that between 1850 and 1879 Spain had to issue a new stamp every year to stay ahead of the forgers.

Forgers not only counterfeited stamps they altered stamps to increase the value of the stamps. These stamps are called fakes, which are original stamps that have been altered to add value to collectors. Many of these stamp forgers were legitimate stamp dealers. One noteworthy forger was Jean de Sperati whose forgeries and fakes are often of a better quality than the original stamps.

Jean de Sperati was able to produce some 566 varieties of stamps from over 100 countries. He was able to flee Italy before being arrested by government officials and was able to continue his work in France under the existing laws at the time by selling his stamps as fakes. During World War II he smuggled stamps out of France into Spain and was arrested for exporting stamps for profit. He proved his innocence by producing five more sets to show he did not export real stamps. In many cases, his original fakes today sell at a higher price than the original stamps.

Another area of the stamp market is the production of propaganda stamps that fall into two categories — Cinderella and Black Propaganda stamps. Cinderella stamps only represent original stamps, and they are used for promotional purposes. The black propaganda stamps were named for their relationship with the Black Market and other negative connotations.

Many of these stamps have a high value and these bogus stamps have also had forgeries made of them.

During conflicts, governments have used stamps to disrupt and make fun of the other side.

PROPAGANDA AND CINDERELLA STAMPS

Above on the left is a postcard of Hitler and a young girl holding flowers that was later used in a stamp designed in 1940. In the center is an example of a 1940 German postal stamp issued that year. The stamp on the right is a propaganda stamp produced in Hollywood, California to portray a different meaning of a little girl spitting into the face of Hitler.

Both sides before and during the Second World War used stamps for propaganda purposes. The Germans printed stamps connecting the British to the Jews. Another connection of the Soviet Union with propaganda copies of the British Jubilee stamp of 1935 with King George V on a 1939 war stamp replaced with Stalin. Then the 1937 Coronation stamp of the King and Queen with the Queen's image was replaced with one of Stalin in 1943.

Not to be outdone the British produced a booklet of the German *Winter Relief Fund* stamps, as a parody of a German stamp in 1943.

The Americans entered the war with their propaganda operations. Operation Cornflakes produced a parody stamp of the German stamp *Deutsches Reich* (German Empire) with an image of Hitler's profile with the words *Futshes Reich* (Ruined Empire) and Hitler's face decaying.

Many of these Forgeries and propaganda stamps have real value today to collectors.

Another area of the value of stamps is in printing errors. These are stamps that have been printed incorrectly and have inadvertently been released to the public. The errors can range from the color, double impression, inverted centers, offset printing, wrong overprint, imperforated and watermarks.

INVERTED   **SHOULD**   **PERFORATION**
                   BE BLUE   **MISPLACED**

Overprints were used for several reasons from adding value to the stamp, to honor an individual, or to making stolen stamps harder to sell.

VALUE   **HONOR**   **LOCAL POST OFFICES WERE**
                                  TARGETED BY ROBBERS.
                                  OVERPRINTS LIMITED
                                  THE THIEVES' SELLING
                                  STOLEN STAMPS.

Many of the forgers in the past used the legal system to hide their illicit trade in various stamp frauds for many of their methods were acceptable at the time. The sentencing for the crime of forgery was light with many sentences being less than two years or the individual being given probation. The stamps shown here are identified as forgeries for simplicity. However, many were counterfeits to deceive the government and individual collectors.

The phrase "History is written by the victors" is often quoted. Many attribute this quote to Winston Churchill, Yet Robespierre made a similar statement during the French Revolution. Then Ken Hirsch said something similar in 1842 as did the ex-Confederate Senator of the American Civil War, George Graham Vest in 1891. Also, Hermann Goring at the Nuremberg trials is having said *"Der sieger wind immer der Richter und der*

Besiegte stete der Angeklagte sein" which translates into something like, "The victor will always be the judge and the vanquished the accused."

> *The part that always shocked me was the inter-community violence among the chimps: the patrols and the vicious attacks on strangers that led to death. It's an unfortunate parallel to human behavior - they have a dark side just as we do. We have fewer excuses because we can deliberate, so I believe only we are capable of true calculated evil.*
>
> — Jane Goodall

History is a collection of facts that are linked together by historians to be interpreted for a new generation with various interpretations. They take old facts and new facts and reinterpret them to answer new questions and provide answers for the next generation. History does not repeat itself, but each time evil is defeated it works its way back into life. Evil is Evil. The Holocaust was defeated only to be replaced by Balkanization and Ethnic Cleansing.

CONTENTS

Evil preaches tolerance until it is dominant then it tries to silence good.

— Archbishop Charles S. Chaput

CHAPTER ONE

Jean-Baptiste Phillipe Constant Moens began his career around 1868 in several philanthropic activities in the stamp world that would not be considered ethical today. In 1864 he published one of the first illustrated stamp catalogs that was used by other members of the stamp trade for their models of reproduction.

GENUINE

FORGERY

Despair is typical of those who do not understand the causes of evil, see no way out, and are incapable of struggle. The modern industrial proletariat does not belong to the category of such classes.

— Vladimir Lenin

1924 - In a locked boxcar on a train to a Siberian gulag

The train moved slowly along the cold countryside passing the recent scars of the civil war and famine. Many of the burned-out buildings had individuals living in them. Dogs could at times be seen eating the carcass of a dead horse or cow. The villages they passed through had women standing around in groups holding babies or walking along the tracks looking into the cattle cars as they passed by. It had been some two years, and the land still held the scars of the turmoil of war — communism ruthless Soviet policies.

The cattle cars were filled with men and women packed so tightly that it was difficult to sit down or get up. The passengers in the cars had no privacy and the dead remained until the soldiers unlocked the doors. The cold wind blew through the cracks in the walls of the car and the noise of the train and wind prevented the people from talking to each other except in whispers. Even these conversations were guarded for one did not know who could be trusted. The person next to you could be a Cheka informer, which was now named the GPU — the new Soviet name for the secret police. If one wanted to talk, the talking was done mouth to ear.

Alexei and Viktor were sitting up against the wall of the car in a corner. Both still wore their Red Guard uniforms Bogatyrkas without any identification marking. The soft wool hats that peeked at the top with earflaps to cover the ears and a strap under their chins were all they had left of their belongings. They had both been arrested on the street and taken right to the train station. Alexie was born in 1910 and Viktor in 1911. They both had joined the Red Army as children and over time became low-level leaders in the Bolshevik party. Now they were being transported to a labor camp.

"Alexei, what are you thinking?" asked Viktor into his ear.

"Viktor, do you know why we were arrested, stripped of our rank, weapons, and placed on this train?" replied Alexei.

"Yes, of course, it is a mistake. Our friends will wonder where we are and soon correct this big mistake," said Viktor.

"You are wrong, my friend! We are here for one reason and that reason is because it is the will and plan of Comrade Stalin!" said Alexei as he looked around to see if anyone was listening or watching.

"What about him? He is a nobody of power in the party!" said Viktor.

"Yet, that is the reason we are being removed from view. Stalin is clever and more ruthless than Lenin ever was if that is even possible. He has learned important lessons from Lenin, and he is following Lenin's methods and policies in his ruthless effort to expand and remove all opposition to his leadership," said Alexei.

"Then, why us? We are not important!" asked Viktor.

"Simple, how long have you been working with Comrade Trotsky?" asked Alexei.

"Ever since he took command of the Red Army and went on to defeat the Whites and Green Thugs with their Western capitalist allied armies," said Viktor.

"You worked around Trotsky. What does he think about Stalin?" asked Alexei.

"He thinks Stalin is a small, corrupt and brutal individual with no real brains. That is why the other members of the Politburo allowed Stalin to hold the office of General Secretary in the Party with no real power. That is the last position anyone in authority would want. It has no authority over anything but the Party membership," said Viktor.

"There, that is my point! He has built a power base in the party. More than any of the other leaders and they do not see it. He controls who is in the party and what place they hold in the Party. He is placing his people in select positions within the Party. He is moving his supporters around like pieces on a chessboard building a loyal following. At the same time, he is playing the others against each other. Do you remember who he joined forces with to keep comrade Trotsky from succeeding to leadership after Lenin's second stroke?" asked Alexei.

"Yes, yes! Comrades Kamenev, Zinoviev, and Stalin voted together. They used comrade Trotsky's absence from the funeral of Lenin to push him to the back of the party leadership. I also know that comrade Stalin sent a message to comrade Trotsky that he should not rush back to Moscow when Lenin died," said Viktor.

"What does that tell you about Stalin, Viktor?"

"I don't understand?"

"Stalin is playing chess with us as the chess pieces, and he is twenty moves ahead of other leaders and they do not realize what is being done. You and I are being sent out of the way so that Comrade Trotsky will be isolated without any real support when his time comes to go. Comrade Stalin is already siding up with comrades Bukharin, Rykov, and Tomsky. Soon the Left in the Party will be removed from office. Then Stalin will turn and remove those against him on the Right. Comrade Trotsky will be isolated without any support in the Party. Comrade Stalin will become the sole power in the Soviet Union and there will be no more real opposition," said Alexei.

"You're saying everyone has comrade Stalin figured all wrong?" said Viktor.

"Yes! He is working behind everyone in plain sight within the Party and building his power by appointing his people to important positions. In no time, he will be in total control. You and I have not been the first to go and we will be a far cry from the last individuals that comrade Stalin removed from the playing board. I am done using the term comrade and the Party. So, when we get to the camp, we need to work together to stay alive," said Alexei.

"What? How can we do that? I have never been to one of these new Soviet work camps. They're filled with socially undesirables, criminals, and counterrevolutionaries," said Viktor.

"Well, I have been to many, and they are as dangerous inside the camps as they are on the outside. When I worked with both comrades Andrei Rykov in the Sovnarkom (Committee of Commissars) and Mikhail Tomsky in the trade unions, I was assigned as a member of a Troika group and the three of us would decide the fate of individuals on the spot. We sent many off to the camp for almost any reason to protect the revolution and the Party. Many of these individuals had no idea why they were questioned. Many I believe were on the list for no reason, other than someone did not like them or wanted revenge.

"Later, I was posted to establish a new camp. Many of the camps were just the camps the Tsar had established for exiled citizens. The revolution needed more camps. New camps were built by the inmates with only their hands and a few tools. Many died from the cold or hunger. The hunger took most of them in the first six months. Those who survived took the clothes of the dead to stay warm. That is what you and I are going into my friend, and we will need friends in the camp.

"There are three groups in the camps. First, there are the opposition Socialist Party members that are called 'politicos', you know, what we call fallen socialists. They are treated a little better than the others by the guards. The second group is the group that is the common everyday social screw-ups that are sent to the camps for anything identified as anti-Soviet behavior. Finally, there are the Thieves-in-Laws, and they are professional criminals (urki).

"The Thieves-in-laws have their hierarchy and they have only one rule – No Thieve is to work with the State apparatus. That rule is enforced with a sentence of death. We need to build a relationship with all the groups and become a valuable connection between the groups. The number one group inside the camp is the Thieves and they run everything inside the camps and have influence outside the camp," said Alexei.

"What about the guards?" asked Viktor.

"They stay outside the wire for the most part for their protection and most, if not all, will take brides. We need to become the go-between the guard, Thieves, and fallen Party members. Then maybe we will be able to stay alive until something happens to get us out of this mess that Stalin has tossed us into," said Alexei.

"How long will that take?" asked Viktor.

"Viktor, we are young, and I think we are going to be here for a while. It took Stalin three to five years to gain complete total control over the Party. By then all the current leadership will be eliminated or under Stalin's control."

"Trotsky will not let that happen. He has the support of the Red Army!" said Viktor.

"Viktor, the Red Army is controlled by the Party and Stalin controls the Party. Every unit in the Red Army has a political commissar. As I said, Stalin learned from Lenin how to control the party and its people. He is using Lenin's method of the purge now with us being removed."

"I do not understand?"

"Remember Lenin purged the Party every once in a while, to remove selected individuals slowly over time. Stalin is removing anyone who has a link to the opposition to him. Besides we both know Trotsky can be ruthless, but he is an intellectual and is always thinking and talking about the cause of World Communism. Stalin is ruthless, and cruel and is only thinking of his path to power in Russia first. Stalin knows the power in Russia is within reach right now and that revolution in the world is just a dream for now. Lenin saw this also and signed that treaty with the Germans giving up parts of Russia."

"What about the west?"

"Yes! The Allied governments will allow the Bolsheviks in Russia. They withdrew their troops by 1921 and one year later the Japanese pulled out of Russia. Now the West will allow Russia to remain in the hands of the Bolsheviks. Besides, remember Lenin tried to expand the Red Revolution in the West and failed to establish it for any period in any other country in 1918 and 1919. No, we will be in this situation for years I am afraid," said Alexei.

CHAPTER TWO

George A. Hussey was involved in producing questionable reprints as early as 1854. The Hussey reprints and counterfeits are said to make up 95% of the 5 and 10-cent stamps in Providence, Rhode Island.

GENUINE　　　　**FORGERY**

If you want to control other people, first control yourself.
— Abu Bakr

PALESTINE 1929 - BY THE DOME OF THE ROCK

The two men stood together looking back at the Doom of the Rock in the Plaza of al-Haram al-Sharif. It was beautiful with its octagon shape holding up the Golden Doom with sixteen piers and columns. Surrounding this circle are 24 piers and columns. Each section of the octagon is 60 feet wide and 36 feet high. The interior has many windows, and the marble and mosaics have no human or animal forms. At the southern end of the Plaza is a mosque.

Most Westerners think the Dome is an Islamic Mosque, but it is a holy shrine. The Muslims believe that the Mosque at the southern end represents the place where the Prophet Muhammad ascended to heaven.

The two men were standing so they could look down towards the wall that the Jewish people believed was the last part of their holy Temple of the Mount. That is now called the Wailing Wall where the Jews said their prayers and placed papers of wishes or prayers in the cracks between stones in the wall.

To enter this area tourists and Jews had only one gate that they were allowed to enter. True believers of Islam had other gates that they could use to enter the holy site. The Jews and Christians called the site the Temple Mount and the Muslims held it as a shrine where Mohammad made his way to Heaven with other prophets. The Western Wall or Wailing Wall and the Dome of the Rock are considered a holy site for the three religions of Jewish, Christian, and Islamic faiths.

As the men stood there, one turned to the other, "Why do we need to meet like this and what are we doing here, Nasir?" asked Ibrahim.

"I needed to tell you what is being planned. We are going to rid our homeland of these filthy Jews once and for all. They have come to our land and brought back their stinking religion and thieving ways to steal our land. They ignore the word of the Prophet and after tonight they will be gone!" said Nasir.

"They have not brought anything back, Nasir. They and their religion have always been here. They have only increased their presence. Besides, the British will not permit any attack on the Jewish quarter. If it is attacked, all that will happen is damage to both sides and everyone will lose in the end," said Ibrahim.

"Not this time! The British know they cannot protect the filthy Jews and have issued them weapons to defend themselves. We will defend ourselves and rid ourselves of this festering sore tonight. After all, they ignored the law and started to build the structures at the base of their so-called Wailing Wall in violation of the 1925 law," said Nasir.

"They have set up a few benches for the old to sit and a screen to separate men and women, while they worshiped at their Wailing Wall. This is also done in our religion to separate men and women. Besides this is not a violation of the 1925 Law and they are not beginning any building construction nor is it an insult to our faith. I will not go with you," said Ibrahim.

"The Mufti of Jerusalem has just had leaflets distributed that claimed that the Jewish Zionists are planning to take over the Dome of the Rock Shrine where our Great Prophet Muhammad started his journey to heaven. The filthy Jews insult our faith every day. We must make a stand to correct the wrongs that are done to us and our faith!" said Nasir.

"Yes, I think, are you referring to that poor Sephardic Jewish boy that was recently stabbed over some small slight to a Moslem person the other day that set off more violence in demonstrations and counter demonstrations. Is that the wrong you speak about?

"You also seem to forget it was Moslem demonstrators that massacred the village of Hebron killing women and children along with the men. Fighting continues as we sit here talking, Nasir," said Ibrahim.

"Yes! You forgot to mention the Jews attacked and desecrated the Nebi Akasha Mosque. Ibrahim, you seem to think the filthy Jews want to live together with us and you fail to see them as invaders who want to control us just like the Imperialist British. Tonight, we will end the Jewish occupation," said Nasir.

"Go and do what you want, I will not go with you, my friend," said Ibrahim.

That night the fighting started and continued through August and ended by September. There were some 13 Jews killed with over 300 wounded and over 100 Arabs killed with 220 wounded, many by the British trying to stop the fighting. After the battles had finally stopped, Ibrahim was standing at a bread vendor's stand and turned around to see Nasir with another man entering the marketplace.

"Well Nasir, now your nights and days of fighting are over and what have we gained? The rioting lasted weeks and was a three-sided battle. What happened was the British had armed the Jews and many of these individuals were ex-British soldiers who took up arms for protection of their communities from roaming bands of Arab troublemakers.

"At one point the British troops were caught between both rioting sides and fired into both groups of Arabs and Jews. The result was simple for both sides are more radical. Now each has their demands for independence with both sides increasing their push for the end of the British foreign influence in Palestine with the Jews pushing harder for their nation. Yes, Nasir, you have settled nothing except to create another great European investigation into the Palestine issue.

"Once more the British have set up a commission to investigate the rioting. That commission will report that after weeks of rioting the Jews had to evacuate 17 of their communities and both sides have lost hundreds of dead and wounded. They will list destruction that is everywhere. The report will be turned in and a study group will be set up to look for a solution. Then what will be done? Not much Nasir, so was it worth it?" asked Ibrahim.

"Yes, we showed the Europeans and their Jewish dogs that we will not give up our homeland without a fight. Tell my friend Ibrahim here, Professor Aizza, about these British and European Jews!" said Nasir as he turned to the man with him.

"It is good to see you again Ibrahim. Of course, I will be glad to share my knowledge on the subject if you like?" said the Professor.

"I would be pleased to listen from such a learned scholar," replied Ibrahim.

"Well, I should start with the history of the Hebrews before and after the Romans, but I will not and give a shorter version. I will jump centuries and start with the 19th Century and the state of the world at that time. At the time Palestine lived under the thumb of the Ottoman Empire during the Century and all societies were in a period of rapid change with the political ideas of the Anarchists and Socialists that were pushing for a world society without a government. At the same time, the Imperialism of the European nations was spreading and expanding their power along with their religion around the world.

"The change in part was due to their desire and need to create a greater national ideality with the collection of colonies for markets and natural resources with the industrial age. Of course, these colonies created the demand for naval coaling stations around the globe.

"During this same period, Charles Darwin developed the idea of evolution on natural selection that some interpreted as the survival of the fittest. His idea of natural selection morphs into what is now called social evolution where societies were ranked by their standing in the world at that time. The evidence for support of this social evolution was simple for the Europeans. The Europeans had taken control of both of the Americas, Asia, and India by the 19th century and they were in the process of taking control of Pacific Islands and Africa.

"These newly colonized peoples were gathered into the various empires without consideration for the existing tribal boundaries or cultures. Geographically, new nations were created, and local tribes were divided with new leaders put into place. This in time caused a power struggle in the local native populations for leadership between the traditional leaders and the new colonial leadership. Moreover, these new subjects of the empires were often the objects of suspicion that called into question their loyalty to the new empire.

"The Germans and Belgians rulers were brutal to their native populations and took all the value they could from the land without consideration of the people or environment. The Germans committed horrible brutality against the Herero peoples in southern Africa and the Belgian's treatment of the population was as bad, if not worst, in the Congo.

"The Germans and Belgians provided little support for the native population and limited education for the young. The government was direct and indirect at the same time based on commercial aims.

"Then there are the French who gave their colonies an illusion of uniformity in teaching the natives through college level in the French language and academics plus giving the natives French citizenship. I say illusion because the problem with the French is the closer to Paris the more French they are so colonial French and natives were looked down upon. The cloak of uniformity was an illusion for that reason. The best and brightest left the colony for France draining the skilled individuals off to France.

"The British in my opinion were the best in providing education and government skills for their native populations. Yet, they were also arrogant and looked down on the people they said they were helping to bring up into the modern world – Darwin's influence.

The British and Europeans built railroads for their commercial needs, not the native populations.

"Thrown into this mix of imperialism came a greater demand for nationalism and cultural identity. The Jews of Europe, who were never trusted in Europe and anywhere as good citizens for the faith, were always seen as outsiders and the killers of the Christian God on the cross. The question often asked was if Jews were loyal to their religion or the country where they lived. They had been driven from one country to the next from 1492 in Spain they moved to Portugal then to Brazil and when the Inquisition caught them they went to Holland with the diamond trade. Each time a new form of pogroms of organized attacks on the Jews followed them. In Russian the Jews were locked in the Pale after the First Partition of Poland in 1772. The pogroms were so violent and repeated so often that by the late 19th century the Jewish leadership set out looking for a place to call their homeland to live in peacefully. Palestine was one site they spoke of as a homeland.

"That idea was advanced by a French Jewish businessman, Baron Rothschild, who tried to help the Jews of Europe by providing funds for the Zionist movement to establish a small community or a national homeland in Palestine in 1882. The Jews of Europe started to return to Palestine to live with other Jews that had stayed in Palestine after the Roman diaspora had sent many of them off to distant places centuries ago.

"However, the argument among the Jews for this new Jewish State was not settled on the location of Palestine within the Jewish community. That soon began to solidify with the pogroms in Russia and the trial and conviction of Captain Alfred Dreyfus in what is known as the Dreyfus Affair. The Russians also were asking the Ottomans to allow the Jews to settle in Palestine.

"Theodor Herzl had suggested in his publication, Der Judenstaat, for a Jewish homeland in either Palestine, Argentina, or in East Africa as possible locations in 1896. The First Zionist Congress held in 1901 decided on the location of Palestine and made plans to buy more land for the settlement of Jewish settlers. By that time the Ottoman Empire was in decline and nationalism was spreading in the Arab communities and tribes. It was not a good time to introduce a new national identity to the region.

"Then during the Great War Arab leaders signed a letter with the British agreeing to create an Arab state out of the Ottoman Empire after the war. However, this Hussein-McMahon letter did not spell out the details precisely. At the same time during the war, the British and French had made a secret agreement with the Sykes-Picot Agreement to divide the Middle East at the end of the war with no Arab state.

"During the war, the British then approached the Jewish leaders to win their support for the war and agreed to bring about a Jewish homeland in Palestine. This was known as the Balfour Declaration and the Jews of America entered with money.

"At the end of the Great War, the peacemakers met at Versailles and two Americans (Henry King and Charles Crane) were sent to investigate the possibility of a Jewish homeland. Their report was later dropped and kept secret for three years.

"All this time Jewish immigration continued to flow into Palestine and riots broke out in 1921 and forced the British to reduce the number of Jewish immigrants that would be allowed into Palestine between 1922 - 1925 and then the peace was broken by the riot at the Dome of the Rock. The two sides, Arabs on one side and Jews on the other, were becoming more agitated and the shouting was increasing with violent threats. The location of resentment was focused around the Qubbat al-Sakhran Shrine built on the second Jewish Temple that was destroyed in 70 C.E. by the Romans. An agreement in 1925 permitted the Jews to pray at the Wailing Wall, but they could not build any structures at the site. Zionist leaders soon began making demands for a Jewish state.

"Then in 1928, the Jewish worshipers at the wall set up a screen to separate the men and women. The Arabs saw this as a violation of the agreement of 1925 that the Jews were not allowed to build any structures at the site. Palestinians Muslims and Jewish Zionists were facing each other at the shrine. On that day the Jewish leader Vladimir Jabotinsky gave a speech calling to create a Jewish State and colonizing Transjordan into a Jewish homeland.

"This Zionist demonstration and speech at the Dome of the Rock was too much for many Arabs. The riots that followed were in part because of many broken promises made by the Allied Powers during the Great War to all sides. But the Europeans did what they always do after a crisis, organized a commission to investigate. This was the Shaw Commission and was later followed by the Hope Simpson Commission. They held that the Grand Mufti of Jerusalem was responsible for the rioting," said Professor Aizza as he finished his story.

"See! We are going to lose our land. The Europeans hate the Jews, but they hate and disrespect us more and will send their unwanted Jewish scum here," said Nasir.

"No, Nasir! We will only lose our homeland because we fail to see the world as a connected community and our failure to work together for a peaceful solution is the problem," said Ibrahim.

"What do you think, Professor?" asked Nasir.

"Well, from my point of view, violence has never worked in the past and neither has peaceful negotiations. So, I would say all sides must find a way to work together," said the professor.

"I must say professor you answered that very diplomatically," said Ibrahim.

"Professor you and Ibrahim are intellectuals and do not live in the real world. You both think that everyone wants to be reasonable. You are very wrong! Everyone is out for an advantage, and we need to stop being taken advantage of by others like our brothers the Ottomans, the Europeans, and the Jewish Zionists from stealing our homeland," said Nasir.

"Nevertheless, I must be off Nasir. I have a meeting at the university," said the Professor.

"I must be off also. You both give your families my best," said Ibrahim as he stood up.

Nasir stood and watched both men walk away. Shaking his head thinking to himself they were fools that did not see the real world.

CHAPTER THREE

James A. Petrie was arrested and arraigned for stamp counterfeiting in 1869. He later claimed that on one of his buying trips through the American southern states, he discovered the first known copy of the Confederate Greenville, Alabama, stamp provisional with the printer's ornaments minus the lead type. Today he is known for his fakes and counterfeit stamps of the Confederated States of America.

BLACK PENNY

FORGERY

There are a thousand hacking at the branches of evil to one who is striking at the root.
— Henry David Thoreau

A Small Strip Mall Structure Fire – 2002

The fire was noticed at 4:01 a.m. by a neighbor who was leaving for work. He rushed back into the house to call 911 and asked for the fire department that received the call at 4:02 a.m. The Dispatch alerted the fire company at 4:05. Two engines and a truck company pulled out their doors at 4:07.

The first engine arrived at 4:12 a.m. to see a fully engaged fire at the end of the strip center. At 4:13 a.m. a second alarm was called by the first engine company — the fire was located in the last shop in the strip mall shopping center and could have spread to the connecting store by a common ceiling. The fire crews had knocked the fire down by 4:42 a.m. when Chief Franklin arrived on the scene.

"Good work, Captain Williams," said Department Chief Franklin.

"It looked a lot worse when we came into the parking lot. The whole end of the building was a ball of flames. We were lucky to get into the shop next door and stop the spread of the fire into that shop and the rest of the stores or we would have had a major problem. Lady Luck was with us. There is mostly smoke damage to that shop next door with a little fire damage in the ceiling above. The end store is completely gone except for the exterior walls with just a few hot spots now," said Captain Williams.

"Why were you lucky to get into the shop next door?" asked Chief Franklin.

"The front door was open. I went over to it as the engine guys were putting water on the fire. I wanted to check to see that the fire hadn't spread. This old type of strip center was built with common ceilings without any firebreak stops in the attic space. Anyway, I tried the door and it opened and I could see flames just starting in the ceiling by the connecting wall. I called for a crew to get in there and knock it down. The place was filled with smoke. I called a second alarm as insurance if this thing should go wild in the attic space," said Captain Williams.

"Well, good work again Captain. Do you have the business owner's names?" asked Chief Franklin.

"The owner of the print shop that has burned is standing over there with the truck captain. He did give me the name and phone number of the owner of the stamp shop next door. I called and did not get an answer," said Captain Williams

"Chief Franklin, you better come look at this!" called a fireman,

"What's the rush, Bob?"

"We have a body in the stamp shop in the back-office room!"

"Captain Williams, go over to the police unit and have him call it in. Let's not make this a public show, at least for now," said Chief Franklin.

"I am on it Chief," said the captain.

"Now, Bob let us go see this body. I hope nobody touched the body," said the Chief.

"No, we were opening windows to ventilate the smoke so we could see better. I then went into the little office in the back and found this guy sitting with his head down on the desk. I checked for a pulse and found none. Then I came out and looked for Captain Williams and you," said Bob.

"Alright you stay by the office door and keep everyone outside until the police come and take charge," said Chief Franklin.

"O.K. Chief."

"Bob, that was good work and I hear you are signed up to take the next captain exam."

"Yes, sir I made the list last time but there wasn't an opening before my name came up on the list."

"I am glad you are still interested. There will be several openings this time around," said the Chief as he walked back over to Captain Williams, who was just punching off his phone.

"I still cannot get the owner of the stamp shop, Chief!"

"That's O.K., I think we may have the owner over in the shop. He is slumped over a desk. It looks like a heart attack or stroke. We will know more after the police and coroner get here and do their investigation," said the Chief.

"Since we have a body that is connected to the fire, should I call C.E. to investigate?" asked Captain Williams.

"That may be a good idea. Besides you said that this fire was well involved in what seems to be a very short period. I would like to have its source checked out. Yes, give C.E. a call," said the chief.

Just then a police unit with the Chief of Police pulled into the parking lot. "I heard the call over the radio and came by to see if we needed more manpower. What is this about a body?"

"The shop adjoining the shop where the fire started had some smoke damage and the fire began to spread into the common ceiling. After the fire was knocked down and the smoke was being cleared out, my men discovered a body sitting at a desk," said Chief Franklin.

Just then the Corner pulled up and parked next to a police unit and she got out of the passenger's side and C.E. got out on the driver's side of the car.

"I heard that you two had become an item," said the Police chief.

"It has always been hard to keep you in the dark Chief," said C.E.

"That is why I am the Chief of Police."

"You boys have your fun while I do my job," Elaine said as she walked toward the fire crew.

"It is good to see you and Elaine together C.E. and it looks like it is getting to be more than friends," said Chief Franklin.

"Yes, it is, and this is not what it looks like. I was just picking her up for breakfast down the coast when the call came that she was needed here. Then before she left, my phone had a message that I was also wanted at the site. So, we came in the same car. Now you both can forget what you were thinking."

"It is still good to see you in a relationship," said Chief Franklin.

"Well, I am going over and look around the fire. Unless you two want more personal information I am not going to give it to you. You two are the biggest gossip in town."

"Now! That hurts C.E. and what would Mabel say about that?" asked the Police Chief. "The town gossip always seems to show up everywhere!"

"She would agree for she is innocent as a lamb in her mind. If you remember she blamed you for the human smuggler incident last month," said C.E.

"What human smuggler incident? That woman saw five storefront dummies floating in the river and called everyone saying that human smugglers had dumped bodies in the river. Before I got there a dozen T.V. crews as well as several government agencies had arrived. There was Mabel there in the middle of the cameras telling everyone that she had warned me of the smuggling," said the police chief.

"You have to admit it was funny when the one news reporter ran down the bank to the water with his cameraman to film the bodies. When he realized they were manikins he tripped and fell off the rocks into the river screaming and you went to the rescue," laughed Chief Franklin.

"The other station ran that segment of the rescue so much the national media picked it up. I laugh every time I see it with you being pulled into the water by the falling reporter. The look on your face was priceless chief," said C.E.

"We have that picture on the station's wall of shame," said Chief Franklin.

"You guys have your fun and you know that both of you have photos in the department locker room of you being hugged by Mabel," said the police chief.

With that C.E. walked over to the fire and studied the outside before entering the structure. He noticed that the fire inside looked to be evenly distributed around the main room. Inside the source of ignition seemed to be everywhere. The fire did seem to have one complete source of origin all around the room. C.E. took out some sample bottles to collect materials for testing. Then he walked back to the Command unit.

"I can say that the fire was an arson fire and it had one ignition source, an acceleration that was spread completely around the room. I need to do some testing for the liquid used. But it smells like plain diesel gas. I need to talk to the first unit and the shop owner."

"The owner of the print shop is right over there talking to the captain of the first unit to arrive," pointed out Chief Franklin.

"Thanks" and C.E. turned and walked over to the two men. "Captain, can I speak to you for a moment over here?" asked C.E.

"Sure thing C.E., will you excuse me a moment Mr. Burns."

"No problem, Captain," said Mr. Burns as the captain walked over to C.E.

"What can I do for you C.E.?"

"Tell me what you saw when you pulled up at the fire?"

"The shop at this end of the building was engulfed in a wall of flame or rather a cube of flames and the roof was pretty much gone on the far end. It was a wonder that the fire had not spread into the attic more. I called in a second alarm right away. It looked like this could get away from us. The windows were out, and the front door glass was gone from the heat from the fire inside the print shop. So we hit it with water from outside. I went to check the shop next door and the door was unlocked." said the captain.

"What did you see?" asked C.E.

"I could see a lot of smoke and flames in the adjoining ceiling wall. When I opened the door there was no alarm, which seemed odd at the time. That is why I am talking to the owner of the print shop right now."

"Good let's both ask him some questions," said C.E. as they walked back to Mr. Burns, who was in cargo shorts, a bathrobe, and slippers.

"Mr. Burns this is C.E. Hall our independent Fire Inspector. He would like to ask you some questions," said Captain Williams.

"Sure, it is nice to meet you, Mr. Hall. I hope you can find out how this happened. That was my only source of income and I have three kids in college," said Mr. Burns.

"When were you last in your printing shop?" asked C.E.

"I close the shop at 6 p.m. every night, set the alarm, and walk home just across the street."

"Did the alarm go off tonight?" asked C.E.

"No, I was awakened by the sirens, looked out the window, saw my life going up in flames, and came right over."

"Did you lock the door to the shop last night?"

"Yes, I always check it twice. I have a mild OCD condition if OCD can ever be mild."

"So you are sure you locked the door?"

"Yes, I must check it at least twice before I leave, and many nights have come back over to be sure."

"Do you have insurance on the shop?" asked C.E.

"Some, but not nearly enough to cover this total disaster. The insurance will most likely not cover the cost of my machines and computers. Then there are the orders that were done and those waiting to be done. I'll be lucky if customers do not sue me over their lost work. I do not know what I am going to do now."

"What about the stamp shop owner? Can you tell us anything about his shop hours?" asked C.E.

"Sure, we were neighbors for 10 or more years. He was always open until 5 p.m. every night except on Tuesday nights when he was open until 8 p.m. for a stamp club he started."

"Was he very careful?" asked C.E.

"I do not understand! About what?"

"In locking his door?" asked C.E.

"Oh, yes! There have been a few break-ins on the other side of this little center in the last few weeks. He had a security system being installed. I think it was to be installed this week. He wanted to know if I wanted to have the system also to share the cost. He said they would give a break on the cost if other shop owners signed up."

"What did you say?" asked the captain.

"That I was low on cash right now. The printing business has been a little slow at this time. You know kids and college. We were to talk about my doing it later if the security company would still offer the reduction. Have you gotten ahold of him?" asked Mr. Burns.

"Yes, we have. It looks like he had a heart attack over there in his office," said the captain.

"What! He is dead?"

"Yes, I am afraid so," said the captain.

"Oh my God, how did this happen?"

"Did he have any family?" asked C.E.

"No, he lived alone. I think he had a wife that died a year or two before I moved here," said Mr. Burns.

"Well, thank you for your time, Mr. Burns. We may be in touch with you later. Oh, one last thing, did you do any printing for the stamp shop owner?" asked C.E.

"Yes, I did some printing for him now and then. Why?"

"Just curious," said C.E.

"I know, I said one more question, but did he work late at night other than his meetings on Tuesday?"

"Not that I ever saw. Most of the time he was locking up right around the time I did."

"You said you locked up at five and he locked up at six?" said C.E.

"I locked my door at five and then had to get things done around the office to set up for the next day and order supplies. I usually was ready to walk across the street by six when he was locking his door."

"Thank you. Again I may have some questions later, if that will be O.K. with you," said C.E. as he turned and walked back to the command unit just as the coroner Elaine walked up.

"I think all of you should come back to the stamp office. C.E. I would like you to come and give your opinion," said Elaine.

"What's up Elaine?" asked the Police Chief.

"I'm almost positive we have a death by unnatural causes. I will know for sure once I get the body back to the lab, but I would like C.E. to look at some stamps."

"What does that have to do with the death and fire?" asked both Chiefs together.

"You'll see! First, the body seems to be staged at the desk and I would say the death is right about the time the fire started. I will know more after some tests," said Elaine as they walked back to the stamp office.

"So what do you want C.E. for?" asked Chief Franklin.

"C.E. is into stamp collecting and he talks about it all the time. So, I have a little knowledge of the subject, and this caught my eye," she said as she pointed to sheets of stamps," said Elaine.

"Those are Penny Blacks, and they were the first stamps ever issued and they are very rare in this condition, and it is impossible to be originals. The others are United States 24-cent Inverted Jenny stamps. Since they are on uncut sheets, I would say they are all forgeries, if not counterfeited. This other group of stamps are United States $2.60 Graf Zeppelins stamps from 1930," said C.E.

"What is the difference between forgery and counterfeit?" asked Elaine.

"A forgery is an original stamp that has been printed or altered as a page filler or used without the intent to defraud and the counterfeit stamp is the creation of a stamp from scratch that is an unauthorized imitation of the genuine stamp with the intent to defraud. That is a simple explanation, but you get the point I am trying to make," said C.E.

"What value could these stamps be worth?" asked Chief Franklin.

"A single Penny Black can bring $500,000.00 to several million dollars at auction?" said C.E.

"So maybe these are real?" said the Police chief.

"Not in full sheets of stamps and, if they were real, they would not be in unprotected full sheets. They would be single stamps and in protective covers. I know of only two full sheets of the Penny Black stamp, and they are both in London under lock and key in some tower over there. Here we have two full sheets of each set of these stamps in this pile. No stamp dealer would ever allow real stamps like these to sit around without protective covers."

"How big is the counterfeiting of stamps?" asked Elaine.

"Anytime there is value there will be a market. The first postage stamps were those that are called the Penny Black. They were issued on the first of May in 1840. The books on forgeries were in circulation by the 1860s and some collectors and dealers wrote books on how to identify forgeries were the forgers themselves. Two early books on the subject were ***Forged Stamps How to Detect Them*** by Thornton Lewes and Edward Pemberton in 1863 and ***How to Detect Forged Stamps*** by Thomas Dalston. Many of the forgers were also involved in the stamp trade and the ethics were lost. One dealer was so good that his forgeries and counterfeits were better than the originals. He considered himself an artist and not a counterfeiter," said C.E.

"Wow, you just rolled that off from memory. I am so impressed," said the Police Chief.

"Just be glad you were not trapped on a fire engine with him after inspecting a stamp store," said Chief Franklin.

"How about being trapped in a car." laughed Elaine.

"Hey, you asked about my collection on that small trip. I am hurt! Maybe we can get back to the situation at hand."

"You're right C.E. I think I'll give the FBI a call. How about we all meet at my office at lunch," suggested the Police chief.

"I should have the autopsy preliminary report by then," said Elaine.

"Then it is agreed we will meet at the Police Chief's office," said Chief Franklin.

"I still have some work inside the print shop," said C.E.

"Oh, now I have to find a ride?"

"That will teach you not to make fun of my stamps," said C.E.

"Alright that's O.K. I'll ride back to the office with the P.D. unit," said Elaine.

"I'll stop by before the meeting," said C.E.

CHAPTER FOUR

Giovanni Patroni was arrested in 1875 in Philadelphia on charges of attempting to defraud the government. This was his first trial related to philatelic forgery. He admitted producing the stamps just for collectors, was found guilty, and the jury recommended mercy. He served no jail time and soon left for South America.

GENUINE　　　**FORGERY**

Solitude is better than the society of evil persons.
— Abu Bakr

TRANSJORDAN 1948

The men were old friends sitting in a small café drinking coffee. One wore a Western European-style suit and carried a briefcase. The other had well-worn military pants, boots, and a colorful shirt.

"It is good to see you again Nasir," said Ibrahim.

"I wish that were so, Ibrahim. You left the cause for our freedom after the riots in 1929 and went to work for the British oppressors," said Nasir.

"No, I worked for the people of Palestine in my way. Not the way of radical firebrands like you that want to blow everything up. We need to find a way to peacefully obtain control over our land and hopefully, that will not be with violence!" said Ibrahim.

"You are no closer to our freedom your way than we are by our way!" replied Nasir.

"Nasir, we were friends and still are as far as I am concerned. We did take different paths to the future of our nation of Palestine. You and others like Nasser in Egypt sided with the fascists against the British even when those same fascists saw the Arab people as inferior to the Germanic and Italian races. So what did your cooperation with them get us?"

"What did your work with the British get us? Nothing!" said Nasir.

"Not true, the French withdrew from Syria in 1945 and Lebanon in 1946. The British left Egypt, Iraq, and Transjordan by 1946 and today they are pulling out of Israel. Within a few years many of the Arab states will be independent and, hopefully, so will Palestine," said Ibrahim.

"Ibrahim, you are a misguided fool to think Palestine will ever be free of European influence and Jewish outsiders. Jews are pouring into Palestine every day and the British do little to nothing to stop it. The world feels sorry for the Jews because of their fake made-up story of the Holocaust. We will lose our country if we do not fight back to stop this flow of Jews from Europe."

"Nasir, you surprise me. You served with the German military and saw what they did and yet you talk about the Holocaust as if it never happened."

"That was war!" said Nasir.

"No, Nasir. That was pure hate. Do not try to justify mass murder as a cost of war."

"The quest for our nation at times needs to work with the Devil."

"Nasir, your group talks about Arab nationality and yet does not practice it. Your Arab League formed in 1945 gave the illusion of uniformity without actually believing in it. The Egyptians for their part want to regain the glory of the past with the Pharaohs and take the place as the leader of the Middle East, while leaders in Iraq want to rebuild the power of the Mesopotamian Empires of Babylon and become the leader of the Middle East. Of course, there are the Iranians who are thinking about the rebirth of the Persian Empire and the leadership of the leaders of the Middle East. Let us not forget the Turks who have adopted many Western ways to rebuild the Ottoman Empire. None of this will end the struggle for power in the Middle East for it is just one part of the struggle.

"Added into the mix are our religious groups involved in the infighting of Sunnis, Shiite, Druse, and those radical Wahhabism of Salafism. They attack each other over their beliefs and pit the rural Muslims against the urban Muslims. You, my friend, think you are making things better as you help destroy any hope of a nation. The only good thing I can see for now is that you still allow me to talk to you while you are pushing for more war," said Ibrahim.

"Ibrahim, be careful of what you and Professor Aizza are saying. Many in the group see you as enemies of the cause and you both should be removed. I say this to you as a past friend."

"A past friend! It finally has come to this. Then I am truly sorry Nasir! We have known each other from childhood and now your hate of others has driven a wedge between us. I am afraid this is the last time we will have this type of talk – God be with you," said Ibrahim.

"God be with you - Ibrahim."

CHAPTER FIVE

Jean De Sperati may be the best of all the forgers. He produced stamps from more than ninety countries and wrote books that criticized the philatelic experts that he fooled with his work by using the correct paper, the correct watermark, the right perforations, and genuine cancellation. He created the 'Livre d' Or' a collection of 234 rare stamps from around the world. The stamps were certified by some 17 experts as being genuine. They were his artistic forgeries.

GENUINE

FORGERY

Cursed is the man who dies, but the evil done by him survives.

— Abu Bakr

FRENCH ALGERIA – EARLY 1942

The French occupation of North Africa took three decades from 1830 to 1860. The conquest took the lives of perhaps a million lives of a population of three million in a scorch-the-earth policy. Emir Abd al Qadir agreed to surrender with an agreement of safe conduct to Egypt of Palestine. The French broke the agreement and sent him to France, because of a defeat the minister of war suffered two years earlier at the hands of Abd al Qadir.

The economy of Algeria was controlled by grandsons colons European colonists. The system was designed for the markets of France. Europeans held 30% of the arable land and by 1900 Europeans produced two-thirds of agricultural output with half of that in wine production. The French colons (colonialists) worked through the beni-oui-ouis (a derogatory term for Muslim collaborators). In 1870 France granted Algerian Jews citizenship, but not Muslims. Citizenship was granted to some Muslims after 1919.

The Vichy government was working with the Germans and in 1941 Hitler sent General Erwin Rommel's North Afrika Korps to Tripoli to save Mussolini's Army.

The two men sitting at the market had a meal and as one got up to leave, "Ismail what are your plans and where are you going?" Abdul asked.

"I told you. I am off to join the fight against the Russian dogs with the Germans."

"Why? How? Where?" asked Abdul.

"This guy, Otto Fischer, is asking Muslims to fight for Germany. He is a Muslim from the Balkans and said there are thousands of Muslims in the German Army. He had another Muslim soldier in a German Uniform with him. His name is Ahlam, also from the Balkans. He tells stories of the German Army rebuilding Mosques, prayer halls, and Madrassas as they moved into the Soviet Union. They are rebuilding all those things that the Communists had destroyed during their civil war and under that thug Stalin. He is trying to wipe out the Muslim faith in the Soviet Union. It is a good and just cause."

"Ismail! Do you think the Germans like or care about the Muslims?" asked Abdul.

"I do know that they hate the Jews and make them wear the Yellow Stars of David so they can be easily identified. The French have also done it with the Jews here in Algeria. Only that fool King Mohammed V over in Morocco has refused to make the Jews wear the Star," said Ismail.

"So, you are going to join this fight, because of your hate of the Jews?" asked Abdul.

"No! I am going to fight for the freedom of Muslim people with the German army in a unit called the Freiwllige, their volunteers. It is a jihad against the Jewish communist Zionists. Besides Haj Amin al-Husseini is working with the Fascist for our independence and it is very near," said Ismail.

"I hope you are right, and I hope to see you when you come back, Ismail. God be with you."

"I will come back to our new nation when this is all over."

ALGERIA 1946

Abdul was sitting in a café when he noticed an old friend a few tables away. He got up and walked over. "Ismail, I see you made it home. I am sorry to see that you lost your right arm," said Abdul as he thought that losing the right hand made life difficult for the left hand was unclean. Communal eating has rules and one should not be impolite.

"Abdul, it is also good to see you well and I am lucky it was just my arm. The Russians were far worse than the Germans when it came to killing. They would cut down their people to get them to fight us. One time as we left a small village, I heard the Russian soldiers shooting the villagers because they were alive when the Germans were there.

We were told when the Russian POWs were rescued by the advancing Red Army in the German-occupied territory, they were considered to be traitors by Stalin and were to be shot on the spot or placed in front of the next offensive attack. The real lucky ones were sent to one of the prisons they call a gulag. I heard it was a living death," said Ismail.

"It must have been bad," said Abdul.

"Bad would have been nice. We would cut down hundreds of the Russians and more would just keep coming. One time they stopped rushing us and turned back and were cut down by their side.

"The Germans were always short of supplies and at times sent the wrong stuff to the front. I had to unload a train of Champagne and beer during one retreat so we could load the wounded soldiers. The Champagne and beer had frozen, and the bottles were worthless to the troops," said Ismail.

"How did you get home?"

"After I was wounded, I was in a field hospital and one day I just got up from the bed and walked away. I was in the Crimean and down by the water I found a Muslim fisherman, who took me in his boat across the Black Sea and from there I walked home with the help of the Brotherhood."

"I see that you are still a believer that violence will rid the country of the French?" said Abdul.

"How do you see that?" asked Ismail.

"I saw who walked away from your table as I walked up. He is a hunted man for acts of terror against the French military and civilians with bombs he set. Some of those killed civilians were good Muslims. One of his victims was a young Muslim child only nine years old," said Abdul.

"Yes, it is sad, but the cost of freedom is paid in part by the innocent," replied Ismail.

"So the cost of a few innocent children is the price you are willing to pay?"

"Yes! You should also say that. The French are not going to leave. We just had a mass protest demonstration in Setif and Guelma. What do you think the French did? I'll tell you! They fired on the crowd killing as many as they could. Then they arrested the leaders of the Algerian nationalist movement.

"The funny thing is that last year on May 8, the Germans surrendered ending that horrific episode of world history. Now we have a new horrifying episode to replace it — the French are returning as colonizers," said Ismail.

"Yes, I remember the parade to celebrate Germany's surrender and how the extremists tried to grab the colonial banners from the French Gendarmerie that started a riot. Then over the next five days, the French committed their share of atrocities with the police and military summary executing individuals on the spot. Vigilantes broke into jails and lynched prisoners and French warplanes bombed remote villages. We have been in rebellion against the French for over a hundred years and what has violence gotten us?" said Abdul.

"What has pacify gotten us? The French began to colonize us in the 1830's and started a French land rush grabbing our land for the production of cotton. The bey of Constantine Ahmad ibn Muhammad led a revolt until he was captured in 1837. Then Mohamed ben Abdallah, Sherif Boubaghla, the Prophet took up arms with that woman Lalla Fadhma until he was killed some say by his treasonous allies in 1854. The French say they pacified Algeria with negotiations. They used violence, locust plagues, famine, and the cholera plagues in 1866 and 1868. Is that what you call fair negotiations?" asked Ismail.

"It is better to talk rather than to be in constant violence fighting for an idea, Ismail. What will you end up with after the fighting?" asked Abdul.

"Our Nation!" shouted Ismail waving his arm.

"Run by who? Those of your leaders that I see fill their own pockets with cash and ride around in their limousines. Yes, Ismail, you will have a new nation in name and still live as you do today under the yoke of an oppressor. Only that oppressor will be of your people with a corrupt leadership," said Abdul.

"Yes! But it will be my oppressive leaders; not some foreign imperial nation or Jewish dogs," said Ismail.

"I am sad for you Ismail!" said Abdul.

"Do not be sad for me. It is I, who is sad for you and those like you that are willing to live under the French colonial power. I am more than sad for you. You disgust me for your ignorance and trust in people who only see you as an inferior human. You are the perfect lap dog for the foreign masters," said Ismail.

"See there, Ismail you show your hidden contempt for people with different points of view. It is true I did not go off and fight with the German colonizers for what you call the fight for our freedom from the evil French masters. Your contempt of the French did not stop you from joining with other colonial Europeans that you say you despise. You, Ismail, are blinded by your hate!" said Abdul.

"If I was you Abdul, I would be careful," said Ismail.

"Why?"

"There are those of us that see traitors in words that you use," said Ismail.

"Well Ismail, I see we are no longer friends. Your hate has taken reason from your heart and mind. I will leave you now, God be with you," said Abdul as he turned and walked away.

Ismail watched Abdul walk away and made a note to himself to talk about Abdul to the group that night.

CHAPTER SIX

Francois Fournier was a colorful forger who viewed himself as a creator of art. His 1914 price list offered over 3,500 different stamps. After his death, to keep the stock of his forgeries from falling into others, his stock of stamps and equipment was purchased by the Union of Philatelique de Geneve. The forgeries in that stock were said to weigh over 800 pounds. The equipment was donated to the Geneva Museum of History.

GENUINE

FORGERY

Be good to others, that will protect you against evil.
— Abu Bakr

ALGERIAN WAR AND FRENCH INDOCHINA WAR 1954-1962

SEPTEMBER 18, 1956

"Captain Boucher there is a man here with a message for you," said the orderly.

"Send him in and close the door," ordered the captain.

The man entered the room and stood at attention saluting the captain, "Sergeant Moze reporting on my mission, Sir!"

"Sergeant Moze, stand at ease. What do you have to report on these radicals?"

"My sources are telling me that the NLF is planning to move from their guerrilla war to a full-scale conflict at the end of the month. Last night I was told that a shipment of guns was smuggled across the border."

"Do you know where and how this new phase will take place?" asked the captain.

"My source has said the Casbah will be the main area that they will hit for the coverage of international press," said the sergeant.

"I have expected this after the peace negotiations were called off. Do you know what their first targets will be?" said the captain.

"No, but there is talk of attacks also being planned on the soil of Europe. It is just a rumor and another rumor of targeting the pied-noir civilians to break French power," said the sergeant.

"I am afraid this is going to become a big and dirty bloody civil war, sergeant," said the captain.

"I think you are right, Sir. There is a saying going around in the NFL that one bomb is as effective as a French battalion.

"Then you need to forget the undercover assignment that you are on and return to your unit. We will need to be on full alert. Inform the other Harkis agents to return to their units also. You and the others have served France well Sergeant."

"Yes, sir, and thank you."

SEPTEMBER 20, 1956

The Arab women were not searched by the police in Algeria, because of religious social norms. The reason the three women were recruited by the NFL was to carry the three bombs into the Casbah. The bombs were to be placed where the European presence was most noticed in the Casbah. One bomb was to be placed at a milk bar, another at a cafeteria, and one at the Air France terminus.

Two bombs had detonated at the first two sites killing three people and injuring some 50 others. The bomb at the Air France terminus did not go off, because of a failed timer.

The bombs were meant to draw international attention to the freedom fighting in Algeria. The bombing of civilians horrified people on both sides of the conflict. The radicals did not care and set off a brutal colonial conflict with no concern for life. They followed Lenin's idea of breaking a few eggs.

Terrorist actions were met with actions that many saw as activities outside of the French legal system with brutal interrogations, torture, forced disappearances, illegal executions, and mass arrests. Later the collapse of the government of the Fourth Republic of France created a mass exodus of a French colonist known as Pieds-Noirs (Black feet) and the Harkins, who were native Algerians who fought alongside the French colonists.

"Ismail, the world has noticed our cause. Now we must intensify the attack. I want you to set up small bomb-making factories so we can keep the colonists and their lap dogs off balance," said Yosef.

"I have already set up several and we have plans to move them around to different locations," said Ismail.

"Good! We will give the French a war that will scare them out of Algeria," said Yosef.

OCTOBER CONFLICT IN A CAFÉ IN THE CASBAH:

"Jamar, we need to hurt the Pieds-Noirs in their shops and businesses. We need to strike terror in their everyday life and win an Algerian battle much like the Viet Con did at 'Dien Bien Phu' in French Indochina in 1954 and at the same time take care of those traitorous Harki," said Ahmed.

"That will cause the French army and the Pieds-Noirs vigilantes to increase their campaign to end the war with more violence, Ahmed," said Jamar.

"Yes, and that will bring more world attention to our fight. The French people are tired of the wars in Asia and here in North Africa. The Casbah will be the focus of our activists," said Ahmed.

"I do not understand, Ahmed?"

"It is simple. The French had to choose between Algeria and Indochina. The French nation could not fight battles in Indochina and North Africa at the same time. One colony had to be abandoned and that was French Indochina now Vietnam. The French focused their attention on Algeria, while the Americans took over the conflict in Vietnam. They were already there since they were supplying and paying for the French to fight to hold off the communists there.

The Americans will pick up the fight and save their interest in stopping the communists from expanding into all of Indochina. They will protect their economic interest from communism. That fear will make the Americans and Europeans create their reverse of what President Eisenhower called the Domino Theory. That theory is their Achilles Heel and will lock the West up into many conflicts without any victories.

Yes, the French will have their hands full in this war and the battle in the Casbah will be our Dien Bien Phu," said Ahmed.

"Allahu Akbar!" shouted Jamar.

1958 ALGERIA

The political uprising in May had turned into a coup d'etat by the French Algerian Army. Colonel Paul Paquet sitting at his desk read the message sent from French army headquarters in Algiers. The French government had collapsed, and General Charles De Gaulle was forming the Fifth Republic and stated that he would end the Algerian War. Pieds-Noirs resistance to the French government went underground with its efforts in Algeria.

1961 ALGERIA

The OAS (Organisation Amee Secete) was organized and used sabotage, bombings, and assassination to keep Algeria in the French colonial world. L'Algeria est francaise et le restera (Algeria is French and will Remain So) was the motto. Many of the recruits were from the old French Fascist group before the Second World War. Some 2,000 individuals would die in OAS terrorist acts between 1961 – 1962.

FRENCH MILITARY HQ IN ALGERIA

The Colonel placed his hand over the phone. "Caporal Emilian, get in here! I need you to go and have Captains Boucher and Julien St. Martin report here NOW," said Colonel Paul Paquet.

"Yes, Sir," said the orderly as he saluted and rushed out the door.

The colonel returned to the phone. "Thank you for the information general. I will see that perpetrations will be established."

"It is most important colonel there is no paperwork and no mention of this activity! Is that clear?" said the general.

"Yes, sir!" said the colonel as there was a knock on the office door. "Come in."

Two captains entered the room, stood at attention, and gave a smart salute together, "Captains Boucher and St. Martin reporting as ordered, Sir."

"Sit down. Gentlemen, there has been a change in Paris. There is going to be a new change in the government policy in France with the new government being run by General De Gaulle. He will no longer support our policy in Algeria no matter what he says about it, but it will be in part because of our recent support here in North Africa for the Vichy government during the Second World War. Plus, our resistance after the war to his leadership, and that will be his number one, unstated reason, for the withdrawal from Algeria."

Both captains stood and said together, "Long live French Algeria!"

"Sit down and stop the dramatics. The time has come to plan and work together. That egotist De Gaulle has never been popular in North Africa. We need to organize a loyal opposition within the army and with the Pieds-Noirs to control the situation. You were both born here, and this is your country. I hope you agree with me," said Colonel Paquet.

"Tell us what you need, Colonel. You have our complete support," said Captain Boucher.

"I agree! Sir" said Captain St. Martin.

"Good, there can be no written communications on what we discuss. All orders will be delivered by selected trusted men. You both understand what is being done here and some might consider this treason."

"Yes, understood," replied both men.

"Then be careful of who you talk to and bring into the group. We need true patriots of Algeria. This cannot be done with just loyal officers to Algeria the rank and file need to be included."

"What about the Pieds-Noirs?" asked Captain St. Martin.

"That is being taken care of by others. We are to focus on the military rank-and-file members. Others are working with the patriot civilians side of the effort to save Algeria for France. Gentlemen welcome to the Organisation Armee Secrete," said the colonel.

1962

The Evian Accords were signed in March 1962 and the exodus from Algeria began in earnest. One last attempt was made by the OAS to reverse the withdrawal. Then the Oran Massacre in July of 1962 sealed the fate of the French in Algeria. Over half of the Pied Noirs had left Algeria and on July 7, a Muslim mob had rushed through the area attacking individuals cutting the throats of men, women, and children. The death toll ranged from less than a hundred to over 300 deaths by various accounts.

In August 1962 the OAS organization attempted to assassinate President de Gaulle once more. The OAS had become just another terrorist group made up of French officers and men setting off their bombs to make a point. These bombs also killed innocents. It was seen as just part of the cost for a French Algeria. The OAS organization was locked in a violent clandestine war with the NFL Moslem nationalists and the French government. The attempted assassination failed, and Captain Boucher sent an aid for Sargeant Moze.

"Sargeant Moze reporting as ordered, Sir."

"Yes, have a seat, Moze. The time has come for us to leave Algeria for France. You and your family will not be safe here. So, Moze get your family ready. I will make sure they get to France safely. De Gaulle has not yet permitted for the Harkis to be evacuated to France. Time is running out and the Arab nationalists are telling the Pied-Noirs to 'leave with a suitcase or in a coffin'. Who knows what they will do to those Harkis that stay behind? You and your family have been loyal supporters and fighters for me and France.

"Now France is deserting the field and leaving the Harkis behind to the new rulers of Algeria and they see the Harkis as nothing more than traitors. So, get your family and meet me at the air base tonight at 8 p.m. This has to be kept quiet. I can only offer this to just your immediate family. If word gets out, the moment will be lost. Do you understand Moze?"

"Yes, and thank you, Captain Boucher."

"I am sorry I cannot do more for the Harkis we leave behind. Some, I am sure, will reach France on their own. I will meet you tonight, Moze."

The Algerian War had set the design pattern for later Arab revolts in North Africa and the Middle East. The French withdrew from Algeria and out of the 250,000 Harkins (native Algerian Soldiers and family members) who fought for France in Algeria only 90,000 would make it to France. Once in France, they were treated as second-class citizens. They still seek full recognition of their part in French history.

CHAPTER SEVEN

Louis Dumonteuil (Dumonteil) D'Olivera was an active swindler of other philatelic dealers and the general public. He was connected with Enrique Gainsbourg with the fake newspaper stamps of Bolivia. By 1894 his swindles of other stamp dealers had the police Commissioner raid the shop Louis used to sell his forgeries seizing the stock and equipment. His associates were apprehended and prosecuted for forgery. Later, he went on to continue his illicit trade unrepentant. The extent of his forgeries is unknown.

2ND ZIONIST CONGRESSES
1898

1ST STAMP OF ISRAEL
1948

For evil to flourish, it only requires good men to do nothing.

— Simon Wiesenthal

RUSSIA 1900

The sun was high overhead, and the fields were ready for harvest. There was a slight breeze moving the leaves of the nearby trees. If one listened, the leaves could be heard talking among themselves. Aaron and Izzy just sat down and were opening their meal for afternoon break when they heard the gunfire and screaming. Aaron jumped up excitedly and yelled, "Come, Izzy, let's hurry, something is happening in the village!"

They ran as fast as they could and when they reached the edge of the village, they saw the last of the Russian mob riding off laughing. Parts of the village were on fire and several bodies lay in the street.

"Where are Mother and Ruth?" yelled Izzy.

"Izzy, you go home and look for our mother and sister. I will try to help those that are hurt here," said Aaron as Izzy ran off down the street.

Aaron grabbed people standing around to help him organize the survivors into fighting the fires. "Saul get some people to form a line to get water on the Temple. We can save it and keep it from spreading to the others nearby. Elijah you and your mother start helping the injured," said Aaron.

A few minutes later Izzy came back and joined in the effort to save the Temple. The fires were almost extinguished, and people were standing around when Aaron walked up to Izzy. Did you find Mother and Ruth?"

"Yes, they are all right, Aaron. They were in the woods collecting berries when the mob attacked. Our neighbor Naomi was not so lucky she was grabbed and taken by one of the men on horseback. She swung her egg basket and hit him in the head. He yelled out in pain and tossed Naomi off his horse. She hit her head on the ground, and she is with her mother right now, but she is unconscious," said Izzy.

"We must leave this country if we are ever going to be safe!" said Aaron.

"The elders and our uncles will never agree to that!"

"We will have to convince them at a meeting tonight!"

Later that night the meeting was held and Moshe, the community leader, spoke of the need to accept the things that just happened. "It was and is the way things happen for our people and this present time will also pass as the bad times have always passed for us Jews."

"Moshe, we need to take charge of our lives. We cannot wait for things just to happen and then just accept the results as if it is just the way life is!" said Aaron.

"Aaron, you, and your brother Izzy are always wanting to change our ways. The Jews of this world have always been persecuted. The Catholic and Orthodox Churches have used us as scapegoats for everything bad that has happened in their history since the death of their Jesus on the Roman cross.

"The Republic of Venice in 1516 hated and feared us so much that the city forced the Jews there to live in a small area every night. That area had been a copper foundry. In the local Venice dialect, the word for foundry was Gheto. That was the first ghetto and was created by the Doge of Venice Leonardo Loredan. Once outside the ghetto, the Jews were forced to wear a yellow cloth around their outer clothes and then later a yellow conical hat 'Dunce hat' so they could be identified as Jews.

"Yes! The Christian governments have never trusted us because of our religion. They see us as disloyal people in every country. They call us the killers of Jesus Christ and that we deserve what happens to us. They say that since the Jews have no country, they cannot be loyal to any country. They even blamed us for the Black Death.

"Over the years, that fear has caused the Jews to be driven out of Spain and England leaving us to find safety in other countries that would allow us to settle and take roots. Then each time the whole process began all over again.

"Now, you are saying we must find a new place that will welcome us to build new homes. I tell you that this is the way things have been done in the past, so what would you have us do Aaron? The process will be the same wherever we go," said Moshe.

"You are most likely right Moshe, if we just go to another country, and that is the reason we need a homeland where we can make our laws. Here in Russia, we are required by their laws to remain in the Pale. — The place that was established by Catherine II for us to settle during the First Partition of Poland. Now we are still required to get their permission to move around within the limits of the Pale.

"Of course, they have now allowed us to fight and defend Mother Russia. That same government under the Tsar Nicholas I calls us Zhids, Yids, or Kikes and has passed some 600 Decrees against the Jews in Russia. Each year that privilege for us to fight for Mother Russia has forced the Jewish communities to provide quotas for the military. When those quotas were not met, Our Pious community leaders and rabbis sent Khappers (Jewish thugs) to collect Jewish men, really boys, to fill the community quota. Young boys of 10 or 12 years old in the past were grabbed and sent to the military.

"These young boys were said to be 18 years old by the elders. The army knew the truth and kept the boys anyway. They kept these boys and placed them in what was called Cantonist (juvenile conscripts) schools. When the boys turned 18, they were transferred to the military for their 25 years of military service. Today we sing a folk song about these young boys that have been taken away," said Aaron, as Izzy began to sing a Yiddish folk song in a beautiful tenor voice:

Tears flow in the streets
One can wash oneself in children's blood
Alas! How great is our dismay
Will never dawn a brighter day?
Little babies from school are torn away,
And dressed up in soldier's grey
Our leaders and our rabbis
Even help turn them into Gentiles
Rich Zushe Rakover has seven sons
Not one a uniform dons
But poor widow Leah has an only child
And they hunt down as if he were wild
It is right to draft the hard-working masses
Shoemakers or tailors, they're only asses!
But the children of the idle rich
They must carry on without a hitch

The room was silent when Izzy finished the song. Everyone looked at Moshe, whose face was red with anger and hate for the two brothers.

"Aaron, you sound like that radical, who calls himself Lenin and those radical fools that follow him. Russia is making progress and things are changing. You are in rebellion against our community, and you wish to destroy our unity and way of life!" said Moshe.

"You are right, Moshe, in only one thing and that is those Cantonist schools have ended. Yet, we are still resented and hated by the Russians who see us as enemies of the state. They will continue to attack us and suffer under their new pogroms. So, here we are in Russia and still being the target of a Christian government that takes out its frustrations of their failure on us," said Aaron.

"What would you have us do? Become a terrorist like that thug from Georgian, Dzhugashvili who calls himself 'Koba' after that legionary King of Georgia who was seen as their Robin Hood. That is if he has not already chosen a new name to call himself," said Moshe.

"We are not terrorists Moshe! We are just tired of being scapegoats for the failures of Russian leaders and our leaders. As for what we can do is simple, we can go to Palestine. There are twenty or more Jewish settlements there that are sponsored by the Baron Rothschilds in France. We can follow the example of the First Aliyah and return to our traditional homeland. The Zionist Theodor Herzl has written about a Jewish state," said Aaron.

"What are you trying to imply? What is this Zionism and what is this State?" asked Moshe.

"Zionism, Moshe is a Jewish state where the Jews can live and control their fate and government," said Izzy.

"That is just more intellectual claptrap thinking of the communist and socialist writings of that radical German Karl Marx. Those people would have us turn away from our culture and religion. Marx was an atheist. We have our government right here in Russia!" said Moshe.

"No, you have your government here, Moshe. My mother, sister and brother are coming with me to Palestine. We will not stay in a country that publishes lies about the Jewish people," said Aaron.

"What are you talking about? My government? What lies are you spreading now?" asked Moshe.

"You know Moshe, stop pretending you don't know about The

Protocols of the Elders of Zion that were written and published by the Tsar secret police, the Okhrana, last year," said Izzy.

"Why would you say I know?" asked Moshe.

"Because Moshe, I saw and heard you talking to that chief Russian officer the other day. I was just wondering if he warned you about the pogrom that happened here today. Was that the reason your family was not in the village today?" asked Aaron.

"What! What! Are you accusing me of – YOU, YOU, simple dung peddler!" yelled Moshe.

"You know very well what I am saying. You and your family have benefited during hard times. While others have suffered, you and those who control this community do so through religious intimidation. Our religion and principles seem to be ignored by you on several occasions," said Aaron.

"You bastard of a whore!" With that Moshe rushed at Aaron and the room erupted into a brawl that turned into several smaller fights and arguments and a few more pushing matches before everyone left. Moshe was pulled from the room yelling back at the brothers that they would pay for the insults.

Before they were able to leave the community, the Russian police officer began to make life difficult for Aaron and Izzy in small ways that delayed their daily activity and progress to leave the village to work in the fields. During the simple act of walking to the field each day, they were stopped, and their papers were checked. Each day it was a new issue that caused the stop.

"Aaron and Izzy, where were you last night?" asked the Russian police officer.

"At home, why do you ask?"

"Someone broke into a barn and ran off with some tools."

"Why ask us?" said Izzy.

"There are rumors about the two of you in the community. The rumors are about you being the source of many of the problems," said the officer.

"Who is making the statements? I guess it would be Moshe," said Aaron.

"I was told to keep a watch on the both of you from the office. I am just following, well you know. Yet, you are right. I think it is Moshe, who is telling my superior to stop and check you each day. I like you two for being Jews — you are good men. If I were you two, I would be very careful," the officer said as he turned and walked away.

"Izzy, we need to leave before Moshe and his group have us removed to one of the labor camps or moved to Siberia," said Aaron.

"I agree, when?"

"I know and I have been setting a plan in motion with that Russian that runs the Black Market in this area. He will get us out for a high fee tonight," said Aaron.

"Can we trust him?" asked Izzy.

"He is a member of the Thieves, and they have one rule. That rule is they must never work with the government. Do I trust him? No, but if we stay here, it will only get worse for the family. That Russian officer made me think that something is being planned to happen soon to us. If not tomorrow, the next day. I saw Moshe was talking to the chief officer when we left for the field this afternoon," said Aaron.

"Then make the arrangements. The sooner the better," said Izzy.

That is why the family left that night after leaving notes with the black-market Russian on Moshe's activities with the head police officer and other community elders about the payments made and favors given to Moshe.

The Black-Market Russian was good as his word to the family in part because Aaron and Izzy gave him the same information that could be used against Moshe and the Police officer for blackmail.

The Thieves' network took the family to Odesa on the Black Sea. Then they were taken by a fishing ship through the Dardanelles to Greece where they changed to a ship for Cyprus. A week later they were on their way to Palestine in another ship. That summer Aaron and the family re-searched Palestine. They were the last part of the first Aliyah, that helped establish a Kibbutz at Degania in Palestine.

CHAPTER EIGHT

Edward Stanley Gibbons engaged in less than reputable practices in the stamp world in today's ethical world. He sold his stamp stock and business in 1890 to Charles J. Phillips. Charles reportedly said that if the trade in fake stamps continued it would ruin the stamp trade business. Gibbons went on to become a world traveler and popular in the stamp world. The company became the Gold Standard in Philately.

CURTISS JENNY

INVERTED JENNY
$500,000 TO
$1 MILLION

It is best to avoid the beginnings of evil.
— Henry David Thoreau

CORONER'S OFFICE 2012

"You called and I hope you have something good for me today, Elaine?" said C.E. as he walked into the coroner's office.

"Well, how nice! No, hello Elaine, or you look nice today. I guess this relationship has fallen into that old comfort zone people always talk about."

"Oh, no! That is not happening at all. I just finished talking with the FBI about the stamps you discovered at the fire. They were all very high-value stamps. A stamp collector would be willing to pay top dollar for any one of them. What we saw was just the surface of the forgeries. There were stamps from all around the world that were stuffed in a hidden drawer on the desk. The agent said that most files in the desk and cabinets had been removed. The hidden drawer was discovered by accident when an agent turned a handle in the opposite direction. So, my mind was just thinking of stamps," said C.E.

"You are not making this any better. Stamps before me?" said Elaine.

"I see I am in a no-win situation. How about I admit my faults and we get back to the topic at hand?"

"Yes, now that you have admitted your faults. However, why the secret compartment? Why would the stamp dealer have all those stamps in a secret compartment if they were forgeries?" asked Elaine.

"Many of the early forgers were also stamp dealers so I guess this guy was just following the old stamp collector for in the early days it was not that uncommon," said C.E.

"Now I remember you telling of a French forger who was good. What was his name?"

"Jean de Sperati and he was the best at least to many in the trade."

"Yes, his story was interesting, but back to the topic at hand. What did the FBI say?" asked Elaine.

"They are thinking it was a way to hide or launder money by important individuals or an organization. They think this stamp dealer was skimming stamp sheets for his use and was caught doing it by the people ordering the printing and that would explain his death," said C.E.

"Then you might want this autopsy report. Our stamp dealer did not die of a heart attack. He died of a massive drug overdose. That is why I called you. I thought this might be important and I know that you cannot let things sit around. I also sent copies to the fire and police chiefs just before you got here," said Elaine.

"What do you mean by a massive drug overdose?"

"The guy was pumped full of enough drugs to kill an elephant and that caused the heart and other organs to shut down. No one could have survived that dose of cocaine."

"I guess we better go over and talk to them and see what we can piece together," said C.E.

"I know you said some of these stamps were worth close to a million dollars or more, but how expensive can any of the other stamps be?" asked Elaine.

"Like I said, the Penny Black is expensive. Some of the other stamps they discovered are just as expensive or even more. For example, an 1851 Hawaiian Missionary's stamp just sold for around $600,000. Then there was a Benjamin Franklin stamp from 1851 that sold for $3 million, a Swedish stamp of the 1855 Treskilling Yellow sold for $3.8 million, a block of four China One Dollar stamps from 1897 went for $4.6 million, a rear Inverted Jenny Stamp was sold for close to $3 million…just to name a few that I know about. Our dealer must have been following the sideline work of many past dealers in forgeries and somehow got mixed up with the wrong group," said C.E.

"You've got to be kidding – stamps! I thought they were just a pretty little picture hobby and not a real investment plan," said Elaine.

"Yes, stamps! They can be both. I collect them as a hobby and enjoy their artwork, plus I am fascinated by the history behind them and who owns them. The nice thing about stamps as a hobby is that one can collect and make a little money at the same time. I like the old Soviet Union stamps because the color quality begins to fade as they run off more and more in the series of stamps. At the beginning of a series run the stamps would be a bright color, say red, and that would slowly fade to washed-out pink by the end of the series run. Thus, the color of the stamps adds or decreases the value. The Socialist system demands quantity over quality for more was the goal."

"I will have to pay more attention to your stories on stamp history. They were just plain old stamps that you put on an envelope to mail before we started talking about them. I started to see them as something to collect as a hobby and now I am starting to look at them as little pieces of valuable art," said Elaine.

"Now who is falling into that comfortable habit of just listening to someone's stories."

"Touché, I see we must continue this discussion at a later time," said Elaine.

"I agree maybe we could do that tonight?"

"I'd like that to start with dinner," she said with a smile.

"Home or out?" asked C.E.

"Chinese at my place," said Elaine.

"I'll bring the P.F. Chang if you provide the wine," said C.E.

"Done! Now shall we go see the Chiefs and ask them for their wisdom?" asked Elaine.

"Wisdom, I think not, but we will get a solid policy from them both."

CHAPTER NINE

Andre Frodel was a master of forgeries, overprints, fakes, fake imperforates, imitation cancellations, and fantasy stamps. At his death, the Canadian government seized a treasure of Andre's craft. It is unknown how many of Andre's excellent reproductions are in the hands of collectors. He may have done this work as a hobby and not to defraud buyers.

FOUR EMPIRE LOST IN THE GREAT WAR.

What happens when good people are put into an evil place? Do they triumph or does the situation dominate their past history and morality?

— Philip Zimbardo

PALESTINE 1922

The ship had docked, and the troops were walking down the gangway. Many were tired from the Great War and Allied intervention that had ended the year before. They were part of the British Army that was sent to Arkhangelsk and Vladivostok in northern Russia to prevent the allied military supplies from falling into the German hands after the Russian Reds had withdrawn from the war at Brest-Litovsk in 1918. Now, after many years of their service, the Russian Jewish translators were being sent to Palestine to help the colonial government.

Aaron was one of the translators used by the British. He and his officer had been assigned to the Estonian front in the intervention working along with White Army Units in an Operation called White Sword. Its purpose was to capture Petrograd from the Bolsheviks.

The operation failed when many of the different units failed to work together. The White units were pushed back, and the Estonian Army and Navy decided to withdraw from the resistance. The Reds began pushing forward and the troops of the Allies British started to withdraw their armies from Russia. Then a small unit with Russian Jewish translators was sent to Poland during the Soviet-Polish War that ended in 1921. Aaron was with the Polish Army in the victory over the Reds, who were under the command of a Bolshevik commissar who started calling himself Stalin after dropping the name of the Georgian folk hero, Koba. That commissar would not forget the defeat.

Now they were sent back home to Palestine to be discharged or work with the administration in Palestine. Aaron was halfway down the ramp when he heard his name being called out. He looked to the left of the ramp and saw his brother Izzy waving and jumping up and down."

"Aaron, Aaron, over here, over here," yelled Izzy. Aaron looked and waved back and pointed to the place they should meet. Once they met, they embraced in a huge hug.

"Aaron, why did you go to help the British in their war against the Germans? The British are better than the Germans and Russians, but they see us as Jews and not to be trusted," said Izzy.

"Yes, you are right Izzy. However, the British attitude is shifting slowly towards our people and a Jewish state. It is our best chance to win our state," said Aaron.

"But you were in Poland this last year with the British and you are still the only Jew that can help them," said Izzy.

"Yes, that is true. But the Allies in the beginning were worried that the Germans would get tons of war materials they had sent to aid the Russian Army before the Revolution. Then the Bolshevik government surrendered to the Germans and that fear of a Red Revolution became a real worry in the West. The Reds controlled the government in Russia, but not the country. Groups and events soon had the different elements in Russia struggling for power and control of the nation.

"The Civil War increased the Ally's fear that a Red victory would increase the spread of communist revolutions. There were crises in Berlin, Hungary, Finland, and Sweden, and there were bombings in New York City just in 1919. It was for this that I was assigned with a British officer to coordinate with a Whites Army in an Operation called Sword that was to capture Petrograd. It failed after all of our successes because the allied partners failed to work together, and we were pushed back. Then the Estonian army withdrew to their territory lines. At the same time, the Allies started to withdraw from Russia and the civil war.

"After that collapsed a few of us were sent to Poland to be advisors to the Polish, who were fighting the Bolsheviks in Ukraine. They had taken the city of Kiev for a time until the Bolsheviks counterattacked, dividing the Polish back to Warsaw. Somehow the Polish army pulled off a miracle at the Vistula River destroying the Bolsheviks and forcing the Russians to end the war. The Bolshevik leader of the operation in that sector was someone calling himself Stalin. He was able to place the blame for the defeat at someone else's feet.

"The rumor was he vowed to make Poland suffer if given the chance. The Russians had problems at home at the time when the Kronshtadt sailors revolted in March and the Soviets withdrew from the Western wars.

"I'll tell you one thing, we are lucky to be out of Russia. The Reds and Whites are killing anyone in opposition, especially Jews. The Bolsheviks were attacking and sacking their churches while they killed every religious Jew they found. At the same time, many of the Bolsheviks are Jews.

"The white armies in Russia mistrust each other while they fight the

Reds. At times they go on a series of pogrom killing sprees. At Fastov, Kyiv, Tetiyev, and other places the synagogues were burned, and men, women, and children were killed just for being Jews.

"I was told on the ship by a British officer, who was a professor at a university, that there were perhaps half a million Jews murdered by the Reds and Whites after 1919. He went on to say that Jews like Leon Trotsky and Rosa Luxemburg had joined the Bolsheviks as socialists to make a better world. That decision placed them in conflict between their religion and their political philosophy for a better world," said Aaron.

"I do not understand the conflict?" said Izzy.

"I did not understand either and the professor went on to tell me that the Bolsheviks see all religion as the greatest weakness, and they therefore plan to create a government and a better world without any religion.

"He went on to say that the Jews are not united on how they are to win their homeland for they are divided between the Zionists of old, socialist, assimilationist, and nationalist that are not part of the Trotskyist — just to name a few of the different ideas for the homeland," said Aaron.

"Trotskyist?"

"He explained to me that the Zionists of old wanted a homeland for Jews. Trotsky is a nationalist of a different kind and he wants a better socialist world. Therefore, Trotsky is a radical nationalist who wants to create a better world for the working class, not just Jews.

"The Bolsheviks are creating this new form of government not based on the Karl Marx idealism, but on Lenin's of elite revolutionary leaders. That in time Lenin will remove those that oppose his political views. He said that process is underway now in the new Soviet Union with Lenin's New Economic Policy. The civil war in Russia forced Lenin to create what he called War Communism and the peasants suffered under this policy. Lenin signed the treaty with the Germans, the Bolsheviks, turned their focus on Russia, and created a new government there. Now the country is in economic chaos and Lenin is trying to get the peasants to support the new government," said Aaron.

"The Western powers have also created some new governments," said Izzy.

"Well now that the war and the civil wars are over, we see we are no further towards our independence. The Europeans have been lying to everyone in the Middle East. They agreed in secret that after the Great War, they would allow the Italians a share of parts of North Africa in the Saint-Jean-de-Maurenne agreement. Then they turned around and agreed to share the same territory between France and Great Britain with the Sykes-Picot agreement.

"Plus, they offered the Arabs their independent state in a correspondence between Hussein and McMahan. That was followed by the Americans at the Balfour Hotel that continued the discussion for a Jewish state in what is called the Balfour Declaration," said Aaron.

"Aaron, you are a misguided soul. As you just said, the war did not improve our situation. I see that it did open a renewed wave of Arab nationalism at the same time and renewed or increased the hate for our people in Palestine," said Izzy.

"President Wilson's 14 points and self-determination will provide for our independence. You are right for now Izzy, but the 14 points will change the world for the better," answered Aaron.

"That was four years ago he made those points. Do you think the Europeans were ever going to allow President Wilson to implement his full 14 Points? Don't be foolish, they will never allow that. Look how they used the 14 points to get Germany to surrender and then the Germans were not even allowed to sit at the Peace Table. God only knows how that will turn out in Germany. The American President Wilson wanted his League of Nations and was willing to give up all his other interests and our desires for his desire for the League of Nations," said Izzy.

"You are wrong. The war is over and calmer heads can now take charge," said Aaron.

"You are forgetting the Bolsheviks you just left in Russia are starting to cause trouble around the world and the West is beginning to worry. The Bolshevik slogan calling for 'Bread, Peace and Land' is beginning to resonate in the Arab world for the end of the colonial powers.

"Our Jewish homes here and elsewhere in the world will be in more conflict than ever. In the end, the Europeans will control the Middle East as before. Only this time it will not be as an Empire, but as a declared protection from radicalism, nationalism, and Bolshevism. Plus, it does not help that the Russian Revolution was filled with many Jews in its leadership. Bolsheviks or now the Communists will be seen as a Jewish conspiracy to dominate the world like the fake Protocols of the Elders. This will only increase the attacks on the Jews outside of Russia," said Izzy.

"Izzy, you need to think more positively, things will get better. This is nothing like the world of the past," said Aaron.

"You're right and yet that Bolshevik Leon Trotsky, who is a Jew, will bury the religious Jews with their Torah along with the Christians and their Bibles. These Bolsheviks will not tolerate any dissent and the Middle East will become part of a new struggle for power between the capitalist and communist of Europe. At the same time, the Arabs will be at each other's throats trying to obtain power while they try removing the Jews from this earth," said Izzy.

"Izzy, you sound like the prophets of the past. I hope you are wrong. Our hope is in building a modern industrial financial system so we can control our fate," replied Aaron.

"See that is what I mean, Aaron. In our past before 1100 A.D., we were the money lenders of Europe's financial world and that was only because the Christian Church did not allow Christians to loan money for interest. Then the Knight of the Templars became bankers and the church discovered there was money to be made. We were accused of controlling the banking system back then as we are now.

"Added to this today we are accused of being behind the Communism movement and its spreading. If we want to be free of antisemitism, we must have our homeland. We tried to assimilate and are still seen as Jews and not to be trusted," said Izzy.

"You are right we did try assimilation in a dozen nations and have been driven out of each by hate. Yet, there is one nation where Jews are welcome and that is America," said Aaron.

"America, are you kidding me? Men like the industrialist Henry Ford hates the Jews and publishes a paper *The Dearborn Independent* that accuses the Jews of being the controllers of world banking and interest.

"In the Southern states of America, Jewish individuals are lynched alongside the blacks and others. Even in the other states in the north and west, the Jews are not allowed in their elite country clubs, schools, or other organizations simply for being Jewish. No, for all their so-called tolerance Americans dislike Jews. They just do not have Pogroms. They just have lynching!" said Izzy.

"Our cousin Marty has a family and home with a dealership selling Ford automobiles in America and has asked me to come over and help him. He said that life there is good," said Aaron.

"Wait a minute! Are you going to separate the family and go live in another place where you are going to be disliked?" asked Izzy.

"No! I'm just saying he seems to be doing well for his family. Working and selling cars for the man you say hates Jews," said Aaron.

"I will give you this Henry Ford may just express an undertone in the American mindset about Jews. I doubt that very much. I have read his newspaper, and he expresses hate against bankers who are controlled by Jews.

But I am glad you are staying here. Now, let's get back to work. I would not like to lose my best brother," said Izzy.

"I am your only brother!" said Aaron.

"See! There it is. I did not have much to choose from. I think we both are working out what we want and how to achieve it. You felt that the British were changing their position of a Jewish state and now it seems you are with my side that the only solution for us Jews is our state," said Izzy.

"You are right, I think we differ on how to get that Jewish State," said Aaron.

"It is good to have you home brother. Let's go find our family and celebrate your return."

CHAPTER TEN

Adrien Champion had several aliases he used to defraud London stamp dealers. After being arrested in England he fled to France and was arrested. Then in Geneva, he was arrested once more and placed on trial for forgery charges. In his defense, he argued that stamp forgeries were no different than selling imitation jewelry.

He was sentenced to nine months and 10 days in prison. Since he had served that time already, he was free, and he moved back to France to continue his trade. His stock was confiscated and sold at auction. He bid on the confiscated stock, won the bidding and resumed business in Geneva under the name Frederic Champion.

GENUINE   **FORGERY**

In our country the lie has become not just a moral category but a pillar of the State.

— Aleksandr Solzhenitsyn

A Soviet Gulag in Siberia July 1941

On June 22, 1941, Hitler broke the Nonaggression Pact he signed with Stalin in 1939 that divided Poland between the two nations. Hitler decided that the British were out of the way as a threat to his western front and launched the largest military invasion in history with some 4 million men, 23,000 pieces of artillery, 600,000 horses, 600,000 vehicles that included almost 4,000 tanks with 4,000 aircraft divided into 153 divisions of 104 infantry divisions, 19 Panzer divisions, 15 motorized divisions with 9 security divisions called Einsatzgruppen (police units) in three army groups that would conquer Russia before Christmas.

Stalin refused to believe that Hitler would attack, while the British were still in the combat field in the west. Stalin had read *Mein Kampf* and knew Hitler was fearful of a two-front war. The Einsatzgruppen units would clean up the areas behind the battlefield.

At Babi Yar in the Ukraine, the Einsatzgruppen units began the mass murder of Jews and the Death Camps were established to remove the Jews from Europe.

"Alexei something big has happened – come quickly," yelled Viktor.

"What? I am trying to get some rest."

"They want everyone to assemble at the front gate. The guards are in the camp," said Viktor.

"Now? That is something! They never come into the camp unless it's big. We need to be careful. Come stay close with me," said Alexei.

At the main gate, a new commissar stood on a raised platform with a bullhorn walking back and forth waiting for the guards to assemble all the camp inmates. There were more guards than usual. Everyone around the commissar stood in a state of anxiety fearful of his wrath.

He was a little man who had ruthlessly followed orders and the Party line to get to his current position in the power chain of command. There were thousands of little commissars just like him in the Soviet Union. Each one waiting to make a name for himself with a job well done by overfilling quotas that were sent down from Moscow.

This was his chance to impress his superiors by filling his quota and doubling it or even more. He looked out at the mass of prisoners, stepped to the front of the platform and raised the bullhorn.

"I am Commissar Isaak Rykov and I have come to set you free of this place and your past crimes against Mother Russia. The German international criminal Hitler and his gang of thugs have invaded Mother Russia, and your country needs its patriots who are willing to fight for Mother Russia. Comrade Stalin is willing to grant a full pardon to any prisoner willing to fight for Mother Russia. You will be given your freedom at the end of the war. Those who will stand with Mother Russia will leave this camp today and join our glorious Mother Russian and Red Army today.

Those of you that stay, your life will become more difficult for you must do the work that is needed for the war effort. Mother Russia is at war and all resources will be directed to the war effort, even the work of criminals and reactionaries. So those who wish to fight for Mother Russia line up at the tables by the gate now! We will be leaving today! Long Live Mother Russia!" The commissar turned and walked off the platform giving orders to those at the tables.

"Commissar, the trucks are lined up outside the gates and ready to move to the train station," said a guard as he ran up to the Commissar.

"See that they move as soon as the last man gets on board. Mother Russia and Moscow need every fighting man they can get," said the Commissar.

Alexei was deep in thought when Viktor asked, "What are we going to do, Alexei?"

"First, I want to talk to Mikhail. Wait for me here. I will not be long."

Alexei walked around the assembled group looking for a group of men who had been their protector since he and Viktor walked into camp that first day. Mikhail was the leader of the camps' Thieves-in-Laws, and he always had his enforcers with him. Few prisoners could approach Mikhail without asking permission and Alexei was no exception.

Alexei saw who he was looking for as he approached the group — one of the enforcers who was covered in tattoos that told his history as a member of the Thieves. The enforcer looked at him and asked, "What do you want Alexei?"

"I need to speak with Mikhail!"

"Wait," the enforcer looked back at Mikhail who gave the enforcer the sign to allow Alexei to approach.

"What can I do for you, Alexei?" asked Mikhail.

"The offer of freedom is being given. What should Viktor and I do? You have been good to us, and we know your code about working with or for the government. I do not wish to lose your trust," said Alexei.

"Alexei, you are not a member of the Thieves. You have no tattoos and have never taken an oath to us. You are a 'Politico'— one of the government's fallen socialists and for that you have had a real value to me in the camp. As for this war, it is going to change things in Russia for a time, and we are going to have to adjust to new situations, once again. In the end, we will need people on the outside like you and Victor. So go and save Mother Russia as the commissar mentioned and, if you can survive Hitler and Stalin, maybe we will meet once more," said Mikhail.

"Can we trust Stalin?" asked Alexei.

"Nothing is for sure! Remember you need to adjust to the situation. Stalin is the leader of a different group of 'Thieves' and they have no code to follow at all. They will adjust to situations with no need for loyalty by just climbing over those in front of them.

"Did you notice that the Commissar did not mention the Soviet Union once in his speech? He did however mention Mother Russia several times. A Russia where all Russians shared in good and bad times. They are scared and need to rally the nation to their side by using Mother Russia as the hook. The Russia of the past will begin to reappear in very small details to win public support for the nation in the fight against Hitler and his army of thugs.

"I will say this, Alexei, things will get better. The number of arrests will drop, and more freedom will be allowed until the end of this crisis. Then it will shift back to the old pattern of terror with the Bolsheviks controlling what freedom is allowed and to whom. So, go and win your freedom. When this is over, let's hope we meet again Alexei. Who knows - maybe we can work together once more after this war?" said Mikhail.

"What about trusting Stalin?" asked Alexei.

"What choice do you have? Learn to adjust Alexei because it will change with you or without you."

"Thank you, Mikhail, you have been a good friend to Viktor and myself. I hope to see you again when this is over." With that Alexei turned and walked back to Viktor.

"What did Mikhail say?" asked Viktor.

"He said to go and win our freedom and he implied we should not trust the communists. Let's go to the tables and sign our lives away from the war and for Mother Russia," said Alexei.

Alexei and Viktor walked out of the camp and loaded into trucks. When they had come to the camp, they had been forced to march to the camp from the train. Now they were given a ride to the train. "Viktor, things must be bad!"

"Why do you say that Alexei?"

"Remember when we came here, we had walked. I think things must be bad!" said Viktor.

"Well, we are in it now!" said Alexei.

"Where do you think we are being taken?" asked Viktor.

"Some place they need bodies to die. We will have to stay close together and watch each other's backs," said Alexei.

They were driven to the waiting train and once again locked in a cattle car with others. They were sent west to face the German Army at Leningrad. There they were each given a rifle and told how to load it and pull the trigger as their only training and sent right into battle against the German machine guns in front and the Russian machine guns that were set up behind them. There were no retreat orders and those who tried to retreat were shot by Soviet special units and political Commissars.

"Get down Viktor! We have taken our objective and driven that advanced unit of the Germans out of the city, no thanks to the brave commissars hiding behind the wall over there."

"If I knew who the German sniper was who shot that idiot commissar, I'd give him a medal! Once he was shot that army officer took complete command and worked the unit into positions that commanded the street. That commissar cost us half of our men when he had us rush the Germans lined right down the middle of the street," said Viktor.

"I doubt it was a German sniper, he stood there in the back by that machine gun yelling at the men to rush the Germans. When the Germans opened fire, the commissar was hit but fell forward," said Alexei.

"What do you mean?" asked Viktor.

"How many men have we seen killed since we came into the city?" asked Alexei.

"Too many to count. This place is a blood bath," replied Viktor.

"When a man or woman is hit by a bullet, which way do they fall?" asked Alexei.

"I don't know, they just fall," said Viktor.

"Have you seen anyone jump forward?" asked Alexei.

"No, they slump or just drop backward away from the path of the bullet, I guess," said Viktor.

"The commissar did not just fall forward it looked like he jumped into and over the sandbags he was behind. No. Someone behind him shot that kill shot. We need to be careful. Never say anything about what I just said," said Alexei.

"Why?"

"These commissars are paranoid and always looking for conspiracies and people to take the fall for their poor decisions and failures. The commissar that was killed can be used to place the blame for the failure of more ground being taken. It will be best to know nothing that happened. Just say we were moving forward if asked," said Alexei.

A junior Lieutenant ran up and yelled, "You two go back and get more anti-tank mines to place out in front of our lines."

Both men saluted, kept low, and rushed to the rear without saying anything.

As the battle went on, the city of Leningrad was surrounded, and Alexei and Viktor were assigned to protect the road across the frozen lake which was the only way into the city during the winter. Those civilians and soldiers who were forced to stay in the city were hungry and dying. The ground was too hard to bury the dead except for the holes made by German artillery shells. Everything was white or grey.

1943

"Alexei, we've been here for over a year and a half and are still trapped in the city. Why have the Germans not tried to enter the city?" asked Viktor.

"They are in just as bad of shape as we are. Their artillery makes it seem as if they are strong. Yet, remember that Spaniard we captured? He was from the Spanish volunteer's Blue Division in the German army. He was in a summer uniform last winter and was also hungry. He almost seemed happy when the commissar shot him. I think the Germans hope that starvation in the city will break our willpower to resist. They do not understand that if we stop resisting, we will be shot," said Alexei.

"The people of this city are stooping to murder others for their ration cards and there are rumors that NKVD units are arresting individuals for cannibalism. Nobody is talking about it. I overheard two commissars talking when they were relieving themselves last night. Everyone has a 'dull look' to their eyes and if it was not for this Ice Road across this frozen Lake Ladoga and the water boats in the summer, this city would be done for in days or weeks," said Viktor.

"Be careful of what you are saying. The wrong word can get you shot Viktor. This month there is another planned campaign to break the encirclement. Its code name is Operation Iskra and an attack will be a faint made against that same Spanish Blue Division and those idiot Fins. Then the main push will be against the German fortifications in the south of the city to relieve the city to make a land path for supplies. That is if the plan is followed by the commissars," said Alexei.

"Those idiot Fins, as our great commissar calls the Fins, are real fighters. He fails to remember the Fins kicked the stuffing out of Stalin's armies in the Winter War in 1939 and 1940. So I was told by a soldier that was there. So do not underestimate the Fins, my friend," said Viktor.

"Viktor, my friend, we better get some sleep. We are going to be busy trying to stay alive from the enemy in the front and our friends behind us," said Alexei.

CHAPTER ELEVEN

James M. Chute was a member of what was called the 'Boston Gang', a small group of swindlers. He specialized in the false authentication of stamps and other documents. In 1886 he was elected to be the first editor of The American Philatelist publication. Then at the same meeting, the association's constitution was amended with an adoption that the editor's office be by appointment of the official board. Therefore, James never served in his elected post. He was denounced in 1892 for his fraudulent activity by several philatelic publications.

GENUINE   **FORGERY**

A state of war only serves as an excuse for domestic tyranny.

— Aleksandr Solzhenitsyn

AUGUST 1945 IN WESTERN POLAND

The countryside was in ruins from invading armies that had moved back and forth across the land causing mass human and material destruction. The first invaders were the German Wehrmacht and Waffen-SS units that struck on September 1, 1939, with their combat units pushing through the weak Polish defenses. Following the Wehrmacht were the Einsatzgruppen units that rounded up Jews and organized ghettos at lightning speed. Then in a shock invasion on September 17, 1939, the Soviet Union military entered the war claiming they were there to protect the Polish people. The Poles, believing the Soviets were there to help, failed to recognize that it was an invasion to take territory.

The Wehrmacht and Red Army coordinated their advance until the Red Army reached Bug River meeting the Germans and the Soviet troops shook hands in cooperation with their victory. The city of Warsaw surrendered on September 28, 1939, and on October 6, 1939, the last resistance to the invasions took place. The Polish government surrendered to the Germans and the Nation was divided between the two invaders by a secret protocol between Hitler and Stalin.

The killing did not stop at the end of the battles. The Germans in the West still used the Einsatzgruppen units that were rounding up the Jewish population for isolation in ghettos. The mass killings that would be called the Holocaust would not start until Hitler invaded Russia in 1941.

The Soviets in the eastern part of Poland immediately began their plans for the elimination of perceived enemies of the Soviet Union with the NKVD creating an atmosphere of terror with murders and deportation. They began to remove any opposition to their control with mass killings and then blamed the Germans for the slaughter.

To remove any opposition to the Soviet rule, the NKVD squads gathered Polish Officers and other Polish leaders at a place in the Katyn Forest massacred them, and buried the victims in a mass grave. Photographs were then taken of the process and used by the Soviets as an example of a German atrocity. The world accepted what they saw in the photos. The Germans were seen as beasts in Western propaganda news press and films.

The Germans in the western part of Poland began pushing the Jewish communities into the small neighborhoods called ghettoes to starve them to death and later used Poland as a place for other European nations to send their Jews to the Polish Concentration death camps. They were described as relocation settlement camps for the Jewish community.

The Germans and Soviets continued to cooperate waiting until their military forces were strong enough to remove the other side. Both leaders knew that a war between them was coming, and Hitler could not wait, while the Soviets built up their military.

Stalin believed he had time to build his forces as long as the Germans were still fighting in the west with Great Britain because Hitler was fearful of a two-front war. When he was told of German military buildup for an invasion, Stalin refused to accept the facts. In June of 1941, Stalin was shocked to learn German troops were invading and collapsed into inaction for days.

Operation Barbarossa ended the Hitler-Stalin Nonaggression Pact between Germany and the Soviet Union. The eastern front of the war allowed the Germans to begin plans for the Final Solution with mass killings of the Jewish population in Europe.

The Germans once again sent their "Death Squads" Einsatzgruppen to follow the Army as it moved into Soviet control zones and systematically wiped out Jewish communities as they moved forward. The mass killing began at a place called Babi Yar in late September 1941. The process began with German troops shooting the victims in pits. That killing process caused the German executioners to break down mentally. A way had to be found to correct this problem with the executioners.

The second stage of the killings began with the gassing of the people in the back of truck vans used to transport the victims. It was begun to save the executioners from the trauma of the killings. However, this new process caused the breakdown of the drivers who had to remove the bodies and finish off those still alive. All of the early methods of killing had caused far too many mental breakdowns in many of the killers, and many ended up killing themselves.

A new method of killing, the Final Solution, was soon developed for faster mass killings in Death Camps and to ease the psychological effect on the killers. The workers of the Jewish and social undesirable did 99 percent of the work in the killings in the camps. The Concentration (Relocation) camps soon became Death camps for the sole purpose of the extermination of the European Jews and other undesirables for the new German Empire in gas chambers.

The Germans were not alone in these killings. The local populations often helped in the process, or they watched as if it was a spectacle for entertainment. Many of the killing sites would go unrecorded for years, because of the shared guilt of what happened. Only the Death camps would be shown to the world as the real "evilness" of the Nazi regime.

The world leaders knew of these mass murders and did not want to divert war materials to prevent the further transportation of Jews or the destruction of the Death camps. The rationale was that ending the war as fast as possible would save more lives. The camps went on and continued their evil work and became better at killing right up to the end of the war.

The German war crimes would be splashed across the front pages of newspapers and magazines as the camps were liberated. Nazi war crimes were on full display while other crimes committed by the Soviets were ignored or blamed on the Germans.

In the Pacific, the Japanese war crimes like those of the 'Comfort Women' and 'Camp #731' would be quietly talked about and only come to light 40 years later. The comfort women were some 200,000 women (sex slaves) used by the Japanese military from 1932 to 1945. The U.N. estimated 140,000 died of sexual abuse. It was not until 1992 that the survivors came forward and talked about the abuse during the war.

Then at Camp #731, the Japanese conducted experiments on human beings like the Germans did in their concentration camps. The experiments were from hypothermia to spreading infectious diseases like the plague and Cholera. Much of the current knowledge on hypothermia comes from these experiments that were done by German and Japanese medical researchers. The ethical questions asked today are about the use of the knowledge collected in this way.

On April 25, 1945, Soviet and American troops as comrades-in-arms exchanged souvenirs in their cooperation for the destruction of the Third Reich ending the war in Europe at the Elbe River. The first handshakes were not filmed, so the Soviets demanded a second meeting to be filmed for a visual record of the event and also did the same for the surrender of the German Army.

In time, the old enemies (Germany and Japan) would become new allies and an old ally (the Soviet Union) become the new enemy. The Soviet Union began to spread the idea of Communism and at the beginning of the Cold War a limited war of proxy combatants between the Eastern Bloc and Western Bloc.

This was the beginning of a new kind of war that was made possible on August 6, 1945. A Nuclear Age war was born with the USA and their control of the atom until 1949 when the Soviet Union entered with their own A-bomb. The arms race began with ever-increasing weapons. The fact that the Soviet A-Bomb looked a lot like the American bomb and other top-secret ideas and plans turning up in the Soviet Union created another Red Scare in the West.

The Second World War had broken down the rule of the colonial powers and this added to the problems of the Cold War. Independent movements swept across the globe and the East and West Cold War players played a major political and economic part in these conflicts.

The Cold War victors used war criminals and Nazis scientists who were useful and valuable workers in the technology struggle of the arms race and Cold War.

MAY 1945 ON THE RUSSIAN-POLISH BORDER

"Alexei, it's over, the Germans have raised the white flag. We can go home as free men. I cannot believe that we have lived through this nightmare," said Viktor.

"Home? Where is home for you, Viktor?" asked Alexei.

"I guess it's Kyiv, that is where my family lived until the Revolution. Now, I do not know. I was with Trotsky in Moscow until we were arrested. What about you Alexei, where is your home?"

"I do not have a home. The Party was my home, and I joined the Bolshevik party happily. Then Lenin and his stooges like Stalin ended that when they started to take absolute power and removed any opposition to their rule. I say Stalin because he continued Lenin's policies and improved and expanded the brutal methods. I regret I played a part in a revolution that did not change anything but the people in power who were worse.

"The Cheka replaced the Tsar's secret police, and it became more than just a secret police agency— they became a killing machine for the Party. Then when the killings became an excess, Stalin changed the Cheka name to the NKVD under the leadership of the criminal Beria who continued the State-sponsored terror. We are lucky to survive the camps and this war, Viktor.

"The day we left the camp Mikhail told me that things would change even in the smallest details. Do you remember the uniform we were given at the start of this war? The collar was worn flat like that of the Bolsheviks at the start of the Civil War. Now today it looks more like the collar worn by the old Imperial Russian army with the rank markings and the rank is also more prominent now. I think it will change once more and not before too long. I do not trust Stalin," said Alexei.

Just then a Commissar joined the front of the group and called for attention. "I have two lists of names my glorious Soviet comrades. The first list is those of you who will be transferred to the eastern front to face the yellow devils of the Japanese Empire. The second list of comrades will be going home today to the Soviet Union."

"Alexei, let us hope we are on the second list and the war is over for us. This day could just keep getting better."

"If your name was not called for the first list, report to the rail yard for the journey home. Thank you for defending the Soviet Union!" yelled the Commissar.

Alexei and Viktor's names were not called, and they started to move towards the train yard.

"Viktor look around, tell me what you see?"

"Happy faces waiting to board the boxcars. Why?"

Just then the boxcars doors were pushed open by commissars and armed Soviet soldiers yelled for groups to move faster. "Hurry up! Everyone gets into the train!" was broadcast from a loudspeaker. A soldier stood at the head of the line and counted 50 men for each carload. The count was always the same when moving people in boxcars. Alexei and Viktor were numbers 22 and 23.

As they jumped into the boxcar Alexei said, "Who do these faces belong to Viktor?"

"Soldiers!" replied Viktor.

"Which soldiers?" asked Alexei.

"I don't understand – they're our soldiers," said Viktor.

"Yes, they are and where did they come from before the war?" asked Alexei.

As the doors were closed, Alexei grabbed the fellow next to him and asked, "Where were you before the war?"

"Hey! Watch what you are doing! I was in the camps, and I wanted my freedom," said the soldier

Alexei turned to another soldier and asked the same question. "I was in the camps – why?" came the reply.

"Viktor, all these men I am sure are from the camps and many have the tattoos of the Thieves. These commissars that closed the doors and the army guards are taking us back to the camps," said Alexei.

"Alexei, do not be so cynical. Stalin gave his word we would have our freedom after the war. We have always been transported in cattle cars. We will be back to the heart of Mother Russia in no time, Alexei. Stop your worrying my friend," said Viktor.

"Victor, do you notice how the Commissar addressed the men at the end of his speech when he said we were going home," said Alexei.

"Yes, he said thank you for defending the nation," said Viktor.

"NO, he did not! He said thank you for defending the Soviet Union!" said Alexei.

"SO!" said Viktor.

"When they first came to the camp to get fighters it was Mother Russia, not the Soviet Union and during the worst part of the war, it was always Mother Russia. What were the Commissar's actual words?"

"You are right. He said thank you for defending the Soviet Union. Have we been fools?" asked Viktor.

"We are not alone. This train is full of fools. Get some rest while the train is moving. We will need to be alert."

The train moved through the countryside and the passengers could see the devastation through the slats on the sides of the cattle cars. They passed through villages and towns missing the major cities for they lay in ruin. The climate turned colder each day of travel. When they were at their destination the doors were opened. The men looked out of the train doors, and they saw the train was ringed by guards and a commissar ordered them out of the train.

"Welcome, to your new home of freedom. If you do not follow orders, you will be shot, if you do not move fast, you will be shot, if you talk in line, you will be shot, if you make remarks against the Soviet Union, you will be shot. Now! you will move to the camp on the double or be shot," yelled a commissar.

"You were right Alexei; we have been betrayed by Stalin," said Viktor before they jumped down from the boxcar.

"Do you plan on getting shot our first day back? Stop talking and stay close to me Viktor, the camp is not going to be safe for us."

"Why?" asked Viktor.

"Some of these men are members of the Thieves-in-Laws and they broke the rule of not working for the government. A harsh penalty is going to be paid. We want to stay out of the crosshairs of the fight that is coming," said Alexei.

A shot was fired and a man fell to the ground. "No talking and line up and answer when your name is called for the roll. Then we will march double-time into your new home comrades," yelled a guard as he pushed the men forward.

"Be careful of what you say Viktor. Say nothing about Stalin or the Party," whispered Alexei.

"Let's hope to see some of our old friends here in this hell hole," said Viktor.

The roll was called, and the men moved to the camp at a fast pace. Those who fell on the run to the camp were shot where they fell. One of those shots wore an American Flyers uniform. As Alexei looked around, there were half a dozen in a similar uniform. Later, he was told by another man that that group of men were members of an American bomber crew that crash-landed in Soviet territory after being hit and damaged during a bombing raid in Rumania in August of 1944.

There were also British soldiers in the group that were taken to the camp. Of the 1,500,000 Allied POWs held in the Soviet Union after they were liberated from German POW camps only one million returned to their home countries. Reports indicated that 50,000 POWs disappeared in the Soviet Union. There were some 20,000 American POWs lost in the Soviet Union prison system. Those with Russian or Ukrainian names were executed as Soviet deserters. The British and American governments knew the men were alive and being held in the Soviet Union as hostages for Soviet POWs held in the hands of the Allied governments. To get the return of the Allied POWs the Western powers forced Soviet POWs to return to the Soviet Union at gunpoint against their will. Many of these POWs were shot soon after stepping off the ships.

THE GULAG AND OLD FRIENDS

"Alexie, I saw Mikhail talking to some of the new arrivals that came with us yesterday. The talk did not seem that friendly, but Mikhail did not seem upset. The guy with Mikhail did push one of the guys that came in with us and yelled that he was a traitor. Mikhail stopped him and the two groups walked away."

"Viktor, do not go anyplace tonight and stay close to me. The killing will start tonight."

"What killing?"

"The Thieves are going to war with each other, so we need to stay clear of both sides so that we are not seen as one group or the other. The next few days we will see how the wind is blowing," said Alexie just as Mikhail entered the barracks.

"Alexie and Viktor, what a surprise to see you both survived the war. I am sorry that you both have decided to return to this little home of ours. But Stalin is Stalin."

"You were right. Mikhail said that things would change for a while and then return to the old Soviet way," said Alexie.

"Yes, and the old way is gone. So, my friend, trouble times are coming so stay neutral and you both will be as safe as one can be in this camp," said Mikhail as he turned and walked away.

"What was that all about?" asked Viktor.

"He was warning us that there is danger and to stay away from both sides in the struggle for power between the Thieves. I think Mikhail will be the winner in that struggle," said Alexie.

CHAPTER TWELVE

James A. Croy was arrested in 1983 for possession of counterfeit United States stamps. He agreed to cooperate with the government and help law enforcement after the seizure of some five million dollars of forged twenty-cent stamps and eighty thousand dollars in counterfeit U.S. currency. At the time James was arrested, it was found he had a warrant issued from 1976 for parole violation for a conviction in 1973 for counterfeiting.

GENUINE   **FORGERY**

History never really says goodbye. History says, 'See you later.

— Eduardo Galeano

ARGENTINA 1946

"**P**edro, we need to clean up the streets of the neighborhood. Eva Peron is coming to talk to the poor children later today. The photos must show clean streets and the area needs to look nice," said Edelmiro.

"Edelmiro, I have already told the boys to get to it. The streets will be decorated in the national colors of blue and white. Plus, I have the most beautiful young child to present our next First Lady with a large bouquet," replied Pedro.

"Perfect, now we need to talk about these new German immigrants that are entering the country. They will need papers and identity cards," said Edelmiro.

"Who are these people? I was at the coast a year ago when a group came ashore from a submarine, and they were wearing German military uniforms. Now this new group came at night off a cargo ship. They also were Germans. Are we taking in Nazis?" asked Pedro.

"Do not let anyone hear you say that. Never mention it again. Do you understand what I am saying?" whispered Edelmiro.

"Yes, yes! You are right! I am sorry for bringing it up." said Pedro.

"Now I will tell you this one time and just for your information. The government has agreed to help these individuals. They are bringing vast amounts of money and technology along with experience that will help us develop our business and industrial sectors. If it takes European fascists to help get the economy growing, so much the better. How many Nazi criminals do you think the Americans are running through South America for their new rocket program?" asked Edelmiro.

"I have seen dozens. Some were still in their uniforms," said Pedro.

"The Allied powers in Europe are also using the so-called ex-Nazis in the counter-espionages operations in central Europe and the Soviet Union. Besides, Peron has always been in the fascist political sphere," said Edelmiro.

Outside the cheers could be heard, "Evita, Evita, Evita."

"Pedro, the people love that woman. She is the best thing that happened to Juan."

"We all know that. Listen to that crowd. How did the two of them meet?" asked Pedro.

"It was that earthquake in 1944. Eva was a popular radio hostess and she invited Peron to a fundraiser. That was their first meeting. Then early in 1945, Juan was ousted in a coup that had him sent to prison. When he was released in October, he was with her, and they were married soon after that.

Once they were married the rumors started about her past. Juan resigned from the army in protest of the treatment of Evita and ran for President. The elite class did not like a person who was born to a mistress and raised in a poor neighborhood who may become the first lady. They did not think Juan could win an election with her beside him.

Juan and Evita outwitted them and played to the poor working-class part of the county – those that are called the 'Shirtless Ones'. It will be Evita who wins the vote of the poor and the women for Juan. Listen to the public out there. That woman is loved," said Edelmiro.

"What about the Americans? They were investigating our close ties to Germany during the war," said Pedro.

"You mean the investigation called the U.S. Government Blue Book on Argentina?" asked Edelmiro.

"Yes!"

"The book was published to discredit Juan, and he has turned it against the Americans with his slogan 'O Braded O Peron' (Braden or Peron). Remember that the American Ambassador Spruille Braden is known for interfering in Latin America's internal affairs and is not popular in Argentina.

"Besides there are other Latin American nations that have deep connections with these Germans, and it is so wide and deep that no report of those events will ever come to light in our lifetime or at least until we are very old.

"The allied nations knew that Heinrich Himmler was setting up an escape route in Spain as early as 1944. We have taken advantage of that network, and it has helped us with our economic plans along with the aid from the Vatican. The Vatican fears the communist more than the Nazis and has also helped develop the escape line called the 'Rat Line' to Africa.

"My friend, there is money to be made in the world peace. Even the Swiss bankers and Western intelligence agencies were willing to allow this to happen for various reasons," said Edelmiro.

"Why?" asked Pedro.

"The Catholic Church and the Soviet Union have a different understanding of the function of religion. The church was a source of salvation; plus, the Roman church saw the Nazis as a stop to the spread of communism. The Soviet Union viewed religion as a source of control and the church as a hindrance to the social state that they were building. The church provides hope outside the government and the communists want the government to be the only hope.

"Then there are the capitalists that are the Americans and their bloc of Western countries. The Americans are the driving force for individual wealth and building a stronger society, while the Communists view money and private ownership as holding back the development of a utopian society.

"Let's face it, money is the strongest political, economic, and social force. Swiss banking came out of the war with unclaimed wealth from the Jews of Europe. The Jews placed their money in Swiss banks to protect it from the Germans before they were murdered in the death camps. When the relatives tried to retrieve the funds, they were told they needed a death certificate to withdraw the funds. There were no death certificates issued in the camps. It will take years of legal battles for the relatives to get the funds released. The Swiss banks will use those funds to make more funds for the banks. Money and technology make strong economic societies. That is why these Germans were let into the country. It is what they bring with them wealth and knowledge. We, like the Americans and British, are willing to overlook that these were war criminals and stolen art and gold as well as lives. These Nazis can provide valuable knowledge to our industries.

"The Western intelligence agencies see these Nazis as undercover agents inside the Soviet Union. I have been told that it is a poorly kept secret. The West and the Soviets will not get along for very much longer. The American's A-bomb and the issue of POWs is already causing concerns in Washington with President Truman," said Edelmiro.

"What about POWs?" asked Pedro.

"The Allied powers are forcing Soviet POWs to return to Stalin in the Soviet Union, knowing those men and women will be executed or at best be sent to prison labor camps once they arrive back in the Soviet Union.

The West is beginning to understand that Stalin cannot be trusted," replied Edelmiro.

"Then why force the POWs to go back?" asked Pedro.

"Stalin has a large number of Allied soldiers and will only return them when he is given all of his people back. These Soviet POW's will be sacrificed for the return of Allied POW's.

"Many of these Soviet POWs did work with the Germans and Stalin's claims to surrender was treason. Many of the POWs hated Stalin and his regime and did not want to return home. Stalin wants to make an example of these individuals," said Edelmiro.

"But you said the West does not trust Stalin. Why would they think he will follow with a fair exchange of POWs?" asked Pedro.

"They don't! The leadership knew there were false numbers in the counting of Allied pows in Soviet control areas of Eastern Europe and Asia. The Allied powers were not allowed to go into the POW camps in Soviet Territory so they had to rely on the Soviet numbers.

"The public in the West is tired of war and a new war will not win anyone an election. Just look at what happened to Churchill. He stood against the Nazis almost alone at the beginning of the fight against Hitler. Then he had Great Britain hold off the Germans for two years alone. Then in 1941 the Soviets and Americans joined the fight. Winston Churchill was the reason the Allied world was the victor over Hitler. Then the British public voted him and his party out of office.

"So, my friend, the military and political leaders will see the return of most of the POW's as only a small defeat that they will keep quiet. They know Stalin is using POWs to collect technology and engineering skills. There may be thousands of allied POWs that will be left in Soviet hands when all this is done. It will be seen as the price Western leaders are willing to pay for peace. Just as we are willing to take in so many of these murderous thugs, you saw getting off the boats, for our economic interest," said Edelmiro.

"But with the Nazis and their murderous actions in the death camps how can we justify taking in these people?" asked Pedro.

"I just told you. It is the price that we are willing to pay. You know war crimes go both ways. The German crimes are very visible today to the world. The Japanese government committed the crimes as bad; yet, their crimes are buried in the press. The Nuremberg Trials are being held now and are open to the news media. This public knowledge will be circulated in the world's public press.

"Trials are being held in Tokyo for Japanese war crimes and most people will not even know they are going on or of the brutality of the Japanese Army committed or their actions against the local and military populations they controlled. Their prisoner camp number 731 in North Korea did a medical treatment on prisoners and the U.S. wants to keep that information on the Japanese atomic program, hypothermia as well as other scientific studies out of Soviet hands. I would not be surprised to see Japan and Germany becoming major parts of the West in the conflict between the Soviets and Western Europe.

"If our role in the ex-Nazis ever comes to light, we will just say that other governments were the ones to move these people into and through Argentina for their national security or various other reasons. No one will want to bring us up for public view.

"The Americans wanted the German technology on rockets and grabbed them so Russia could not grab them. The Soviets had already grabbed as many of the Nazi scientists that were left or stayed in the eastern zone as the Soviet army advanced," said Edelmiro.

"What will happen if the Americans call us Nazis and anti-Jewish?" asked Pedro.

"If the West then attacks us for our hard-liners and calls us anti-Semitic, we will just point out that Argentina has taken in more Jewish refugees than any Western nation," said Edelmiro.

"Let's just hope Juan wins the election," said Pedro.

"The election is already won Pedro!" said Edelmiro.

CHAPTER THIRTEEN

Lucian Smeets was part of a little-known gang known as the 'Belgian Gang'. Lucian was at his best covering his activities, which equal those of Fournier and Sperati as a major philatelic forger. His downfall came in 1912 with his arrest in Berlin for fraud. He was sentenced to one year in prison; however, he fled from Germany and never served a day in prison there.

GENUINE

FORGERY

The biggest danger of this terrorism and extremism is the tarnishing of the reputation of our beloved religion… We will not allow this to happen.

— Abu Bakr

PALESTINE 1949

The Jews in Palestine (the Yishuv) were split on how to win their nation. There was the Lehi (Stern Gang) led by Yitzhak Shamir, who wanted to bloody the British. Then there was the Irgun led by Menachem Begin, who wanted to embarrass the British. These two were opposed by David Ben Gurion of the Haganah, who used the British to remove the Lehi and Irgun from the playing field in what was called the Hunting Season.

Things escalated on November 6, 1944, when the Lehi fighters assassinated Lord Walter Moyne the British minister of Palestine at his home in Cairo. Lord Moyne was a friend of Sir Winston Churchill and the British. The assassination caused the place to put a hold on the partition of Palestine.

David Ben Gurion used the opportunity to work with the British to remove the Lehi. David Ben Gurion set in place Moshe Dayan and Yigal Allon to weed out the Lehi terrorist. Next, he took the opportunity to also weed out his opposition in the Irgun. The 'Hunting Season' was a bloodbath where the Yishuv were fighting each other for the same cause of a homeland. The season ended with Lord Moyne's assassins being hung in March 1945. The two assassins sang Hatikvah when they died. The song would become the national anthem of the new State of Israel.

"Izzy, I see that you have joined the radicals of the Lehi Stern Gang?" said Aaron.

"Yes, brother and you are a member of the Haganah militia, and we want the same thing; yet here we are in a dispute with each other over a common goal," said Izzy.

"That is true, and our cousin David has joined the Irgun with Menachem Begin. It seems our family is fighting for the same cause from a lot of different angles. At least the "Hunting Season" and for a time the Lehi, Irgun, and Haganah were working together instead of fighting each other," said Aaron.

"Yes, we tried to work together and then the Irgun went off on a terrorist campaign against the British that broke the partnership between the groups. We were still able to create our very own nation. Despite the Irgun and its acts of terror and retaliation.

"The British made many mistakes in their public relations campaign. That whole fiasco with the Exodus blew up in their face just because they tried to control Jewish immigration into Palestine for various political reasons.

"When they stopped the ship Exodus in international water and told the people on the ship that it would be boarded, the 4,500 Jewish refugees that were on board refused. The British had two British destroyers put next to the ship and rammed each side of the ship's hull. Troops then boarded the ship where the passenger fought back under a blue and white flag of Zion. The struggle ended with two passengers being killed and dozens injured. Then came the lies.

"The British deceived the passengers saying they would be taken to Cyprus for transferring to Palestine after they were transferred to naval transport in the port of Haifa, Palestine. The transport instead took them to France where the passengers refused to disembark. The French government refused to use force to remove them. The British made another mistake and decided to wait for the passengers out. The passenger then began a hunger strike for 24 days.

"The British then moved the ships to the British zone in Germany and had the passengers forcibly removed and took them into internment camps and set off protests on both sides of the Atlantic.

"The pictures of the ship in France and the people refusing to disembark were bad, but then having the ships in Germany where the passengers, men, women, and children, being dragged off the ship and placed in displaced person camps was even worse. Memories of the Death Camp were brought up in the press. That was a very bad public relations image for the British," said Izzy.

"You forget, Izzy, we have also hit some low spots. For one thing, the lynching in 1947 of the two British sergeants in retaliation for the Irgun fighter's death earlier. The sergeant's bodies were hung with booby traps that would explode when the men were cut down. That one act created a lot of anti-Semitic feelings and rioting in England. Then there was our part in the letter bombs that were sent to public officials, plus the terrorist attack at the King David Hotel in 1946 and the explosion that killed 91 and wounded 46 individuals of different nationalities. All this has caused a public outcry and has not won us much world public opinion for a Jewish State, Izzy. At times, I wonder who we have become. We are acting more like the Germans at times," said Aaron.

"How can you say that? The anti-sematic world now is pushing their hateful propaganda that we are acting just like those murderous Germans, Aaron. When in fact we are forging the new state of Israel that is standing up for Jewish rights in a free nation of our own!" said Izzy.

"What about the rights of the Palestinians?" asked Aaron.

"We are now the Nation of Israel, Aaron we won!" said Izzy.

"Yes, but at what cost?" asked Aaron.

"Like I said we have a new nation. Our Homeland now! The Palestinians are welcome to stay," said Izzy.

"Stay? That is easy to say, but the reality is how many Jews and Arabs will be forced to move from their homes? How will these refugees be treated? We have thousands of Jews flowing into our new country from Arab countries and the Palestinians have fled this new nation to the nations around us and they are being placed in refugee camps.

"These Palestinians are being placed into refugee camps with the promise of Israel's soon-to-be destruction in the next war. Those Palestine refugees will only be able to return to claim what they call their land if we lose the next war.

"Those refugees are also being isolated from other Arab populations in the surrounding nations. There will be no assimilation of these Palestinian Arabs into these host nations, unlike the Jewish refugees who are being assimilated here.

"Every day the Palestine refugees are being told that the next war will remove us from the face of the earth. Over time the hate in those camps will fester. This will be a problem for a long time for us and the Arab nations," said Aaron.

"We will assimilate our Jewish brothers and sisters and the Arabs can do what they want with their neighbors and brothers. I do not care!" said Izzy.

"Yes, we will assimilate our brothers and sisters. Then we will debate with each other on how to live. Then the Orthodox, Reform, Conservative, Reconstructionist, and secular elements in the community will argue over religious practices, the socialists and conservatives over the structure of government, taxes, military service, the workdays, and any other things. All the things that they will think are important to build a Jewish nation.

"Many of these ideas will come from their old countries and situations. They will only band together in a war against the Arabs. The Orthodox will question any action on the sabbath, holy days, or some other religious topic. Plus, I asked you! Will we assimilate the Arabs that are willing to stay in our new nation?" asked Aaron.

"Aaron, you think and worry too much. Everything will be fine. We have a homeland, and we can now finally control our fate," said Izzy.

"I hope you are right. Our history has not given much hope of our people working together. The Kingdoms of Judah and Israel vanish in history and the Romans spread the Jewish people around Europe. Even in Russia, we disagreed on what to do within our community. That is why we left with the family. We will have to work together for we are surrounded by enemies and as of right now we have no real friends in the world," said Aaron.

"The Americans have assisted our cause," said Izzy.

"Yes! That is because their political leaders see us as a stabilizing factor in the Middle East. There is still antisemitism in America and is only hidden from view by their Jim Crow Laws against the negros in the South and unspoken racism in the North and Western parts of that nation. America is a religiously free nation to worship, but not to mix socially.

"Then there are the Europeans who see us as a balance between Arabs and European interest in the Middle East as the links to the Suze Canal and connection to the oil fields under the land. Our friends, as you call them, have strategic concerns they must worry about.

"Plus, on top of all this, the British and French are still trying to hold on to their Empires. The Americans are still trying to figure out their place in this post-war world, while Stalin is making a more complex effort to undermine the political and economic stability in Eastern European and Western nations. You see, Izzy we will be given aid only because we provide stability in this unstable area of the world," said Aaron.

"You have a valued point. The Arabs are not going to set back and allow colonialism to remain in their world. They just see us as another colonial power. The Second World War showed Arabs and other peoples in Asia that modern war is a war that is destructive to colonial powers and empires. The colonial men who fought in the two great wars now understand the image of the Western world power was an illusion. That the use of public images can be used to shape public opinions. For that reason, Ho Chi Minh the communist in French Indochina is creating problems for the French. His Declaration of Independence he issued is a mirror image of the American Declaration. He is a communist showing American idealism to win support for his cause of freedom from French colonialism.

"The Allied powers are already breaking apart between the West and East. The crisis in Berlin and the British and American response to an airlift will only widen the split and don't forget the American Marshall Plan to Europe. The Americans included the eastern nations in Europe knowing that the Soviets or should I say Stalin would not allow the participation of any Eastern European country.

"The Soviets will start to offer help to many of the Arab nations. This new Cold War will soon be right here in the Middle East and our new nation will be in the bull's eye and be one of the first targets. I'm also afraid our path forward will be rough. However, for now, my brother let us enjoy our new nation and celebrate," said Izzy.

"I still worry about our ability to work together as a community. The Reform Jews and the Conservative Jews do not worry me that much. It is the Orthodox Jews and their adherence to the observance of the Shabbat. Will they fight on the Shabbat? Or worst will they be willing to defend the nation in time of war," said Aaron.

"What are you talking about now?" asked Izzy.

"During the war of liberation some members of the Orthodox communities failed to fight or just refused to fight for religious reasons," said Aaron.

"That may be true, but let's first build a nation then worry about other problems later," said Izzy.

CHAPTER FOURTEEN

Peter Winter formed an association for the production and marketing of stamp forgeries. The British Library started a legal action against Peter. Peter and the Library agreed to an out-of-court settlement. After the settlement, Peter said he was no longer going to deal in the forgeries market and sold his stock to a company in Switzerland that is still selling the 'Winter's forgeries' today.

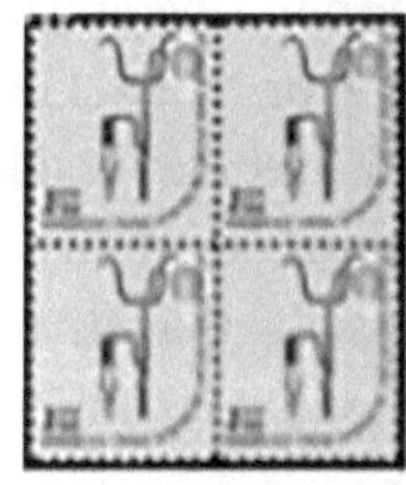

RUSH LAMP   **CIA INVERT**

Enlighten the people generally, and tyranny and oppressions of body and mind will vanish like evil spirits at the dawn of day.

— Thomas Jefferson

MEETING AT THE FBI OFFICE 2002

After C.E. had passed through security at the front door he was told to wait there by a receptionist, and someone would be there to take him to special agent Thomson's office.

C.E. watched the people come in and out of the lobby and it seemed that the FBI was like most government departments and large businesses with a lot of staff that seem to be just walking back and forth. Most of the individuals were clerks and messengers carrying folders and paper.

He noticed a man in a dark blue suit and dark tie walking towards him. C.E. wondered why all FBI agents wore dark or blue suits. Just then his thoughts were interrupted by the man in the dark suit saying his name.

"Mr. Hall, I am Special Agent Thomson with the counterfeiting and fraud investigations team. I wanted to come and meet you personally."

"It's nice to meet you and it's C.E. to my friends."

"We just met?" said the agent.

"True, but for me we are friends until we are not. It's best to start positive," said C.E.

"O.K., then it is Nick. The title 'Special Agent Thomson' seems so formal when we will be working together."

"What? Working together? I thought I was asked to come in to follow up on what I saw at the stamp store and fire."

"Yes, that was before we noticed your experience with the department on that secret fascist organization last year and your knowledge of stamps. The leadership decided you would be a good resource for us with you on board to follow up on this incident," said Nick.

"Well, I do not know how much help I can be. You must have people who are more knowledgeable about stamps and forgeries than I am," said C.E.

"We do and I am one of them with a very limited scope of knowledge of stamps. The leadership was impressed with your investigating skills last year. You brought down a whole international organization with links in the present and its links to the past criminal activities of Nazi Germany. I think they are going to try to recruit you into the Bureau."

"That is nice, but it will not happen," said C.E.

"Never say no, C.E. The Bureau could offer a consultant position you can't refuse."

"Isn't that what you are offering me right now?" asked C.E.

"See, that is why the higher-ups want you on board. You are sharp. How about it? Will you work with us on this case?" asked Nick.

"I still do not see why you need me?" said C.E.

"The simple fact is I am an art historian more than a stamp guy. I know the history of art counterfeiting, but not so much about stamp counterfeiting. Our stamp experts are back east and are on other jobs right now and we need someone out here who knows stamps and you seem to be our guy - I hope," said Nick.

"Well, I do have some open time on my hands with no jobs scheduled right now so, guess I am in. I hope I do not regret this," said C.E.

"Great! Come with me and we'll get you signed up with an identification card and take care of some paperwork."

"What about a background check?"

"That has already been done. Remember you once applied for the CIA after you left the military. We just updated that file. You have an impressive history and reputation C.E."

Later, as they were waiting for the paperwork, C.E. asked Nick about his interest in counterfeiting. "I was doing a Doctorate in early American art history when I ran across a counterfeiter who was part of a British Plot to assassinate General George Washington and other leaders of the revolution army. As luck would have it, at the same time the Bureau had come to me and asked for my assistance on a case of early American art. The next thing I knew I was an agent. I love the job."

"What was this early American counterfeiting plot?" asked C.E.

"Well, as you might guess, as soon as the first coins were minted in the Lydian Kingdom some 3,000 years ago and used as money counterfeiting coins were not far behind, and the same with paper money. By the 18th century, the English counterfeiting of money was in full swing. Copper coins were really easy to counterfeit. Some say that close to half the copper coins in England at that time were counterfeit and that was just one type of coin in circulation.

"When the British arrested counterfeiters, they were sent to the colonies as punishment. Once they were in the colonies many of these individuals resumed their old trade. During the wars of empire between the European powers the colonies were allowed to print paper money because of the lack of gold and silver coins. Counterfeiting of paper money was cheaper than coins. As soon as colonial paper money became legal tender during these war years counterfeiting followed. Foreign governments and forgers entered the game of counterfeiting with gusto for money and to destabilize the other side.

"Once the war ended, Parliament decided to remove colonial paper money until the next war. The removal caused the coin counterfeiting to become the sole focus until counterfeiters moved to counterfeit tax stamps.

"The Stamp Tax area was a constant for the counterfeiters for the custom stamps were required on several different items. These stamps became big business in counterfeiting trade for legal documents. Plus, another big business in the colonies was the occupation of smuggling. The smugglers also found that counterfeiting custom stamps could verify their goods with the required documentation. The smugglers were small-time criminals up to big businessmen. John Hancock was said to be a big smuggler in Boston.

"Then during the American Revolution, the British began printing counterfeit colonial money to disrupt the inter-colonial commerce trade. The local counterfeiters also saw an opportunity at the same time. Newspapers in the colonies began issuing warnings about phony forty-shilling notes.

"The British and Colonial counterfeiting gangs were busy printing paper money. Then one day a counterfeiter by the name of Isaac Ketchum was arrested and his printing press was confiscated. After he was convicted and placed in a jail cell, he told the authorities of a plot he overheard in jail from another prisoner, that the individual had a friend who was someone very close to General Washington's protection unit. That person was Thomas Hickey, a member of Washington's elite Life-Guard squad. He was identified as a member of a group of British and Tories, who were plotting to assassinate the General and other American leaders.

"Thomas Hickey was quickly arrested along with some others. The royal governor William Tryon and the city mayor were just missed and avoided being arrested in the plot. They were able to flee to safety behind the British lines.

"At the trial, Thomas claimed he joined the plot to get money out of the British and he never planned on going through with the plot. He said he had planned to expose the plot after he received the money. He just wanted and needed the money.

"He was convicted and sentenced to hang the next day. The hanging was viewed by 20,000 spectators who came to see the first American traitor executed in what is known as the "Hickey Plot" and that is how I became an agent," said Nick.

"I am surprised I never heard of this plot," asked C.E.

"Well, poor old Thomas Hickey died in June of 1776, and as I said he was the first. Benedick Arnold would be more infamous. However, the same year of Hickey's execution he was overshadowed by the young American patriot named Nathan Hale. He was executed by the British in September. His statement '…of only one regret…' took center stage in American folklore history. You might have heard of that story for it does overshadow the 'Hickey Plot' in every American history book. Hickey was a small-time fool or criminal and Hale was a national hero," said Nick.

"I see your point. I also see you have a copy of another piece of American stamp history. The CIA inverted stamp on your desk. Any special reason?" asked C.E.

"Yes, it reminds me that trust is elusive. Those particular stamps were purchased legally at a local post office by a federal agent. The postal clerk did not notice that the stamps were a printing error inverted making their value far more than the one dollar of their face value. That agent and others in the CIA noticed the mistake and decided to make a profit with a stamp dealer.

"The whole thing fell apart and the agents were told to return the stamps. In the end, five agents agreed and were allowed to stay with the agency, and four agents were terminated for failing to return the stamps. I have only a copy of the stamp, which is not an original, to remind me that good men sometimes do fall into evil actions. Thomas Hickey may have fallen into that group."

"I agree with you that trust is elusive. Leadership can be good at meetings, but when the chips are down, and when their careers or money is involved, usually career and money will win over what is right," said C.E.

"I know where you are coming from. I read your file, you are impressive and were left out in a void with your injury by your old agency's management," said Nick.

"That is all water under the bridge. Now what about this case?" asked C.E.

"O.K. let's get to it. I or I should say we, the Bureau, think that the print shop was a major money laundering scam with stamps by one of the Mexican Cartels. They were doing it much like it is done in the art world to launder and clean money by various illegal means," said Nick.

"Do you have any evidence to suggest that?" asked C.E.

"Very much so, it seems that Mr. Burns, the print shop owner, was working with the stamp dealer on making the counterfeits for some time. At first, he denied the printing, but he broke down when we showed him the stamp plate we found in the ashes of his shop. He said the stamp dealer offered him $100,000 to run the stamps off. He said it started with the idea that they would be sold as copies with the word counterfeit or copy stamped in red ink on the backside. That is legal. Then once he was involved in the scam he could not get out and the money was good. Now we are looking into the customers for connections."

"Something is wrong here! Why burn the print shop and not the stamp store? The murder was in the stamp store. Why there?" asked C.E.

"See there again! That is why we need you in this case. We think the stamp dealer had the printer printing more stamps than he was told to print. The secret compartment held two sheets of all the stamps the printer told us he printed, and he printed five sheets of each. So, we think the printing was to be for three sheets of each stamp. The sheets your people discovered that were left on top of the desk were five sheets each. We think the person that murdered the owner and collected all the stamps out of the cabinets was in a hurry and overlooked the sheets on the desk that was under the stamp dealer after he staged the body there," said Nick. "Wait, you said plates, how many were there?" asked C.E.

"Good question, we found only plates for two stamps. Our guess is the arsonist took the other plates."

"Then I think we better find those other plates because those stamps were top-of-the-line forgeries," said C.E.

"Also, on our list in this case." "Well, let's go look at the file you have put together," said C.E.

CHAPTER FIFTEEN

Doctor Bernard Assmus was head of the Universal Academy in Paris, published novelist, and the proprietor and editor of the *German Gazette* in Paris. Around 1890 he had lost all his money for various reasons. He decided to then use his knowledge of chemicals to produce several fakes and forgeries of stamps from different countries. He was arrested after selling an altered 'Black Penny' stamp. He was found guilty and sentenced to three years. The judge told him that the more serious crime rather than his forgeries was the offense of dealing with the Queen's effigy in the way he had done.

GENUINE

FORGERY

Death is the solution to all problems. No Man? No problem.

— Joseph Stalin

"SUKA WARS" IN THE GULAG'S 1945-1953

As the returnees entered the camp, they were met with a quiet silence and many men who were already in camp stood with their backs turned to new arrivals. Alexei and Viktor moved along with the others. "Stay away from those with tattoos, Viktor. There is going to be trouble within the Thieves-in-Law between those who stayed and those who fought in the war. Let's wait and see how the wind is blowing before we take a side," said Alexei."

"What if we do not have a choice?" asked Victor.

"We will have very little at first and that is why we must stay together for preservation and stay away from any of the tattooed individuals, so you do not get in the crossfire. We go to no place alone. Is that understood? In time, we might be able to be neutral and serve both sides." said Alexei.

"Yes! I understand."

By the second day, the Thieves who fought in the Great Patriotic War were being attacked and beaten to death by the old guard Thieves. The sides were formed quickly into two warring groups. The old guard Thieves that stayed behind had felt they were betrayed by the returnees. They gave the returnees the name Suka (Bitch) or Suki. The Suka had the advantage in this war for three reasons when the Suka Wars broke out.

First, the Suka used their military experience in fighting with military tactics and strategy. They set traps for their opponents to pick them off in small groups. The Suka were a small well-organized minority in the camps. But soon they built alliances with the guards and then over weeks with a few of the old guard Thieves.

The second factor was the Suka had no code that forbade them from working with the government. They soon learned they could work with the guards and administrators of the camps to gain an advantage in their fight with the old guard Thieves.

Finally, the Suka had their new contacts with individuals outside the camps and they began using the guards as their conduits for gifts and bribes. Slowly, the Sukas became the victors breaking the hierarchy of the

Thieves. The top members in the camp were now uneasy at peace between the old Thieve leader and the new Suka leader. The rule now was who was the most ruthless with no limit to violence.

Over time contacts were made on the outside with middle- and upper-party members and this included several members of the new KGB. It seemed that NKVD killings were being noticed by the public, so Stalin had the organization reorganized under the new name KGB. The name changed but the organization did not, and a new leader was named. Sergei Kruglov was in charge of the KGB and he was no supporter of comrade Beria.

This set off a struggle in the Security Services until 1948 when Lavrenty P. Beria and Georgy M. Malenkov used the Leningrad Affair to purge supporters of Comrade Andrey A. Zhdanov. Few knew that Stalin was behind the plotting to create the conflict for a new purge that executed and imprisoned thousands of party members.

After the executions were carried out, Beria still did not feel secure in his new position for some of his opposition was left in place. Beria began building a network to support his bid for power once Stalin died.

In the Glugs the new leader controlling inside the camp would use Alexei and Viktor as a go-between. The new leader was their old friend from the past camp Mikhail. He saw the new shift in power and adjusted to the change to use it to his advantage. The Suka were a violent group without any long-term direction. Mikhail stepped in to provide a new direction. Mikhail used Viktor and Alexei as the link between the Suka, old Thieves, the guards, and outside contacts. His authority expanded throughout the glug system.

By 1953 the Suka and new Thieves were in control of the Black Market and could provide Western goods to those inside the camps and those outside the camps who could pay for them. They had contacts with members of the Party and the KGB. It became a working relationship that mutually benefited all parties.

One day an enforcer approached Viktor. "Mikhail wants to see you Viktor and Alexei, so find Alexei now. Then both of you come and have a talk with him," said an enforcer.

"Yes, Alexei is over at the main gate bargaining with two guards over medical supplies. I'll go and get him," said Viktor as he ran off.

"Alexei, Alexei, Mikhail wants to see the both of us now," said Viktor as he walked up to the three men.

"This will have to wait," Viktor heard. The guards also heard Mikhail's name and the negotiations ended.

"We have been back in the camps for some eight years and things have changed don't you think? The guards are less aggressive and seem to be watching on which side to stand," said Alexei as they walked away.

They approached the areas that were Mikhail's seat of power. "I wonder why Mikhail has asked us to come and see him," said Alexie, an enforcer who looked back at Mikhail.

Mikhail waved that Alexei and Viktor were both allowed to come over. "Alexei gets a message from the camp commissar that his package is at the station. He should not pick it up in person. He should also know that one of his guards is working with Zoya and is trying to get evidence that the commissar is corrupt," said Mikhail.

"You're kidding me - everybody is corrupt here," said Alexei.

"True, but Zoya was on the wrong side in the Suka war. He did not want to change from the old ways, lost his bid for power and was replaced by me as the leader. I told you that things have to change with the times. So, I allied with the returnees to adjust to the new situation."

"Why have you still allowed Zoya to have a say in the camp politics?" asked Viktor.

"It's simple, Zoya has a large following of the old Thieves in this camp, and we are at peace for now. If I remove Zoya, there will be a continuation of the wars. I need to persuade the old Thieves that my way is the best way to grow our power inside and outside the camp. Zoya cares only about what happens inside the camp and has very few contacts left outside the camp. He can see no future on the outside. That is why he is trying to remove the Camp Commissar," said Mikhail.

"It is true Zoya is a thug who is smart enough to know how to bully prisoners and buy off a few of the guards. The commissar has used him against you on several occasions only to lose the contest. It is good that the commissar likes what you can provide for he constantly undermines his plans to remove you as a camp leader," said Alexei.

"Yes, the Soviet system has always allowed the brutes to climb to power and only a few of them have some intelligence. The thug Stalin is in a league of his own. He built elaborate strategies to remove people. Some of the things he did took years for the action to take place. The new Doctor's Plot was his latest masterminding that has been in the works for years. His fear of the Jews was behind the whole plot. He saw comrade Trotsky's beliefs in every one of the Jews. Stalin worked well with the Jews in the party and that in itself is funny because many of the early leaders were Jews and they were eliminated by Stalin from high party leadership. Each new leadership of so-called smart leaders from the beginning reacted out of self-interest and not a long-term plan.

"When Moscow set a quota, these brutes went out of their way to double and triple the quota. Just so they will look good to the leadership back in Moscow. Look around this camp many of these individuals are here for no other reason except for the whim of a petty bureaucrat's desire to look good to his superiors.

"Then there are the ones that had upset a neighbor or a fellow worker at a plant getting even for some small incident by whispering a complaint to the right person. Then the neighbor or worker woke up with an early morning knock on the door and off to the camps.

"Finally, there are those of us called the Thieves and the political inmates that are here for a real reason. The leaders allow us to survive for the benefits we provide. So, you are right, the whole system is corrupt, Alexei. The one thing we can count on is change and it is coming faster," said Mikhail

----

Later that night a guard walked up to a bedside in the barracks and said, "Zoya come outside so we can talk without others listening."

"What is so important that you get me out of bed in the middle of the night to talk in the dark?" asked Zoya.

"I have a message for you!" said the guard as they walked outside.

"A message, from who?"

"That would be me," said Mikhail, who came up with two of his protectors.

"What do you want Mikhail? We agreed not to bother each other and keep the peace in the camp. So what do you want?"

"Zoya, you tried to have the KGB set a trap for my group and the commissar. Unfortunately for you, I also have contacts in the KGB and it is your people that have been taken to Lubyanka to be dealt with tonight. Now it is your turn to be dealt with my old friend," said Mikhail.

"We were never friends. I never liked you Mikhail, you are a traitor to the organization. What are you going to do in here?" said Zoya.

"That should be obvious by now Zoya, the guard came and woke you out of your bed and I stand here with my people. The guard has walked off and where are your people?"

Two men grabbed Zoya covering his mouth and carried him to the middle of the open space into the rain. Then the enforcer grabbed Zoya's head and gave a violent twist breaking Zoya's neck. The body was allowed to drop in the mud.

The next morning the body lay in the mud for all to see. Nobody approached the body not even the guards.

"What should be done with the body? The Commissar wants to know?" asked a guard the next morning to Mikhail.

"Leave him in the mud. It will be a message that things have changed once more. They can bury him tomorrow night," said Mikhail.

A week later the news came to the camp of Stalin's death.

CHAPTER SIXTEEN

Alfred Baguet was a prolific forger and made millions in French Francs before his arrest in 1922. At his home, the police found a printing press and items for gumming, and perforating stamps. He was found guilty and served three months in prison for forgery.

PROPAGANDA

DEATH

One death is a tragedy; one million is a statistic.

— Joseph Stalin

MARCH 20, 1953 DEATH OF STALIN

A few weeks later a new body lay in the mud until late in the day. The guards and prisoners did not look in the direction of the form that had molded into the mud. A point was being made once more to others that life was easily taken. The body belonged to Yuri Kirov, an enforcer for the Thieves. He had made the mistake of not following his orders to the letter and paid the price. The rules had changed in the "Bitch Wars" —— the Thieves and Suka had merged into a new more sinister criminal organization. The camps had become a larger breeding ground for evil and survival was at any cost.

Mikhail had become a powerful leader in the Thieves during the "Bitch Wars" and saw the need for a change. Alexei and Viktor were the means for that change since they were 'politicos'. They had contact with the Thieves, the Party, and the KGB on the outside. He called for an enforcer to get Viktor and Alexei.

"Alexei, I want you and Viktor to help me change things outside the camp," said Mikhail.

"How? Why? You already control the camp and have a strong link to the outside. Look at the body over there. The guards will not touch it because of the influence you have inside and outside the camps," said Alexei.

"What a nice way you have to put my ruthless methods into words that sound innocent. You have been important to me in the past by being my go-between us and the government officials. You have helped me to keep my honor to the Code of the Thieves by not working with the government. But times are changing, and the old code is gone. The death of Stalin will cause a new political power struggle within the Party and the individuals in that struggle will try to win the support of the people. When that happens, prisoners will soon be released and some of the camps will be closed in the spirit of a new Soviet order. It will still be the same regime filled with ruthless individuals who will sell their fathers to win favor with the powers to be. You and Viktor will be my door to that new open society."

"What are we to do? We have been in this place for years and most of our contacts in the Party were eliminated in the Stalin Purges of the 1930's. Those that we know are from the Great Patriotic War."

"Trust me you will be released soon by that master Soviet criminal Beria in his bid for power. Those Party members that you knew are still there and have been joined by some of your comrades from the war and they all want things we can provide. They did not stay alive and outside the camps by being honorable individuals. Some of them may have been the reasons you are both in the camp system. Plus, your friends during the war years are still out there. They will also want things we can provide."

"What can we offer them?"

"Things from the West capitalist world. If it is new and well-made, they will desire it. Find out what they want, and we will supply it for a small piece of the price."

"What about the KGB?"

"Those murderous thugs are opportunists that hide behind the ideas of the State and Party. Their greed for wealth and power controls their behavior for self-preservation.

They do not know it, but their great Soviet society ended with Lenin taking power. Stalin even referred to himself as "like a Tsar" to his mother when she asked what he did. The Soviet great society just put a new arrogant and stupid elite in power.

"The Soviet system is dying and will be gone most likely in the next fifty years. You and Viktor will be my link to this greedy bureaucracy that is dying and the new one that is now developing. We already have contacts within the KGB, so you will have some protection."

"How do you know this will work?"

"Look around Alexei, the body in the mud was an important man in the camp and a friend to the guards and what do they do now! They did what everyone does when that early morning 'knock on the door' comes at their neighbors next door. They are hoping that they are not next.

"That fear of the knock on the door in the early morning was so great that they were silent about the people that were removed during the night. Those individuals were never spoken about to anyone out of fear they would be overheard. Lenin created the corrupt fear system and Stalin perfected the perfect corrupt society."

"So, what do Viktor and I do when we are released?" asked Alexei.

"You both go to Moscow and see Ivanna Popov, give her this," said Mikhail and handed Alexei a piece of paper. "She will set you up with funds and other arrangements. Alexei, please remember the guy in the mud. I do not suffer displeasure."

"I have no other plan other than to work for you and do my best, Mikhail. Viktor and I are loyal to you for all your help, security, and guidance. We both owe you our life, Mikhail."

"Good and set up the connections with caution. The old system has not broken completely."

The very next month the reforms started in the camps and within the Soviet society. Mikhail's predictions were proven right. Georgy Malenkov took control of the government and pushed for an increase in the production of consumer goods.

Lavrentiy Beria made his bid for power by passing liberal reforms for releasing political prisoners. Acting to build a base of support in the party. Georgy Malenkov and Nikita Khrushchev conspired to remove Beria from any power. Then on June 26, 1953, they accused Beria of anti-party and anti-state activities.

He was arrested and tried. Beria was one of the last of the old guards to suffer the same fate that he delivered to so many at the Lubyanka the KGB building in Moscow, on December 24, 1954, he met his fate.

In time Khrushchev became the real power in the Soviet Union and took charge of the collectivization of farming in the Soviet Union and Eastern Europe, seeing himself as an expert in agriculture. He pushed for the Virgin Lands project to increase the food production of the Soviet Union. Unfortunately, he allowed Stalin's top biologist Trofim Lysenko known as the 'barefoot biologist' to stay in power with fraudulent scientific facts that backed Soviet agriculture for twenty years. Trofim policies and Nikita's Virgin Land project did not end well for Soviet agriculture.

Khrushchev's plan had a good start in 1954 and Khrushchev increased the quota. Then in 1955 crop production fell short of the quota, but in 1956 a record food crop was produced. That record was never met again. The plan fell short for several reasons. There was no increase in shortage capacity and there was a high percentage of grain lost to these inadequate storage facilities. There was a lack of available machines to work the fields. The fact that the labor force was not available caused the program to force many individuals to be moved from important work in industry to work the land. Finally, the single-crop production decreased the soil nutrient content to levels that it caused a further reduction in the food production.

Khrushchev's enemies were waiting for their time. Khrushchev surprised them all and slowly worked with other party members to isolate Malenkov and removed him from office in 1955. Then all opposition to Khrushchev stayed buried in the Soviet bureaucracy waiting for its turn to grab power.

Prime Minister Khrushchev felt strong enough in 1956 to deliver a speech denouncing Stalin and his brutal policies. The old guard resented it but kept quiet. The Soviet Union had become stronger with A-bombs and H-bombs that would later be carried on ICBM missiles. The military kept other peoples and countries in line with brute force and the threat of Tanks to force others to the Soviet side of issues.

One reason Khrushchev was able to stay in power was his push to be first. In 1957 the world saw the Soviet launching of Sputnik I and later that year launched Sputnik II with Laika the dog. Next in 1961, the Soviets sent the first man in space with Yuri Gagarin followed in 1963 with Valentina Tereshkova the first woman in space. The American reaction was fast with math and engineering programs developed and JFK's plan to reach the Moon by the end of the decade.

Nuclear war was on everyone's mind. Khrushchev had moved the Soviet Union into a world power equal to the U.S.A. Then in 1961 America under JFK blundered into a fiasco in Cuba with the Bay of Pigs. Khrushchev saw an opportunity to move ICBMs into Cuba which created a crisis in 1962 with the threat of a Third World War with nuclear weapons. JFK and his brother RFK made a deal with Khrushchev for him to pull the missile from Cuba in exchange for the American agreement to protect Cuba from any invasion. The world press made it look like Khrushchev backed down and JFK a winner of the Western world. Khrushchev was now on borrowed time as the leader of the Soviet Union — the hardliners were ready to pounce.

CHAPTER SEVENTEEN

Alfred Benjamin was part of the 'London Gang' a group of forgers that included Julian Hippolite, Sarpy, and George K. Jeffryes. They produced fake surcharges, forgeries, fiscal postal, and forged perforation. All three men were arrested and convicted of conspiracy to defraud. Benjamin and Jeffryes were sentenced to six months and Sarpy to four months of hard labor. Benjamin continued to sell his forgeries after his release from prison. Where he doubled the price and sold them this time as forgeries.

GENUINE

FORGERY

A person may cause evil to others not only by his actions but by his inaction, and in either case he is justly accountable to them for the injury.

— John Stuart Mill

Northern Ireland 1999

I t was a summer day and not too hot with a slight breeze in Dublin. Two men sat at a café table outside and talked in low tones. One man sat with a green Trinity cap on his reddish hair and wearing a green Aran sweater with Brooks Brother's tan trousers. The other man was wearing an Italian Armani charcoal suit and Hermes-Kennedy black loafers. The guy in the sweater put his paper down. "What can I do for you Abdul?" asked Duffy.

"We would like to work with you in a mutual common cause."

"What is that? What common cause could we have together and why would we be doing that?" asked Duffy.

"We both have similar outside influences. Northern Ireland has the 'Troubles' as you call them with a deep history of discrimination against your religion by the British protestants. The same has happened in our history with the British and our religion," said Abdul.

"What do you know about Irish history?" asked Duffy.

"I know that the Troubles began in 1968 when the Catholics of Northern Ireland were discriminated against in housing, voting rights, and various other things. It started in that year when a home came up for a new tenant and it was given to a young single Protestant woman, over the needs of a large Catholic family by the housing committee. That simple act started a riot over the housing rules and discrimination against the catholic community.

That began a campaign of mass protests and bombings that took some 3,500 lives over the next three decades. Your own Ulster paramilitaries finally came to the peace table against the wishes of your small faction within the origination. Yes, we have done our homework, Duffy. We know you are being hunted by both sides in this conflict now that you have refused to stop the fight."

"I see you have done some work. So, what is it you want from me and those that agree with me?" asked Duffy.

"You have expertise in some special areas we need to develop to make our point to the imperialistic powers. They control our lives, and we want to send messages that will get the world's attention!" said Abdul.

"That is very nice, but you and your friends have not been all that warm to my religion. You would just as soon kill all of us Christians, if I am not mistaken Abdul."

"We have no desire to impose our belief on Ireland. We only want the West imperialist out of our lives and out of our countries and territory. We are willing to pay and provide you with certain materials you may want to use in exchange for your tactical training."

"Give me a number to contact and I will think about your offer and discuss it with my friends."

"Very well," said Abdul and handed Duffy a card with a number on it and no name.

Across the street in an apartment window sat two United States CIA agents with electric equipment pointed toward the café. They had been listening and watching Abdul for the last month and identifying his contacts inside and outside his organization.

"I guess the old saying has merit for it looks like politics do make strange bedfellows. What do you think?" asked Moses.

"About what?" asked Eric.

"To start with, will Duffy join with the Arab radicals?" asked Moses.

"I doubt they would be able to work together," said Eric.

"You could be right, but Duffy claims he is low on funds or so that is what he tells the others in the group. The people he controls have no real cause other than money and their funds are low. On the other hand, Duffy's bank accounts in different offshore banks are in the millions and we are watching for who shows up at those accounts," replied Mosses.

"If we know that much about him, why not just pick him up?" asked Eric.

"We do that, and we lose our unsuspecting leader as a decoy to bag the other like-minded members to his way of thinking. Right now, it looks like his circle of friends just got a lot bigger and more dangerous. We need to get on this fast.

I want you to take this tape and photos to the Embassy and give them to our station agent there, Mathew. This is a top priority so no stops on the way and only hand it personally to the station agent — give to no one except Mathew," said Moses.

"What if…"

"Stop, I do not care about any what's! This is going to be very important and the fewer people in the know of it the less risk for the information leaking out. Our intelligence agency seems to have far too many leaks. So get going and you are to give that material to only one person. You know the number to call, if you have any problems, if push comes to shove.

Arabs and Irish terrorists teaming up together would make this a really big game-changer. This new change, I think, is about to bring in some new dangerous radical terrorist players into the game," said Moses.

CHAPTER EIGHTEEN

Chauncey L. Young was a practicing minister in Iowa. He could turn a common stamped envelope into a rare envelope. At the same time, he could create nonexistent types of stamps to sell to the unexpecting public. A stamp dealer noticed the Young envelopes were fake and sought help to stop the selling to collectors. After an investigation, it was proven the envelopes were fakes. There was a quiet agreement reached between all parties to keep it from becoming a scandal. The parties agreed and a settlement was reached that Young would stop the sales of these envelopes as long as his position as a minister and his standing in the community was not jeopardized for as long as he lived.

HEROES USA

The object of terrorism is terrorism. The object of oppression is oppression. The object of torture is torture. The object of murder is murder. The object of power is power. Now do you begin to understand me?

— George Orwell, *1984*

DECEMBER 14, 2002 AT THE FBI

September 11, 2001, was not the first attempt to bring down the World Trade Center in New York. The previous event took place on February 26, 1993, when an Islamic extremist drove a truck bomb into the underground parking area and detonated a bomb.

The plan was to collapse the North Tower into the South Tower. The bomb failed to bring down either of the towers, but it did kill six people and wounded 1,000 others. The investigation led to the arrest of several individuals and the possible involvement of other Middle Eastern Islamic nations in the plot.

Then the nation fell into its old pattern of feeling safe behind two oceans. Movies and stories were made of Americans fighting radical Islamic terrorists and winning on the Muslim's home territory.

"Moses, the director, would like to see you in his office five minutes ago, so you better get up there," said agent Kirk Thorne.

"Any idea what it is about?" asked Moses.

"You have to ask the director! Now you better get going."

Moses walked over to the elevator, stepped in and went up to the director's office. As he walked in, the secretary said, "Go right in Moses, they are waiting for you."

"They?"

"Yes," was her reply as he opened the door.

"Perfect, gentlemen, here is our man now," said the director as Moses stopped in mid-step in the room that was filled with major players in the American intelligence world.

"Sorry about the quick notice Moses, but agent Eric Miles of the CIA said you were aware of Abdul and the connection between the Irish terrorist Duffy. Is that true?" asked the Director.

"Yes sir, I was in Ireland on assignment with the CIA station agent looking into a breach in security. One of the embassy employees was in a relationship with a female British reporter and he was a little lost with his 'pillow talk' at night. However, there were no security leaks.

"It was more about the attitudes of the staff at the embassy towards the Catholic Irish public. It became a public relations problem when the reporter wrote about the unflattering comments made about local leaders. Fortunately, the comments were made by a Protestant Irish cook who worked at the embassy. He was interviewed and admitted to the comments and said his words were taken out of context — that they were made in answering a question in a joking manner.

"He was sorry that anyone took offense to a private conversation. The internal interview ended, and he went out to a press conference. Then the individual once more stated he was the one who had the loose tongue as he stepped up in front of the gathered groups of news reporters. Once more he said that he had made the comment as a joke and that the reporter who reported the story misrepresented the whole thing. He was then sent home, and the reporter was given a promotion at her tabloid paper."

"Thank you, but that is not why are asking for you to be here. What we want to know is about the meeting between Abdul and Duffy?" said the Director.

"I do not know that much about Abdul, but I did investigate Duffy. After their meeting at the café, Abdul had Duffy go to Libya and Abdul went off to recruit more mujahedeen fighters for the fighting in the Middle East and Afghanistan.

"I was sent to the states and Caribbean to trace the funds that Duffy was being paid to train foreign fighters in Libya. I would say Duffy would have made a very good financial advisor. He started by banking a share of the money received from Abdul for Irish groups, service in a Delaware bank, and another share in a bank in South Dakota. The money stayed there for a month and then the money was moved to the British Virgin Islands and days later it made its way to Belize. After a few more transfers all the money ended up in a few selected banks in Switzerland."

"Delaware and South Dakota banks! Why there?" asked the director.

"Banking secrecy laws in states like Delaware and South Dakota allow individuals and shell companies to hide money from creditors, government authorities, and their partners. It is like having local offshore banking in Switzerland here at home."

"Nice to know? Now, what about Duffy?" asked the Director.

"A year after setting up his training operation, Duffy was killed by the father of a young girl in Libya. It was reported by our people there that Duffy got drunk and made advances in public towards the young girl at a market.

"The father saw the exchange and confronted Duffy, who pushed the father away and laughed at him calling the father names and the young female an Islamic whore. The father then stuck a long knife into Duffy's chest.

"It was at that time we decided to freeze Duffy's business accounts immediately that we had been able to identify. There were some 66 different accounts which at the time totaled close to 20 million Euro. I then was assigned to a different investigation and moved on to that case," said Moses.

"Well then Moses that current assignment is now someone else's problem to worry about. You are once again assigned to join the FBI-CIA task force and work with Agent Mathew on the terrorist financial network we have just uncovered. You have been selected, because of your knowledge of the terrorist financial network," said the Director.

"Sir, if I may, I did not do my work on the finances by myself. I could not have done it without the help of Kirk Thorne. He is a genius with numbers," said Moses.

The FBI director looked at the CIA, "What do you think?"

"We'll take both. This is going to be a lot different than the Cold War idealism and bluffs. This enemy is going to fight an urban guerrilla war like that in the Algeria war with no central leadership. Plus, with no regard for the lives of their followers, innocent bystanders, or others. The only way to fight them is to control their funds and that will be hard. Some of our so-called current friends in the world support the radical movement through their governments and with private individuals. Pakistan and Saudi Arabia are the major sources of their funds," said the CIA director.

"If I may ask, do we have any leads? I will need to read the background of the case to get up to speed," asked Moses.

"Yes, there is a report with my secretary for you so pick it up on your way out. Keep us informed and this is a top priority."

"Yes, sir."

"Welcome to our little band of merry men Moses," said Mathew as the group got up and walked out of the office.

CHAPTER NINETEEN

Albert J. Rabinowitz was arrested with thousands of fake overprinted stamps. He pleaded guilty to the overprinting of the stamps in 1941 and was given three months in prison. Then in 1943, he was arrested once again with four other dealers for possessing and counterfeiting stamps. In 1949 he was arrested once more for selling altered stamps and was sentenced to one year and one day in prison.

GENUINE   FORGERY

Even philosophers will praise war as ennobling mankind, forgetting the Greek who said: 'War is bad in that it begets more evil than it kills.

— Immanuel Kant

2002 Meeting with Professor Hellen

"Good morning, Helen. Thank you for taking the time to see me today. How are your classes this year?" asked C.E.

"A little different since I finished that paper on Arab radicalism and the women's movement in the Islamic world. The administration now thinks I am the "Bee's Knees" on the subject and they have me holding a class on the subject each semester."

"The Bee's Knees" is an old term way before your time and not heard much today. The new class seems like a wide topic," said C.E.

"You mean women or radicals?" asked Helen with a smile.

"Well, I guess both now that you bring it up. But seriously, are not radicals and women trying to get the same answers and solutions to their issues?"

"You are right they are the same to some degree, but with different outcomes and methods of dealing with the change. For example, the "bra burners" of 1968 were women protesting the image of women presented at beauty pageants. The protesters had with them some items of their clothes that they considered forms of torture for women. They planned to show their displeasure with image identification.

"A 'Freedom Can' was set up to throw mops, lipsticks, high-heels, girdles, curlers, and bras into as a symbolic act for the new woman. I do not think the world of women changed that much with this simple act of protest. However, the reporting of the event made national news that night with the headline "Bra Burners" at a Beauty Pageant. It made it sound like women tore off their bras and other items and tossed them into the can to burn. There was no taking off of their bras or the burning of their bras at that protest. The event issues were ignored, and the news was about the so-called 'Bra Burning'," said Helen.

"I remember the news reports. They made it seem like a big deal for feminism and women's rights have been getting better," said C.E.

"If you compare the 'bra episode' with Iranian women marching in the Islamic Revolution of 1979 with women wearing the hijab and the chador during protest marches, these marches were against western modernization of Islamic society and women's rights played very little. The Iranian women were willingly going back in time to cover up themselves either by design or force," said Helen.

"That was surprising, and I just learned the other day that women in Saudi Arabia are still not allowed to drive. That got me to look up a few things on the net. It was a real surprise to find that in France women did not get the right to vote until after the Second World War. I guess the French Revolution and the Rights of Man were just that. The demand for liberty did not include women; although, she is always pictured as liberty," said C.E.

"Why is that a surprise to you? When in this very country with all the feminist movements for the Equal Rights Amendment, that amendment has not passed the U.S. Congress? Women are divided on the issue of equal rights. To some, they see it as a major gain, and to others, it is the loss of courtesy rights.

"They are claiming that equal rights will cause women to lose some of the privileges such as the courtesy of going first and having the doors opened for you or by being given a seat to name a few. Everything has an action and a reaction that may bring a different result than the one that is believed would be the result.

"Any behavior changes will cause an effect on the social life and that change may be popular or unpopular. For example, would providing free drugs to drug addicts decrease the drug problem? Or would tougher drug laws end the drug problem? Another example is the civil rights issue that started with the civil rights movement. Is it an individual movement or a group movement?

The case in California Mendez vs. Westminster School District in 1947 was over a Mexican student being allowed to go to the closest school to her home. Then seven years later the Brown vs. Board of Education in 1954 and 1956 case ended the "Jim Crow" laws that had legalized discrimination. That still has not answered my question of individual civil rights or group civil rights," said Helen.

"That is true. Civil Rights is becoming an issue for other groups," said C.E.

"You are right and that is a much bigger issue for another day. Now what about you C.E.? What are you working on? I think you stopped by for more than to say hello. So what can I do for you? I love improving your knowledge," said Helen with a smile.

"I am just doing some consulting work on stamps for the FBI. What can you tell me about the radical fundamentalist in this country and around the world?"

"Now, we are back to a wide topic. The radical fundamentalists do not want to move into the modern world. Tradition is their way of life in their culture group or tribes. That tradition has been disrupted by modernization and Imperialism during the 19th and 20th Centuries and even more with the political power struggles between the Europeans and their colonies in modern wars.

"The colonial groups began to remove the colonial powers from their territories. In this power vacuum, many groups in the Middle East started to re-establish their traditional culture and demanded control as the main source of power in the Middle East. The Egyptians wanted to bring back the power of the Pharaohs. Iraq wanted to bring back the power of the Babylonian Empires and Iran wanted to re-establish the power of the Persian Empire. Finally, the Turks wanted to hold on to their power as the Ottomans in the eastern Mediterranean.

"Each is dominated by the religious and political powers of the past and present. Each one wants their power back to exclude the others and they are willing to use the fundamentalist to obtain that goal. They are not the only ones wanting to bring back the past glory.

"The Italians and Germans in the first half of the 20th Century looked to re-establish their past glory that led to the Second World War. The Italians under Mussolini saw the fascist Party as creating a new Roman Empire in Africa and the Germans looked to building once more the Teutonic Knights glory and tried once more to move into eastern Europe.

"Then after the Second World War, the Western powers created new nations in the Middle East. These nations seek to expand their power base with the economic control of resources. The two main resources were oil fields and the Suez Canal.

"The new and old Arab nations had one thing in common and that was their hatred for the new nation of Israel. That has been the center of all conflict in the Middle East for the last fifty or so years and brought the Islamic world together for that one issue, but tribalism is still a major issue in the Arab world.

"Most of today's politicians fail to understand the power of tribalism. A very good example of the power of tribalism is the break-up of Yugoslavia after Tito's death and the beginnings of the Bosnian Wars with the Slovenians, Croatians, and Bosnians and the fighting at Kosovo. The world created did not create a new form of evil actions in that war. They replaced the term Holocaust with a new term called Ethnic Cleansing.

"It was repeated in the Rwandan during their Civil War conducted between the Tutsi and Hutu. Individuals were hacked to death for the only crime of belonging to a different tribe. That tribal connection was so strong that Catholic Nuns were involved in the murders. Many leaders today are using ethnic identity and separation to gain power and influence.

"The Bedouins have an apothegm that goes 'I am against my brother, my brother and I are against my cousin, my cousin and I are against the stranger' and that saying can apply to the whole human race. So, C.E. what I am saying is this topic is difficult to explain in a short period for all of the aspects of it are intertwined," said Helen.

"I see your point, but now I do have a little better understanding of the topic. I hope I have not kept you away from your other work and I do thank you. It is always a pleasure to tap your mind for information on history. I'll talk to you later," said C.E.

"It is always my pleasure C.E."

CHAPTER TWENTY

Leon Armanak Hadenkian of Egypt was arrested after two local stamp dealers turned Leon in to the police as a stamp forger. When the police went to Leon's home, they entered while he was busy making overprint stamps. After his arrest he admitted to making stamp forgeries since 1927 and that several postal administrators were implicated in the scheme.

GENUINE   **FORGERY**

With guns you can kill terrorists, with education you can kill terrorism.

— Malala Yousafzai

AFGHANISTAN, MAY 1, 1988

The Evening News started at 6 p.m. on each coast with nationally known anchor Chet Butler.

"Wake-Up America this is Chet Butler with the important news of the day. We start with the news that the Soviet Union is withdrawing from Afghanistan. We start tonight's program with a special report on the war in Afghanistan beginning with the history of recent Soviet policy up to the invasion of that country. In recent years the Soviet government and the Soviet leadership have used the Brezhnev Doctrine with the cooperation Warsaw Pact to keep their satellite nations in line.

"The Warsaw Pact is the Soviet Union's defensive counterpart to Western Europe and the United States defense pact that is NATO. These treaties state that a threat to one is a threat to all. Both the Warsaw Pact and NATO are defensive organizations for protection from outside forces.

"The movements for more liberal government in Warsaw Pact nations began in Czechoslovakia in 1968 and then once more in Poland in 1980. Each time these liberalizing movements were met with Soviet tanks that were sent in to maintain the current control leadership of Soviet Union puppet governments.

"The Warsaw Pact treaty that was created to protect one nation from outside threats is now used to justify the intervention of one communist country into another communist country. The tank has been and continues to be the best method for the Soviet leadership to control the unruly population.

"When the Afghanistan military had thrown out the centrist government in 1978 and the re-establishment of the Socialist People's Party, the country had split into two different parties — the Khalq Party (Peoples' Party) and the Parcham Party (Banner Party). The Soviet leaders once more sent in tanks to secure a pro-Soviet government. On December 24, 1979, the Soviet leadership helped set up the new government in Afghanistan.

"This invasion was met with resistance from tribal and urban fighters that joined together to resist the foreign invasion. These fighters became known as the Mujahideen or as the American President Reagan called them Freedom fighters.

"These fighters came from around the world to fight the Soviet Red Army in a guerrilla-type war that was being supplied by the United States through the CIA with weapons. One of these new weapons was the Stinger missiles that would help bring down the Soviet airpower on the battlefield.

"These guerrillas were not unified as a single group. The Nuristani in the north, the Hazara in the central mountains, the Pashtun the largest group, and the Tajik the second largest group all joined together to fight the one common enemy — the Red Army.

"Then there were nontribal different groups that claimed leadership in the war. Two of these groups were the Taliban and Al Qaeda which later would emerge as the two most dominant groups. Some of these resistance fighters were financed by Saudis through Osama bin Laden and by other individuals and nations that were locked in this political and religious conflict. The Cold War was used by each side to collect military and economic gains from both major powers.

"The Nightly News media and the major networks covering the war with reporters were embedded in the field with the rebels. Reporting from the field made many reporters national celebrities in the news media. All the major networks had reporters in Afghanistan and some rich independent reporters went there to make names for themselves. The evening news presented the story as a David and Goliath struggle with reports of the freedom fighters standing up against the massive Red Army and their huge war machines. Many claimed that the Soviet war in Afghanistan was and was the Soviet Union's Vietnam.

"That is a summary of the history up to today and now we have a live report on the ground from Afghanistan. We now turn to a report from the mountains of Afghanistan with our reporter on the ground there," said the evening news anchor Chet Butler as the screen turned to the reporter in the field.

"Good evening, Chet and America, this is Bill Ranken reporting from the mountains of Afghanistan with members of the Mujahideen. We can hear a big Soviet helicopter gunship coming slow and low through the valley. When it gets within range, these brave fighters will try to bring it down with a weapon supplied by the United States..." The camera cuts to the view of the valley leaving the reporter's voice with the picture.

"THERE, THERE, SEE IT! AND THERE IS ANOTHER! those

are Stinger anti-aircraft missiles that have just been launched by the Mujahideen members. You can see the trail of the missile as it tracks and targets its prey. WOW, LOOK AT, THAT WAS A DIRECT HIT! See that chopper has been hit dead center. The huge thing is falling from the sky on camera.

"If we turn the camera around, you can see the freedom fighters are all cheering and jumping up and down with this success. The cheering will not last long and the fighters will disappear into the mountains once more, for it will not be long before more gunships come into view. This is a hit-and-run war with no big battles.

"The Red Army is stuck in this war much like the Vietnam War was for the Americans. There seems to be no plan by the Russians on how to win this war. The plan seems to be for both sides just to go on with killing and hoping the other side will quit.

"Millions of Afghanistan's have left the country for Iran or Pakistan as refugees. Many will return to fight during the summer and then move back across the border for another rest period and resupply their weapons during the winter months.

"Then today's news was that the Soviets are withdrawing troops. This is Bill Ranken reporting from the battle zone in the mountains of Afghanistan Goodnight." The screen cut back to the network.

"That was our reporter in Afghanistan with an update. Now we move to our panel for their evaluation of the situation in Afghanistan. We have with us retired General of U.S. Army Brigadier General Lee Major and noted Professor Hashem Khan, who has written several books on Pakistan and Afghanistan.

: First, I must ask General Major, what do you think the outcome will be of this war and the withdrawal?" asked Chet.

"Well, Chet the Russians are in trouble. The death toll is greater than the Russian public knows, and the government wants to keep it that way. There are rumors of the bodies of Soviet troops killed in Afghanistan being taken to other Soviet Bloc nations in eastern Europe for burial to avoid calling attention to the high loss of life in Afghanistan.

"The Soviets are in a war that they are not prepared to win politically or militarily. Their military tactical skills it seems are the same as when they fought the Germans in the Second World War which, to put it in simple terms, was just to use pure blunt force of mass weapons and men.

"The economic resources needed to support this kind of warfare are draining away resources from the domestic side in the Soviet Union. The shortages at home and the rumors have the Russian public beginning to ask questions about the war," said General Major.

"What do you say, Professor Khan?"

"I agree with the general. This area of the world has been difficult for foreign invaders for centuries. This time it is not just the mountain tribes that are in arms against invaders. It is the Islamic world that is in revolt against the modern world. I think the Soviets will be completely out of this war within the next two months, if not before, because of other pressures on the Soviet Union.

"For example, the SDI program that everyone is calling 'Star Wars' proposed by President Reagan has caused the Soviet leadership and military to worry and expand their missile defense budget to keep pace with the Americans. The effort into missile research did reduce their military effort in Afghanistan and further reduce their domestic economy. The economic fact is that the Soviet Union could not afford the cost of both 'Butter' the domestic goods or 'Bullets' for military production and defense. The Soviet leaders pick 'Bullets' over 'Butter' and for that, they are in trouble at home and in the war," said the Professor.

"Can you give an example of this Bullet and Butter thing so I can understand your point better?" asked Chet.

"Take for example when President Reagan proposed that the government should have a supply of medical morphine so that every American would be able to get say 200 injections of morphine. That simple statement sent a message to the leadership of the Soviet Union that the American leadership believed they could survive a first nuclear attack," said the Professor.

"What? How?" asked Chet.

"That one statement caused the Russians to increase their underground shelter program and other things that would be needed in case of a first strike. They recently reported they have enough shelter for the entire Soviet population in case of a nuclear strike." said the Professor.

"That seems like a stretch. How could the morphine statement be taken as a threat?" asked Chet.

"It is simple, Chet if you look at the big picture. For example, Morphine is used for the treatment of burn victims. If you know this, what happens in a nuclear strike?"

"Burns!" said Chet.

"So in the Soviets mindset, the leadership had to increase their production of the drug and also increased the production of bomb shelters for the public and at the same time improve the missiles preparedness. That all requires money and that has caused the Soviet Union more economic problems. Either it focuses on butter or bullets to do both could be runniness," said the Professor.

"O.K. I understand that better. Now back to Afghanistan, you and the general seem to agree the Soviets will be out of Afghanistan in two months. Is that too optimistic professor?" asked Chet.

"No, not in a country that has been at war for centuries with itself and others. Two or three years is not that long," said the Professor.

"I agree with the professor on Afghanistan and the fighting, but the Russians cannot keep this war going and still project an image of the perfect society. I said two months as an upper limit. I would not be surprised if they are out in the next six days," said the General.

"Would you agree professor?" asked Chet.

"Yes! I would say that is a very good possibility, but when that happens things will fall into chaos in that country," said the professor.

"Why?" asked Chet.

"All the warring parties or tribes will then turn their attention to each other using the modern weapons that the Soviets and the Americans will have left behind," said the professor.

"What do you think general?"

"Chet, Afghanistan is a third-world country and has no real strategic importance to the United States. Our reason for being there was to stop the Soviet Union aggression and we will have that if we leave," said the general.

"If I may point out, we should consider the Islamic fundamentalist position in this war. These people were not fighting to stop the spread of communism. They were fighting the modern world and its impact on Islamic culture. No, I think Pandora's Box has been opened!" said the professor.

"Well, we must have another conversation on that issue another time.

For now, we are out of time gentlemen. I want to thank you both for being with us for this discussion tonight. This is Chet Butler for Wake-Up America and the Evening News. Good night and be safe."

AT A MEETING ON THE BORDER OF PAKISTAN IN AFGHANISTAN – OCTOBER 2001

The last man of the Soviet Army left Afghanistan on February 15, 1989, and the mujahideen groups began fighting among themselves for power. The Taliban won the struggle, and the Taliban began to brutalize the population and destroy historical monuments.

The leadership's order to the destruction of the Buddhas of Bamiyan was a fulfillment of Koranic Law in March of 2001. This one act shocked the world and was referred to as the Bamiyan Massacre.

The tribal warfare continued with Ahmad Shah Massoud's 'Lion of Panjshir' the guerrilla leader in the north battling the Taliban and Al-Qaeda. Osama bin Laden ordered the execution of Ahmad. The assassination was carried out on September 9, 2001, by two men posing as Belgium reporters. Two days later Osama bin Laden and Al-Qaeda conducted four coordinated attacks on U.S. soil.

"Nasir, why have you asked me to you in Afghanistan?" asked Abdul.

"The movement needs money and Osama has moved on to other plans with his vast resource of funds. So, we need a new benefactor or an increase in our resources of money. The poppy fields can be expanded and with routes into the European market added to ours, we can increase our funds and feed the growing Western demand in the drug market," said Nasir.

"I see your point and there is another area for a huge cash profit available to expand our market by developing connections into the Cartels in Mexico. The decadent North American societies will pay for all the drugs we can deliver to the Mexicans and their routes will allow us to expand our route into North America with little effort on our part. The packaging and shipping will be the only part of our process here and in the Asian drug market," said Abdul.

"That is good because with Osama off on other things, we need a new source of money. Will the Mexicans allow us to enter their routes?" asked Nisir.

"I will find out when I go back. Do you know what Osama is planning next?" asked Abdul.

"I do not know, but I doubt it will happen soon. I was told he is with the Taliban at some training site. His idea is to attack Western culture to free Islam. He needs to be focused more on building nationalism in the Arab world rather than on attacking the Western culture," said Nasir.

"He is free to follow his path. I will go to Mexico and make contacts for our arrangements. This will take some time to build an understanding with the cartel leaders. These people have no allegiance to anything but money and power. The drug money is difficult to hide, but I have an idea of how to clean the funds by using government postage stamps. We will use the valuable collectors of these postage stamps much like the black-market individuals who use valuable art. I have an artist working on engraving the plates now," said Abdul.

"I do not understand?" said Nasir.

"The black market used valuable pieces of art to help launder their money and stolen art. For example, someone has a valuable artifact, say a cuneiform tablet from Babylon. They take the artifact to a middleman in Lebanon who creates documentation for the artifact. Then he sells the piece to someone in Turkey who then transfers the artifact to a dealer in Western Europe. That dealer knows of an American who is building a Museum for the Bible. The artifact is then purchased for the museum with all the legitimated documentation," said Abdul.

"How is that laundering money?" asked Nasir.

"Alright, let's say a valuable painting is sold at auction. That art is taken to a storage facility for valuable art and other things. Then it is sold to an anonymous buyer without ever leaving the facility. The same thing is done in banking with lots of transactions leaving a transaction trail. The sales in artworks have less of a paper trail with the anonymous buyers of the art world. Simply put all the transactions clean the money with each transaction," said Abdul.

CHAPTER TWENTY-ONE

Robert Haisman was an excellent forger of air mail covers and cards. He was never indicted, because, on October 9, 1985, police found Robert and his wife dead of gunshot wounds from a murder-suicide. A search of their home discovered the fake paraphernalia used to make the fake postal canceling devices.

GENUINE

FORGERY

The line between good and evil is permeable and almost anyone can be induced to cross it when pressured by situational forces.

— Philip Zimbardo

2002 - TO "CRY WOLF"

At the FBI building Nick and C.E. were walking in when Nick asked, "C.E. did you ever hear the story of the boy who cried wolf?"

"Sure, most parents would tell it to their children to get them to tell the truth and not to tell tall tales. Why do you ask?"

"Mass social media is filled with the 'Wolf' stories today. The internet, these new blogs and other social media forms are filled with information and stories that are less than accurate. I can only guess there will be more types of these information sites in the future. It is becoming difficult to know whether a story is based on facts or just made-up fiction just to get noticed. It's hard to tell the truth from fiction today." said Nick.

"Yeah, that is a common belief today. Back in the 1960's Ronald Reagan gave a speech about the horrible detestable tactics of the colonial American patriots in 1776 published that year in the London Times. The next day everyone was talking about what a great speech Ronald gave. Only later, did someone point out that the London Times did not start publishing until the 1780's. Reagan made up the story. With more media that comes on the information market, the truth will be more difficult to find," said C.E.

"I see your point and once the story hits the internet it is repeated so often that it is believed and picked up by major news networks that do not want to miss out or be the last one on a good story. Nobody will question the validity of the story. They just run with the story until it just dies then it is off to the next story. However, it is also true that the public's view of the press has dropped since 1985 and those of us at the national security agencies have to monitor all communication sites for any threats to the nation. That can work in our favor at times for it allows us to gather more information quickly.

"That brings me now to the sale of stamps on the web. I had no idea how widespread the collecting industry was in stamps. There are hundreds of sites selling stamps from vintage stamps to current stamps. Recently a British Guiana stamp of a One Cent magenta sold for nine million dollars. Now, our discovery at the print shop has opened or should I say expanded an area of our concern," said Nick.

"Why? Counterfeit stamps now? They are not new to the illegal trade. They have been forged almost as long as they have been printed," said C.E.

"True, but now they appear to be used to finance terrorist operations. Just as priceless pieces of art have been used to hide money. Now it also seems to be the case with stamps. The reason for stamps is a history of the ownership, that is providence of the stamp, is not required. When one sells art in the United States, buyers will want a legal title document for the artwork. In the 1990's a law was passed to protect art.

"One problem with the use of Black-Market art is that the artworks are at times large and not easy to transport or to store. So the art is held in storage until it is taken or resold and never leaves the storage house. Stamps on the other hand are smaller and are almost as valuable, if not more, and can be stored in small places or carried on the person. Plus, stamps are sold legitimately daily for large sums, while valuable art that is stolen or forged is not sold on the open market every day.

"The simple fact is that a good market creates a market ripe for talented forgers. Art forgeries and art hoaxes will flood the market through auctions, galleries, and now online. Remember the film The Thomas Crown Affair? It put a spotlight on the world of the art theft. Now we understand stamps that are part of that market we need to adjust," said Nick.

"So how do we start and who is working on this?" asked C.E.

"That would be us as one part in the field of alphabet government agencies and their agents. The systemic looting and the illicit trading in antiquities is a constant struggle for us to stay up with and the new ways of criminals trying to avoid our efforts to control their efforts. Once we figure out one kind of method they adjust to new criminal patterns. Many agencies are working at the same time on this illegal trade and, unfortunately, none are working very well together.

"We have the Anti-Money-Laundering (AML), the Banking Secretary Act (BSA), Combating Financing Terrorism (CFT), and the Department of Justice all working on this criminal activity. At one point the DOJ seized a painting worth millions being shipped into the United States on an invoice that claimed that the painting was worth just a hundred dollars. DOJ only caught the artwork when a private security company notified them that the art was stolen and was in that particular shipment. Private Security has become a major industry and at times works for the wrong side.

"Part of the problem is that the security industry is built on their representation of what they can provide for total security once their system is installed. Then the criminals work around that new security system. When a criminal network is broken and the criminals are apprehended, the news media will expose their method in details of their criminal activity.

"The exposure of the method causes more theft and another surge in private companies to come up with a new method of protection for the general public and business industry from criminal activity. The result is the 'Wolf is at the door' and security loses its impact after a while. The security industry loves it for they get to update the systems and the cycle starts over.

"Then over time people become once more relaxed and stop looking deeply at things. They will over time miss those small indications of something bigger that is about to happen. A good example is a group of foreign students learning to fly large commercial aircraft at a private flying school and not putting in the time or effort to learn the skill for landing the craft.

"The warning flags were there. They were just missed being picked up. Each day there are millions of things the national security agencies are looking at and once we discover a problem a new method is created to avoid detection. It may be something small like this stamp connection we discovered at a small fire in a printing shop. We now think this has a connection to an international terrorist plot," said Nick.

"Wow! I guess, I have just seen the tip of the iceberg. Where and when is this terrorist plot to happen? Where do we start?" asked C.E.

"That is our major problem we do not know. It is a matter of us putting the pieces we have together and coming up with a scenario. Right now we have a known terrorist who has been dealing in stamps. So for now why don't we go to the site of the fire and start from the beginning? We'll take my government car and I'll bring you back here if that is O.K. with you," said Nick.

"Let's do it."

CHAPTER TWENTY-TWO

David Cohn was a Berlin stamp dealer and forger, who reprinted some 50,000 sets of a Hanover stamp. When his activity was discovered, the Berlin *Philatelisten-Klub* paid Cohn 500 marks for all of the materials that he had used to reproduce and reprint forgeries of the stamps. The equipment and materials were donated to the German Postal Museum in 1895.

GENUINE

FORGERY

Violence can only be concealed by a lie, and the lie can only be maintained by violence.

— Aleksandr Solzhenitsyn

RUSSIAN MAFIA 1991

"Alexei, you and Viktor have been our face to the new business corporate world. Now that the old Soviet system is in chaos and has fallen rapidly apart, the state-owned businesses will need to be financed to run and many will be sold to individuals or groups. I want you to make connections we have within the KGB and buy into these industries and businesses. Be careful with your inquiries for there are those in the KGB that have their plans to take over the state-run enterprises," said Mikhail.

"I think you are right for Colonel Fedorov and Sasha Vasiliev have both contacted me about business opportunities. They say that with a supply of funds they can buy or payoff officials for a few of the good state-operated industries," said Alexei.

"Who are the individuals you mentioned Colonel Fedorov and Sasha Vasiliev?" asked Mikhail.

"Sasha is a party leader in Leningrad or should I say Saint Petersburg. That city has changed its name many times since the original city was named by the Tsar Peter the Great. It was Saint Petersburg then became Petrograd to sound less German. Then after the Socialist Revolution, it was renamed to honor Comrade Leningrad and now it is back to Saint Petersburg," answered Viktor.

"This Sasha must be new or young for I do not know of him. Why would you think he is a possible person for this enterprise?" said Mikhail.

"You're right! First, he is young, but also a climber and if the party had not collapsed, he would have been a major player in a very short time. Secondly, he also knows members of the different small gangs in the city. He told me that these gangs are eyeing each other and will turn the city into the crime capital of Russia within the next few years.

"He knows your organization will be the big winner in the long run and wants to be on the winning side. It is with his knowledge of the state industries we will need to snap up the better-run businesses," said Viktor.

"Alright bring him into the loop and keep a close watch on him for he is a climber, and they are difficult to trust. What about this Colonel Fedorov?" asked Mikhail.

"He was in charge of the section in the KGB that inspected the records of several State-owned industries. He knows which ones are run with efficiency and can function without the state funds to hold them up in business. In other words, those that will survive in a profit center society," said Alexei.

"Alright, we'll go with that. Alexei, you, and your son Popov are to establish banks in Leningrad and Moscow. We will fund the cost from outside the country and make it look like foreign capital is being invested in the Russian economy. If I remember right, you told me you worked with a German and an American banker before you were sent to the Gulag," said Mikhail.

"Yes, that was a long time ago, but I reconnected with the American banker's son who was connected to the German banker. The American banker was in the Soviet Union with their President on the last recent official visit. They were part of the economic team. We met briefly in the hotel. That is how I met Colonel Fedorov. He questioned me on my meeting with the American banker. I told him the banker's father was a friend of the Soviet Union in the twenties," said Alexei.

"Is he still a friend?" asked Mikhail.

"The thing is that the banker was working with the German and Soviet governments in the 1920s and continued to work with Germany through-out the 1930s. He once told me that one of the American Presidents said 'The business of America is business'. These Americans chase money and money will always make strange bedfellows.

"I think he would be a good conduit into the American banking sys-tem. These people are all about money, so if you ask me if I trust them, I say No! However, we would have strong leverage to hold them in line. They have laws that he will be able to bend and that will be our hold on them," replied Alexei.

"Leverage is good. Just because this state is in a state of collapse and that drunken Boris Yeltsin is taking power in the long run, he will not last long. The so-called liberal democracy in Russia will not last. I have word from a good contact within the KGB that a young Lieutenant Colonel named Vladimir Vladimirovich Putin is building a political group. Let's face the simple facts that in all of Russian history the fact that government changes with no real change. Look at the recent history.

"The Tsar was replaced with a series of troika's starting with Lenin, Trotsky, and Lenin's bitch wife. They set up a pattern of constant terror just to stay in power. Lenin purged the party of anyone who could stand in the way of his dream of a new society.

"The troika of old was replaced with Lev Kamenev, Grigory Zinoviev, and Stalin after Lenin's death. Then that group shifted to little dwarf Lavrentiy Beria, Alexie Malenkov, and Vyacheslav Molotov, who were controlled by Stalin until he died in 1953.

"Nikita Khrushchev, Georgy Malenkov, and Vyacheslav Molotov took charge and brought great success with the Soviet space program at the cost of domestic development.

"The joke about domestic products was the first thing you did when in a new home was called a repairman. Yet, the poor quality of goods and the reduction of domestic production did help our growth in our economic activity in the Black Market.

"By the time Khrushchev was removed from office by the next troika of Alexei Kosygin, Nikolai Podgorny, and Leonid Brezhnev the system was deeply connected to us with the goods we brought in from the West. By then the whole system was completely corrupted. There was not one part of the government that was not connected to our black-market system. Brezhnev appeared to be a righteous Communist as he moved around the country in his Western-made suits and western-built cars.

"He defended the Soviet Union during Czechoslovakia's Prague Spring in 1968 with tanks that brought up memories of the Hungary Revolt in 1956 to the world. Once again, the world's public opinion turned against the Soviet Union.

"Later he used the Warsaw Pact organization that had been established for the common defense of the Soviet Bloc nations. That one act demonstrated to the West just how weak the Soviet Union had become. Communist leaders had turned the Warsaw Pact into a weapon, for the hardliner, to crush political opposition in Czechoslovakia. The weakness was greatly demonstrated when it was learned that East Germany and Romania were two eastern members of Warsaw that pushed hard for the Soviets to act and send in the tanks.

"The Solidarity Movement caused concern in the Polish leadership in 1980. The trade Unions at the Gdansk shipyard forced the Polish government to give in to the workers' demands. The workers listed twenty-one demands for the government to approve.

"The fear of a Soviet military invasion caused the Polish military to declare martial law by the end of the year. Members of Solidarity were arrested including Lech Walesa. This prevented the Soviet military from taking direct action in Poland.

"Poland was in a stalemate between the government and the citizens until 1988 when Solidarity and Lech Walesa reappeared. This was followed by another poor Soviet decision in the leadership that hurt their Soviet image in world opinion. The Soviet system was falling apart way before Brezhnev died.

"After Brezhnev's death, we saw a parade of old men in leadership. Yuri Andropov did not make it a full two years before death took him. We should be thankful that he died before he could have made any real reforms that would cause our organization any real trouble for, he was a real idealist in the Soviet view of the world.

"He was replaced by another old man waiting to die, Konstantin Chernenko, who did not live long enough to do anything of importance. He was followed by the next younger generation of the revolution Mikhail Gorbachev, who had bad luck for him and good luck for us to come into power when the state was already in a complete state of collapse.

"Mikhail Gorbachev tried to remove our influence within the government by his restructuring (*Perestroika*) program and the policy of openness (*Glasnost*) in government. He also tried to reform Russian life and tried to reduce drunkenness and the consumption of Vodka with increased production of beer and wine, which gave us a larger market in the sales of Vodka.

"He also had some bad luck with President Reagan's Star Wars (SDI) plan. That forced the Industrial-Military complex people of the old Soviet world to re-thinking and shift more and more funds into military spending and away from domestic goods. The old members couldn't change to new situations when something did not work, they just did the same thing over again with the same results. If small worked, then bigger was better, and large was great.

"Our public worldview was damaged when the military shot down KLA flight 007 with a U.S. government official onboard. That was followed by a young German kid flying right through our great air security network undetected with a small plane landing right in the middle of

Moscow's Red Square. That did more damage to the public image of the military here at home. That was all followed by the worst nuclear accident in history at Chernobyl which almost resulted in a nuclear meltdown. As it was, it did spread radiation across the world and made the area around the plant unlivable. Poor old Gorbachev did not have a chance. Yet, leaders come and go, and we are still here!" said Mikhail.

"Mikhail, you surprise me with your understanding of Soviet politics and national history. You were in the camps for almost fifty-five years and still know more than most of us of our history," said Alexei.

"Not so surprising when you know I was the youngest scholar at the university when the Bolsheviks murdered my family for being in the way of the revolution. Lenin and the communists saw the proletariat as just the industrial workers. The communists saw the peasants as capitalist thieves who would hide their wealth from the state.

"My father was a village elder and leader who spoke out against Lenin's plan that took food away from the peasants to feed the industrial workers and military. Lenin called the plan 'War Communism' and the food went to the military and industrial workers first.

"Our village was non-essential and left to starve. My father protested and was dragged out of our home and shot with his mother in front of the whole village. The village was then told not to help my mother or any of her children who were still home. I returned the next year to find they had all starved to death because of Lenin's actions of war communism. I turned to the Thieves for revenge.

"Of course, Lenin won the civil war and later changed the policy to a capitalistic economic system he called the New Economic Plan that allowed the peasants a small plot of land for their use, and they could sell their small food products in the open markets. All that was too late for my family and millions of others. The Soviets were political thugs with no honor.

"So you act surprised I know our history, but one must know his adversary to defeat him or join with him. Today that adversary is this young Lieutenant Colonel from the former KGB. He will work with the National Defense and Security people along with the new business technological oligarchs to grab power. He will become the new Tsar of Russia.

"Until then, Russia will have power struggles between politicians and the different groups that have evolved out of the Bitch Wars. We will win because we are going to get tied into the new elite oligarch and that young colonel. That is my history and I believe that is the first time I have told that story so completely," said Mikhail.

"Thank you for telling it to us. I know the past is hard to bring up," said Alexei.

"What about now?" asked Viktor.

"We will watch and wait and make moves with the future in mind. The new Russia will see some violent times for the next few years and we will play our part in that while everything changes and nothing will change.

"Today my friends, with the collapse of the Soviet Union there is a power struggle going on for a new social order in Russia. I agree with your man in St. Petersburg that that city and government will be in chaos, gangs will assassinate leaders, and the homicide rate from gang violence will increase at such a high rate that films will be made based on the violence. St. Petersburg will look like the American gangster city of Chicago in the last century. Money will be made in the power struggle and that will be made by us," said Mikhail.

CHAPTER TWENTY-THREE

Josef Riesa began counterfeiter as early as 1865. His main counterfeited stamps were valued at (2) Mexican reals (coins) stamps in yellow-green and 8-reals red-lilac stamps of 1856 and the 4-reals stamps of 1861 all with various cancellations and overprints.

GENUINE   **FORGERY**

People like to say that the conflict is between good and evil. The real conflict is between truth and lies.
— Don Miguel Ruiz

2001 MEXICO AND DRUG CARTELS

Mexican cartels to avoid the U.S. border and customs agents started using tunnels. The border agents discovered 12 tunnels connecting Mexico to the United States between 1990 and 2001. One tunnel was four feet wide with an elaborate rail system, a ventilation system, and an electrical supply generator. The length of the tunnel was 3,309 feet long and six stories deep. After 2001 border agents increased detection and used ground-penetrating radar to locate the tunnels.

"Mateo, did you take care of that little thing?" asked Diego.

"Yes! The body is placed so that others will know not to betray you," said Mateo.

"Good! Now tell Santiago and Juan to start two new tunnels into California and one in Texas or New Mexico and no more mistakes," said Diego.

"What shall I do with that politician Matias?" asked Mateo.

"Nothing for now he has sold his soul to us with his betrayal of the U.S. DEA individual. We need to discover how he was able to get into our organization undercover. For now, we have the photos and tapes of our good honest politician taking the money. Plus the 'honey pot' video is also available," said Diego.

"O.K., one last thing, the mules that Liliana is running north have had a slight problem. The woman, Lucia, had a problem with one of the bags when it broke open inside her and she is now in a hospital in Texas. I have sent someone to take care of that little matter by tonight," said Mateo.

"Is the woman conscious?" asked Diego.

"No! She had no identification when they picked her up off the bus. Plus, she was taken to the Austin hospital unconscious," said Mateo.

"What about the others? Where are they?" asked Diego.

"They were all on separate forms of transportation to reduce exposure for us and to have a lesser chance for the women to get together to compare notes. Of course, they were all told that their family would pay for any mishaps. The reward in money they are paid and the fear for their families will keep them in line," said Mateo.

"So, the system is not in danger of exposure?" asked Diego.

"No, but just to be safe I established a second transport system through Florida for the next trip. They will move from Columbia to Puerto Rico to Florida instead of the Mexico route," replied Mateo.

"Good!"

"There is one more thing, the meeting with that Moslem Abdul has been changed to tomorrow. These guys keep changing locations and times. They seem to be so concerned for precautions and yet, they still do stupid things that could get themselves exposed to the people they are trying so hard to hide from!" said Mateo.

"That is their problem. I do not care as long as they pay the money and keep their promises. You still have Isabel and Ana keeping tabs on our friend and entertaining him. Even with all the precautions he takes, he is still easy to identify and follow. He may blend in up in the North, but here in Mexico he just stands out," said Diego.

"It is funny how these guys seem to ignore their religious beliefs on alcohol and women. Isabel and Ana say this guy is uptight but enjoys wine and women more than once in a while. They say he is rough and a mean drunk. That if you had not told him to not hurt the women they would have been hurt," said Mateo.

"Why do they say this?" asked Diego.

"He has gone off on his own a few nights and found some women, but mostly young boys on the street a few times. One or two of these unlucky souls, that we know of, went to the hospital," said Mateo.

"WHAT! This could lead back to us if the victims can identify Abdul!" shouted Diego.

"Not to worry, we talked to his victims, and they know the cost if they talk. Then we talked with Abdul and said next time he will be paid in kind if any more such behavior of that kind happens in Mexico. He was also made to make payment to the individuals he hurt, and we took a percent of the payment as their agent," said Mateo.

"Did he do it?" asked Diego.

"Of course, he denied everything at first. Then we showed him photos and that they could be made public, and he became quite compliant. He made the payments, and I distributed the funds to the individuals. I think this guy is willing to send others to their death, but not at his own risk," said Mateo.

"No, he knows his organization is much like ours. Toleration is not something to be accepted. Give the photos to him. We need him happy and not worry about us and his public exposure. The leadership over there tolerates indiscretions as long as it is not in the public eye. You see we are similar," said Diego.

"Very well. Should I also give the negatives?" asked Mateo.

"Of course only after you make copies. It is always best for us to have a little insurance," said Diego.

"Copies are already made, and I will see he gets the photos and negatives this afternoon," said Mateo.

"Good and have the meeting here with Abdul. My family will be out of town visiting with my mother. I do not want to travel to see him. I do not like the jerk," said Diego.

"Understood and I'll tell him the meeting will be here," said Mateo.

"Good, now I must go and see my children before they leave," said Diego.

CHAPTER TWENTY-FOUR

Kotaro Wada was an excellent forger of stamps. He sold them to foreign travelers as 'Tourist Sheets'. He also offered them to European and American dealers. It is hard to determine a fake from a genuine stamp. There are still forgery copies in circulation as genuine stamps that outnumber the genuine stamps 10 to 1. He ended his practice of counterfeiting in 1911. The counterfeit plates he used were supposed to have been destroyed in the earthquake in Tokyo before in 1923.

GENUINE   **FORGERY**

Human nature is evil, and goodness is caused by intentional activity.

— Xun Kuang

1995 China's Plan

At an office in the city of Tianjin in northern China, a select small group of business and city government officials of the upper leadership sat around a table discussing the future of the city and the country.

The city of Tianjin in 1860 was one of the foreign Treaty Ports established after the Second Opium War. The war started with the British and French demanding that China accept payments for Chinese goods in opium instead of gold. The Chinese refused and were defeated once more and forced to accept the establishment of more Treaty Ports.

This was a humiliation of China that continued between 1841 and 1914. There were close to 80 Treaty Ports forced on China during this period. That all changed in 1949 with the victory of Mao and the Communists over the Nationalists.

Now Tianjin was one of the first state-level economic and technological zones established in 1984 by the People's Republic. The port was located on the Bohai Sea which was open to the Pacific trade. China was becoming a modern world power, and the leaders were playing the long game. The meeting was to discuss current plans and operations.

"Mayor Bo, we will soon join the World Trade Organization and China will become a major business and industrial player in the world. I have asked Professor Wu to introduce you to the plan that he has developed from the studies he conducted at Yale University. His plan was developed at their business school," said business leader He.

"Thank-you Chairman He. First, let me start with a little history. For centuries China has been a leader in the world of business with just five basic rules. These five rules we need to focus on to understand the present.

"First, there is the traditional Chinese top-down management structure. We will keep that with a decentralized structure that will allow a rapid response to the shift in the business markets.

"Second, we need to identify, recruit, and retain the best teenagers who are capable of growing into the new business organizations we are building.

"Third, and most importantly we need to move from a central planning economy to a private enterprise model with a minimum of oversight controlled by the state.

"Fourth, a key element is to expand our development with reverse engineering of foreign products so we can get around international patent issues. Then once we redesign the product, we can begin marketing the product in foreign markets.

Finally, we are planning for today with the understanding we are preparing to double the economic structure in three to five years," said Professor Wu.

"Are you saying we are to ignore international patents?" asked Guo.

"Who are you?" asked Wu.

"I am the lead engineer in research and development, Zixuan Guo, sir."

"Engineer Guo, for centuries the Western world has taken our inventions and never paid any royalties to China's ingenious inventors. They took our noodles and called them spaghetti, our fireworks and made weapons of destruction, our compass, waterwheel, and clock just to name a few. So, what I am saying is that we reverse engineer their ideas into our ideas just as they did with ours," said leader He.

"Gentlemen, we have already decided a way around any international problems. We have a billion people who will be working for a lower wage than any other industrialized nation. The Western business world wants access to our one billion people for their marketing. We will provide them with an increase in access to our market at the cost of their intellectual property and a share of their profit.

"We will remain a socialist country and shift to a series of selected economic enterprise zones. Expanding the economic and technological zones into commercial joint ventures with foreign capital for export. This will be an orientation that will react to the market forces," said Ying.

"Will the West allow this?" asked Mayor Bo.

"The West is filled with individuals that will see profit and nothing else. Their political elite needs to provide for their families, and we can influence those families with business opportunities. Besides, most of their leaders only look at short-term success in the business world.

"The Japanese government and business community after the Second World War saw this and started to see a profit in the 1950s by targeting specific industries in the American market to take over. The television industry was one of their first industries targeted. Television manufacturing soon became a Japanese industry and that industry left America in a few short years. The Americans do not even manufacture a single T.V. set today. The slogan American made soon became American assembled.

"The same happened with the steel industry that is almost gone in the United States. So, Mayor Bo the West has no long-term plan except to make money. We have a long-term plan to dominate the economies of the world within the next two generations," said Ying.

"What happens when our economy grows, and wages increase? What will happen to cheap labor costs?" asked Guo.

"A good Socialist system has a way to find low-wage workers – engineer Guo!" said Ying.

Guo sat there thinking that now he was worried that he might have caused undue attention to himself and his family. He had known fellow workers who had made innocent comments and were sent to re-education places. It was a known fact that camps were forced labor and that those in the camps were never mentioned in conversations.

One's freedom in the Chinese legal system was always one step away and one had to be careful of what was said to others. That is the ugly beauty of the socialist system, thought Guo as he was brought back to the discussion.

"We will always have workers gentlemen - our long-term goal is to have the Western world educate our young so we can compete with the West in the next 25-30 years. Their Western businessmen and leaders are interested in making a profit. They will use our students to help build their system of marketing. We will have what the West calls a 'fifth column' being built in their very backyard by their leadership.

"They only see a billion customers that are willing and ready to buy. Their leadership will be willing to do just about anything to get into our markets. Then in time, they will be committed to our resources. They will follow our rules, or they will lose their place at the business table. Their talk of individual freedom will be ignored over their profits.

"We will make them bend to our demands to share and follow our guidelines. Their greed is so great in their business they have allowed us to buy into their companies for our advantage. We will take command of the economic market of the world from within slowly," said Mayor Bo.

"Yes, and one more thing we need to look into is that the Americans allow foreign investors to purchase land in the United States. We need to start on a small scale in that area," said Professor Wu.

"I have a group already looking into that area of development," said Ying.

"Good! Now if that is all let us move to have some tea and company," said Leader He as they all stood up.

CHAPTER TWENTY-FIVE

Joseph Britton printed all five of the Wells, Fargo & Company Phony Express stamps. He copied and printed them in the approximated original colors of the government runs. The stamps in the original color are all forgeries or at best re-printed forgeries. The stamps in different colors are bogus.

GENUINE   **FORGERY**

When we believe in lies, we cannot see the truth, so we make thousands of assumptions, and we take them as truth. One of the biggest assumptions we make is that the lies we believe are the truth!

— Don Miguel Ruiz

1996 China's Western World College Network

The *gaokao* is China's National College Entrance Exam. It is one of the most difficult entrance exams in the world and to avoid the *gaokao* one can study abroad. The number one place to study abroad is the United Kingdom followed by the United States. Between 1985 and 1990 two-thirds of Chinese students that went abroad to study failed to return to China. The Chinese government underfunded these students and encouraged them to seek financial aid from other sources — private and foreign governments. The Chinese government shrunk support from 54% in 1979 to 17% by 1989.

Professor Clark was the head of the chemistry department at the university which had several federal grants to work on new formulas in organic chemistry. One of those grants was now a byproduct of another grant. The original grant was at first established on a heat resistance material that could be used for firefighting. That changed within a week when new properties of the material were discovered. Now the grant was part of a Pentagon program looking for a new body armor that would be lighter and bullet resistant and cut production costs by more than a third.

The preliminary test showed good results and the best thing was the new material could be used in many different industries. The new material was stronger than any material now in use and had the property of being more heat resistant than any material now in use. NASA and the Pentagon were in discussions to increase the funding for the grant. The research was top secret; only a few selected individuals had the security clearance and even fewer were allowed access to the program.

Outside the university, a man sat on a park bench when another man approached and sat down.

"Good day, Professor Clark, we have transferred money to your account in Switzerland. However, the flash drive you gave me did not have the latest test results on the new material. When can we expect this information?" asked Jing.

"I have to be careful this information is closely watched. My lab research assistant Mei is from Hong Kong and holds strong ill feelings against mainland China. Her grandmother died in the Tiananmen Square protest in 1989. Now that the Hong Kong agreement of 'one nation two systems' is being slowly disregarded by your government, she is very vocal in her resentment of mainland China. If she ever saw me talking to you, her resentment would lead to an investigation with her asking other questions," said the Professor.

"Yes, we are aware of her views. We have been able to place a grad student, Su Wu, as another research assistant in the program. She has passed your security clearance check and her background also shows she is from Hong Kong. She will become friends with Mei. So, you will be able to pass information to Su," said Jing.

"What about Professor Qing?" asked the professor.

"Professor Qing will not be a problem any longer. He has become an informant for us. It seems we have a film showing his relationship with certain students and he also has a policy of having certain students receive better grades for donations to him. He is worried about his job and that his wife will find out about the affair and ruin his life. For now, he is only providing small amounts of information. Later we will expand his role," said Jing.

"But Professor Qing has been asking questions that may have exposed our deal," said Professor Clark.

"True, but now Qing will no longer ask those questions. If asked about them now, he will say he was wrong and upset at losing his grant funds to your section in the department. He will stay away from Organic Chemistry. Our plan is long-term, we can take our time, but still demand results," said Jing.

"What should I do about Mei?"

"Nothing, for now, she and Su Wu can work together. Later start giving Su more responsibilities, but slowly so as not to show concern. This is a long game and time is on our side. Mei is not a problem as long as you do not give her any reasons to become suspicious. Her work at the university is almost over and she will graduate and move into the business world. We have a company offering her a very good position in Hong Kong and she will be taken care of in Hong Kong," said Jing.

CHAPTER TWENTY-SIX

H.E. Macintosh sold a dozen or more forgery stamps from the Confederate States of America. They were not genuine stamps for Macintosh had a deal with August Dietz who designed the patterns for the stamps in 1918. When Dietz informed Macintosh that the stamps were in violation of copyright laws and U.S. Postal law, Macintosh claimed to have destroyed the equipment and continued to sell the stamps with *Facsimile* on the reverse side. He continued to sell the imitation into the 1950s.

GENUINE

FORGERY

It is necessary for him who lays out a state and arranges laws for it to presuppose that all men are evil and that they are always going to act according to the wickedness of their spirits whenever they have free scope.

— Niccolo Machiavelli

MAY 2002 THE RAID IN MEXICO

The adobe hacienda sat behind the outer walls that surrounded the home and courtyard. The house was constructed with thick walls covered in white stucco with exposed thick heavy dark wooden beans. The roof finished the Mediterranean influence with red clay tiles. The courtyard was surrounded by walls that allowed for outdoor privacy.

Diego stood up, but did not offer his hand and said, "Abdul, welcome to my home."

"Thank you, Diego. Your people have been very easy to work with. It is nice to finally meet with you in person. I am sorry for all the changes in the schedule. Our Russian friends have their way of doing things. They are very close to the leaders in the Russian government if they are not running most of the agencies. It is not like the old days of the Cold War with KGB, who were just ruthless. These guys make that ruthlessness look tame," both men laughed.

"Am I missing something about our business - Abdul?" asked Diego.

"No, No! The Russians have agreed to work with us in driving up the price of oil. The Americans in the next few years will flood the market with their shale oil reserves. We have decided that when that happens, we will need to drive the price down so that the American industry cannot afford to produce shale oil at a lower cost. We think that will be a distraction for the Americans while we put our other plan into action." said Abdul.

Just then the door opened, and Diego and Abdul turned to the door. "Diego, we just were warned Federal police are planning a raid on the house right now. The information comes from two sources. One ranking official said the raid is scheduled to start in 20 minutes. I went to the roof and saw they were assembling down the street. What should we do?" asked Mateo.

"Abdul it is best you leave right now by the tunnel." Diego turned and said, "Mateo have Juan take him now and put the call out that we will make a stand and have those at the warehouse assemble behind the police line. When the first man in the raid enters the gate, we will open fire from both directions. Then we will have them in a crossfire from the front and back."

Mateo rushed out of the room saying to Juan, "Juan, you take Abdul out through the tunnel then come back and help set up."

Minutes later the Federal police slowly approached the house with three armored vehicles. Two to cover each side of the villa and one to break in the front gate. Once they crashed through the gate they were fired upon from inside and from behind. The gun battle soon became a stand-off with the cartel members from around the city behind the officers and then those in the building.

The police had called for reinforcements. Before they arrived, the popular Legislative Representative Matias showed up and he negotiated a solution to the firefight between Diego's men and the police. Both sides agreed to cease the shooting and the police withdrew after collecting the dead and wounded. They left the location in frustration and anger at the leadership that allowed the cartels this power. As the police left the location Representative Matias walked over to the reporters and gave them the story of how he had personally de-escalated the situation.

The story reported the next day was the police had made a mistake on the address which led to a shootout and Representative Matias was able to calm down the situation and have the sides agree to end the stand-off. There were three Federal officers wounded and one resident in the house slightly wounded. There was no reporting of the ambush from behind the police. One of the police officers died two days later which was the only reported death in the shootout.

The night of the shootout Diego walked into the warehouse for a meeting. "Matias, I want to know who set up the raid on my home and I want to know now!"

"Yes, already done. I have the name of the individual. He was the American ATF agent Felipe Garcia," said Matias.

"Juan, have some people pick him up. We are going to send a message to the Americans. They have their ATF agents sent down here to stem the flow of firearms. If they can cut off our access to the semiautomatic versions of AK-47 and AR-15, our competitors will be better armed. I have heard they are planning an operation called Project Gun Runner. It was just an idealist plan put on the shelf. Then some genius saw it as a good working plan, and it is being implemented. We need to turn this attack back on the ATF as a 'Black' operation of rouge agents," said Diego.

"I'll have the ATF agent taken to the ranch," said Mateo.

"Good, and have Jose get that reporter we have on our payroll in Texas to report on the story of the guns. We can make the Americans have doubts about their government and cause more chaos along the border," said Diego.

"The internal conflict with the political parties in the United States will be a distraction from our business interest," said Mateo.

"Let's hope they will be so busy in their political arguments they will lose their attention on the border. We need to increase immigration into the states. We can use the coyotes and start a campaign in Central America for them to look for better jobs in the United States.

"Immigration always divides the American political parties. Remember President Reagan passed the bill to allow illegal aliens to remain in the country with the agreement that Congress would develop a plan to secure the border. Well, where is that plan? One party got what it wanted and both parties failed to follow through with the plan for the border security. No, I think, illegal immigration will not hurt our efforts or should I say undocumented people. It might increase our business interest," said Diego.

"I do not understand?" said Mateo.

"We will charge everyone we take to the border and then control their lives in the states until they pay for the passage. This might become more than just running mules in the drug trade. I think we can bring families into the trade business," said Diego

CHAPTER TWENTY-SEVEN

Robert Steinberg was a stamp and postmark forger who was arrested and convicted in Duesseldorf, Germany, and served a term in prison. Later he was arrested once more in 1959 in Paris with his colleague, Hannelore Rosenberg who posed as a sales agent. They were detained for stealing at a stamp dealer's shop store. Then both individuals fled to Switzerland and were arrested again in Basel in 1961. The search of their apartment revealed several devices for forging stamps. Robert was also very capable of forging signatures. They fled to France by car supporting themselves there with the sale of forgeries.

GENUINE

FORGERY

Good is positive. Evil is merely privative, not absolute: it is like cold, which is the privation of heat. All evil is so much death or nonentity. Benevolence is absolute and real. So much benevolence as a man hath, so much life hath he.
— Ralph Waldo Emerson

June 2002 U.S. Ambassador's Office in Mexico

At 0734 on a Bridge in Central Mexico, a human body with a sign around the neck and an American Flag draped over the shoulders. The Federal police cut the body down and notified the American deputy clerk at the Embassy.

"Sir, we have a notice from the Federal police that a body was hung from a bridge and that it appears to be an American. I sent an employee to investigate. What do you want to do?" asked Gloria Mills.

"You better contact the Ambassador and see how he wants to handle this before we know for sure if it is an American."

An hour later the identification was made of an American ATF undercover agent that had not reported in for the last 12 days.

"Ambassador, the body on the bridge was agent Felipe Garcia with the ATF on assignment to the DEA. He had been tortured and…," said Beth as she broke down and could not finish the statement.

"That is alright Beth I can imagine. These people are sending a message to our government. I want everyone who had a connection to Felipe sent home. There is no reason to believe he did not break under the torture and give up other names. Before they are sent home, I want protection for them. We do not know how big a message these people are willing to send," said the Ambassador.

"I'll get right on it, Ambassador. Is there anything else?" replied Beth through tears.

"Yes, have Agent Thomson come to my office," asked the Ambassador.

"He is outside now, I thought I should bring you up to date on the situation first. I'll send him in," said Beth.

"That's fine Beth and thank you. I know you and Felipe were friends. I am so sorry?" said the Ambassador.

"If you do not mind, I would like to call his parents. I have become very close to them." Beth started to cry harder. The Ambassador walked over and hugged her.

"Beth I am so sorry I did not realize you were both that close. I think you need to go home also," said the Ambassador.

"We were going to get married after his assignment. I do not know how I am going to tell his mother and father. They live in New Mexico," said Beth through the tears.

"You go to New Mexico today and tell them in person. Set up everything in my name and office. I can handle things here. You go and be with people you love and give them my deepest sympathy," said the Ambassador.

"Thank you, I'll send in Agent Thomson."

"Ambassador, I am surprised that Beth can work, she and Felipe were in love. I think they were going to get married. She is a real trooper," said Agent Thomson as he walked in.

"You are right about that. She just informed me that they were going to be married. I am sending her to his parent's home to inform them. Now what have you learned about this whole mess?" said the Ambassador.

"The best I can figure out was that Felipe had set up a raid on the Diego home. The Federal Police entered the gate, and a firefight broke out. The officer in charge of the police unit believes that Diego had been warned about the raid and was ready within minutes.

"As soon as the police entered the gate with the first officer he was fired upon. He was wounded and died days later. The police were attacked from the rear at the same time and trapped in a crossfire situation. They called for reinforcements that were slow to react and before the reinforcement arrived a local political representative showed up.

"That was Representative Matias who said he showed up to negotiate a deal. If I had to say what happened, it would be that the tip of the raid came from Representative Matias who has contacts in the Federal Police and was at the planning meeting before the raid. Who knows how many in that organization are on the cartel's payroll?" said Agent Thomson.

"Why do that to our agent?" asked the Ambassador.

"A message was sent to us and the other cartels because Diego is in trouble with the other cartels."

"Why?"

"There was an undercover DEA agent that was discovered in his groups not long ago and left in the street last month. Diego's group was beginning to look weak. When an undercover agent gets discovered and is that close to the leadership in any cartel, it is a sign of weakness. Diego needs to show his power and what better way than to show that than with the death of a second American agent? That shows he can reach into our organization and do whatever he wants."

"Then your main assignment here from now on is to find any laws that this Diego has broken in Mexico or the laws of the United States and see if we can get him to the United States for trial," said the Ambassador.

"We have that information now. The problem is getting the government here to act. The cartel's reach into the political system here is vast. Small bribes are a way of everyday life, and it is expected or tolerated even by the reformers," said Thomson.

"O. K. then I want to make an example of this Representative Matias and make him very unpopular with the cartels. I do not want this incident to fall into that nothing void of the bureaucracy back home.

"If Diego wants to send messages, we will send bigger messages. I am off to Washington to talk with everyone there and this has just become my highest priority issue," said the Ambassador.

"Matias has started a run for President in the next election. It would not be wise to make an example of him right now. But we are planning to set the stage to deal with both Diego and Matias. That is part of the reason I am here. I received a call just now and was told to pick you up to go to Washington," said Thomson.

"What? Why is this news to me?"

"I am afraid I cannot answer that at this time, Ambassador. I have a chopper on the roof waiting to take us to the airport in 15 minutes."

"O.K. Washington calls. I will be ready in ten minutes."

CHAPTER TWENTY-EIGHT

Manuel Rivadeneira and his sister Emilia Rivadeneira de Heguy made new plates to reprint forgeries of stamps. They also produced excellent outright forgeries of many national stamps.

GENUINE   **FORGERY**

In the Age of the Almighty Computer, drones are the perfect warriors. They kill without remorse, obey without kidding around, and they never reveal the names of their masters.

— Eduardo Galeano

2002 FALL-OUT FROM THE MESSAGE

"**D**iego, Jose has returned from his trip to Israel and Argentina. The stamps were a success, Abdul was right. The stamps are a convenient and better way to launder money. We should be able to have the system back up in a short time," said Mateo.

"What do you mean back up?" asked Diego.

"There was a small problem with the stamp dealer up north. He was printing more sheets than he was told. Our man there took care of the printing office, and the stamp store copies," said Mateo.

"Who was this? Was there a need for the cleanup?" asked Diego.

"It was Ramon Luis, he did the clean-up," said Mateo.

"Ramon Luis is a dimwitted brute. I hope someone was with him to make sure everything was done right," said Diego.

"No, he was alone, but he has assured us that he has all the stamps from the stamp dealer's office and those from the printing shop which was burned to the ground," said Mateo.

"Did he get the plates?" asked Diego.

"What plates?" asked Mateo.

"The plates are sometimes called dies for printing the stamps," said Diego.

"Oh, yes, yes, he said, he collected dies from the print shop before he torched it," said Mateo. He was glad Ramon had told him he had some dies.

"That is good. Abdul may want them back, but we'll tell him they were lost in the fire or transit," said Diego.

"Very well. Will that be all?" asked Mateo.

"No! I want an update on two things. First, has the situation with the mules been taken care of?" asked Diego.

"Yes, the female that became sick did not make it through the night," said Mateo.

"Then next, it seems that fool Matias is a hero for the way he ended the raid on my home. Let us play that up and support him for President in the next election," said Diego.

"He has already put that into motion. It seems he has had bigger plans for himself than we realized. He has on his own been talking to the newspapers and is on T.V. talk shows explaining the need to end the cartel's wars," said Mateo.

"Very well let him be the big shot for now. I am late for dinner with my family, but one last thing, are we still watching the Arabs?"

"Yes, I say again for individuals that are religious they whore and drink a lot," said Mateo laughing.

"They project an image of moral leadership and then justify their indiscretions under the idea of their superiority in leadership. They can justify most things, or they just hide it by not talking about it. Keep a closer watch on him. That man has no loyalty to anything but himself," said Diego.

"I think you are right and will see that it is done."

CHAPTER TWENTY-NINE

Kamigata was a stamp dealer and bookseller in Tokyo, who sold forgeries of Japan, China, Shanghai, Taiwan, Korea Argentina, Belgian Congo, and the United States to name a few of his forgery productions. He was one of the most prolific forgers in the world. He offered postcards, and envelopes along with high-priced stamps and may have had links to Kotaro, who also was a forger in Tokyo at the time.

GENUINE   **FORGERY**

MANCHUKUO

Evil prospers when good men do nothing.
— John Philpot Curran

2002 TOP LEVEL MEETING WASHINGTON D.C.

"**W**elcome everyone, I am Assistant Director Howard Mills, and this meeting has been limited to this small number to keep a tight lid on this operation. So let me introduce everyone. Then we can get down to business. To my right is agent Nick Thomson next to him is agent Eric Miles. The gentleman on my left is Ambassador Joseph Morgan and I believe everyone here has worked together before. Except for our newest special consultant. Ambassador this gentleman is C.E. Hall who is working with Agent Thomson on a money laundering scam with stamps as well as the financial aspect. We think there may be a connection between the situation in Mexico and one here in the States. So this meeting is to organize a plan to capture the individual that murdered one of our agents," said Assistant Director Mills.

"So, that is the reason agent Thomson showed up on my doorstep without my prior knowledge and to bring me here. It is nice to meet you Mr. Hall," said Ambassador.

"It is C.E. to friends."

"Good, you can call me Joe. The title Ambassador is so formal with friends. My dad was an auto repair mechanic, who knew all his customers by their first name. Now what can I help with to find out who murdered and tortured a fine agent assigned to my embassy," replied Joe.

"We have a lead on an individual that we believe murdered a printing shop owner and is also connected to the death of a stamp shop owner in this country. After the killing, he set a fire in a printing shop. We have him on a private security system getting into his rental car. He is our strong link, and we have his record of arrest in this country and having been deported last year. During his arrest, it was established that he belonged to Diego's cartel. We have him under surveillance and will pick him up when he is alone and out of plain view, so nobody will know he is in our custody," said Assistant Director Mills.

"So why am I here?" asked the ambassador.

"We need to know who in the government down there is trustworthy?" said Mills.

"Well, that is a real question. One never knows for sure who is with or against you down there. Every time a reformer comes into leadership the whole mess seems to stay the same. The real reformers are intimidated or removed from this life. There are two individuals that I believe are true reformers. There is an officer in the Federal Police named Rodrigo Ortega.

"He was the leader of the failed raid a little while ago on Diego's home and is Diego's unofficial headquarters. The raid ended in a gun battle between the police and cartels. That raid is most likely the reason behind the murder of our agent for he set up the raid. So most likely Diego was not only sending a message to us, but to the other cartels. Reprehensive Matias brokered a cease-fire during the shootout." said the Ambassador.

"How about this reformer Representative Matias who became a hero for ending the shootout episode?" asked Mills.

"Yes, he is the one. Now there is talk about him running for President. However, I am sure he is in the pocket of Diego, and Officer Rodrigo would love to arrest Diego and Matias together. Officer Rodrigo has a good team and one of his men died of wounds he received during the failed raid," said the ambassador.

"Why do they think Matias is linked to Diego?" asks C.E.

"Matias was at the meeting that planned the raid. He left the meeting when the troops were suiting up. The raid was to be a surprise and they were met with heavy fire as soon as they came through the gate. They were waiting! So there was no surprise. The wounded man who later died had a family including a two-year-old child. He was the first man into the compound. Officer Rodrigo had to go tell the man's young," said the ambassador.

"Who is the other person you think is honest?" asked C.E.

"That is Catalina Diaz an independent reporter. She is new and dedicated to exposing corruption in government. She is from Argentina and did some stories on the links of drug traffic between the two nations. She also referred to a group of Arabs seen in Argentina recently with some cartel people. It was just a rumor in the cartel's circle of friends. I would say these individuals are the best two for you to seek out for information on the cartels. Rodrigo and Catalina are a solid foundation for good reform.

"The Representative Matias is a fool who thinks he can use Diego and the Cartels for his political advancement. Diego will support Matias and then control him or remove him. Diego is a smart and vicious individual," said the ambassador.

"What is this about the Arabs? Did she name the Arabs?" asked Nick Thomson.

"No, the article was about the wide reach of the cartels in the drug trade in the world," said Joe.

"What is her motive for this research?" asked C.E.

"I have been told her sister became hooked on drugs and then sold into the sex traffic trade by her dealer. When Catalina found her in Eastern Europe, it was too late to save her life. Death was slow and Catalina then vowed to God to expose the link between drug trade and human slave trade traffic. Her reporting is more on the sex traffic trade than the drug trade, but the two go hand in hand," said the ambassador.

"What are we doing about this Matias guy?" asked C.E.

"Agent Thomson told me on the way up here he set a rumor in motion that Matias was working with the Americans and the other cartels had put out a contract for his head. Just before I came into this meeting, I got a call from the embassy that said that Matias was there. It seems he heard of the rumors and came to the Embassy and asked for protection. I instructed to offer it with the stipulation that he come clean on the Diego organization and his part in the leaks," said Joe.

"Who knows he is at the embassy?" asked Mills.

"I am sure everyone in Mexico City knows by now," said Joe.

"Nice, so you put out the rumor and then let the bad guys do the dirty work," said C.E.

"Well kinda, we knew he would seek help from us. We just did not think it would be this fast. He knows what happened to the ATF agent for he was there. It was one of the worst things I have ever seen. Hard to believe that anyone could do that to another human," said both Nick and the ambassador at the same time.

"How many in the embassy know he is there?" asked C.E.

"Just the Marine guards. They took him to a secure room to hold until I returned," said Joe.

"Why do you ask, C.E.?" asked Nick.

"Maybe, we could use him to our advantage. That's all," said C.E.

"In what way can we use him?" asked Mills.

"Let him hear a planned attack before we let him go. Then he will run right away to this Diego guy with the plan. It will be a perfect distraction for the real operation we plan," said C.E.

"I now see why everyone was so interested in bringing you in as a consultant. That is what we have been planning to do," said Assistant Director Mills.

"Then let us get back to Mexico and get this thing set in motion down there. I want this bastard placed in the darkest hole for the rest of his life," said the ambassador.

"How will we get him to agree to do this?" asked C.E.

"We will not have to. This guy is so sleazy that once he hears the plan he will run to Diego," said the Ambassador.

"When we get back there, I will have him placed in an office to wait. Then we will discuss the plan outside the room. He will then tell us he has changed his mind and leave the Embassy," said Nick.

"Alright everyone this has top secret priority and is limited to as few individuals as possible," said Mills.

CHAPTER THIRTY

Doctor Hugo Hahn and the mystery disappearance of a 20-centavo stamp of Chile, issued on January 1, 1862. The plates for the stamp had disappeared from government control and were later found in Europe. Dr. Hahn had purchased the plates and returned them to Chile. He proposed that the government use the plates to reprint several sheets, which they did with a decree issued on May 13, 1910. It was then that collectors and the public began an outcry that forced a second decree on April 5, 1910, canceling the run. Doctor Hahn was able to collect the sheets that had already been run. He began to sell these new prints. There are some dozen different colors and shades of the reprints.

GENUINE   **FORGERY**

Each time a new war is disclosed in the name of the fight of the good against evil, those who are killed are all poor. It's always the same story repeating once and again and again.
— Eduardo Galeano

2002 THE TRAP FOR RAMON

The meeting was held at a building site on Centinela on the West side of Los Angeles with Santa Monica on the other side of the street. Everyone was dressed for the part they would soon be playing. The meeting was set up as a low-budget movie film as cover.

"Agent Thomson the teams are ready to take down the suspect," reported each lead member of the teams.

"Good, we do not want anyone to see the grab tonight. Nobody must know he has been removed from the playing field. Is the decoy body and everyone ready to do their part in the false narrative we designed for the cover and removal of Ramon? Why not walk me through it once more," asked Thomson.

"Our grab team has the exercise down to 43 seconds from the time the car stops. They will leave the site within one minute," said the driver of the extraction car.

"That is a precise time?" said Thomson.

"We have run the exercise twenty times and 43 seconds is our slowest time."

"Good, what about the replacement body?"

"Yes, the body will be in a car following behind Ramon, and within the minute after Ramon is taken from his car, the body will be placed inside the vehicle. Another of our agents will be walking with a dog. She will call 911 after the body is set in the car and the car is set on fire.

Then our ambulance crew will be dispatched at the same time the engine company is called out. Our crew will remove the body to the coroner's office where the body will be lost in the system," said another agent.

"Perfect, let's hope this goes as we wrote the script," said C.E.

"So little faith C.E.!' said Nick.

"Like Tyson said, plans are good until you get hit in the face."

Everyone laughed.

Later that same night on a deserted road in the Santa Monica mountains of Los Angeles the trap was set on the route that Ramon always took after every meeting with his cartel contact. This place was picked since the route never changed during the time the team had been following him on his twice-a-week meeting.

The plan was set in motion that Ramon would be followed to his cartel contact that evening then they would take him on his return trip to his apartment. Ramon left his contact and headed home. The tail car sent the message that Ramon was on his way.

As Ramon's car rounded the mountain curve everything happened fast. A car coming the other way suddenly seemed to lose control and cut in front of Ramon's oncoming car without hitting it. Before both cars came to a stop four men jumped out of the car, rushed up to Ramon's car, and pulled him out of the car.

"Hey! What the 'Hell' is this? Let go of me! Who are you guys?" yelled Ramon.

"Ramon, just be quiet, and nothing will happen to you. Now, look into the camera," as an agent took a photo to verify that this was Ramon. The man with the camera turned and said, "It is him!"

"Take him to the van and let's get set up for the rest of this little play." The car was pushed completely to the side of the road and a body was placed behind the wheel. Then everyone, but one person with a dog, left. The dog walker moved away from the car as the fire started to consume the vehicle. She took out her phone and dialed 911.

"911 what is your emergency?" ask the operator.

"I am on Canyon Road by the turn-off that went to the old movie ranch and there is a car fire."

"Is there another car involved?" asked the operator.

"No, just the one and it is on fire."

"Is there anyone in the car?"

"I cannot tell, the car is fully in flames. It looks so bad!"

"O.K. Please stay there the police and fire engine have been dispatched. They should be there in less than 5 minutes. If you would like, I will stay on the phone with you."

"Thank you. That would be nice. This is so horrible. I hope it is just a car fire and nobody is inside," said the caller.

"Just stay where you are, and the emergency units will be there soon.

You need to stay safe. Stay away from the fire because the gas tank might explode. Do you live in the area?" asked the 911 operator.

"No I am just visiting, I hear the sirens now and see their lights," said the caller with a little tremble in her voice.

"Good, when they get there, they will want to ask you questions. Are you O.K. now?" asked the operator.

"Yes, thank you for talking with me. This is so horrible. The police just pulled up," said the caller.

"I am hanging up now. Take a few deep breaths. You stay safe," said the operator.

"Thank you," said the caller.

The fire engine pulled up and the crew grabbed a hose and went to work putting the flames out just as the police unit rolled up. A firefighter called the officer over to the car. He looked inside, went back to his unit and made a call for the coroner's unit. Then he walked over to the dog walker.

"Are you the person that called 911?" asked the officer.

"Yes, the car was just sitting there and broke into flames as I walked towards it," said the woman with tears running down her cheeks.

"Were there any other cars on the road?" asked the officer.

"None passed me either way and that was the only one I saw. It was sitting half off the road just like it is. I hope, if there was a driver, that he did not have a heart attack. That happened to my uncle last year. He was lucky and a passer-by stopped and did CPR until the paramedics arrived. Was there someone in the car officer?" asked the woman.

"I am afraid so. May I have your name and address if the department has more questions for you," asked the officer.

"Oh, I'll be glad to help. I am Linda Foote spelled with an 'e' at the end. I used to get mixed up with another Linda Foot at school, so I always say with an 'e'. I am sorry. I just moved here to visit a friend before I take my new job. I am staying in the motel at the bottom of the hill. Do you know the one?"

"Yes, thank you for your help. Did you see anyone else on the road?" asked the officer again.

"Oh no, do you think the car driver suffered any pain?" asked the woman.

"I do not think so. The body did not look like he tried to get out of the car. So he most likely had a heart attack and died before the fire," replied the officer.

"I am so sorry. It was horrible," said the caller.

"Do you need a ride to the motel?" asked the officer.

"No, I think I need to walk to collect myself. This has been such a horrible experience. The walk back to the motel will help me to collect myself."

"All right Miss Foote with an 'e' you be careful and thank you for your help."

"No, thank you, I wish I could have helped that poor person in the car," said the caller as she turned and walked away with her dog.

The officer watched her walk away thinking the public can sometimes be helpful and compassionate.

LATER BACK AT THE BUREAU FOR THE DEBRIEFING MEETING.

"Mary, how did it go out there?" asked agent Thomson.

"I think it went just as we planned. I planted the seed of a heart attack and saw him write it in his notes. He also told me it was most likely a heart attack when I asked if the driver suffered any pain."

"That was good thinking. What about an address?"

"I told the officer I was new in town and staying at the motel at the bottom of the hill. I had checked in there earlier and checked out before I came here. There were no cameras in the motel lobby or parking lot, so if they want to find Linda Foote there will be little to no evidence."

"How did the ambulance part of the plan go?" asked Nick.

"Could not have been better! It has been a busy week for bodies. We took the body down the coast to a major hospital there. It will take a couple of days to sort out what to do with it," replied the ambulance driver.

"Good job everyone. Tomorrow we will begin our interrogation of Ramon. Let's all go and get some sleep and relax," said agent Thomson.

CHAPTER THIRTY-ONE

A. Saatjian had purchased a chest just filled with Persian stamps most likely through a bribed official. He'd been permitted to overcharge the stamps and he issued nine new stamps with a surcharge. A few sheets were sold in Teheran to give the stamp an official image. Most of the stamps were sold in France as legitimate stamps. He was able to buy the original lithographic stone for a Suez Canal stamp in 1907 he made appropriate alterations for three more stones. The original stone stamps are "private reprints." The other three stones are outright forgeries. When Saatjian died, the printing stones passed to a forger in Brussels that produced forged surcharges and cancellations. When that dealer died, the stones passed to another known forger. The Suez Canal stones are lost to history.

GENUINE

FORGERY

False words are not only evil in themselves, but they infect the soul with evil.

— Socrates

2002 TERROR IST PLOT IN CHICAGO

"Is Karyme ready?" asked Bassam

"Yes, she has the last part of the bomb in her cleaning supplies. She will place the bomb in a closet by the modern art exhibition tonight," said Fazil.

"What about her cleaning partner? Don't they always stay together during their shift?" asked Bassam.

"Karyme, said her cleaning partner is a party girl and takes a lot of nap breaks," said Fazil.

"What about the guards?" asked Bassam.

"They have become friendly with the cleaning crew and leave them alone at times," said Fazil.

"Wait! What do you mean they leave them alone?" asked Bassam.

"When a new cleaner first shows up, the guards stay pretty close and watch. Now they have become comfortable and friendly. Karyme thinks her partner Gabriella is sleeping with one of the guards on those naps," said Fazil.

"How did Karyme get the bomb into the Museum?" asked Bassam.

"For the last week, she has taken in parts and hidden them in the supply room. She will take the last of the C-4 in tonight, then assemble the bomb and set the timer for 10 a.m. allowing for the tourist groups to have the time to enter the Modern Art exhibit," said Fazil.

"Good, now what are the plans for Karyme's exit?" asked Bassam.

"Once her shift is over, she will be picked up outside right down the block after she makes a change in clothes at a fast-food place. Then she will be taken to the airport for her flight to New York," said Fazil.

"What about her identity?" asked Bassam

"Her identity as Elena the cleaning lady will lead back to the South side of Chicago and there is a Latino gang community there," said Fazil.

"Will that be a problem?" asked Bassam.

"No, Karyme gave her address there and she has never set foot there. That's the funny thing about this country. Lower skilled level workers' background check times just have a superficial background check as if they are not smart enough to do anything else. There is even a rumor going around that a United States senator has a Chinese spy as her personnel driver.

"All one needs in this country is a social security number and green card or birth certificate. There are more than 12 million illegal aliens from Latin America and then there are many others that just overstayed their visas.

"If one looked at the numbers of so-called legal immigrants, those that came here to have their babies born in the United States, the immigrant numbers would be even higher. This country and its freedom have corrupted itself. God be Praised we will defeat this Satanic Empire," said Fazil.

"Good! All is set as planned. One more thing, Fazil, your father Abdul wants to see you before you leave the country. Rahim will take you to see him as soon as we are done here," said Bassam.

"This must be important to say my father Abdul. Is there more you and I need to talk about?" said Fazil.

"Yes, the girl Amira. I believe that is what your father wants to talk about," said Bassam.

"Yes, that was very unfortunate," said Fazil.

"Unfortunate! You had a young girl with the mental mind of a six-year-old wearing a bomb jacket going into a mall. She started running around yelling Bomb! Bomb! a full minute before the bomb went off. That her life was the only life lost was a waste of our time and effort.

"That is the best that can be said about what you call unfortunate. The only best thing about it is she died and cannot be linked to our organization. It did, however, bring up the issue of the news of terrorism. The Americans are beginning to focus their attention to terrorism on their home front once again," said Bassam.

"I don't understand, the Palestine groups have used the young people with bombs and allowed those individuals with mental and physical problems to serve God's will and win their place in heaven," said Fazil.

"Do not let your religious fever cost the movement its goal, Fazil! Our goal is to crush the Satanic West, not to win heaven for the less fortunate. What would have happened if Amira had done something else and the bomb did not go off?" asked Bassam.

"But it did go off!" responded Fazil.

"Yes, and we are still sitting here planning our next move to bring down these infidels, and yet, you could have placed the organization in a dangerous position, if one thing went wrong. I think your father wants to talk about that very issue with you. I am telling you this now, so you can think about a solution before you see your father. He is not a tolerant man with mistakes. Do not think you are safe from his wrath because you are his son," said Bassam.

"I understand and thank you, Bassam, for your wisdom," said Fazil.

"It is not wisdom, Fazil. It is a warning to you that your youth may cost you things that you love. We are in a struggle and personal things may have to be sacrificed for the final victory," said Bassam.

"Yes, I understand," said Fazil.

"I do not think so, Fazil. You are young and, well, let's just let it go for now," said Bassam.

"You worry too much, Bassam."

"Then, go in peace!" said Bassam.

CHAPTER THIRTY-TWO

James Mc Donald Field produced inexpensive overprints converting low-value stamps into higher-value stamps fleecing collectors from 1942 to 1949. The American Philatelic Society notified the police, who then arrested James for using the mail to defraud people and for possessing items with the intent to counterfeit stamps in 1950. He pleaded guilty and was given one year and a day in prison.

GENUINE **FORGERY**

If you try to cure evil with evil, you will add more pain to your fate.

— Sophocles

2002 Chicago 9 a.m. - The Bomb at Museum

Outside the museum, people were getting off buses with their tour groups of senior citizens, young school children, and a university art class. The professor on the art student bus was saying, "When you get off the bus stay together. I have my big colorful hat so you can see me. This is going to be the best art field trip you will see during your time at this college. Almost all the best modern artists in the last hundred years are displayed in this one place. So, make sure you have your tablets and pens and please do remember to take notes. Now! let's go see the art," said Ms. Walker to her university art class.

"I do not understand what that woman thinks. Why does she need to wear that purple and yellow giant hat? The red-rust colored hair that feezed out making her head three times its normal size is enough to spot her in any large crowd," said Billy.

"Oh, be nice," said Jane.

"I am, she is a wonderful teacher and is a little bit odd, but she knows her stuff. When I was told I needed this class to get my degree, I just knew I would hate it. Then she came into the classroom and made art exciting and hilarious. Do you remember the story of Sandy Skoglund and the raw bacon room? I still laugh when I think about the way Ms. Walker told the story. She had me laughing on the floor," said Billy.

"My favorite was Salvador Dali on the Merv Griffin show. She not only told the story, but she acted it out with a real diving helmet. To think Dali almost suffocated wearing a helmet, while he tried to explain what Surrealism art was about. I still do not know how we could hear her through that deep diving helmet. Oh! Then there was the ocelot she pulled out when she was finished saying Dali had one just like it," said Jane as she laughed.

"Remember the mystery story of Mark Rothko. She had people coming into the room with missing pieces of artwork, bundles of money, backstabbing each other, and at the end that big frame fell exposing the body of Mark. She should be on Broadway," said Billy.

"She is funny and down to earth. That first day she looked around the lecture hall pointing out the real artists in the room. They all tried to look the part of the original independent. When she was done, she pointed out that in the search for their independent identity they all kind of looked the same as artists in style…," said Jane as she was interrupted by Ms. Walker talking.

"All right everyone. We will meet back here at 11:30 sharp for our lunch break. I have arranged a special presentation for the afternoon," said Ms. Walker as they walked in the front doors of the museum.

As they entered the museum Billy turned to Jane. "I wonder …," said Billy

Just then the fire alarm sounded at 9:47. The guards and employees started moving everyone to the exits. The first fire engine arrived at 9:53 and pushed through the people coming out. The building was empty by 9:57 and the firefighters checked out the rooms.

One firefighter opened a storage room door and stepped inside and then backed out. At 10:05 the police bomb squad was called. Some of the crowd had left and others stayed around to watch and wonder what was happening.

"May I have everyone's attention, please? I am afraid the museum will be closed for the rest of the day. I have been asked to tell you to please go over to the table that we have set up to take your name and give you a refund or new tickets for another time. Thank you for your cooperation," said the director of the museum.

"Officer, what has happened? Will we be able to get back into the exhibit soon?" asked Ms. Walker as she approached him.

"I am afraid not Miss. The museum is closed for the rest of the day or longer," said the officer as he moved away to join a group of police and fire officers who had gathered just inside the tape that was placed a distance away from the front of the building.

"Why have we called for the bomb squad on a structure fire? asked the fire chief.

"We were checking for the source ignition of the fire when a firefighter opened a closet and saw what looked like a bomb on a timer. His captain called me over and we backed out and called the police and notified them of a possible bomb. The dispatch notified the bomb squad," said the battalion chief.

"Why did he think it was a bomb? asked the police commander.

"He is a recent veteran and was familiar with bombs in Afghanistan and that this one was a similar pattern like those he had seen over there," said the patrolman. A bomb squad member walked up, "Are you the officer in charge?"

"Until the mayor shows up. What can you tell me?" asked the fire chief.

"It is a bomb on a timer and looks like it was set to go off at 10 a.m. I think the sprinkler head in the closet may have shorted the wiring. We have deactivated the bomb and will transport it to a safe location to study it and then dispose of it," said the bomb technician.

"Was the fire part of the bomb?" asked a police officer.

"No, there was no fire. One of the workers had set a lamp at the top of a ladder right under a sprinkler head. He told me he was going to come right back, but a supervisor stopped him and sent him off to do another small job and he forgot the lamp was on. The heat from the lamp set off the alarm and sprinklers," replied the technician.

"So, we have a fortunate accident that saved a lot of lives today," said the fire Chief.

"The FBI will have a team all over this place in an hour or so and they will want to interview everyone," said the police commander.

"That may be a little difficult. The museum was by appointment only today and there was a college class that got on the bus and went back to their campus a few minutes ago. Some people stayed around to watch, but they were mixed up with all the onlookers. We do have the names of the individuals who booked the time. The director had people sign a list for refunds or new tickets," said a patrolman.

"That's OK the FBI has resources, and they will want to interview the units and men that were the first to arrive," said the police commander.

"I will have them notified and make the arrangements for them to be taken to headquarters where they can be interviewed. The fireman that saw the bomb said it was a copy of the ones he saw when he was a Marine in Afghanistan," said the fire chief.

"Let's not get ahead of ourselves. This may not be a terrorist plot, but it will be treated as such for now. Gentlemen, there is no need to repeat this information to anyone until we find out for sure. So, no reports of terrorists to the press," said the police captain.

"I'll see that everyone understands, Chief."

"One of the security guards told the art teacher what he had heard. So you may want to inform the FBI," said a patrolman.

"Is she still here?" asked the Chief.

"Yes, she sent the students back to the campus and she stayed to make different arrangements for a program that was planned for this afternoon. That is her over there. The one with the fiery red hair under the big hat," said the officer.

"Wow! That is a lot of red hair under that big hat. I'll go over and talk to her and get a list of the students from the bus," said the Chief.

"O.K. then I will send a couple of men to go over to the college and try to control the gossip channel. However, I think that cat is out of the bag by now," said the Police commander.

"I was to give you this list of names commander," said the patrolman.

"Thank you, what is your name, officer?"

"Ron Evens, sir"

"And your partner?

"Sargeant April Morgan, sir. This is her walking up."

"Sergeant Morgan, you and this young partner of yours take this list to the college and find these students so the FBI can interview them as soon as they arrive."

"Yes, sir! Ron lets you and I get over to the college. You have just had a big break. The top commander in the department asked your name," she said as they walked off to their vehicle.

"Is that good or bad?"

"He most likely forgot both of our names as soon as we walked away. We are low in the chain of command. I was joking. But be ready for the jokes back at the station in the locker room."

CHAPTER THIRTY-THREE

Henry C. Needham was an advisor to the Scott catalog. He wrote articles and at times made up facts to include misinformation. Needham was a skilled faker of local covers. One buyer of these covers was Elliott Perry who set out to expose Needham with factual information. Only his anger was such that the facts were lost in his arguments. Henry's misinformation on stamps remained in the catalog for several years.

GENUINE   **FORGERY**

Not to punish evil is equivalent to authorizing it.
— Leonardo da Vinci

2002 INTERROGATION OF RAMON

The interrogation room held only Ramon and the interviewer who was a psychologist. Nick and C.E. were in the viewing room watching. The psychologist reached over and turned on the recording machine.

"I am agent Saul Miller, and this interview is with an individual known only as Ramon. He has stated only the name Ramon with no last name at this time. The time is 9:38 a.m. Ramon this interview is being recorded. Would you like to make a statement?"

"NO! Why am I here? I have rights!" sneered Ramon.

"I am a psychologist with the Bureau of the FBI, and I have been asked to ask you a few questions, Ramon."

"You can ask. I do not have to answer!"

"That is also true. Shall we begin?"

Phycologist: *"Ramon, have you ever talked with a man called Abdul? We believe he is a terrorist and if you are working with him that will change your situation here a great deal. You will be charged as a terrorist and not as a member of a drug cartel. There is a place like the one in Cuba that will be your new home in isolation. Now would you like to talk about Abdul?"*

Ramon*: "I want a..."*

Psychologist: *"Before you say that last word Ramon, that may be a problem you do not want to get involved in. Once you lawyer up, the cartel will know you have been with the FBI and they will not take kindly that you are talking with us."*

Ramon: *"I have not talked with you!"*

Psychologist: *"True, but we will not say anything, and they will believe you did. Then it will be your word against what they believe. Ramon your position in their organization is way down the list of importance. You have a chance to stay alive by talking to us."*

Ramon: *"I will take my chances."*

Psychologist: *"You are welcome to take that chance! But, what about your family? We have a report that is saying that the last member of your organization who talked with the FBI had his whole family pay the price for his betrayal. It was not pretty. You may have been part of the punishing group!"*

Ramon*: "I was not part of that. I have done bad things, but never to innocent family members!"*

Psychologist: *"You do not have a large family Ramon and your sister, and her family do not have anything to do with you. We know this. However, do you think the organization will care about that?"*

Ramon: *"Leave my sister and her family out of this. They have not talked to me in years, since they moved to this country. They moved here because of what I do."*

Psychologist: *"We know that Ramon and we will not be the ones to bring your family into this. You know your bosses better than we do. We do know they love to send messages to those inside and outside the organization. You know that better than most since you were a major enforcer for these messages."*

Ramon: *"O.K., O.K., I will talk with only one condition. My sister and family are protected in this country."*

Psychologist: *"It has already been done, Ramon. We do not want to have individuals living in America subject to cartel punishments."*

Ramon: *"What do you want to know?"*

Psychologist: *"Tell us what you know about Abdul?"*

Ramon: *"I have talked to him and his son Fazil on several occasions."*

Psychologist: *"His son?"*

Ramon: *"Yes, and a woman called Elena — I think that was her name."*

Psychologist: *"When was the last time you saw them?"*

Ramon: *"Abdul a week ago and the son and woman maybe two weeks."*

Psychologist: *"What else can you tell me?"*

Ramon: *"I think the couple were off to Chicago and then New York. That is all I know about them. Abdul was around Diego's home now and then before I came up here. I talked to this man Abdul and did not like him. He was cruel to the women, and I had warned him after he sent a young boy about eight, and a young girl about 14 to the hospital after he was done with them. At first, he denied that it was him. I showed him photos of what he had done and then I showed him some of my work. Told him that any more such action on his part would be dealt with in a like manner. He started to tremble when I informed him that his actions were not permitted unless permission was given - You know public relations."*

Psychologist: *"What about the son?"*

Ramon: *"He was also weak and I think he was in love with the woman. I also, think he is afraid of his father."*

Psychologist: *"O.K. with that for now. What can you tell me about the print shop?"*

Ramon: *"I was told to remove the print shop owner and collect the plates and stamps. I had the plates and set the fire to the print shop before I went to the stamp store. Just as I got there the stamp guy was locking his office. I pushed him back inside and took him back to the office then set him at his desk and started to collect the stamps. The guy grabbed his chest collapsed and died right there. At first, I thought he hit his head when he fell out of the chair. I put him back in the chair and took the stamps. The fire was moving too fast, and I needed to go."*

Psychologist: *"What happened to the stamps and plates?"*

Ramon: *"I had just delivered them to my contact here and was on my way back when that the car stopped my car and forced me here."*

The psychologist looked into the mirror. The door to the interview room opened and Nick walked in with C.E.

"Thank you, agent. You can take Ramon back to his new home for now and that was well-done agent Miller." Then after Ramon was out of the room. "C.E. go pack a bag. We are off to Chicago and then New York. There was a bomb at a museum in Chicago this morning that had been set to go off at 10 a.m. today. I thank God, we were lucky it failed," said Nick.

"Why Chicago? They are most likely headed for New York by now. Remember, Ramon said, two of Abdul's people were off to Chicago and New York. Do you think New York is the escape route," said C.E.

"C.E. that is why the bureau needs you. You think several steps ahead and I agree with you. We will not be in Chicago long. Just enough to get a picture of what happened before we are off to the Big Apple. We need to locate these two individuals. I have people working the case in New York checking the airport."

"We need to book flights now," said C.E.

"Today we use the company plane. We will be in New York within hours ahead of the commercial. When we land in Chicago, I have a chopper waiting and we'll be on the ground less than three hours if everything goes as planned. We will have sent a description of the bomber to the office in New York. Now, let's get to Chicago," said Nick.

CHAPTER THIRTY-FOUR

Lieutenant Colonel Charles Mottes was a producer and a distributor of fake stamps, postmarks, overprints, and errors of Persia during the 1870's. A. Larisch a collector warned the Dresden Philatelic Society of Mottes' swindle. Then Colonel Mottes sent documents that verified the forgeries were genuine and Larisch was expelled from the Dresden Philatelic Society that both he and Mottes were members.

Larisch began collecting evidence on Mottes' forgery activities and unfortunately died before the publication. To suppress the scandal the society purchased the entire edition of Larisch's evidence. The truth was made public with F. Schueller showing how Mottes manipulated the official document evidence to cover his forgery activities. Then Mottes' name was quietly removed from the Dresden Philatelic Society.

GENUINE   **FORGERY**

The Lord is known by his justice; the wicked are ensnared by the work of their hands.

— Bible, Psalm

2002 New York and Failure

The office was large and had a huge Persian rug on the floor. Abdul sat behind a large hand-carved desk with lion heads at the corners. The chair was of carved words with two figures of peacocks facing each other at the crown of the chair. He was lost in his thoughts of the once again rise of the Persian Empire and his place in the new Persia. He was interrupted when his son walked in. Abdul looked up, "What happened in Chicago Fazil?"

"There was a fire in that part of the museum that set off an alarm and sprinkler system and somehow the bomb did not go off," said Fazil.

"Fazil, we have talked about your failures to follow through with your assignments. First, there was that idiot girl with the bomb in the market, and now this episode. You are very close to being of very little value to the organization. There will be no more excuses for your failures. Do you understand?"

"Yes, father!"

"Now where is the person who set the bomb in place?"

"She is in the other room," said Fazil.

"Get her. I want to talk to her and ask why the bomb did not go off?" A few Moments later Elena, the bomb expert, walked into the room. She was in a tank top with the word PINK across the front and wore shorts and sandals.

"So, you are the one who set the bomb?" asked Abdul.

"Yes, excellency," Elena.

"I see you are willing to dress the part of a Western whore even in my presence," said Abul.

"I am sorry for the way I am dressed. I did not have time to change. When my plane landed from Chicago, I was met and brought straight here without my luggage and clothes to change. Please forgive my appearance. I do not mean disrespect to you or our religion," said Elena.

"Tell me about the bomb," said Abdul with a little waving of his hand.

"The bomb was set. I am not new to this. I placed many bombs in Afghanistan, and none failed. The only thing I can think that may have happened is when the fire alarm went off and the sprinklers system sprayed water that shorted out the timing device," said Elena.

"Why didn't you take into consideration the sprinkler system?" asked Abdul.

"The sprinklers are for fire and if there was a fire the need for a bomb would have been unnecessary. I was given the parts for the bomb and told to assemble it. I did bombs just like it in Afghanistan," said Elena.

"Are you pushing the blame off onto others?" asked Abdul.

"Not at all. I am just giving you the facts. I mean no disrespect,"

"Well, we now have a problem in that you can be identified. What should we do?" asked Abdul.

"I wore a wig, different contacts, thick glasses, cheek implants, and make-up when I was with anyone at the museum. That would fool most facial recognition machines. Plus, I always wore gloves so there are no prints left to trace me. Anything, my lips touched was taken with me so no DNA would be left. I am at your and our religion's pleasure," said Elena.

"I am impressed with your answers. However, we cannot take a chance on you being identified. You are being sent to Spain and from there you will make your way to Turkey, then to your home and family. Rahim has a plane ticket and money for your journey home. You leave in 3 hours. I will have Rahim take you to the airport. Be careful on your journey. Peace be with you," said Abdul.

"Thank you, peace be with you." Eliana walked out of the room with Fazil and Rahim. At the door, Rahim turned and walked back in and closed the door.

"Well?" asked Rahim.

"She is good, but now she is a liability, and she is developing a Western female attitude that women have their place inside and outside of the home. She challenged me on every point I brought up. No, you and Fazil take her to the plane and watch her get on. Then contact our people there and have her picked up when she gets to Spain," said Abdul.

"What do they do with her then?" asked Rahim.

"Have our people there contact the Serbs and they can take her to Serbia. They have places for whores like her. She seemed very comfortable in those whore clothes, and she looked into my eyes as if she was an equal. Women like her are dangerous," said Abdul.

"Very well, I will do as you say, and I will not tell Fazil," said Rahim.

"What? Is there something I should know?" asked Abdul.

"Yes! I believe that Fazil is bedding her and has developed a very strong attachment to her!"

"Then I was right, the West has made a whore of her and she has made Fazil weak. The whore is going to a place she is suited for her and nothing more. You better keep an eye on Fazil until she leaves." said Abdul.

CHAPTER THIRTY -FIVE

William B. Peters was an engraver who entered into a stamp scheme with John Voney and Alpha Bodkin to produce forgeries of two-cent United States stamps in 1896. This was known as the Second Chicago-produced forgery. The First Chicago forgery was produced by Warren T. Thomson a year before. The forgers were arrested in April of 1896 by the postal service. Bodkin and Voney pleaded guilty and were given eight months with five at hard labor. Peters jumped bail and was arrested in New York a year later on other charges.

GENUINE　　　**FORGERY**

When justice is done, it brings joy to the righteous but terror to evildoers.

— Bible, Proverbs

CHICAGO FBI 2002 CONFERENCE CALL

"We have a good lead. One of the museum cleaners was a woman, who was known as Karyme, and she had disappeared. We were looking at the cameras around the museum and found her on one of the cameras going into a restroom at a fast-food restaurant down the street. When she came out, she had a complete makeover. We circulated a photo of her new image to all the transportation hubs and got a hit at the Chicago airport," said Thomson

"Then let's pick her up," said an agent.

"She has left the city on a flight to New York under the name Eliana. We have agents looking for her in New York. Plus, after a little digging, we found that a woman using that name was responsible for several bombings in Afghanistan last year. So, we can consider her dangerous," said Thomson.

"What should we do when we find her in New York?" asked an agent.

"We don't need to find her. Once she lands in New York she has a ticket to fly to Spain this evening. We are planning on taking her before she gets on that flight without anyone noticing. Agent Edgar here will you give us the details about the plan to take her," said Thomson.

"The plan is simple to take her in the isolated passageway we created in the tunnel to the plane. The tunnel bends just before the cabin door and she will be out of sight of anyone following or watching her. The ticket person and flight attendant at the plane door will be our agents. The person at the ramp will hold up the line so that there will be a vacant gap. The attendant at the door will delay her entering the plane so that our people can make a quiet take-down that nobody will notice. There is a small door and platform at the side of the ramp we will cover so that it hides anyone from seeing our people and her while they wait until the plane takes off. We have agents in the setting area watching her arrival until she boards the plane. If anyone follows her, we will stay on them," said Edgar.

"Then we will have at least two people from this organization. The problem is we do not know if the events at the print shop and Chicago are connected," said C.E.

"That is true. We may be chasing our tails. Ramon did say he was told by his contact that he was to remove the owner, destroy the printshop and collect the stamps and prints.

"It was our luck that whoever sent Ramon did not tell the genius how many plates there were, and he did not take all the stamps in his rush to leave after the fire he started. Plus, he has also seen Abdul with Diego. It is a weak link, but it is something," said Nick.

"So, now we must question the bomber if it is her!" said C.E.

"We got lucky again. We intercepted a message with Elena's name and the time of landing in Spain. So we know it is her. The message gave instructions to a criminal group in Spain that is known to us. They have been hired to kidnap Elena once she gets off the plane in Spain and then sell her to a Serbian mob for the sex slave trade. The message referred to her as a whore. I think someone is upset with her over the failed bombing. So, wrapping up this meeting everybody, C.E., and myself are headed for New York. If our flight goes well, we should be there an hour before Elena's flight departs," said Thomson.

They were getting on the plane when an agent walked up to C.E. and handed him a briefcase. "These are all we have on the stamps and plates from the fire. My boss thought you might want to review them on your flight to New York."

"Thanks, I am flying for the government so I guess there will be no entertainment," said C.E.

"That is where you are wrong again. The bureau has upgraded the use of the director's plane. However, there is still no entertainment, but a lot more comfortable and faster than other government forms of transportation," said Thomson.

CHAPTER THIRTY – SIX

Enrique (Simon) Gainsbourg was a mastermind of philatelic forgeries starting in 1892. His reprints succeeded beyond anyone's expectations and caused a lot of confusion between genuine and fraudulent printings. An investigation was conducted with one member of the committee, David Cohn, a known reprinted and forger, who legitimized the stamps as official. The report was a Machiavellian masterpiece that convinced careful scholars. That act helped to convince Dr. Herbert Munk, an expert, to report and mark the prints as 'guaranteed'.

GENUINE   **FORGERY**

Evil draws men together.

— Aristotle

2002 - Madrid-Barajas Airport Spain

"I told you Andrei we should have taken the A-1 to the airport instead of the A-2. The A-1 is faster this time of day," said Dafo.

"We have plenty of time, Dafo. We have her photo and will keep watch for her until we pick her up. This has to be done with careful planning. My instructions were that she must disappear from here without a trace," said Andrei.

Andrei and Dafo had formed a partnership after their former gangs were busted up in coordinated international police raids a year ago. Andrei had been the contact between his Romanian gang and Dafo's Bulgarian gang. They were lucky to have been small-time thugs and not rounded up in the sweep that broke up the large British sex slave ring in Bulgaria. Arrest warrants were issued in England and Bulgaria for the same day and Andrei was across the street when Interpol agents entered the Brothel. It was a week later the two men connected and became independent contractors.

"Where shall we set up to spot her when the plane lands?" asked Dafo.

"We don't need to worry. The people who were sending her to Europe paid for her flight and a driver to take her to the hotel tonight. All we need to do is wait and follow the car she gets into. Then later we will take her," said Andrei.

"Do we know the car?" asked Dafo.

"Yes," said Andrei.

"Is he…?" Dafo started to ask as he cut off.

"No, he will not know anything about her activities in Madrid, if there is any reason for an investigation. We are not to take her to Madrid. They gave her an itinerary to stay in Madrid for two days and then pick up a rental car and drive to Italy. We are to take her before she gets to Italy," said Andrei.

"I spoke with my contact in Bulgaria and was told that there had already been several bids for her," said Dafo.

"WHAT! This is to be a silent grab and no trace of any contact. What have you done?" asked Andrei.

"Do not worry there was no photo of her and just a short description," said Dafo.

"This was to be very hush-hush. I was told she is a favorite of some big wig's son, and the big guy wants her out of his son's life and their organization. So, if you have done anything to upset this job our new boss will not be pleased. Do you understand what I am saying - Dafo?" said Andrei.

"Yes, not to worry. The feeler I put out is blind. They were told the location she would be placed for view, and I have a second place for the actual exchange. I did not like the idea of there being a chance discovery at the first site. So, once we have her ready for shipment a message will be sent that will change the location. I needed to get them to see that she had real value, or they would not take the risk with just this one unknown female. These guys trade in volume," said Dafo as they walked up to the pickup spot.

"Over there is the driver right on time. See his sign?" said Andrei.

"The passengers should be coming out in ten to fifteen minutes. Do you want a drink?" asked Dafo.

"No, let's stay close by. Things always go wrong after a plan is set in motion. We need to react to any variations fast. See, here comes the first passengers now," said Andrei.

"Do you see her?" asked Dafo.

"No! But watch the driver is holding a sign with her name."

Thirty minutes later the driver took out his phone and made a call. He put the phone away and walked over to the car and just as it started to drive off. Andrei walked up to the car window and said, "Excuse me, sir, did your passenger miss her flight?"

"No, I just called my office and they said she just called in and said she had different transportation and was sorry for the inconvenience," said the driver.

"What a shame to lose a ride," said Andrei.

"No, it was prepaid, can I offer you a ride?" said the driver.

"No thank you, I was just curious. How often do you get stood up on rides?" said Andrei.

"It is rare, but once in a while. They missed a connection or something like that. Sometimes when they land, they just take alternate transportation. Excuse me, I have to get going. I have been given a new rider," replied the driver.

"Well, Good Luck!" said Andrei.

Back at the car "Well, what happened?" asked Dafo.

"She called and said she had other transportation. He did not know anything else."

"What do we do now? We have a contract to complete."

"I know! I know! Let's get to the hotel and see if she checked in before we make any calls. This could be bad for us if we do not find her."

Three hours later Andrei made a phone call. "Hello, the woman canceled the car and took some other form of transportation from the airport," said Andrei. He listened to the other side of the conversation. "No, we did not see her come out of the terminal. We went to the hotel, and she had not checked in there yet. She has just disappeared. What should we do?" Andrei closed the phone.

"What did they say?" asked Dafo.

"That we better find her or someone who looks like her to complete the contract you started Dafo," said Andrei.

"Who did you call?" asked Dafo.

"The Turks - they are the ones that are expecting her. They made the deal with the Bulgarians who worked with the Serbs. This thing is a nightmare of complications," said Andrei.

"What about the guy in New York?" asked Dafo.

"We do not know him or his organization. They put her on the plan, all we need is to provide a replacement," said Andrei.

Later that night the police were sent to a local café with reports of shooting in the street. It started with trying to abduct a young woman. As the men tried to push the woman into a parked car a guard across the street came out to see what was happening when he saw the men pushing the woman into the car trunk. He called out at them. One of the men turned and fired a shot at the guard. The guard returned fire hitting the guy in the middle of the chest. The guy let go of the woman and drew his revolver. The guard fired again, hitting the thug in the neck.

The young woman was hysterical and kept thanking the security guard. He had been hit in his left arm. The police arrived and called for medical assistance. They checked the kidnappers for life — both were dead when the police arrived. They had false papers of identification from Italy. The woman was transported to the hospital to check on the head injury she suffered when her head banged the trunk cover. The security guard was also taken to the hospital for the gunshot wound. They were met at the hospital by a large group of the news media.

The attempted kidnapping was reported in the news that night and on the morning shows.

The report was that two thugs had picked the wrong woman and the wrong place to apply their trade.

Later, an American embassy official sent a report to the FBI in New York about the incident. The story turned into a major international media blitz about an American woman saved from international slave traffickers. The Ambassador's office in Spain had no comment.

"Well C.E.! It seems things are looking up. I just received a report from Spain that a woman matching Eliana's description was saved from an abduction by a security guard. The woman was leaving the café when two men grabbed her and shoved her into the car. The guard from across the street from the café came out and the shooting started. The two thugs were killed, and the guard was wounded in the arm. They were well-known small-time players in a gang known to be active in the sex slave trade in Europe. The woman's description of the men matched two members of the gang that were to take our lady to the airport. The links are getting better," said Nick.

"That should give us a little leverage in the interview," said C.E

CHAPTER THIRTY-SEVEN

Oswald Schroeder in Leipzig, Germany produced a large number of forgeries from dozens of nations and locations. In 1891 a report listed 56 different forgeries of his were published without naming him. Later when he was named, he fled to Zurich, Switzerland. His forgeries were displayed at the London Philatelic Society in 1904. After he died in 1920 the Swiss police listed some 34 more of Schroeder's forgeries.

GENUINE

FORGERY

Knowledge is the life of the mind.

— Abu Bakr

2002 THE TURKISH CONNECTION

In 1934 the Turkish government passed the Surname Law that required every citizen to have a surname. Under the Ottoman Empire many people had no surname and were called by their hometown, or as a teacher, or as a pilgrim, or lady or madam. The new surnames were many times based on one's physical appearance, skill, or for many historical Turkish events. Demir Pehlivan's grandfather looked like a Pehlivan (a wrestler) and because of that one fact, it became his new surname.

There was a reaction to the Surname law by pan-Turkish true believers. They said that the modern Turks were attacking the Europeans and failing to honor their culture. That the law made Turks have a lack of confidence in their own culture. Yet, many Turks moved into the modern world rapidly and others at a slower pace. The reluctance by traditionalists, who wished to hold on to the old ways was strong.

These individuals formed into radical groups like the Grey Wolves, who also had ties to the Turkish crime syndicates that were involved in illegal gambling, human trafficking, prostitution, money laundering, drugs, and extortion. The syndicates had links to the Bulgarian Mafia and the Cartel of the Suns in Venezuela. A major connection to Western Europe was through Cyprus to London. Into this mix were the Kurds.

The Kurdish people are located in Turkey, Syria, Iraq, Iran, and Armenia and have been fighting for years for their nation. Every country they are in fears their presence and nationalism. Crime syndicates in Kurdish territory are very sophisticated with drugs and human trafficking along with terrorist activities of the Kurdistan Workers Party (PKK). Money makes crime blend.

"Demir we have heard from our man in Spain. It seems the two men that were to bring the woman to the Serbians have been killed and the woman has vanished," said Ali.

"How did this happen?" asked Demir.

"All we know is that the woman called the company of the driver for the car that was provided to pick her up and canceled the ride. When we asked the driver about it, he said that she called the company and said she had other transportation and that the driver was not needed," said Ali.

"Did the two men collect her?" asked Demir.

"That is unknown. They were shot trying to shove a woman into a car that same night. A security guard across the street interrupted their attempted kidnapping. Witnesses said the guard asked what was going on when one of the kidnappers drew a pistol and fired at the guard. The guard fired back, killing the guy. The other guy dropped the woman and drew his pistol and was also shot by the guard," said Ali.

"What about the woman?" asked Demir.

"She was not the one they were to collect for us. Although, she looked like our targeted woman. These two may have lost the right target and tried to cover their failure with a look-alike," said Ali.

"Do we know where the right woman is?" asked Demir.

"No! I have people looking for her. If she knew what was in store for her, we may not find her. She was a big-name freedom fighter in Afghanistan and had a lot of friends and family in the fighters there," said Ali.

"I better call Ivan and give him the news. Abdul will not like the news either. The good thing is we did not set up the trap or use our men. Abdul and his people will have to accept that for this was all their plan," said Demir.

"These people are careless, and they only have success because the Western governments are careless and fighting among themselves. They allowed us into NATO and now the Syrian crisis with the Kurds put the Western powers off balance because Turkey is an important ally in Western defense. The PKK will pay a price for their terrorism," said Demir.

"The West is worried about terrorism and still supports groups that they list on their terrorist list. The Kurdistan Workers Party (PKK) was on that list twenty years ago and now are given military supplies and support in Kurdish territory," said Ali.

"Do not try to understand the West Ali. We don't work together either. Look at the Kurds they are divided into the artificial nations of Iran, Iraq, Syria, and Turkey allowed to keep a section of that land after the Great War in 1918.

The Kurds have divided into many different groups the (PKK), the

Free Syrian Army (FSA), the Syrian Union Party (PYD), The People's Protection Unit (YGP), The Peoples' Democratic Party (HDP), and the Syrian Democratic Front (SDF) all fighting for the same thing. There may be some 40,000 people neutralized in the last twenty years in the conflict in those nations," said Demir.

"Neutralized?" asked Ali.

"I mean killed or captured. At one time the Turks went into Iraq to attack the Kurds there. The Kurds want their homeland back and that began the movement to get it back in 1978. They were in part backed by the old Soviet Union as a way for them to get into the Middle East. The old Soviets had influenced certain communist groups in the Middle East to take power. Their support of the communists in Afghanistan was a political victory that helped bring down the Soviet Union with their misunderstanding of the religious and tribal nature of Afghanistan.

No, Ali, we cannot wonder about the West and ignore our lack of political understanding. However, our business would not be as successful if both sides ended their conflict, said Demir.

"What do you mean?" asked Ali.

"It is simple, they would stop going at each other and focus on our activities. Our life would become more difficult," said Demir.

CHAPTER THIRTY-EIGHT

Salama said he had a supply of genuine sheets of watermark paper of the first issue of the 1866 Egyptian stamp, plus genuine cancellation dyes. He notified the firm of Stanley Gibbons of the items and was willing to sell or buy forgeries printed on the paper. Gibbons informed the Egyptian postmaster who arranged for the confiscation of the paper and devices.

Salama had additional resources and went on to print and sell forgeries. Albert Eid confronted Salama, who confessed and promised to turn over his stock in exchange for not being prosecuted. However, Salama held back some of his stock and continued to produce excellent forgeries after Albert mobilized for the Great War.

AZERBAIJAN

GENUINE   FORGERY

The evil that men do lives after them; the good is oft interred with their ones.

— William Shakespeare

2002 CASPIAN SEA

Ivan Smirnov was visiting his grandfather Mikhail in the city of Baku on the Caspian Sea. Since the collapse of the Soviet Union, the city was in a major rebuilding to support trade with Iran and the Middle East. "Grandfather, we have had news on the woman from Abdul's organization. It appears she has slipped away and is in the wind. Demir called to give me the news."

"What do you mean she is in the wind?" asked Mikhail.

"There has been no trace of her once she boarded the plane in New York for Spain," said Ivan.

"Was any of it our fault?" asked Mikhail.

"No, it was Abdul's plan and his organization set up everything right up to the moment that she was handed over to the Turks for transportation from there."

"Then we are done with it!"

"What should we do about the payment?"

"They paid upfront - right?"

"Yes, should I return the funds?'

"Why?"

"To keep everyone happy!"

"Happy, who do you think we are working with? These are religious fanatics – they will never be happy. We cannot show any weakness that they will exploit. Tell them that if they find her, we will fulfill our part of the deal. Now, I must get back to my old friends from the past," said Mikhail as he walked off into another room.

"Alexei and Viktor, it is so nice to see you both. How is the new government doing?" asked Mikhail.

"Mikhail, your vision back in the camp was right on. Although, it took longer than we expected to fall apart. But you were so right about the corruption in the Soviet system being very deep. The guards took the western items we smuggled into the country. They told their commanders who wanted in on the goodies. Then it was not long before the Party bigwigs wanted their share. The Black Market was killing the Soviet economy. Kids had been recording and copying western rock-n-roll songs on the x-ray plates of their parents before the 1970's," said Viktor.

"Poor old Nikita Khrushchev was so worried that the West was winning the hearts and minds of the world that he did everything he could to be first in what was called the space race. The first man-made satellite, the first man in space, the first woman in space. His big kitchen debate with Vice President Nixon made the world news. Then came the Bay of Pigs, a small victory for his foreign policy, followed by his bullying of that young President JFK.

"He went on to push too hard and fast by sending those missiles to Cuba almost starting a nuclear war. The old guard became nervous, and he was removed from office for his weakness. He was lucky they did not take him out into the woods like many of those he sent to the woods in the past. The system was becoming more human," said Alexei and they all laughed.

"Wasn't Alexei Kosygin a relative of yours Alexei?" asked Mikhail.

"No, the Kosygin were old family friends, and the name Alexei was given to the first-born boys in each family. I think it had something to do with what the families did together during the Crimean War. I am not sure. They never discussed anything before the Revolution in our family unless they were drunk."

"So, you mean every night," said Viktor, and they laughed once more.

"Kosygin was not as reactionary as Brezhnev. Yet, Brezhnev tried to undo the Khrushchev policies of economic and political reform. However, they both sent the tanks into any country that showed opposition to Soviet rule.

Khrushchev sent in tanks in 1956 into Hungary and Brezhnev sent tanks into 1968 Prague. It was under Brezhnev that the system fell off the Soviet socialism wagon.

Brezhnev was wearing western clothes and driving around in western-made vehicles. After his death, the old guard continued to take control with the two old men Andropov and Chernenko. Yet, they died so fast that nothing was done. The leadership in the last years discussed which old man would take office next," said Alexei.

"Yes, if Gorbachev had been in office a little sooner, things may not have worked out like they did. His Perestroika for the restructuring government and his Glasnost openness in policies for reforming the society might have worked, except for the disasters of Chornobyl, Poland solidarity movement, East Germany demonstrations like the one in Leipzig, and that young German kid landing a plane right in the middle of Red Square right under our military security network. My God, what else could go wrong?" said Viktor.

"That reminds me. Do you remember when they cracked down on youth wearing Western styles in the 60's? Young people with long hair and tight jeans were stopped on the street by security details. Then the security people cut the jeans off and shaved the heads of the youth. I think they began calling it the 'Trousers War' wasn't it?' Yes, a few of the less important individuals ended up in the camps where we found out about the whole thing. We laughed at them," said Alexei.

"I think the name 'Trousers War' was given to it by the people in the street. It ended when the youth of the powerful were caught and subjected to the same treatment of having their hair shaved off and sent home in their underwear. Several security people were sent to correction locations for stopping the wrong youth," said Viktor.

"Well, it has all worked out for us. Those thugs in the KGB and the corrupt Party leaders were all able to help us slice up the economy. Then they put the profit into their own pockets becoming rich and are now controlling the government with a new Tsar at the head," said Mikhail.

"What shall we do?" asked Alexei.

"Just wait and see what happens. I remember what a great general of the past once said about battle plans. One should just show up and react to the situation or he said something like that. We are on the sideline of this. Let's see what the major players are doing then we can react. Right now, we are also building our power, and the old KGB is gone and now the new FSB vultures understand we are of value to their desires.

"On another subject, how are the negotiations going on the economic side?" asked Mikhail.

"Our people in Leningrad, I mean St. Petersburg, have closed the deal on the two manufacturing plants. Both are key to the military development and are secure from the FSB thugs," said Viktor.

"Why is that?" asked Mikhail.

"The FSB thugs are going after the major industries and businesses. We have targeted the small but essential industries. What we are and will produce will be the little things everyone wants and the small parts everything needs. The FSB thugs follow the style of the old Soviet Leaders for the bright shining objects. We follow Stalin's method and take the hidden items that are needed to make the other things bright," said Viktor.

"Then things are set in place when things change again. Let's keep our people informed and to be ready to react," said Mikhail.

"I have a system to keep our people informed just enough," said Alexei.

"Good let us go and have a fine meal," said Mikhail.

CHAPTER THIRTY-NINE

The A. Scott & Company started with two young boys conducting a stamp business in Birmingham, England by selling mostly forgeries and by 1872 they were selling what is known as the 'Birmingham forgery' and 'Birmingham Counterfeits'. This is according to E.L. Pemberton; however, there is no evidence to support this claim. Yet, early philatelic individuals did many things that today are considered disreputable in the selling or making of stamps.

GENUINE　　**FORGERY**

There is only one good, knowledge, and one evil, ignorance.

— Socrates

2002 Interrogation of Elena back on the West Coast

Nick and C.E. walked into the office, "How is everything?" asked Nick.

"Our guests have been quiet for the last hour. I think the female has lost her voice with all the yelling," said the agent.

"Where is the woman?" asked agent Nick.

"She's in the back room with two agents. After the sedation and transference to this location, she spent the night yelling about her rights. Earlier this morning she was alert, demanding a lawyer with a softer voice," said the agent.

"What did you tell her?" asked Nick.

"That she was in the custody of the United States of America and nothing more. I left her in the room with two agents. I would not trust her. She has the look of a trapped animal," said the agent.

"O.K. and where is Ramon?" asked Nick.

"He is in the room at the other end of the hall, and he is in cuffs and watched by two agents also," said the agent.

Nick turned to C.E. and said, "Well, C.E. shall we go see Elena first?"

"O.K. but give me a second to collect some materials and I will be ready," said C.E.

A few moments later they walked down the hall. Then stopped outside the interview room door and C.E. turned to Thomson, "When we are done with Elena, I want to ask Ramon a few questions."

"Do you want to do that first?" asked Nick.

"No, what she has to say may help when we talk to Ramon," said C.E.

C.E. and Nick walked into the room. Elena sat in a chair behind a large table with an agent on each side of the room. She looked up and looked at Nick and then C.E. "I hope you two have brought me a lawyer and one for yourself. I am going to take this government to court and win a wrongful imprisonment case," said Elena.

"First this interview is not being recorded. That may take place at a later date, depending on you. Feel free to bring the lawyer up at your hearing for terrorism Karyme or Elena. Whichever name we are using today?"

"So, you know I have used other names. What's the big deal?"

"The big deal is let's see for right now, we have you on camera and when we are done, we will have DNA evidence that places you at a failed bomb location. That makes this a terrorist act and a whole different case. However, more importantly, we also have your boss on tape giving instructions that you are to be abducted and sold into the sex slave trade. Plus, we have video of the two individuals that were to pick you up in Spain," said Nick as he placed a folder in front of Elena.

"You might want to look through this material. We'll give you a few minutes," said C.E. and the two men walked out of the room.

"Do you think she now realizes we are her only chance?" asked C.E.

"She is a hard woman. Her record in Afghanistan is impressive for a woman in that male-dominated world. The only thing we have on her is the failed bomb attempt. It is weak but maybe enough to put her away for a few years. If she will not work with us, the alternatives are not very pleasant for her," said Nick.

C.E. took out his phone and looked at the message.

"Do you need to go?" asked Nick.

"No, it's a reply from a professor friend. I had asked her about fundamental radicals and utopian communities. She said to call her tonight, she has a class to give right now."

"Any particular reason?" asked Nick.

"I like to understand the individuals that I investigate. If I understand their motivation and philosophy, it helps to uncover at times their methods of thinking – that's all."

"Do you mind if I listen to the conversation?"

"I was going to ask you to join me. I hope you are not worried that I would let out some restricted information?"

"Not at all, I would also like to know any outside views. Sometimes we get lost in our in-house analysis. The FBI is an intelligence gathering agency and not a criminal investigation organization many believe. Outside information or analysis is one way to keep a good thing on track and that is our strong suit. Well, I think she has had enough time to look through all the documents. Shall we go back in and see if Elena wants to cooperate."

"Lead the way."

Elena sat in her chair looking at the photo of a man as Thomson and

C.E. walked into the room. She looked up at them. "You said you have a recording. May I listen to it?"

Thomson looked at one of the guards and motioned to him. The man left the room. "He will bring back a machine so you can hear the tape. Do you know anyone in the photos?" asked C.E.

She just sat there and waited for the recorder. The tape was played and after it was played, she sat still for a while shaking her head. Then looked at the two men and said, "I am a good religious person who has made many sacrifices to help my religious cause. The men who lead the cause are held in great honor and respect. I have seen them at times violating Islamic laws and excusing them. I thought they were honorable. Now, I begin to wonder why I believed them at all. This is what they plan to do with me after all my sacrifice?" said Elena as she waved at the materials on the table.

"So, you believe what we are telling you?" said C.E.

"Yes, I know that voice. He treated me as a daughter, and he was still willing to do that to me. I have been working for evil. What do you want to know?"

"Who are the men in the photo that were to pick you up in Spain? Do you know them?" asked Thomson.

"The tall one in the photo is Dafo. He delivered some C-4 we bought from the Russians last year. I saw him in the training camp with another older man called Viktor. Viktor spoke Russian and I do not think Dafo was Russian as his Russian was poor."

C.E. took out another photo and placed it on the table. "Do you know this man?"

"No, he is a Catholic."

"Why would you say that?"

"The cross on his neck is not Orthodox or Coptic."

"Why focus on his religion is what I meant?" said C.E.

"Wait a minute I may have seen him in Chicago when I was setting up my false residence there. He was talking to the head of the gang that was providing my apartment. I did not meet him, and he was walking out when I came into the room. He is a killer."

"Why do you say that?" asked Nick.

"I knew men in my country that liked the killing or had become numb to it. They all have a look. As a woman you stay away from them."

"You have killed also Elena," said C.E.

"Yes, for a cause I believed was true and good. Not at all like this man or men like him. They have no soul, and they believe in nothing, but the killing."

"Back to the Catholic – why?" said C.E.

"The Crusades, I guess. As a child, I was told the Roman Catholic religion was the worst of the Christians. The others were bad, but the Catholics were the real evil ones. I learned to tell the differences in their crosses."

"That is it and nothing more?" said C.E.

"Yes, all Christians are bad, but the Roman Christians are the worst."

"Alright, Elena, one last question for today. Then you can get some rest. Now you know what plans they had for you, what can you tell us about the place you were being sent?" asked Thomson.

"I was to go home by way of Spain and then on to Turkey for the trip to my home."

"I'm sorry I was referring to where Abdul planned to send you?" said Nick.

"I think it is run by a Russian named Borya. He came to the camp many times with weapons. There were rumors he collected women to use as whores. I think it could be him, but if the word of my being sold into the sex trade reached home my family would seek revenge and it would be bad. My father is well-known and loved. Now, I will never see him again."

"Why is that Elena, because of talking to us?" asked C.E.

"NO! He was not happy that I became a freedom fighter and dropped out of university. I have blemished the family name in his view. I knew I was cutting the relationship with the family when I joined the fight. Now, I am helping the other side. My family and life are now lost forever. It is one thing to join the fight and another to work with you the Imperialist Christians. I am dead to both my organization and my family."

"You were on the wrong path Elena. Evil men used God's work at times to make evil. Your life is not lost. We'll see you tomorrow," said Nick.

As C.E. and Nick walked down the hall C.E. turned to Nick. "You better have her put on suicide watch and get a religious leader to talk to her now," said C.E.

"Good idea, she seems very distressed about being betrayed by her mentor and the cause she believed in so strongly."

"I think there is something more to her depression. I just cannot see what it is right now. Let's go and grab a bit to eat and then call my professor," said C.EW.

"What about Ramon?" asked Nick.

"Let's hold off on that for a while longer," said C.E.

CHAPTER FORTY

Anton Victor Winter was arrested for counterfeiting stamps in 1923. His arrest was after a group of his stamps were sold in New York to a dealer. The dealer noticed the irregularities and notified the government. In 1907 Winter's was arrested for making and passing counterfeit $2 bills. He served seven years for the money counterfeiting. The new arrest had him sent to Atlanta penitentiary and then deported to Germany.

POSTAL SERVICE WILL NOT SAY HOW THEY IDENTIFIED THE FAKES

The only good is knowledge, and the only evil is ignorance.
— Herodotus

2002 Phone Conversation
with the Professor

"It is so good to hear from you C.E. I've been out of town the past few days at a seminar where I presented my paper on woman radicalism in the Middle East. Now, what can I do for you?" asked the professor.

"Hellen, I have you on speaker so a friend with me can hear our conversation. Is that O.K. with you?"

"Is he FBI? I guess they finally caught you!" she laughed.

"Now that you mention it, he is an FBI agent, and I am working a case with him."

"I was kidding C.E. You are not in any kind of trouble are you C.E.?"

"No, Hellen and this is special agent Nick Thomson of the F.B.I."

"Hello, professor."

"Hello, and please call me Hellen, any friend of C.E.'s is a friend of mine."

"Thank you and please call me Nick."

"Now, what is this I can help you both with C.E.?"

"I need a quick course on modern Islamic fundamental radicalism and Utopian thinking," said C.E.

"As we talked about before that is a broad subject that may take some time."

"I just need a little better basic understanding, if you have the time?" said C.E.

"O.K. I will give you a short general review of the topic. Let's start with the Utopians. They were and are still small groups or societies that believed they could and can change society or at least, their small part of it. The name comes from Sir Thomas Moore wrote a book titled, *Utopia* in the early 1500s about a perfect society called Utopia.

"The term Utopia means 'no place', so what he was saying was that the perfect place was not possible. This thinking was in part the ideas of the Renaissance Humanist period of philosophy. They had expanded the idea that God had made man in his image and therefore man was close to God. An image of this type of thinking can be seen on the ceiling of the Sistine Chapel where Michelangelo depicted God giving Adam life. That image has Adam not standing in terror but relaxed holding out a hand to God. Now that is a simple answer to a very complex philosophy, but I continue.

"The Reformation began as an attempt to reform the church and ended the hold of the Church of Rome in northern Europe. The Church of Rome had split under the Great Schism of 1054 when Rome divided from the Eastern Orthodox Church. One of the questions they argued about was the Holy Trinity — was it three persons or one person?

"Another question centered on the interpretation of salvation. The question challenged the hierarchy system and Aristotle's view of life. The new interpretation was from within. The Catholic Roman church held that one obtained salvation in heaven by prayer and good work. Then the Reformation or Protesters changed how one obtained salvation.

"Martin Luther and his new Protestant ideas held that the interpretation of salvation and heaven were obtained by God's Grace. He went on to produce the Bible in the German language so the common person could read the Holy Scriptures. It was in part a protest of the Roman church's use of Latin that limited the word of God through the interpretations of priests and the educated. "Others followed Luther's example and the Protestants were then split into more groups. One of these was John Calvin who took a step toward salvation further by saying that God knew all and therefore those who went to heaven were already selected by God in what today is known as predestination. In other words, those who would go to heaven were already chosen before their birth.

"Then politics, as usual, popped up with King Henry VIII. He could not get the Pope to give him a divorce, so he removed England from the Catholic Church. Now the Bible was written in the language of each country and the Protestant interpretation of the Bible spread as Papal authority and control broke down more. While all this was taking place, the New World was discovered again. This time by Europeans and it set off with new ideas of paradise and for men to make a name and money.

"Some of these new adventures in the new world were approached by the development of a community activity. The English Jamestown settlement used the community collective (socialism) that failed and within a few years, the land (50 acres) was given to individuals for their management. The same movement from community socialism to individual land management also happened in New England. William Bradford explained in *Plymouth Plantation* how in 1622 land ownership was begun in the English colonies.

"The New England colonies viewed God and Profit as God's Grace and predestination. Then the Great Awakening came and moved individuals into a more natural way to approach communication with God. This period was the Age of Enlightenment. During this time John Locke expanded and developed the 'Blank Slate' idea that one is neither born good nor bad. Humans are born at birth and grow into individuals that are shaped by their environment. They are born into a world of expanding the idea of a community of individual philosophy.

"This thinking was justified in part because of the English Civil War under Oliver Cromwell and the Puritans who ruled with a heavy hand. They had executed the King and needed to prove that Kings did not rule by a Divine Right, but rather by the consent of the people. So, if one killed the king, you did not commit an act against God. Rather, Locke had to justify the killing of the king with what he called the Social Contract. The people gave the King power to rule wisely and that if he did not rule wisely the people had the right to take back the power.

"Locke went on to state that man is born blank and if you change the environment, you change the person. The church, on the other hand, held at the time man was born in sin, and that sin was washed away in baptisms. The church also saw confession as a way to remove sin. Under Locke's philosophy mankind was born blank and the environment shaped him. The American Revolution adopted Locke's ideas in many ways. Most crimes before the revolution were capital crimes and after the revolution, lesser penalties became more common for crimes.

"Then the socialists of the 18th and 19th centuries tried to re-create societies to make man a better human. Utopians like Robert Owens began utopian communities like New Harmony to form a perfect new society. These new collective societies and many like them all failed within a few years of their start."

"Why?" asked Nick.

"Simple — they failed to take into consideration several small things such as human desire, compassion, jealous feelings, or rage. You know all the common natural emotions we all have. Most of these experimental communities failed within a few years of their creation due to these natural human emotions. The only group that did not fail was the Shakers.

"The Shakers made it into the 20th Century. Their problem was that the Shakers did not believe in the human reproduction system. Their membership came from converts and orphans as their sole source of new members. There may be one or two Shaker communities still in existence, but they are care centers for the elderly members.

"The utopian communities are not as common in the 20th century as they were in the 18th and 19th Centuries. The Utopians of the 20th Century fall into two basic types of communes. One that is dominated by a spiritual leader and follows a communal existence of sharing. The other is a more political community idea of workers joining together or the socialist concept.

"The communities began to change by the Civil War with the rapid development of factories and Industrial Capitalism. The worker's relationship had rapidly changed from the old partnership relationship between employee and employer to the cash. This created less personal relations between workers and owners. Workers were no longer part of the family they became a part of the industrial machine to be replaced.

"The Socialists were born out of this industrialization. The workers shared a belief that one could create a Utopian society of workers working together. The idea that the workers needed to form a union together to protect their jobs and the ability to live for the new industrial world made workers just part of a machine. The workers saw their lives shifting back to serfdom conditions. Reactions to the new industrial age came with the Luddites and Sabotage that damaged machines.

"The new socialists did have a faith in their leaders much like a religion in their new societies. There was an understanding of man as he was born bad and that only government and laws were needed to control man's basic instinct human nature of bad behavior."

"How about the anarchist?" asked C.E.

"Well, in my opinion, the Anarchists cannot be included in these groups, because anarchists do not believe in any form of government. So if you organize into any group, that in itself would be a form of government. Therefore, anarchists are just disrupters.

"The modern anarchist just wants to destroy the leadership and that will cause the cultural collapse of society. So, they then can run through the forest in their 'naked glory' as an early philosopher claimed that man would best be served. A return to the time that man lived before modern culture was created with the modern industrial age.

"As with all things they change. The socialist Karl Marx, a German intellectual in the rising industrial power of Germany in the 19th Century, put his ideas to work. He believed the socialist movement needed to change into a radical form of complete government control that he called Communism. That would be a political system that would in the end remove all need for the existing governments and create a society ruled by the proletariat (the workers). It would remove the bourgeoisie (elite) that had held the power and kept the working man down. One small, interesting fact about Marx is that he did inherit money and was able to impregnate a house servant with a baby just like the bourgeoisie elite that he claimed were the oppressors of the proletariat.

"Marx's focus was on industrial workers. He did not see the peasants as part of the working class. They were petty capitalists working in their self-interest. They could not be trusted for their greed. The ultimate goal of communism is to remove the government."

"You mean he was an anarchist?" asked C.E.

"No, they both did have the same goal, but Marx wanted it in stages, not in a big bang. He and his fellow writer Friedrick Engels wrote books on the evolution of the working class through stages of history. That is a vast story in itself I will not go into at this time.

"The next step in the evolution of communism was created by Lenin, who developed the idea of an elite group of professional revolutionaries, the Bolsheviks, that were needed to bring about the new Bolshevik workers society. Lenin believed that the workers were too fragmented and divided to work together for a common cause. They needed professional revolutionaries to lead and take them in the right direction.

"The Bolsheviks took up this new way and began removing anything that stood in their way. One of these revolutionaries was Joseph Dzhugashvili who went by some 30 different names during his early years. At one time he took the name Koba and later he adopted the name Stalin. He was at one time or another a bank robber, thug, and murderer of communism and spent time in the Czar's prison camps in Siberia. The

Bolsheviks called themselves the majority and were never a large part of the socialist movement. Then came the Great War which allowed Lenin and his people to undermine the government and other political groups.

"Once the Bolsheviks obtained power in 1917, they held on to power by crushing all opposition. They then changed their name to the Communist Party. The new leadership would be there to guide the community of workers to a new society without any government over time and that time would be decided by the leadership when they felt that the masses were ready."

"What about other radicals?" asked Nick.

"They come in all forms of extremist from religion to politics – IRA in Ireland, Black September in Jordan, FARC in Columbia, Al Qaeda, Hizballah, and PLO to name a few. The difference between most of these groups from the communists is they want to return to the past no matter what the cost of human life. Which takes me back to human nature. Is man born good or bad or as John Locke said blank?

"By the 19th and 20th Centuries, the rapid industrial age changed in the economic world. The Capitalism of Adam Smith had taken the view that man was born good and would do good in the end. That private property and competition would be controlling factors of human nature.

"That period changed rapidly and did see the expansion of the middle class and wealthy class but left the working man with little power to control over his life. Groups like the Luddites formed to protest the industrialization of workers. At times they would toss a shoe (a sabot in French) into the machinery to break it down. The term sabotage comes from this practice. This is where the socialists and other protesters stepped further into the debate on worker's rights.

"Karl Marx then came along and flipped the socialist argument on its head. He said man was born good but was corrupted by capitalism and private property (greed). Remove the private property and man will return to his natural goodness. Marx believed society was moving in that direction historically in what he called Historical Materialism with stages from primitive communism to slave societies to feudalism to mercantilism to capitalism to finally communism. A pure state 'from each according to his ability, to each according to his needs.' Later Engels rephrased this philosophy to dialectical materialism.

"Lenin set up the dictatorship of the proletariat to guide everyone by force, if necessary, back to the state of goodness. This system still holds many people to the belief that a utopia can be created. Yet, unfortunately, human nature always pops-up in the form of greed and individual desire for power to control the new society. When questioned about these abuses of the workers and their rights, the leaders say a few eggs need to be broken to make an omelet.

"Then today one adds into this mix various elements of idealism, the notions of nationalism, imperialism, and decolonization along with the old elements of religion and territory demands. Israel, India and Pakistan, China's all make territorial demands. Then on every continent, there are conflicts over tribal territory and identity. Just to name a few more trouble spots for radicalism to rise its evil head. That is about it for a quick summary of this topic. I hope that gives you some understanding?"

"Just one more question on Islam," said C.E.

"That could also take a while. However, a summary would be that there are two main groups the Sunni and Shia. The Sunni hold the belief that the political and religious leaders are separate but are to work together. The Shia on the other hand believed the religious leader and the political leader are the same and their authority comes from the Prophets family. That caused a split in the religion around the 7th Century. The Shia lost the struggle and developed the idea of self-sacrifice or martyrs. Creating conflict between the two groups.

"Then in the 18th Century in the Arabian Peninsula, a new interpretation of Islam came into practice known as Wahhabism. This is a radical intolerant form of Islam at times called Salafism. Wahhabism believed that a good Moslem could kill a bad Moslem and it would be permitted by the Quran. That is a short explanation of a very complex topic. Do you have any other questions?"

"I have one about these people and that is when their prophecy fails to come, what do they do?" asked Nick.

"Well, now you open another door to a deep subject. These groups are more like cults and there are studies done on just what you asked, Nick. The bottom line is they seem to double down on the belief rather than realize its failure. A good example is the American Air Corps in World War Two.

"A group of men began to believe a better way to conduct war without the mass slaughter of troops would be to bomb military targets of the enemy that made war possible. To conduct this type of warfare the bombing had to be done in daylight and the war would end faster.

"Well, things did not go the way they believed on the first attempt. They said they needed more training. The second attempt did not go much better and yet they just doubled down and went on with their idea of daylight bombing. Then at the end of the war, they believed they were the reason the war was won. The fact was the bombing did not stop German war production for any long period. The Army Air Corp ended the war believing in strategic booming. All the evidence suggested just the opposite and they just doubled down on the system pointing to Hiroshima.

"I know that is a fast and simple answer to your question. I hope it provided some clarity."

"Yes, I think you explained it very well," said Nick.

"Nick, do you have any more questions?" asked C.E.

"I find the subject compelling and have lots of questions for a deeper study of the subject. However, I think we both have a better understanding for now. Thank you, professor, for taking the time to talk with us," said Nick.

"Remember it is Hellen and it was my pleasure you two take care and come see me when you get home C.E. I will love hearing all about it when you get home."

"I am afraid that will not be possible. This case is very hush, hush," said Nick and C.E. together as they laughed.

"I am sorry, Helen but it is a sensitive case. Take care, Hellen," said C.E. and disconnected.

Nick turned to C.E. and said, "C.E. you are going to make a good agent!"

"What are you talking about, agent?"

"Well, Helen wanted to hear all about the case, and you told her that was not possible at the same time as I did. That was very professional," said Nick.

"I think I will stay as a consultant and not become an agent."

"I am just saying…that's all."

CHAPTER FORTY-ONE

David Allan Gee ran a Chinese restaurant in Australia. The police raided the establishment looking for pornography. During the search, they discovered items for overprinting, surcharging, and cancellations of stamps. Despite previous convictions, Gee was given a suspended sentence.

"ONE COUNTRY ALL RED"

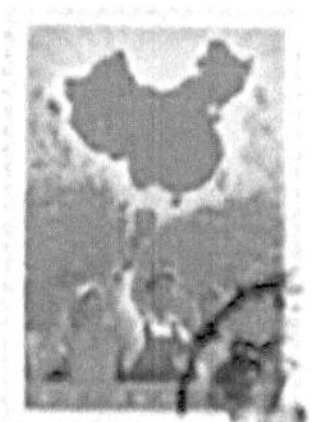

GENUINE   **FORGERY**

Thousands of candles can be lit from a single candle, and the life of the candle will not be shortened. Happiness never decreases by being shared.

— Buddha

1999 China Industry Center

The room had tension when the door opened. "I am sorry to call this meeting so late in the day, please excuse the inconvenience gentlemen," said the leader,

"Has something happened?" asked Mayor Bo.

"No, the committee would like a report on the different operations we are conducting in the United States. The one with Abdul and the other one with that university chemist. So, let's get started with Abdul first. Has that engineer Wu been sent to Iran and when will the shipment be delivered?" asked He.

"He will be there in two days and the shipment will arrive there the day before with the North Korean. They will have everything set up for Wu," said party member Ying.

"Who is the North Korean engineer?" asked He.

"Ji-hoon, their best ballistic missile engineer. He went to engineering school here and was the top of his class and worked with our missile program," said Mayor Bo.

"This Ji-hoon wasn't he the North Korean lead engineer on the 1993 testing of their short-range missile? The one that Iran hopes will place the state of Israel within range of the Iranian missiles?" asked Ying.

"Yes," answered Mayor Bo.

"His father, I believe, was the one who helped the Iranians with the Scud-C missiles and was the conduit we used to send weapons to Iran in 1987. We and North Korea helped provide the Iranians with close to 70% of their weapons that year. As long as Iran kept making noise it took the attention of the Americans off us.

"Then North Korea and Iran's support of Hezbollah also drew the American's focus more on the Middle East and terrorism was even better. That part of the plan is still in play.

"However, now to the other topic now. How are our students doing in the American universities? That is an important part of the overall plan?" asked He.

"They are doing well, and our student agents have recruited a few professors from major research universities. Some by the oldest spy recruitment method, sex, and others by the second-best method, money. Plus, we have placed many low-level individuals in lower positions. There is one that is the driver for an important member of the U.S. Congress. It is amazing how much the American elite talk in front of their domestic workers.

"They remind me of the idiot British when they ran Hong Kong. It is as if the workers were not there. We did not need high-technology listening devices," said Ying

"Yes, we need to keep our goal of being admitted to the World Trade Organization. That will allow more Western industries to enter our markets and will provide us with more industries to take advantage of our low worker's wages. The Americans may not know it, but we will be the top economic and industrial power within 50 years," said the leader He.

"One last thing before we adjourn. What about this Professor Qing?" asked Ying.

"He has taken the bait and is in a relationship with one of our students. We are going to let the relationship develop before we ask him for more favors," said He.

"Good, who is the student?" asked Ying.

"Su Wu, a second-year student at the university. She is very bright and has had some agent training," said He.

"Everything seems to be going as planned. Let us go have dinner," said Mayor Bo.

"One last thing, the new 'Going Out Policy' will start this year, so I would like weekly updates. It's our movement into a global strategy and I have heard of plans to develop a Silk Road project," said Leader He.

"Should I know about this project," asked Mayor Bo.

"No, that project is years away. I just want everyone to remember nothing is permanent and we must be ready for change. Now, let us go and enjoy the evening," said Leader He.

CHAPTER FORTY-TWO

H. Kuroiwa was a dealer in Chemulpo (Inchon, Korea) and is known for the 'Tai Han' overprints. Most of these were in black ink, but some were in red ink of fake overprints he produced. Kuroiwa was at times an advertiser in the *Mekeel's Stamp Collector* and he used the banks in Hong Kong and Shanghai.

GENUINE   **FORGERY**

I do not concern myself with gods and spirits either good or evil nor do I serve any.

— Lao Tzu

2002 REPORT ON NORTH KOREA (DPRK) LABOR CAMP

An Intelligence Report from an American news agency that said it was from an undisclosed source in North Korea was on the desk. Sung-ho picked up the paper and read it to those present.

...The prison camp was crowded and had been since the other camps in the area were closed and the prisoners were moved to this larger camp for what was referred to as re-education. The favored prisoners were allowed to live in a house with their families. All the other prisoners were in barracks that held up to 100 individuals. The camp was surrounded by electrified wire fences, guard towers, and patrols with dogs.

Life was harsh and life-threatening. It was not uncommon to see prisoners with ears torn off, eyes smashed, broken noses, missing limbs, and cuts and scars from beatings. No one was excused from work details. The workday started at 5 a.m. and ended at 8 p.m. unless it was winter when 7 p.m. ended the day's work.

Those who failed to follow the rules or said the wrong thing were subjected to any of the camps torture. Some of these are listed here:

The most common was the water torture, which made the victims feel as if they were drowning.

Then there was the hanging torture where one was hung off the ground for long periods. This is very painful.

Or the Box torture, where one was placed in a box that was so small that standing was not allowed.

Another one is the Pigeon torture, which has the victim's hands tied to the wall about two feet off the floor and the person has to crouch for hours.

The worst was the kneeling torture, where a bar was placed behind the knee and the person had to squat cutting off the circulation to the legs. Many who suffered from this method died later.

Death is not uncommon from starvation, beatings, or killings. Those that were taken to secret work projects were never seen again. Reports of bodies being tossed into coal wagons that were transporting coal for the furnaces at the local power plants or steel mills.

There are reports of human experimentation being conducted in different locations. Our informant was not able to verify these reports.

All the rest of the report was verified by individuals that had escaped or were defectors from North Korea…

Throwing the paper down, the man who was reading it yelled, "Who allowed this person into the camp, and who are these individuals that are referred to in the report?" asked Sung-ho.

"No reporter was ever at the camp. That camp is under total isolation and the strictest guard," said Yun.

"Then where did this report come from, if not a reporter? It is very detailed as to the camp and its practices. The leader wants to know, and someone must pay the price for this public relations failure. We already had to make apologies for the kidnapping of a dozen or so Japanese individuals who had no military, scientific, or political value. They were kidnapped on the whim of the beloved leader, for example, that movie star," said Sung-ho.

"Be careful of what and where you say things like that, my friend. You could be the next person in the self-criticism sessions of one of the camps," said Yun.

"True, and you would be right beside me for giving me that warning. So you and I must stay alive and out of such places. Have our agents in the camp see if we can discover who is responsible for this report. Then they are to be dealt with for disloyalty to the supreme leader. At least find an individual who can take the responsibility.

"I need at least a report that I can take to the next meeting. This has not been a good year. After we nullified the 1994 agreement on nuclear weapons development the world leaders accepted our denial. Everything seemed to be going well.

"However, now the Americans have proof of our nuclear program and we had to admit it to the world. That and the naval battle we had with the South Koreans have made us look like the aggressors. The supreme leader is not happy. Fortunately, I have shifted the burden of that failure off onto that young arrogant party climber Byeol. She will be the target of any retribution," said Sung-ho.

"Well, the good news is Ji-hoon is in Iran and working with the Chinese counterpart on the nuclear program there. Soon the West will be terrified of the nuclear programs that we are helping to develop in so many of the small People's Democratic Republic nations," said Yum.

"Put that in a report for the Supreme leader and I will take it to the next meeting. It should take some of the edge off the bad news. Our push for a missile system is the highest priority to the Supreme Leader. Make sure that the report states that the missile program in Iran is the old program and is not connected with our newest research.

"The Supreme Leader will not be happy to hear that our newest research is out there for the foreign aggressors to see how far we have progressed," ordered Sung-ho.

"That has been taken into consideration and Ji-hoon worked only on the last program and does not know the current program. It is a shame for he is our best engineer, but we have used him to sell the old system to other nations with great success," said Yun.

"Again be careful of what you say, my friend. That could end both of our careers. Have the reports on my desk by 7 a.m.!"

"Once again you are right, and the report will be there!"

CHAPTER FORTY-THREE

H. da Luz specialized in the Japanese Military Government philately. Collectors were looking for the twelve legal postmarks for Kowloon City which were difficult to collect until 1956. Then that year H. da Luz flooded the market with covers with all 12 postmarks. Some of these covers are easy to identify for they are addressed in ball-point pen. H. da Luz remains a mysterious figure in the philately world.

GENUINE   **FORGERY**

It is very important to concentrate on hitting the U.S. economy through all means possible.

— Osama bin Laden

2002 IRAN SECRET NUCLEAR PROGRAM LOCATION

The project leader walked into the room, "Where is that Russian technician?" asked Hormoz.

"I saw him with Zenda in the hall just a minute ago," replied Cyra.

"Then go and get him in here now and also tell the Chinese and North Korean technicians to come in here for this meeting. There is a big wig coming to check on the progress within the hour. We need to get a report ready," said Hormoz.

The Russian walked in with a smile on his face and Zenda followed him. The older woman approached Zenda and pulled her aside from the others.

"Zenda you are playing a dangerous game. That Russian will not stay here long and will ruin your reputation at best, at worst you will be stoned to death for infidelity. You need to stay away from him before the others notice the attention you are paying to him. You are a good nuclear scientist, do not let your youthful passions ruin your life," said Aryana.

"I know, but he has said he will marry me, and we both will go to Russia soon. He is going to see my parents tonight," said Zenda.

"Your father will never agree to the marriage Zenda. He is a strict Muslim, and the Russian is not a Muslim. No, Zenda that marriage will never be acceptable by your father and his powerful family. Save yourself from the heartache of this small adventure. It will cause you nothing but pain," said Aryana.

"We can run away," replied Zenda.

"Your father and his brothers will look for you and deal in the traditional honorable way. Is that what you want? To live a life looking over your shoulder the rest of your life?" asked Aryana.

"My mother will support my choice and tell my father what to do," said Zenda.

"Your mother supported the revolution and wanted to return to the old ways and now wears the Hijab. No, your mother will support your father. They are not ready for the modern world. You, unfortunately, have a good education and know the modern world, but you have to live in a world that honors the past. Please take the advice of an older woman who has seen these things turn out badly for many young women in this country," said Aryana.

Just then the rest of the technicians walked into the room. "Listen up everyone. Now that everyone is here the director of the program will be here shortly. We need to show that progress is being made. So we need to make sure everyone is on the same page. Any questions you have about the project need to be addressed now. Are there any?" asked Hormoz.

"This is not a question as such, but my shipments from Russia are always delayed. That has slowed down my part of the development," said Pyotr.

"Pyotr, it has been discovered that the shipments from Russia have carried contraband that is being sold on the black market. So all shipments are now searched for any items that are not listed on the manifest. We appreciate the help the Russian government is providing and the help of your father's business interest. We are willing to overlook a few minor errors, but we have a limit. Our government has asked that you be replaced on the Russian team. That is another reason for the meeting now. You are to gather your things and be ready to leave within the next hour," said Hormoz. He did not say that it was only because of his grandfather's position in Russia that he was not being shot.

"What? Now? I have things I need to do before I leave this country!" said Pyotr.

"I am sorry Pyotr you will be escorted to your living quarters right now and be out of the country within the hour. Those are the orders I have been given," said Hormoz.

Two security guards stepped up beside him and took him by each arm and walked out the door as Aryana stood beside Zenda. "Be careful Zenda, do not show your grief," said Aryana.

"What am I to do? I cannot live without him." She started to move and was blocked by Aryana.

"I am trying to save your job and your life Zenda. You make a scene now and it will not end well for Pyotr or you and your family. No matter who his grandfather is. Go to your room and cry if you want and I will come there in a few minutes," said Aryana.

After Zenda left Aryana went over to Hormoz as the meeting broke up. "Well, did you get her out of the way?" asked Hormoz

"Yes, I sent her to her room and there will be someone there to watch her so that she does not try to see Pyotr before he leaves," said Aryana.

"Very well, we will keep this between us. She is too good of a scientist to lose over an infatuation. Besides, tell her that Pyotr has a wife in Russia and his father is more than a big industrialist that he is a member of the inter-Russian oligarchy," said Hormoz.

"What shall I do with that part of the project that Pyotr was working on?" asked Aryana.

"Give it to Ji-hoon. He works well with the Chinese and was working with Pyotr. This should not slow down the project and we will have a replacement for Pyotr by the first of next week," replied Hormoz.

Later that day the team was gathered in the conference room and the Director was telling them the latest. "We are satisfied with all the work you are all doing for the nation. As you all know the American president has called us part of the 'Axis of Evil' along with the Soviet Union and Iraq. He has proof of our nuclear program, and it would appear that someone has betrayed the program to the Americans. Photos and documentation were displayed to the Western press. Now we must admit we have the program and agree to international inspections and open talks with the Americans."

"How did the Americans find out about the project?" asked Aryana.

"Someone in the project had contacts with a group in opposition to the leadership," said the Director.

Just then four security guards and an officer came into the room. "Cyra, you will come with us. You are under arrest for betraying the Islamic Republic," said the officer.

"What are you talking about? I would never betray my country. This must be a mistake! I am innocent!"

"Shut your mouth filthy traitor!" said one guard as he hit her in the face knocking her to the floor. She was picked up and dragged out of the room sobbing and pleading her innocence.

Hormoz stood by and watched the poor woman being dragged out of the room. It had been easy to set the direction of the investigation to Cyra. Her conversations with the Russian will be discovered and her guilt will be absolute. Soon he would be out of the country with a nice bank account.

CHAPTER FORTY-FOUR

Charles A. Lyford was part of the 'Boston Gang'. He worked with S. Allan Taylor to defraud individuals and companies. He even acted one time as an interpreter for Taylor when they persuaded a printing company to print bogus Guatemala stamps. At one time Lyford was the editor of *The New England Journal of Philately*. When Taylor was arrested for Counterfeiting in 1890 it was Lyford's mother who furnished the bail.

GENUINE

FORGERY

See no evil, hear no evil, speak no evil.

— English Proverb

2002 New York Fazil looking for Elena

The team was standing in the conference room and Nick asked, "Where are we on this Fazil character?"

"Fazil is in New York and goes from one place to another place," said an agent.

"Do we have a team on him?" asked Nick.

"We have two- or three-men teams," said the agent.

"Why not pick him up now?" asked C.E.

"It is better to follow him to others in the operation. He went right to a banker with high political connections, and we know he is dirty, and this may be the break we need to take him down," said Nick.

"Who is it?" asked C.E.

"You may remember them both. They were part of the case you broke up with the Nazi stamp album. Werner Hoffmann and Rudy Moody. Rudy is the son of Charles Moody," said Nick.

"I remember them. They got a pass by claiming innocence and no knowledge of the evil organization they worked with at the time. If I remember right, only three individuals were charged and two were extradited. One to Germany and one to Poland after a long investigation," said C.E.

"Money, political influence, and good lawyers do have an advantage in the American legal system," said Nick.

"Yeah, I remember the Congressional Post Office scandal in the 90s around the same time. I believe there also was the House of Representatives banking scandal," said C.E.

"You are right. The banking scandal where 22 political careers were ruined. They were over-drawing their housing allotment and not paying them back for months without any penalty if I remember it right," said Nick.

"I do not remember much about the banking scandal, but the Post Office scandal sparked my interest. It was exposed about a year before it became national news after the Postmaster pleaded guilty to charges.

"Members of the House were implicated. They were charged with mail fraud, embezzlement, and money laundering. If I remember right, they would take their Franking privilege and withdraw the stamps and then later take the stamps back for an exchange of money. They also used the Post Office to cash campaign checks," said C.E.

"That's right. The investigation shut down when the House Democrats saw the investigation net was spreading far too wide and stopped the investigation. It became a bone for the Republicans and charges were brought against members. One House member was sentenced to 18 months and given a pardon in 2000 by the outgoing President," said Nick.

"The story did not last long in the national news and was told as a simple Congressional abuse with Franking Privileges and not the actual charges," said C.E.

A clerk walked into the room, "Excuse me, Agent Thomson I was told to give you this message,"

"Thank you," then Nick turned and said, "Well C.E. it seems we can go now and pick up Fazil. He is looking for Elena in what the agents that are following him say is nothing short of a frantic mood. I think she may be more than just another object to use in the cause. Shall we go?"

"Where is he now?" asked C.E.

"He just left Rudy at the bank and we better hurry," said Nick.

"Why?" asked C.E.

"Rudy made a call to Fazil's father, Abdul, as soon as Fazil left the office. Fazil's father was told that his son came into the office and pleaded for help to find Elena. Abdul did not sound happy, said the agent who was listening to the conversation. He said Abdul sounded very menacing. Then he said he'd take care of the problem 'for good' and those were his exact words," said Nick.

"You are right! It sounds like we better pick up Fazil before he goes into a body bag," said C.E.

"That is what the agent who heard the conversation said. He called and said that it might be good to collect Fazil before his father had him picked up," said Nick.

CHAPTER FORTY-FIVE

John Stewart Lowden of London was accused of selling forgeries to L'Estrange Ewen in 1907. Lowden sued Ewen for libel and during the five-day trial, it was found that he did indeed sell forgeries to H. L' Estrange Ewen. Ewen was exonerated and Lowden was ordered to pay the cost. At the same time, Lowden was also involved in another counterfeit case with Rene Careme of Paris in 1909. Rene was later convicted of counterfeiting and fined 16 francs. Lowden continued in the business under the name of George Ellis and was arrested in 1913 for counterfeiting stamps and served 3 years.

GENUINE   **FORGERY**

All human beings are commingled out of good and evil.
— Robert Louis Stevenson

2002 RUSSIA AT MIKHAIL'S DACHAS

At Mikhail's dachas by the Black Sea, he held meetings for visiting members of the industrial international organizations he had built over the years. "What is so important, Alexei?"

"The Arab Abdul now wants to hire our people to remove a problem in his organization," said Alexei.

"You know something Alexei, you, Viktor, and I are getting too old for this. We should retire and enjoy the peaceful quiet. What is the problem?" asked Mikhail.

"He wants us to remove someone in his organization. Someone by the name of Fazil, I think he is the actual son of Abdul and he is unwilling to do the job himself. He wants us to remove this Fazil," said Alexei.

"Or he wants it to appear that outside forces took care of a problem. Tell him no," said Mikhail.

"He will ask why?" said Alexei.

"Who cares! Tell him that Russia has enough problems with the Muslins population in Russia, and we do not need to get the blame for removing the son of an important leader in the radical Muslin world. We have long memories and so do the Muslins. No thanks, have him use those thugs he is using in the Mexican drug Cartels," said Mikhail.

"I'll see that he is told and also your grandson wants to talk to you," said Alexei.

"This is the reason we do not retire my friend. The sons and daughters and their children make more problems than we did at their age," said Mikhail.

"We did have the camps to keep us in line!" said Alexei.

"True, and I was there because I did create a lot of trouble for the new Soviet government. You on the other hand tried to be a good Soviet citizen. Yet, there we were in the same place for years. Of course, you and Viktor took that small, exciting vacation during the Great Patriot War as Comrade Stalin called it," said Mikhail.

"Yes, that was some vacation. The Germans were brutal and when we entered their Death Camps it was an untold horror. That was not much different than the ones we have seen and had been in over the years. The only difference was there were no ovens in our camps, just graveyards. I do not think you or I would send our children to one of those camps," said Alexei.

"You are probably right, but don't tell them that," Mikhail said as he laughed with Alexei.

"Let's not forget, for memories lessen over time," said Mikhail.

"Shall I send in your grandson?" asked Alexei.

"First, how is the weapons deal going with the Chinese, North Koreans, and Iranians?" asked Mikhail.

"The Chinese are stealing every little bit they can. Every package sent has some items missing from our weapons. Two hundred units ended up being 199 or 198 by the time they were unpacked. Plus, they reverse engineer anything they want without paying for it. As for the North Koreans and Iranians, they confiscate our black-market goods and then take them home for their private use. Overall I say the program is going well except for your grandson being sent home and told never to return to Iran. I think it was over a woman," said Alexei.

"You are right, and it would appear that Abdul and I have the same problem with different reactions to solve the problem. Send in the troubled young man," said Mikhail,

Alexei opened the door and Pyotr rushed in. "Grandfather, I know you are upset with me. I cannot help it if I fell in love with a beautiful intelligent woman. I was not allowed to say good-bye. They loaded me into a car, and I was out of the country in less than an hour and placed on a plane home. I was approached in the airport by a young woman who told me Zenda did not know I was married and that her family was very upset. But I do not have a wife. What am I going to do? I can't live without her." said Pyotr.

"You know they sent me a message that you were going to be executed for infidelity with a good young Muslim woman. Her family was in turmoil over the affair. I had to pull in favors and spend a small fortune to get you out of that Stone Age society. You know, comrade Stalin was told he could have his son back after his son was captured by the Germans during the Great Patriotic War and Stalin said to the Germans, they could keep him. You are lucky the Soviet Union collapsed, and Stalin is gone. What do you have to say to that? Why do you find the need to rush in on my meetings?" asked Mikhail.

"Grandfather you are a powerful leader and I know you are no Stalin," said Pyotr.

"You are right! I have too much compassion for my friends and family," said Mikhail.

"The woman I love is in danger and she will be murdered by her family for some idiotic notion of family honor. I must try and save her, grandfather. I am going back to Iran!"

"NO! You will not do that. You will stay right here with me so I can keep a watch on you. I will do what I can. I have a few favors to call in for a recent transaction that I helped with by getting information out of there and to the Americans. Leave it to me or you will get yourself and her both killed by those fanatics. I will work something out."

"How long will it take? Those people will kill her, I am sure. Last week there was a worker at the plant whose daughter was murdered by her brother. He claimed the girl had relations with an infidel and for the family's honor, she had to die. There were no charges of murder issued against the brother. He was seen as an honorable man.

"I cannot help that I fell in love with her, and I was going to ask the young woman's father's permission to marry her that very night. I told that to one of the guys taking me to the plane. He looked at me as if I was a fool and told me that I would have been killed on the spot in the home. These people are truly fanatics Grandfather. I need your help!"

"See, being a member of a thug family, as you call it, is not the worst thing in the world. I am glad to hear I have moved up in your eyes," said Mikhail.

"Don't make light of this grandfather. I am serious and in love with her."

"I know this and the plan to rescue her is already in operation. If everything goes right, you will both be together soon."

"What! You knew all this all the time?"

"Yes, I have my sources and set the operation in motion once they contacted me about you and the young woman. Now, this is absolute, you may not tell anyone of this. We cannot afford any mishaps to ruin the operation. Do you understand?"

"Yes, of course. From what I have been told we will have to hide the rest of our lives from her family. These people are crazy about family honor and kill their own."

"If the plan goes right as we have planned it, you need not worry about hiding. You will just have to have new lives. Now go and let me do some work before we leave here to meet this young woman."

CHAPTER FORTY-SIX

Brewster Cox Kenyon was a philatelist who never missed a chance to defraud stamp collectors. His frauds ranged from bogus Steam shipping company stamps and those of the Confederate States of America stamps plus U.S. revenue stamps. There is still a debate on whether the Steamship stamps are real. In 1895 Kenyon was himself swindled in a Confederate stamp die. In 1903 he published a catalogue of U.S. revenue stamps.

GENUINE

FORGERY

Indifference, to me, is the epitome of evil.

— Elie Wiesel

2002 FAZIL AND ELENA

Fazil was sitting in a bar and showed the bartender a photo of a woman when two agents walked up to him showing their badges and asked him to step outside. At first, he refused until he was told the alternative was being thrown on the floor and handcuffed in front of the crowd. He walked outside with the agents where he was placed in a van and driven to a safe location. Then put on a plane to the West Coast and placed in a room.

"Why am I here? I have a very important matter I need to do!" said Fazil.

"I think you know Fazil. I am a government agent of the United States. My name is Nick Thomson and this gentleman is C.E. Hall and we would like to ask you a few questions about Chicago?" said Nick.

"It is a city in the Midwest. Now may I go," said Fazil as he tried to stand up.

"Very funny, C.E. We have a comedian who does not realize he is in a world filled with lots of different troubles for him. Now, Fazil we know who your father is and all about the organization you belong to, so let's cut to the chase. You have information we would like, and you have a choice to answer or enjoy a trip to a place we have reserved for terrorists," said Nick.

"I have no idea what you are talking about, and I am not a terrorist. I want a …"

"Stop before you ruin any deal you could make Fazil," said Nick.

"I have rights and you government agents are…"

"Fazil, I want to tell you some things you may not know," said C.E.

"What could you possibly tell me – Agent of America!" said Fazil in almost a scream.

"Fazil, I am not an agent of America. I am a consultant called in for my special knowledge on a particular subject. That subject is stamps. You and a woman by the name of Karyme are part of that special subject," said C.E.

"I know nobody named Karyme!"

"Yes, you do, she also goes by Elena. Remember her now?" asked C.E.

"No!"

"That is funny since you have been all over New York looking for her. I believe it was her photo you were showing to the bartender when the agents picked you up," said Nick.

"Alright, so I know her. What is the big deal?" asked Fazil.

"She is the terrorist bomber that had planted a bomb that was set to go off in the Chicago art museum. That means you are also possibly on the hook for that act of terrorism. Fazil you have been connected and it will not take long to make more connections. Are you now starting to get the point?" asked Nick.

"Try and prove that in a court of your law," said Fazil.

"See how little you understand. We don't have to try too hard, for we have an eyewitness that connects you to the plot," said Nick.

"Eyewitnesses are unreliable, and a good lawyer will tear that testimony apart with no direct evidence to make the charge stick," said Fazil smiling.

"You are good. Where did you study law?" asked Nick.

"Harvard and Yale, if you must know. Now may I leave?" asked Fazil.

"I am impressed. How about you C.E.?" asked Nick.

"Wow! Yale that is impressive Fazil. Were you a member of one of the three big secret societies at those universities?" asked C.E.

"No!"

"C.E. our friend here, that is Fazil, was kicked out after his freshman year. I am pretty sure he has no idea of what you just asked him about secret societies," said Nick.

"What about it, Fazil, do you know about the secret societies?" asked C.E.

"Yes, the most known one is the Skull and Bones which is referred to as The Order or The Brotherhood of Death. The other two are the Wolf's Head and Scroll and Key. I was not kicked out of the university. I had personal obligations," said Fazil.

"Fazil, that is not what we were told when we interviewed some of your classmates. It seems your attacks on the Jewish students and Jewish professors were relentless in the classrooms and the administration asked that you leave, or they would withdraw you from the institution. Your law degree is from another country, and you have not passed a Bar exam in the United States. Fazil we do know a lot about you!" said Nick.

"So what, you have no evidence that connects me to any plot you are talking about," said Fazil.

"I wonder how he will explain the connection with the drug cartel?" asked C.E.

"What drug cartel?" asked Fazil

"You know the cartel guy that gave you the C-4 to give to Elena," said Nick.

"You have no evidence of that!" said Fazil.

"We have that vary carrier of the C-4 just down the hall," said C.E.

"That is impossible. He died in a car accident!" said Fazil.

"See there you proved my point. You have been in this room for less than an hour and already telling us about things you said you knew nothing about. He did not even ask what carrier. Is that not amazing C.E. how quickly this tough guy's story breaks apart?" said Nick.

"Well, I see no tape or video equipment, so I guess it is your word against mine," said Fazil.

"That is because we want to make a deal. A one-time offer or it is off to Neverland for you Fazil," said Nick.

"No deal!"

"You have not heard the deal yet; you might not want to be so quick Fazil," said C.E.

"What can you possibly offer me so I would take your deal?" asked Fazil.

"First, we can show you how your father cannot be trusted," said C.E.

"My father is a great man and I trust him with my life," said Fazil.

"Then why did he reach out to the Russian mob to put a hit on you?" asked Nick.

"Nice try, but I know your tricks."

"Oh! Also, there is the little question of why he planned to have the woman you have been looking for all over New York City to be kidnapped and sold into the sex trade in Eastern Europe?" asked Nick.

"That is a lie!" shouted Fazil.

"C.E. would you play the tape for Fazil," asked Nick.

Fazil listened to the tape and C.E. and Nick watched Fazil's face start to drain of color.

"That is not my father's voice. It is someone that sounds like him," said Fazil

"Here are photos of the two men that were to kidnap Elena in Spain. You did put her on a plane for Spain did you not?" asked C.E.

Fazil looked at the photos and shook his head. "yes" he said weakly and slumped in the chair. I heard a rumor that she did not get off the plane in Spain.

"So, Fazil, you are responsible for Elena being placed in the fast traffic lane to the sex trade. How do you feel about that?" asked Nick.

"That is a filthy business, and my father would never be part of it," said Fazil.

"Do you recognize this man, Fazil?" Nick placed a photo of Ramon on the table.

"No!"

"He recognized your picture when we showed it to him a few minutes ago?"

"He is dead!"

"See once again, Fazil did not know the guy, but was still able to tell us the guy was dead. However, that is where you are wrong, Fazil. We have him in our custody after we staged the accident to remove him from the playing field. We can arrange a meeting if you like," said C.E.

"So what! I may have seen him around," said Fazil.

"Oh, did I forget to tell you we also have Elena, down the hall also," said Nick.

"What! She is here and not..." he could not finish and broke down and cried.

"Give him a few minutes," said Nick as they waited.

"Now are you able to talk Fazil?" asked C.E.

Fazil shook his head yes and mumbled what sounded like "Yes, can I see her?"

"That depends on you, Fazil. We have a deal to discuss first."

"I will not make a deal until I see her, and we both talk," said Fazil.

"What do you think C.E. shall we allow these two to talk together?" asked Nick.

"Why not? They are both off to Neverland if they turn down the deal," said C.E.

Fazil walked down the hall to another room. When the door opened, Elena saw Fazil and jumped and rushed up and slapped Fazil in the face and started to hit and kick at him. It took both C.E. and Nick to pull her off her attack. They sat down across the table from each other.

"I do not know what your girlfriend was saying, but I think you may be on her hate list Fazil," said Nick

"FAZIL YOU WERE SENDING ME INTO THE SEX SLAVE TRADE! HOW COULD YOU?" she screamed.

"It was not me! I did not know my love! I am sorry! I did not know! I did not know! I was planning to meet you in Spain as we planned. My father had a different plan than I did. I did not know about his horrible plan," said Fazil weakly.

"I hated you, Fazil. The cause we worked with is more evil than the Western imperialist. You and your father are the worst human beings on earth," said Elena

"Elena, I have been asking and looking for you ever since I heard you were not in Spain. I had a friend there who was to take you to a safe house. He told me you were not on the plane, so I knew you were here. I love you and my father has shown his true self. I am sorry he has failed as a father and as a good man," he started to cry.

Elena softened and reached for Fazil's hand.

"What is your deal? Anyone who tried to put the woman I love in that horrible trade is an evil individual and does not deserve loyalty. Elena, I must do what I can to protect you, if I can. I will do whatever you people want, just let Elena go." said Fazil looking at Nick.

"No, Fazil the deal is with the both of you or neither," said Nick.

Elena sat there with tears on her cheeks, "I love you, Fazil."

"We will talk about that tomorrow. It's time to go back to your room, Fazil. Both of you get a good night's sleep," said Nick as he turned to the guards. "Give the two of them five minutes, not alone. You are to stay and listen to their conversation. Then take them back to separate rooms," said Nick.

Outside the room, Nick said, "Well C.E. that went better than I hoped for. That was a good call allowing them to see each other."

"That is why I am the special consultant."

"Wow!"

CHAPTER FORTY-SEVEN

Raoul Ch. de Thuin produced forgeries and fake stamps over his lifetime. In 1962 at an auction in London 498 lots of stamps of Thuin's forgeries were discovered and the lots were immediately withdrawn. Over the next few years, the American Philatelic Society agreed to purchase all Thuin's stock for an agreement that he would cease his trade in counterfeiting and forgeries. There were 1,636 items he used to create his forgeries, counterfeiting, and fake stamps.

GENUINE   **FORGERY**

All good is hard. All evil is easy. Dying, losing, cheating, and mediocrity is easy. Stay away from easy.

— Scott Alexander

2002 CARTEL PANAMA CONNECTION

"**M**ateo, have you had someone verify the body of Ramon?" asked Diego.

"Not yet, there were a dozen bodies that night and three of them are not where they should have been. In the rush to make room for the bodies others were pushed to other locations and the search is being done to find where they were placed," replied Mateo.

"Still do we know if the body was Ramon?" asked Diego.

"Our informant at the morgue looked at the paperwork and the car was the one Ramon was driving and the body was identified on the police report as a Ramon Luis from what was left of the driver's license. The description of the body was charred, but it was the same size as Ramon."

"O.K. we will have to wait for final identification, I guess. That is if they can make one from what you tell me about the fire. Now about Abdul and why is he in Panama?" asked Diego.

"He is trying to make a deal to use Panama as the transit location for his opium," said Mateo.

"WHAT!" yelled Diego and then immediately calmed down. "That will cut into our cocaine distribution from the Caribbean and South America. If opium starts to go through Panama from the Middle East, that will bring more United States agents into Panama. There will be another invasion of Panama like the one that took down General Manuel Noriega in 1989.

Our money laundering operation and drug trade will suffer a big hit. Find out what Abdul wants and discourage his attempt to move into our territory before he starts a war between the cartels and another one between the Eastern and Western drug trade."

"I already know what he wants. It seems that since 9-11, it has been difficult for his organization to get people into the States. He has been paying us for that transportation," said Mateo.

"Then let us offer a deal where we will transport his people for free as long as his opium distribution trade remains in Europe and Asia. Tell him that a drug war between cartels will not help his desire to get people into the States or increase his money supply.

"When Noriega controlled Panama, he and one cartel controlled the distribution in what was called the first Narcokleptocracy. Everyone was happy to leave things alone until that idiot believed he was beyond reach. Then the Americans took him out.

"Today in Panama there are other cartels in the trade, and we have an uneasy peace with the violence on the increase in cities like Colon and Panama City. The Americans had the country taken off the uncooperative list of the G-7 when the Panama government agreed to sign the FATF treaty. We cannot afford to rock the boat right now," said Diego.

"I'll send Pablo to make the deal," said Mateo.

"Tell Pablo to make it clear that this is not a negotiation. It is an offer for peace," said Diego.

"O.K. Then there is one more thing. It may not be that important to us, but Abdul's son was picked up in a bar by federal agents," said Mateo.

"What does he know about our part in the stamp operation?" asked Diego.

"He was the go-between for only the material for the bomb. He only met Ramon one time and that situation seems to have been taken care of all by itself," said Mateo.

"Yes! O.K. then get rid of the stamps and hold onto the plates. It would be best to use a wide distribution around the world. Do not get rid of all of them at the same time. We do not want to draw attention to any dumping," said Diego.

"What about Abdul, he has a share in the project?" asked Mateo.

"If he complains, give him the stamps. We do not need the problems that are beginning to develop over this small stamp deal," said Diego.

"What if he asks about the plates?" asked Mateo.

"They were lost in the fire. We may use them later when this Abdul thing goes away. What started as a simple deal of transporting items across the border has now become a terrorist problem that will put more pressure on us.

"There may be those in that country that will bring drugs into that country to supply a habit of the Americans, but they may have a different reaction to importing terrorism. NO, Abdul has made himself unwelcome here. The faster we establish control over him and his organization the better," said Diego.

CHAPTER FORTY-EIGHT

Warren T. Thomson produced stamps referred to as the first "Chicago forgery" with two other individuals in 1895. They offered to sell sheets of (2 cent) U.S. stamps valued at $115.00 for $100.00 c.o.d. to customers.

One customer informed the authorities of their activities and in 1896 the group was arrested, and thousands of forgeries and items of equipment were confiscated. Their sentences were less than two years. These forgeries are prized by collectors today.

GENUINE

FORGERY

Whoever fights monsters should see to it that in the process he does not become a monster. And if you gaze long enough into an abyss, the abyss will gaze back into you.

— Friedrich Nietzsche

2002 BARGAIN WITH THE DEVIL

"C.E. what do you think about offering the deal to the two separate or together?" asked Nick.

"To tell the truth I hate to offer these two any deal at all. They should pay for what they have done and spend years in prison," said C.E.

"You are right, but we have a much bigger picture here C.E.." said Nick.

"Don't panic, I know the greater good is needed in some cases. It just rubs me wrong. So, I guess the deal will go better if they both know what each other is saying. They seemed to care for each other and were willing to give up family for each other. I would say my answer is together," said C.E.

"I know how you feel, trust me. I lost one of my best friends to a bomb over there and that woman may have been the one who made and placed the bomb. But if we can collect more information on Abdul's organization and also, take it down and at least weaken Diego cartel's operation then the trade-off may be worth it," said Nick.

"The battle against evil requires witness protection to protect witnesses and inside informers. Some of those witnesses are less than honorable individuals," said C.E.

"Not as many as you think or how Hollywood portrays them. Those few who are in the program have been very important in stopping or preventing serious crimes. Most are just poor individuals who were at the wrong place at the wrong time to see something they should not have seen," said Nick.

"I understand. I just hope these two will change their way of thinking. Let's go and talk to them," said C.E.

"I had the couple placed in the room together a few minutes ago," said Nick.

"Let's hope the loving couple agree to our terms," said C.E. As the two men entered the room the two looked up.

"Fazil and Elena, I hope you both had a good night?" said Nick as he and C.E. sat down across the table.

"Yes," they both said, nodding their heads as they did. They were both handcuffed and sitting apart.

"I am informing you both that I am special Agent Thomson and with me is Mr. C.E. Hall, who is a special consultant, and we are interviewing Fazil and Elena. This interview is being taped. Do you both agree to the taping?" asked Nick.

"Yes," they responded.

"Now I must ask you both if you have been informed of your rights?" asked Nick.

"Yes!" both answered.

"Do either of you have any questions before we get to the deal that is being offered to both of you?" asked Nick.

"No! What is the deal?" said Elena.

"Fazil we need you to answer also!" said C.E.

"No, I have no questions. What is the deal?" asked Fazil.

"The United States is offering you a pass on any charges that you may have committed before yesterday," said Nick.

"What are you saying?" asked Fazil?"

"That as of yesterday you have not committed any crimes against the United States and no charges will be brought against you. Now, back to the offer.

"In exchange for this offer, you both agree to provide us with any information you have on the organizations you worked with up to today. So, you can begin by telling us what you know starting backward from yesterday. That includes any family or personal connections. Is that clear?" asked Nick.

"Yes, I was so naive to believe what I was told. I believe we were working for God and saving our people and faith. To think that my reward for that was to be sold into the sex slave trade! I would like to see them all die," said Elena with her eyes blazing.

"What about you Fazil? Your family is committed to this evil?" asked C.E.

"Family! What kind of a family would send this woman or any woman into the sex trade? At times, I would see my father drink alcohol and go into whore houses, but I would ignore it like many in my religion do now and have done in the past. It was seen as just a few slight indiscretions. No, I no longer have a father or any family. Those who continue to see and ignore these things are not worth my time. So, what is the rest of your offer?" said Fazil.

"The offer is that you will be given new identities and a location to-gether. If either of you breaks the rule of this agreement, you both will go to a security facility we call Neverland. It also means you will never have any more contact with any family members or friends of your past for the rest of your lives. Take some time to think about it," said Nick.

"I do not need to think about it. I was told my family was murdered by Americans. Now, I wonder if that was also a lie. I agree to the offer," said Elena.

"Elena, to be completely honest your family may have been killed in an American operation. I cannot tell you anything differently. We inves-tigated the incident and there was a combat operation area zone, and our records are a little confused about the event in the village. Our vehicle hit an IED killing all inside and its ammo went off in an explosion killing the people in the house next to the vehicle. The confusion is we could not tell who's home the blast killed. All that I can tell you is that it was not an assassination of civilians by the United States. I want you to take some time. This is a big decision that has long-term conditions for both of you," said Nick.

Elena looked at Nick for a long minute. "I am beginning to understand things I have been told are not always clear absolutes. I thank you for your honesty," said Elena.

"What about you Fazil?" asked C.E.

"My family betrayed me and tried to send the woman I love into the sex trade. I agree to the offer," said Fazil.

"I would still like you and Elena to think about it some more. We will leave you to talk and come back for an answer after you two talk," said Nick.

Outside the room, C.E. asked, "Nick why did you hold back on some of the tapes we have on his dad?"

"I did not want him to make his decision in a moment of anger. That tape will make him angry enough to want to kill his dad. Then later maybe regret taking the offer. No, he needs to make this just on what he knows now. I do not want a problem popping up later.

"This is a decision that will change their lives and will be hard to adjust to for them. Prison would have been easier on them in the long run. There they would not have had any choices to make. Those would have been made for them," said Nick

"That's why you told Elena what you did about her parents. That hard surface you display has a weak spot for lovers," said C.E.

"You joke, but I worked in witness protection as a marshal for two years. Some were average citizens who saw the wrong thing at the wrong time and others were low-level thugs who turned evidence on their bosses. It was not like the movies of witness protection. These people in Witness Protect have a hard time making a new life. Normal life itself is filled with normal problems and that is tough.

"Throw in a new identity and a past will just complicate the situation. Some are allowed to leave the program after the trial is over and others are in the program for life. I do have a soft spot for lovers, but these two are not just lovers. They have done very bad things and I want to get the people behind them, so I make compromises for the end that I am trying to get at. I will see that these two are watched and do mend their ways or their deal is broken." said Nick.

"I see you have a deeper knowledge of this than I do, and I agree with you. I was insensitive to joke about it," said C.E.

"Don't be silly, 'Black Humor' gets us through horribly bad situations we face every day. You know that from your time in the fire department and in the military. I just hope we are not moving over to the evil side," said Nick.

"What do you mean?"

"At times those of us trying to stop evil begin to follow the Machiavelli idea of the 'end justifies the means'. In other words, we commit evil to stop evil. At times like this, I feel we do that, and it bothers me. The 'Black Humor' helps with the doubt at times. For example, these two are no angels. Who knows what acts they have committed in the name of their religion." said Nick.

"Yea, I knew Black Humor was a way of coping. There were many conversations we had after a run that would shock the average person on the street. Those conversations could appear evil or incentive to others. But if it was not talked about and laughed over it would continue to mentally fester into deeper issues. Some of the runs never leave your memory. They are always some place deep down in there. The only good thing is that with time the memory of the event faded and was only brought up at times by a smell, image, or comment," said C.E.

"Yeah, we have all had those dreams — ask any combat vet. O.K., I think our new friends have had enough time to talk it over. Shall we go back in?"

As they entered the room Nick asked, "Well what have you decided?"

"I agree," said Elena.

"How about you Fazil?"

"I agree," said Fazil.

"Then now that you have accepted Fazil I want to play one more tape for you that we picked up in Panama. C.E. would you please turn on the tape? I did not want to play before to influence your decision in a fit of anger," said Nick.

The recorded started:

The first speaker:

Abdul what are you asking of me is dangerous and will cost if we find the prison he is being held in. However, we will need half the money upfront so that we can make the arrangements."

The second speaker:

"I know Pablo, the money has already been sent to the account. He must be silenced. He has gone after a woman who is no longer shall we say pure.

The first speaker:

"It will be done if we find him."

The second speaker:

"Make it painful!"

The first speaker:
>*"Abdul this is an American prison. Certain things can be done for a price, but there is a limit to what money can buy. Your son will be killed if he is found. That is all we can say."*

The second speaker:
>*"I understand. Keep me informed. Thank you for the effort."*

Nick turned off the tape machine. "Do you know who this Pablo is, Fazil? Do you understand what is being asked for?" asked Nick.

"YES!" Fazil yelled "The BASTARD OF A FATHER wants me dead and Elena worse than dead. Ask your questions! I will tell all I know. That Pablo is the number two or number three in Diego's operation."

CHAPTER FORTY-NINE

Placido Ramon de Torres was a stamp dealer who was an agent for Miguel Rodriguez's forgeries in the 1850's. He was arrested for forgery in 1886 in Bremen, Germany, and was found guilty of fraud and sentenced to seven months. Before the sentence could be carried out, he fled the country with his stock of forgeries. He was arrested once more in the United States in 1892 for failure to pay customs duties on his counterfeit stamps.

Then in 1893 he started a scheme with others to have Spanish military personnel in North Africa mail envelopes from Morocco with counterfeit stamps and official postmarks. This was to give the impression that the postage was paid with the cancellation marks. The military had free franking privileges. His plan was discovered, and Torres was then once more arrested in 1894.

GENUINE   **FORGERY**

We all have a monster; the difference is in the degree, not the kind.

— Douglas Preston

2002 THE PHONE CALL

"I have a call for you on line one," said an agent in the next room. Nick walked over and picked up the phone.

"Agent Thomson"

"Agent Thomson, this is special agent Juan Patterson in Panama. You asked to be notified of any calls to Abdul and we picked up one with a guy named Pablo. They set up a meeting in a coffee shop. We have a team on-site to listen in on their conversation. Is there anything you need us to do?"

"No. This is a major investigation so be careful not to get noticed and report the conversation as soon as you get it. This could be a much bigger problem than what we started with in the investigation," said Nick.

"You got it," said the agent.

That afternoon Pablo walked around the coffee shop looking for anyone or anything out of place. A ragged beggar was hanging around outside. In the shop, there was a couple in deep conversation holding hands and two very attractive women who looked like models from a photo shoot they were doing across the street. He went inside and sat by the window to observe the street. Moments later, Abdul walked in and sat without looking around.

"Abdul, are you just plain careless or something else?" asked Pablo.

"What are you implying? That I am stupid?" demanded Abdul.

"Take it however you want. First, you call me on the hotel phone for everyone and their mother to listen in on the call. I had to tell you to stop and meet me here. Then you walk right in as if nobody would dare to follow you. I think careless at best is the least I can say," said Pablo.

"Young man, I have been doing this for longer than you've been alive. I noticed everyone in this place and evaluated their need to be here and nothing looked out of place. So do not lecture me on security," said Abdul.

"I may be young, but I have been working at this for 24 of my 30 years of life. I am very good at my job also. Most of your work has been done without the United States agents breathing down your neck. So caution is a word to the wise. I have already tossed that phone you called me on, and I would suggest you toss yours also," said Pablo.

"I change phones every day," said Abdul.

"Good, now what can we do for you that will stop your attempts to move your opium through Panama? We do not want to start a drug war. The other cartels do not know what you are planning and if they find out it will be open warfare and not just these little scrimmages we have now and then. If that happens, you will be the first in line. So what do you want and let us come to a compromise we both can live with?" asked Pablo.

"Since 9-11, it has been difficult to get people into the U.S. without paying your outrageous prices. If we build a drug network out of Panama, our access will be made easier," said Abdul.

"You may think that, but once you open your network the cartel territory wars will begin and that is if not before. Nobody wins when that happens. So our compromise is that we will continue taking your people in now for no charge and just charge a small fee for any material you want to be smuggled into the States. If that is not acceptable to you, then the war starts once I leave this shop," said Pablo.

"Are you threatening me?" asked Abdul.

"Not at all. I am just relaying the facts of the situation in this country. You have your tribal conflicts in your world with a common enemy— the Western culture. We have a major organization, and they are strong but are not any better equipped in weapons than the Americans. Plus, the Americans are on our doorstep and not thousands of miles away. You start a cartel war here and the Americans will get involved and then nobody wins. Also, if you start this proposed new drag route you will be cut off from us at the very least," said Pablo.

"Then this is a fair compromise. I accept your offer. I have one personal request, if I may add it to the compromise," said Abdul.

"It depends on what that request is!" replied Pablo.

"I want your group to remove my son. He is a threat as I said on the phone," said Abdul.

"Yes, another security break. However, as I said it will cost," said Pablo.

"Yes, I believe he is being held somewhere in the Federal Correctional system. He has broken up with the family and is a threat to the group. The quicker the better for all concerned."

"Your son? He is of your blood. What has he done? It is not like a stepson or a relative by marriage or a wife. Is he a danger to us at the same time?" asked Pablo.

"No, it is about family honor. He has broken his oath of loyalty twice. Once by falling in love with a whore and second chasing after the whore," said Abdul.

"As I told you it may take some time to find him in whatever institution he is being held. Then one of our members who is serving a life term will take care of your request. If that is acceptable to you. You will be responsible for the payment to the family of the man who does the favor," said Pablo as they continued to talk about the removal of Abdul's son.

Abdul looked at Pablo at the end and said, "That is acceptable. However, it must not look like I or anyone in the family was the reason for his death. Is that understood?" asked Abdul.

"Yes, then good we have agreed to the compromise, and I will tell Diego it is a go. By the way, the stamps have become too hot and are of little value to us now so we will send those that were collected from the stamp dealer place back to you. The plates were ruined in the fire and were destroyed. So if there is no more, goodbye."

"Yes, and you may keep the stamps. Good-bye."

Pablo watched Abdul walk out watching the eyes of the other people in the café. Their eyes betray no interest in Abdul only then did Pablo stand and start to walk out. He noticed the couple who were in love got up to walk out in front of Pablo. They walked to the corner. Pablo followed them to see where they went. Just around the corner the couple got into a car and started to make out. The beggar was gone before Abdul left and the models were called over to the photo shoot. Pablo was satisfied and walked on.

Moments after Abdul and Pablo had left the coffee shop one of the models returned to the shop, reached under the table, and retrieved the device. She stepped outside and handed the recording to the beggar who came back out of the alley.

The beggar walked around the corner and over to the car with the couple and handed it to the woman. Later, a call was placed to Agent Nick Thomson.

"Agent Thomson this is Juan again I am sending you the recorded conversation from the coffee shop."

"Good work agent. This may be the break we need to break up Diego's operation down there. Thanks for the good work."

"One can only hope that Diego is smarter than the other drug lords. They use only brute force and Diego will use force only to make a point, but he can win local population and political leaders by more than just fear. That makes him more dangerous," said Juan.

"You are right about that. Again thanks for the help."

CHAPTER FIFTY

Harold Treherne was arrested with more than 400 dyes and plates for forging stamps and making overprints. He had produced several overprints on genuine stamps and different stamp forgeries. He is known for having produced the "Brighton '' forgeries. After his arrest in 1904, he pleaded guilty and the sentence was deferred. Then in 1917, new charges were brought against Treherne. This time he was charged with possession of counterfeiting instruments and found guilty and was fined. The next year the case was reopened and Treherne was given four months of hard labor and an additional month for failure to pay a previous fine.

GENUINE   **FORGERY**

Evil begins when you begin to treat people as things.

— Terry Pratchett

2002 ARREST IN MEXICO

The room was filled with American agents and Mexican Federal police as they held the last walk-through for the planned raid on the Diego organization once more.

"Gentlemen, we are going to raid the Diego storehouse at the waterfront in 2 hours. The objective is a shipment of opium that we believe is stored there. We all remember the last raid on Diego so let's be on our toes. Are there any questions and does everyone know his or her part in the raid?" asked Nick Thomson with his counterpart in the Federal Police Captain Alejandro standing in front of the room.

"Yes sir, the men in the room shouted together." Everyone in the room was happy to deliver a little payback for the last raid that killed one of their own.

"Stand easy men and relax, we have a few minutes before we need to move out," said Captain Alejandro as Representative Matias got up and walked out of the room. Then Nick pulled Alejandro aside, "Captain Alejandro may I speak with you for a moment. To prevent a leak, do the leaders of your teams know that the actual location of the raid will change as we leave the compound and there will be no radio contact?"

"Yes, once we leave this room all communications will be done with messenger runners. All these men are trusted members of this unit and they also believe Representative Matias was the leak on the failed raid on Diego's home. So no one will say anything around him," said the captain.

"Good! Let's take this guy down! If everything goes right, we will have a rat caught in the trap," said Nick. He turned to C.E. and said, "C.E. you can wait here until the house is secured."

"I don't think so! I have an interest and did not come along for a spectator's seat!" said C.E.

"Very well, I'll get you a vest," said the captain.

"I want to find those engraving plates and any more of the stamps. I do not want there to be a new flood of bogus stamps on the philatelist market," said C.E.

"That is O.K. with me but stay in the back until I give it all clear," said the captain.

"I will be the last person in. One question, how is Matias out of our embassy and safe with the cartels?" asked C.E.

"We had a rumor circulated that we had set him up and the cartels bought it and removed the hit," said Nick.

"Where is Matias now? I saw him at the start of the meeting," asked C.E.

"He left as soon as we finished the run down on the operation. As soon as he left the room he was followed into his office, where he made a call on a burner cell phone. Most likely to Diego. We will know when Diego's people head for the storehouse. We also taped Matias' office phone," said Alejandro.

"Perfect! Our spy in the sky just reported that Diego's men just left the house and are rushing to the waterfront. Send the runners, captain! We are a go," said Nick.

Within minutes the runners were running up to inform the team leaders that the new location of the raid changed to Diego's home once more. The new instruction was given to each member assigned to each group with smiles around.

"We leave in five minutes and the entry to the home will begin at 1500 hours with two squads at the wall on each side. One minute later the front and rear squads breach the gates and the helicopter will neutralize the men on the roofs. The tunnel squad will secure it to stop Diego's escape tunnel," said Nick.

Diego had sent most of the guards at his home to the waterfront to hold off the raid Representative Matias had just warned that the American and Federal police would hit the storehouse.

The raid on the house went like clockwork. On each side of the courtyard members of each assault team were over the wall before the cartel guards noticed. By the time the guards reacted to the walls the gates were smashed open, and three vehicles entered with men jumping out with guns firing at Diego's men.

Men on the roof were removed from the action by the helicopter that swooped in within 15 seconds of the initial attack. Diego ran out of the tunnel first and was grabbed by two police officers and shoved into a waiting vehicle. The family and two guards were arrested as they stepped out of the escape tunnel. Inside the house, the search had begun before the shooting stopped.

"C.E. over here I think these are what you are looking for and they are in good condition," said Nick.

"You know Nick, some forgers are real artists and many of them were stamp dealers as well in the past. These plates are real works of art. Most artists cannot leave their work unsigned, and this one was no different. See in the top corner he or she has initials hidden on each plate," said C.E.

"Then we can arrest him or her for forgery once we catch him or her. Why are we using all these pronouns?" asked Nick.

"Good question and the answer is the last few years women have begun entering the trade of forgery. Not many, but a couple are good."

"Why leave their initials when it will make their conviction more likely?"

"Arresting forgers is the easy part but proving guilt may be hard. All the engraver has to say is it was done as a work of art. That any stamps printed from them would have the word 'copy' stamped on each stamp before being sold as a piece of art or a historical copy. They were never made to send through the mail as postage. The world of stamp forgery has been in operation for over 200 years and forgers have been getting around the legal systems in every one of those nations. We may catch him or her, but successfully prosecuting is always in doubt," said C.E.

"C.E. sometimes you are a real downer after a great bust. Let's go talk to Alejandro?" said Nick.

"It was a good raid my friends and we have Matias on tape giving Diego a warning on the waterfront raid. He will be going to prison. I want to thank you. This means a lot to the team members of the last raid on this house that cost us two men injured and the loss of a good father to two kids and his wife.

Now, as agreed Diego was not captured in this raid, and I have no idea where he has gone. His family was picked up coming out of the escape tunnel with two bodyguards and are being detained. They did not see the capture of Diego. He rushed out of the tunnel two minutes before anyone else."

"Of course, he was a brave man trying to save his family," said Nick.

"Yes, he did not even put up a fight. He smiled and said he would be released within an hour and that the men who took him into custody were dead men. They just smiled at him and placed him in the van," said Alejandro.

"He is confident right now and that will help break him down when he sees the situation has changed and he has no friends," said Nick.

"The city will be a little quieter now Diego is out of the picture. That is until the other cartels realize there is no longer a Diego. We also have Mateo and Pablo along with several small-time members. I hope you have a safe trip home," said Alejandro.

"I hope this is not going to make your life difficult Alejandro," said C.E.

"Believe me, with Diego out of the picture the government and other cartels will be happy. There will be no blowback except it may take a little longer to get promoted. Some were on Diego's payroll that will resent the loss of their illicit income."

"Take care, Alejandro," said Nick.

"It has been a pleasure and you both have a safe trip home with your cargo."

"Well, now I have only one problem C.E. and that is Abdul and whatever he is planning. Let's hope that Mr. Diego may want to talk to Turkey for a little better location for his time in American custody. I believe his life behind bars in America will not sit well with other members of other cartels. He has been ruthless with them. They may want to take revenge," said Nick.

"Then let's get our passengers and go home," said C.E.

CHAPTER FIFTY-ONE

Geza Tarjan fled from Hungary to Paris when his counterfeits were exposed. In Paris, he was one of a possible 2,000 other stamp forgers. He made a good living off the counterfeits and forgeries and at times he produced more of the stamps than were officially printed. *The Congress of Federation des Societes Philateliques Francaises* in 1930 agreed the stamp price would be that of Tarjan's forgeries. Only once was Tarjan ever arrested and that was in Spain in 1934 for selling counterfeits. His stock of forgeries was confiscated.

GENUINE   **FORGERY**

Men never do evil so completely and cheerfully as when they do it from religious convictions.

— Blaise Pascal

2002 HOME OF ZENDA

Zenda's father stormed into the home, saw his wife, and yelled, "Where is Zenda?" with pure rage in his eyes.

"Locked in her room as you instructed me, my husband. Zenda is a good woman, please do not hurt her, Fardin!" cried her mother.

"Don't you ever dare tell me what I am to do and not to do with my children? You would do best to know your place and stay quiet. Our daughter has acted like a whore with that Russian pig. Our family's honor has been thrown in the mud and dragged through the streets. She must go to the Imam and confess her transgressions and beg for forgiveness. I will talk with her right now and she will go tomorrow to confess," demanded Fardin.

"You are sentencing our oldest daughter to death by stoning. You know the Imam in our community is a follower of the Islamic law in the strictest sense of the letter of the Quran. Zenda has said nothing happened and that they were planning on asking your permission to marry tonight, Fardin. They are in love!" said the mother.

"She only said that after she was caught and now our family is looked upon as a poor example for the followers of the prophet. This community is laughing at us. I must save the family's reputation for the sake of our other daughters. If this goes unpunished, they will not have a chance of finding themselves a good husband. I must think of the family," said Fardin.

"You are thinking of your position in the community— not the family. I know where you go on weekends, and I say nothing. Now, I do. You and others go and drink alcohol and have sex with young boys and girls, so do not tell me about family honor. The whole community knows what you do and what you are! They stay quiet out of fear of the Imam, you, and those evil brothers of yours," she said defiantly to Fardin.

As the last word left Isme's mouth she was knocked to the floor from a punch to the face by her husband and kicked in her side as she went down. She lay there sobbing as he continued to kick and yell at her. "Do not ever talk to me that way again or you will suffer the same fate as that whore daughter of yours," yelled Fardin as he grabbed her by the hair and dragged her to Zenda's room. Unlocking the door, he pushed his wife inside looking at Zenda with rage in his eyes.

"Zenda you will go to the Imam tomorrow and confess your behavior or I will take your mother with you and denounce you both as the whores. You have disgraced the family."

"I will not. I am not a whore father! Nothing happened between the Russian and me except to talk about asking you to permit us to marry!" yelled Zenda.

"I did not ask you to talk and tell you what you will do in the morning. Do not open that whore mouth of yours to soil me again!" said Fardin.

"I will not confess to something I have not done," said Zenda.

"I said, do not open that whore mouth of yours to me," he yelled while hitting her with his fist in the face. "You are a whore and have made the family lose our good reputation. I will drag you both to the Imam in the morning and testify that you are both whores, if you do not confess," said Fardin.

"You have no witnesses, and you need two witnesses according to the Koran and people know who you are, Father! Our family reputation is built on the fear of you and your evil brothers and that devil bastard you call a father," said Zenda.

He walked over to Zenda, grabbed her hair and pushed her into the wall next to her sobbing mother and kicked the mother once more. "Now take care of your mother. I think she has some broken ribs, and she is lucky that is all I gave her and you." He closed the door and locked it. The women cried in each other's arms until sleep came. Later, they woke up and talked and then fell back to sleep.

"I am a sorry mother. I have caused you this injustice and pain," said Zenda.

"It is not your fault my darling Zenda. He is an evil person just like his father and his brothers. They built their power by providing illegal Western goods to the various political and religious leaders. They would have their parties with the young people drinking alcohol with important members of the government.

"Then they took pictures with hidden cameras of all the participants so they could be blackmailed. They were individuals in high and low positions in the government and the brothers called the blackmail their little rewards for showing the individuals a good time.

"I went and tried to tell the Imam last month when I found some of your father's photos and showed them to Iman. He told me to go home and pray that I was wrong and that my father was a good man. He said your father was building a case of corruption against others and the photos were part of that case.

"Your father came home and demanded I turn over the photos and informed me that Imam had spoken to him and they agreed that I was a problem. That if I continued with these lies you and your sisters would be sold into the sex trade in Eastern Europe. Imam is part of your father's group. I looked again at the photos when I came home, and the Imam was in a photo with a young boy. I did not see him the first time.

"You are not the cause of this. It was only a matter of time before your father found a way to remove me as the threat to his political future. I think he is the reason for your young man to be sent back to Russia. Your father is using this to remove me, and I am the one who is sorry you got caught in this mess," said her mother.

"We can tell everyone and stop this," said Zenda.

"Imam and your father will see to it that we are not heard. I am so sorry," her mother said.

"Oh, mother, I did not know. What about my poor sisters? What will he do with them?" asked Zenda.

"They are young. Let's pray it stops with us,"

"We have to get away from here," said Zenda.

"Where would we go?"

"There must be some good people to help us."

"I am afraid the community is too terrorized by your father and his brothers. Plus, they are too afraid of that evil Imam to take any action.

"Remember last summer when the young man accused the Imam of breaking Islamic laws? The next day he was arrested and never seen or heard of again. Nobody in the village ever spoke of him again. Evil has taken hold of the country and the people. What we believe to be a good revolution is to save our culture under the guidance of Ayatollah Ruhollah Khomeini. He came to power and removed the Shah Mohammed Reza Pahlavi and placed these fanatics in power that fed themselves first. Yes, and I was part of this new régime that turned into a corrupt institution of evil men. Oh, my poor Zenda, we are in the hands of the Prophet now."

CHAPTER FIFTY-TWO

S. Allan Taylor was known as the "Prince of Forgers" for the number of fakes and forgeries that he created in the 19th Century. He was identified as the ringleader of the 'Boston Gang' and indicted three different times - 1887, 1890, and 1891 with the sentences dropped or deferred each time. He soon stopped working in the stamp trade altogether around 1892.

FORGERY

Evil is easy and has infinite forms.

— Blaise Pascal

2002 ROMANIA THE RESCUE 2002

The Russian group landed in Romania so that the operation would not be traced back to Russia. This was a group of special forces soldiers and some members of the largest gang in Russia. They were standing in a building on the abandoned airfield.

"Alright before we leave, I want everyone on the same page with this operation. We are flying to the eastern part of Turkey then we load into the Iranian Shabaviz coppers to fly into Iran. Any questions?"

"Why are we flying in the Shabziz, they are poorly engineered American Bell Hilo's?" asked one of the young commandoes.

"The same reason we are dressed in Iranian uniforms. There is to be no connection to Russia on this mission. Once we land, we are to grab the woman named Zenda without harming her. The father is to be killed as if by a vengeful father of a young boy. Is that understood?" asked the team leader.

"Yes!" they all replied.

"How are we to make it look like a vengeful father?" asked the young members of the group.

"How old are you?"

"I just turned 19, Sir!"

"That explains it!"

"What?"

"You are so young you do not remember how we treated our enemies under the old Soviet system. We would cut off his manhood and place it wherever people would notice it to make a point. We wanted to send a message to the family and community. I think I will assign you that job. What is your name?"

"Ivan, sir, thank you for the honor!"

"Young man, you might want to rethink what honor is. Alright everyone, let's load up. We are off to Iran and the home of Zenda, whoever she is!" said the leader.

The Iranian-marked helicopter landed just outside the small town in the dark and made the trip to the home of Zenda in less than 30 minutes. The group was dressed in Iranian uniforms with papers identifying the operation as a training exercise to reduce exposure and cause alarm if they were discovered. They moved through the town quickly. Nobody noticed or wanted to notice the group as it moved through the community.

At the home Zenda, a member of the team opened the front door quietly and slipped into the home. The first door they tried to open was locked with a key still in the door. One member of the team quietly unlocked the door and opened it. They stepped inside and found two women huddled in fear against the wall — Zenda and her mother holding each other in their arms. The team leader placed a finger to his lips.

"Be quiet and no harm will come to you. Where is the woman called Zenda, she has a friend in Russia who wants to save her life?" asked the team leader.

"I am Zenda and this is my mother." Both women stood up with a smile and hugged the man.

"My father is going to have both of us stoned to death in the morning. My sisters are also in danger," said Zenda.

"We must hurry and were told to only take you," replied the team leader.

"Then I cannot leave!" said Zenda.

"Yes, you must go with them. Your sister and I will be fine. I will deal with your father," said the mother.

"Listen we are in a hurry here and I have one more question. Where is your father?"

"Why?" asked the mother.

"We are to deal with him before we go," said the team leader as he looked at the mother. He wondered if she would be a problem.

"I will show you," said the mother and walked out the door. The house was quiet. The mother pointed to the bedroom door, two men entered the room, and the mother followed. They found Fardin lying in bed with a bottle of vodka on the table. He opened his eyes as the blade entered his chest. His mouth tried to scream, and no sound came out. Then as Ivan prepared to do his job, the mother stepped between the body of her husband and that of Ivan. The team leader started to step in and then just let it play out.

"I will do that. Give me the knife. I will teach him not to disgrace the family and beat his wife." She carved a message on Fardin's chest about young boys and then did the deed to his private part, placing it in his mouth. She turned and handed the blade back to the young man and smiled.

Ivan stood there looking at the older woman and took the knife back. The mother turned to her daughter. They both hugged.

"We need to go now!" said the team leader.

"Goodbye my dear daughter, you and the young man have a good life," said the mother. She turned to the team leader, "Tie me up. It will be alright. That bastard left enough damage to my body. There will be no questions except to ask who did this evil thing."

They tied her up and then the team took Zenda with them and left the house.

The next morning the youngest daughter woke up and found her mother tied up on the floor in the kitchen. The screams brought the other daughters into the kitchen. As they were cutting the ropes from her, they were crying and asked, "What has happened Mother? What happened mother?"

The mother looked at the girls after she was free of the rope, "Stay right here! Do not move from here!" She ran to her bedroom and then turned and ran into the street screaming that her husband had been killed by a strange man, who said what he did was to revenge what happened to his son at the hands of this monster.

She said he knocked her down and tied her up before the killing. She laid on the floor all night tied up and her daughters found her when they woke up and untied her. She then ran to the bedroom and found her husband dead and she left him as he was and ran to get help.

Men ran into the home and then came out with the daughters. "He is dead!" they said.

The village later was told of the message that was left on the body and that there was alcohol in the room. Then the resentment of Fardin surfaced and those who supported him became targets of that resentment. The

Imam stood in the back away from the anger of the community. He had lost his most important ally and he turned and went to his home.

The community of women gathered around Isme and her daughters to comfort them. Zenda was never mentioned again.

The Imam and his home were the target of insults after a photo of him was mysteriously circulated throughout the village. The Imam left the village the next week saying he had to care for his grandfather in the South. No one told him goodbye.

CHAPTER FIFTY-THREE

Philip Spiro, the head of the Spiro Brothers lithographic firm in Germany, produced a large variety of bogus stamps. When the philatelic press refused to take his advertisements, he started *Der Deutsche Brief-market-Sammler* to advertise his products.

To help control the flood of these Spiro forgeries on the market that the advertisements made possible, the philatelic community published the 'Spud Papers' in the *Philatelist* in 1871. There were more than 400 forgeries that were exposed to alert collectors.

GENUINE   **FORGERY**

The function of wisdom is to discriminate between good and evil.

— Marcus Tullius Cicero

2002 THE REUNION

Pyotr was waiting for the plane when two vehicles drove up next to him. Two men got out of the front car and told Pyotr to go over and get in the car with his grandfather. Pyotr opened the rear car door and looked in.

"Get in Pyotr we need to talk," said Mikhail.

"Why have you come, Grandfather? I am grateful for all you have done to save Zenda, but you are a busy man and did not need to come."

"As I said, we need to talk, and I wanted to meet this woman who has caused you so much anguish. Pyotr, I will be going back to Russia and you and Zenda will be going to America tonight."

"What? Why?"

"This was a very dangerous, if not stupid, thing on my part. We staged the whole thing from here to hide any connection with Russia. If anyone investigates the operation, it will be traced to thugs in Romania and Turkey. However, if you and Zenda go back to Russia, people will talk, and word may get back to those in Iran that Zenda is alive and in Russia and married to my grandson.

"From now on you are to use the English pronunciation of your name 'Peter' and Zenda will now be called Zoe. You both will be married tonight with the new family name of Devin. Here are your passports and the paperwork allowing you both refugee status to the United States. Memorize the information on the plane," said Mikhail.

"I do not know if she will be willing to do all of this?"

"She has been told on the plane and has agreed to everything. It seems she is as in love with you as you are with her. You both are never to contact anyone from your past again. Is that understood?"

"Yes, but?"

"No there is no BUT about it. If I want to contact you, I will. Nobody else."

"Why?"

"Because Zenda's father was more of an important person than he appeared. His father and family formed a very powerful group of extremists who were expanding their power in the government. The two other brothers are very big in the government. I have placed evidence in this episode that may expose their activity, but I doubt it for that government is as corrupt as the old Soviet Union.

"While we sit here, there are people all over her home looking for evidence of who was responsible for the killing and the message left on the body. The Imam was making noise about the mother to the officials. Then the father's office was searched and the discovery of photos linking the Imam and others to blackmail. The investigators removed the Imam from their report.

"The mother has played her part well and is still hysterical and under a doctor's care. The investigation is now centered on a revenge killing from another family. They just do not know which one for there is a large number of candidates. The discovered photos have caused a major internal problem for those in power. They are running for cover and the best thing will be to ignore any further investigation.

"There is nothing to link any of the operations to us. However, these people have long memories. One brother is in State security as a section head and the other brother is a high-ranking general in the military. We cannot take a chance of a leak that will expose both of you or lead back to our organization," said Mikhail.

"I understand and thank you, grandfather."

"I must be getting weak in the head in my old age. It is good that you leave. Word of this could ruin my reputation as a strong leader."

"You are still a strong leader and with a big heart," said Peter.

"The plane is pulling up to the hanger. Now go see the package you've been waiting to hold. Hurry for we have a wedding to attend before your flight to your new home," said Mikhail.

Peter got out of the car and walked towards the plane. The first few people out were men and then they were almost knocked over by a small rushing object that jumped into Peter's arms. After a few minutes of crying and kissing, Peter walked Zenda over to his grandfather.

"Grandfather, I want you to meet Zenda," said Peter as he was hit in the arm by Zenda.

"My name is Zoe and if you are to be my husband you must learn my name, Peter!"

"I like this woman, Peter. She will make something of you yet."

"Thank you for coming to save me. My father was threatening to have me, and my mother stoned as whores this very morning. My mother and I would not be alive right now if those men had not come. My mother surprised me. I thought she was weak and afraid of my father. I was wrong, she was afraid of a system that did not allow her freedom," said Zoe.

"Peter, I think this woman will fit right into the American lifestyle. There, I hear the women are also telling their husbands what to think. Now, it is time to get married and send you two on your way. Zoe, I do not have an Imam for an Islamic wedding. I am sorry. I only have an Orthodox priest," said Mikhail.

"That is fine with me if it is with Peter."

"Anything she wants is fine with me."

"Peter, I have given you a list of influential people that will help you establish a reputation in finance once you are in America. Then you can help us with our plan."

"How can I help if I am in America? What plan?"

"We want to expand our organization over there. Times are changing and the lines between the nation-states have become blurred with multi-national companies. There is a character flaw in the American capitalist system. The capitalists chase the dollar and not power," said Mikhail.

"Are they not the same? asked Zoe.

"No! For us, power is money and for them money is power," said Mikhail.

"What do you mean? They are the same!" said Zoe.

"No, they are not. Power always gets money and money will not always get power. Many Americans have money and have no real idea of how to use power. So, when they spend money, they think they have power," said Mikhail.

"Yes, that is true. I have seen that in my own country," said Zoe.

"Power is the use of authority and Lenin knew how to use power with authority. He was a master at getting people to follow even when it was not in their own best interest. His slogan 'Peace, Land and Bread' pulled a nation into a totalitarian state with the promise of freedom from their masters. Lenin knew you could give hungry people potatoes and then you would have willing followers.

"Lenin used a political model much like a religion as an example for his new form anti-religious form of government. His new government held the promise of hope to the masses. The religious model provided organization, rituals, and ceremonies for the people to participate in while waiting for a better life. They become believers that Hell was the alternative for those with bad faith. At the same time, the religious leaders continued to live in pomp and circumstance.

"Yes, Lenin was a master of power and knew how to control it. He built a system with one built without a spiritual religion and Hell was replaced with social terror and purges. When Lenin died, he was replaced by a Troika. One of them was Stalin who studied Lenin and expanded what Lenin started.

"Stalin wiped out millions of Kulaks when he collectivized farming in the 1920's. Then during the Great Purges, millions or more of his opposition were removed. Stalin built the perfect bureaucratic killing machine. He outperformed in the number of killings that Hitler had done. Stalin's killing focused on his people. Some estimate Stalin may have killed as many as twenty million Russians during his reign of terror."

"I am sorry to interrupt Grandfather, you said we were to expand our organization. How do I do that in America?" asked Peter.

"Oh! Yes, I was reviewing history. You will help by attacking the flaws in their society. Learn from the old Soviet Union during the Cold War. They set out to undermine the capitalistic society with liberal ideas. Only their plan backfired and came about with the fall of the Soviet Union. There was no longer a need for the Right to resist the Left in America — the enemy was gone. It is very funny to see Western intellectuals today go about expressing the values of the Soviet Union in their idea of real socialist ideas of equalitarian beliefs. The historian Howard Zinn's book on the creation of America, for example, made the Americans look like bad colonizers controlled by the greed and hate of others. In time it will only get more difficult to argue against the Left in the American and Western European universities.

"All of these Americans on the left that expressed the socialist ideas lived in the best places and many had servants as they pushed their ideas of socialism. They act just as the Soviet leadership did while they lived in their Dacha. These Western liberals believed in the image that the Soviet Union placed in front of the world. They tended to see socialism as superior to capitalism regardless of the evidence that was in plain sight from Gulags to long lines in stores for food. Yet, we are glad this Western socialist was bought into the socialist idea. We plan to use it," said Mikhail.

"How?" asked Peter.

"Simple education is the key. Just as the Catholic Church did with indigenous populations and dissenters. Take the children and educate them in the new ways. Destroy the value of the belief system and you crush the philosophy behind it – Capitalism is Evil and Socialism is Good. American power will collapse just as the Soviet Union collapsed.

"The Soviet Union started its commitment to bring down the West in the universities. Look at America today with many ethnic individuals who have made a good life in business and education. Yet, they complain that their ethnic group is not given a fair chance at success. The system they complain about did its best to see they were given a chance over many others in the same situation. We will use that to push the idea that socialism is an equal and better way of life. Give a poor man a dollar and he will be a follower of the new American Way of life."

"Then what grandfather? We are a powerful syndication that works within and outside the legal system," said Peter.

"That is true and so are international corporations and governments. Those corporations have helped governments make laws and rules. Then they turn around and find ways to get around those same laws. A few years from now our country will be in the hands of a few members of the old KGB with our help and influence. We need to expand in a changing world to one of Globalism.

"One last thing Peter, here is a bank account for you to hold until you can work or both of you start to work. I did not forget you, Zoe. You are going to be an American woman!" said Mikhail.

"I am an American woman, you old dinosaur," Zoe said as she hugged him and kissed him.

After the wedding and the couple were gone, the team held a debriefing in the hangar.

"The operation went as planned. Nothing was left behind except one part of the plan had a deviation," said the team leader.

"What was that?" asked Mikhail.

"The mother, my God, what a tough woman. Her husband had beat her and kicked her and I am sure she had broken ribs and lost a tooth or two. We offered her treatment, and she said no that she needed it to be able to say that whoever broke in and killed her husband did it to her. At times she could barely take a step.

"Then when Ivan was starting to leave the message, the mother stopped him and said she would do it. She carved the message we plan to leave afterward. She told me when she was young, she remembered the messages the Soviet Army left with informers and others. She smiled as she did the deed," said the team leader.

"Did you leave the evidence that would suggest the Imam was behind the attack?" asked Mikhail.

"Yes, it will take a few days of going through all the papers. It will also link the two brothers and his close friends, who are also linked to the rest of the family. We should know in a few days. The Fardin brothers will be watched closely by the leadership. It was unexpected that they found the photos and that should help with our plan to bring down the group."

"This little rescue mission allowed us to take care of a much bigger problem. We were able to remove the head of their security and make it look like it was one of their people. It may also bring down a powerful group inside the country. Plus, at the same time help my grandson. Not a bad night's work," said Mikhail.

CHAPTER FIFTY-FOUR

The individual Hazzonpotas had purchased, sometime around 1924, the original Serbian 1880 government plates (of a set of stamps) that had been liberated by Bulgarian troops during the Great War. Then Hazzonpotas was arrested in Paris while arranging the reprinting of the stamps. The plates, reprints, and forged stamps of Georgia, Russia, and Serbia were confiscated.

GENUINE

FORGERY

He who gives away shall have real gain. He who subdues himself shall be free; he shall cease to be a slave of passions. The righteous man casts off evil, and by rooting out lust, bitterness, and illusion do we reach Nirvana.

— Buddha

2002 THE CHINA NETWORK MEETING

"Well, Abdul it would seem your plan to punish the Americans is falling apart. The raid on the Mexican Diego cartel was a setback. Then your contact in the Iranian security service was murdered by a vengeful father for the sexual assaults on that father's young son. That is the report I was given on the subject. Plus, your son has been arrested in the United States and you lost a woman in Spain. Now why should we continue our agreement with your organization?" asked leader He.

"Like all good plans, one has to adjust," said Abdul.

"Yes, China has adjusted for hundreds of years. At different times we were invaded by stronger people and we adjusted by turning them into Chinese. The Moguls broke through the Great Wall and, yet, in time The Great Kublai Khan was more Chinese than most Chinese.

"The Moguls were followed by the Manchu, who also became Chinese. Then the European powers started to grab ports along the coast. Once we threw off the monarchs and formed a republic, the Japanese invaded and took Manchuria and began a long war with us before the Europeans began their Second World War. After that war, we took charge in 1949 and China is on its way to becoming the leader in world trade. So! Do not tell me about the need to adjust," said Leader He.

"I did not mean any disrespect. I was only saying that things begin to fall apart once they are set in motion. Then you can either pick up and go home or you can adjust to the new situation," said Abdul.

"Again, you insult. China has and is playing the long game. While you Moslems fight over that little bit of land in the Middle East, China plays calculated gambles. We have been fighting and winning with India over the Ladakh area. We have taken Tibet, occupied the Parcel Islands from Vietnam, and around the Johnson South Reef in the Spratly Islands. We are playing the long game.

"We focus on the economic road into political control. We will expand the Silk Road into a network that leads back to China. Before America and Europe know, China will be the leading world power," said leader He.

"The U.S. business and economic world is falling apart. Thousands of bankruptcies and defaulting on debt show that the American economy is in free fall and will not recover. Now is the time to cause chaos to create an unstable political environment. I can create that instability," said Abdul.

"How do you plan to do that?" asked Leader He.

"The dirty bomb that you plan to detonate in the Los Angeles harbor - Abdul?" interjected Mayor Bo.

"It is one of the busiest ports in America and shutting it down will cause a blockage of shipping coming from Asia," said Abdul.

"See that is what I mean about your thinking in short terms. You will only slow down their exporting and importing trade. The Americans adjust very quickly. What needs to be done is to attack their morality and their belief that they are special people. Destroy their ideas of their role in the world with culture and economic chaos. Make them think their way of life is a failure and then we win the game," said leader He.

"How would you suggest we play the long game?" asked Abdul.

"I believe you are asking that question in sarcasm, but I will answer it anyway. Many in your world already are playing the long game by educating the West in Islamic history," said Mayor Bo.

"What do you mean?" asked Abdul.

"Well, when you began to introduce Islamic History to American schools you implied that the Crusaders were the aggressors and murderers of all they saw. Never mention the fact that the Islamic world was in expansion at the time and invading every part of the Mediterranean world.

"By suggesting that Crusaders were the aggressor, that started to undermine the basic principles of their Western history that the Crusaders were saving Jerusalem from the Islamic invaders. Your way into the system was you offered these lessons for free as a cross-culture historical understanding. A few years from now, their youth will question their traditional history. They will see the Crusaders as the barbarians, not the Moslems.

"Slavery will become an American problem and America is responsible for its expansion. They will ignore that you, the Arabs, were in the African slave trade long before the Europeans entered the trade. They will ignore the fact that slavery is still a major issue in the Arab world today. That is the long game, Abdul."

"I see your point and will think about what you have said, but for now I need the materials I have asked about."

"You will have all of it from North Korea in the next few days. It will be shipped in the next shipment to Iran. All of our conditions have been met and completed and the payments have been made so have a safe trip home Abdul."

"Thank you both for your time," said Abdul as he got up and walked to the door followed by Mayor Bo.

"Mayor Bo, one moment please, we need to meet with Ying in five minutes. Abdul, it was good to see you once more, and have a safe trip back to Iran," said Leader He.

"Until the next time gentlemen, peace be with you," said Abdul.

Later, in Ying's office, the three men sat, and Leader He said, "I think the situation has changed and we need to adjust."

"I agree," said Ying.

"Those fanatics will never learn that blunt force is always met with blunt force. The ones that are bigger and stronger almost always win. We should give them this last shipment and then cut the ties with that group for they are a loose cannon. Their whole network has begun to collapse, and he does not know it. We listed all the things that just went wrong in his organization, and he still thinks everything is in play," said Mayor Bo.

"You are right. That group is or has fallen apart, which brings me to our people in the United States. I want to bring Professor Quig into a more active role. Instruct Su Wu to have Professor Quig look into Professor Clark's research papers more deeply. She can take photos of the work. It will verify the information we get from Professor Clark. We need to get Professor Quig further under our control," said the leader.

"Oh, I added one thing to the shipment that was being sent to Iran for Abdul. I had the team place a tracer device in it so we would know where they were going. We can prepare for whatever their action will be and when," said Ying.

"Good! There is no sense in leaving anything to chance. If they are setting off a dirty bomb, I do not want our people exposed during or after the fact," said Leader He.

"What should we do with our people in North Korea?" asked Ying.

"What do you mean?" asked Mayor Bo.

"Leave them there or bring them home?" said Ying.

"Let us wait and see what happens next. Their rocket program is a nice deflection off of our moves," said Leader He.

CHAPTER FIFTY-FIVE

Harry C. Heindel worked for the U.S. Postal Service and was a part-time stamp dealer. He was arrested in 1972 for the forgery of stamps and documents from the American Philatelic Society that certified the stamps. On searching his home there were several counterfeit and forged stamps from foreign countries. In 1973 Harry pleaded guilty and was fined $500 and given a two-year probation on condition he stopped any philatelic activity.

GENUINE

FORGERY

There are only two mistakes one can make along the road to truth; not going all the way, and not starting.

— Buddha

2002 OPPOSITION TO REGIME IN CHINA

U.S. Embassy Peru:
"Excuse me, Ambassador, I am sorry to rush in without knocking, we have a message from the June 4th group that should be sent to Washington right now," said the CIA agent.

"Send it and then come right back and bring me up to date," said the Ambassador.

"This may take a while if they want clarification."

"No matter what time it is, come back. I will make the time."

"Yes sir."

Later, at dinner that night an aid approached the table and whispered into the Ambassador's ear. He stood up and told the table, "If you, ladies and gentlemen, will excuse me for a little bit, I have a call from Washington waiting for me." Then he walked out of the room.

"I am sorry Ambassador, Washington wanted clarification and I had to brief agent Thomson on what we know about this subject and the individual Abdul."

"Tell me what is happening and give me some background. Start from the top."

"Well, in 1989 the Soviet communist world looked to be in a free-fall collapse. The Soviet Union, East Germany, and the rest of the Eastern Bloc countries were in turmoil. One communist nation fell to demonstrations, then it was one right after another - Poland, East Germany, Hungary, Bulgaria, Romania, Czechoslovakia, and the Baltic States within three years all independent from Soviet Russian power. Soon, the Soviet Union dissolved into independent states.

"Mikhail Gorbachev had paid a visit to China during this time and Chinese students were demonstrating in Beijing at the death of Hu Yaobang, who was a good reformer. The Chinese students and workers were demonstrating in Tiananmen Square. The workers in cities joined with the students and stopped the movement of military troops to the

Square at the time. When the Communist leadership refused to meet with the students, the students began a hunger strike.

"The government moved tanks up to the protesters. Then when the tanks started to enter the Square an image of a lone man with two shopping bags stood in front of a single column of tanks to block their movement forward. That image was broadcast around the world. As the first tank moved to go around the lone man, he moved with it. It was inspiring."

"I remember that I was with a missionary group in central Africa at the time. We did not have television at the site, but I did see photos in the papers," said the Ambassador.

"As the demonstration continued, the students went on to construct a statue of the 'Goddess of Democracy' that looked like another woman holding a torch. The Chinese government finally decided they had enough and declared martial law and crushed the demonstrator at night. The military kept the Western cameras away. A few images that did get out that night showed the real brutality of the regime that was committed in the square that night.

"Anyways, out of this chaos of that night, a group of those opposed to the ruling class in China formed and they named themselves the June 4th movement. They aimed to bring the truth to the Western world. The official death toll by the government cannot be trusted. They claimed around 300 lost lives. The June 4th group who looked at first-hand reports and hospital records say the number is in the thousands.

"The students go on to claim that many of the student leaders have disappeared or are unaccounted for with just seven of their leaders escaping to the West. The young man with the shopping bags has also been lost to history.

"This event caused a delay for the Chinese government to enter into the World Trade Organization until 2001, which is now causing an economic boom in the economic free zone in China, where a form of capitalism is allowed.

"As far as we know the government has broken up the June 4th group up many times, but it is still functioning and is exposing government policies to the western society. Nobody knows the names of these people or how they get their information. The information just shows up in various locations to be passed on to this office. We don't even know how it gets here.

"There is a question that it may be a trap or misdirection by the Communist party leadership. However, I think it is a real group trying to warn the West of the troubles inside China," said the agent.

"Have we been given reliable information?" asked the Ambassador.

"Many times, a lot of it is just information on re-education camps or how the military is connected to different businesses in the world of high technology. A report on a North Korean re-education camp was leaked to a Western newspaper the other day from the group."

"What do we know about the group?" asked the ambassador.

"I do not think it is a group in the normal sense. I see it as a loose group of individuals that resist the actions of the Communist Party. There is a song that may be an anthem for youth or the group in China."

"What song is it?"

"*Yi Wu Suo You* in English it is (*Nothing to my Name*)."

"Well, what was this latest message?"

"It said that material for a dirty bomb was being or has been sent to Iran. There was talk around the loading area of the material that was shipped had tracking devices placed in it. That same shipment was headed to America after it arrived in Iran.

"Plus, there was a note given to the loading boss that said this was the last shipment to this group. They were to receive and give this material to an individual named Abdul and this organization was being dropped from any further contact with China after this delivery."

"Loose talk, loose security in a tightly controlled society like China. I can only imagine how much information is floating around our security locations. Well, we have done our part and sent it on to the people in the know. That is all we can do. Thanks for the briefing. What records of this have been kept?"

"Nothing, my orders came from Washington. They said to keep no records on this at all."

"Good, this is delicate and loose lips and wandering eyes leak secrets. Again thank you for the briefing."

"My pleasure Ambassador."

"One last question. Why here?" asked the Ambassador.

"I cannot answer that because I do not know. My best guess is that the message is passed through many locations before it falls on our doorstep. This country has a large population of Chinese from anti-Chinese riots in Indonesia. The individuals that fled the Tiananmen Square Massacre turned up in Hong Kong and Australia and of these, a few drifted here."

"Are we the only site receiving this information from the June 4th movement?"

"I do not think so! There is tight security on the messages and source from Washington."

"O.K. keep me informed," said the ambassador.

"I am sorry sir, my orders are to forget everything except to notify you of the message when they come into my office. Washington is keeping this limited to very few individuals and we are just part of the message system. What I have told you is my understanding of the June 4th movement. I could be completely off base with my summary of the events. I wanted to bring you up-to-date on my conversation with agent Thompson."

"Well, then we have done our part. I better get back to my dinner guest."

CHAPTER FIFTY-SIX

Sigmund Freud was the proprietor of a celebrated postal museum in Austria. He sold excellent forgeries that were discovered when he sold an 1856 scarlet Mercury stamp of Austria. After the controversy, he was made to make restitution to certain customers. Then the Austrian courts in 1899 ordered him to make restitution to all parties that he had sold forgeries to. *The London Philatelist* said he was the shrewdest swindler of the 19th Century.

GENUINE

FORGERY

Don't be in a hurry to chase one evil for another.

— Aesop

2002 Interview with Diego

They stood looking into the interview room from the room next door, C.E. turned to Nick and said, "That is one piece of human evil sitting there like he does not worry about the world."

"That is because he has been able to buy or intimidate people to get whatever it is that he wanted. He is responsible for far too many murders and rapes in Mexico. He was, until today, the worst of the cartel leaders only in that he was smarter. Now he is just a prisoner in the custody of the United States government. Shall we go in and inform him that his world has changed," said Nick as they walked to the next room.

"Good Morning, Diego," said Nick as he entered the room.

Diego tried to stand up, but the cuffs would not allow him to stand up to his full height of 5 foot 6 inches. "I want a lawyer. I'll have you sent to the darkest hole in hell for kidnapping me and bringing me to your country against my will."

"Now you may have a problem with that threat Diego since your government signed the paperwork for you to enter the United States. It was all done with legal authority. Your government wants you out of the country, because of your drug smuggling and other criminal activities.

"I also think that another cartel was maybe behind your removal from Mexico, but what do I know about the political operations in Mexico's politics? I do know if the Mexican police that were with us on the raid of your home had their way you would be hanging from a bridge by now," said Nick.

"One other little thing Diego. It seems that you are here with the main charge of conspiracy to commit terrorism as well as ordering the death of an American agent," said C.E.

"You will have to prove that I had anything to do with that murder and torture of the agent," said Diego.

"See, C.E. he is innocent of the lesser charge and ignored the terrorism charge. I would have said terrorism and not said anything about the knowledge of the murder of an American agent. Instead, he said murder and torture of that agent and we only said death. Do you think he already knew it was murder and torture and that there was a terrorist plot?" asked Nick.

"Maybe he thinks the terrorism charge is not real or he is ignorant of what Abdul was planning. What do you think?" asked C.E.

"Should we tell him that we have witnesses to both the terrorism and murder?" asked Nick.

"You two idiots are bluffing and have nothing on me," replied Diego.

"Well, that political person who called you and told you about the undercover agent has confessed. Plus, the thug you had burned down the printing store has made a complete confession and told us about your part in Abdul's plan to plant a dirty bomb in the United States," said Nick.

"What is the matter Diego, have you lost your speech?" asked C.E.

"GO TO HELL!" yelled Diego.

"We are going to send you on ahead Diego!" said Nick.

"We are going right now to talk to our other guest and maybe you will feel more likely to talk with us then," said Nick as he and C.E. walked out the door.

"What do you think C.E., will he help?" asked Nick when they were in the hallway.

"No, he has been a drug lord for too many years and was able to buy his way out of anything. He still holds on to that idea as the cell door is unlockable in whatever hellhole he is sent. I just hope it's the worst prison in the U.S. or if we are lucky Cuba."

The two men walked down the hall to the next room, where Fazil and Elena. Nick opened the door and both men walked in.

"Fazil and Elena, we have a few new questions for you. Remember our agreement is total cooperation and the truth," said Nick.

"Do not worry we will not break the agreement," said Elena, and Fazil shook his head in agreement.

"Alright, do you know a security head in Iran by the name of Rahbar?"

"Yes, my father worked very closely with him. He was very important in the government and lived very modestly. His children were all given good jobs and his oldest daughter is a scientist of some kind," said Fazil.

"Yes, and she is very beautiful. Her father is a very ruthless and callous person. I saw him laugh at the death of a small dog that was hit by a truck when he was at a camp I trained at," said Elena.

"Did he have plans with Diego?" asked Nick.

"I do not know — my father was the link to that part of the operation.

Diego would get the explosives that were sent from Rahbar and then he passed the material along to others, who would then deliver them to the bombmaker," said Fazil.

"What were the stamps for? asked C.E.

"They were to be given to certain people in Iran and other countries as legitimate stamps. The stamps provided real value without money being exchanged at the time. This was a scam Rahbar planned with my father. The Chinese, Iranians, and leaders in North Korea are big stamp collectors, I guess. The stamps were a lot easier for us to make payment with instead of cash. Banks keep records of large transactions.

"Then the word came back that the printer was not following orders. He was printing more sheets than we required of him. A coin and stamp store Abdul had set up reported that the printer had been asking questions about the price of the stamps we had printed.

"Diego panicked and sent one of his thugs to take care of the printer, who we believed now was printing more sheets than he was told to print. As I was told, it was the stamp dealer who told him to print the extra sheets."

"Why do you say that?" asked Nick.

"The thug told his contact up here that the stamp dealer confessed it to him before the dealer died. That is what I heard Diego tell my father."

"Why did he not kill the printer?" asked C.E.

"Simple, the thug did not know where the printer lived. He had started with the printing shop, grabbed the printing plates then went to the stamp shop next door after torching the print shop. At the stamp shop, he was rushed because the fire from the printing shop was spreading faster than he planned. He said the stamp dealer died after he was pushed into the little office. That is what I was told," said Fazil.

"O.K. that fits with what we already know. Now, Elena, what can you tell us about the dirty bomb?" asked Nick.

"I was told there was more than enough material for more than just one bomb," said Elena.

"That is true, but Abdul was planning on just setting off one and saving the rest of the material for a later attack," said Fazil.

"Do you know the location for the placing of the bomb and when was Abdul planning to set it off?" asked Nick.

"He never told anyone his plans. He did not trust anyone. One day, he did make a slip and said the angels would come home here when we were in Los Angeles. I had the feeling he had big plans for the city," said Elena.

"My father was always talking about the big ports. That they were the key to disrupting the American trade markets," said Fazil.

"O.K. thanks. That is enough for today," said Nick.

"Why don't we see what our other guest has to say about the new information?" asked C.E. outside the room.

"Good idea," said Nick as they walked down the hall to Diego's interview room and entered.

"Well, Diego, what do you know about Abdul's plan to set off a dirty bomb?" asked Nick.

"I know nothing about a dirty bomb and where it will be set off in L.A. Get me a lawyer!"

"Thanks for the tip. Nobody mentioned L.A. as the location of Diego, but you just did. I find that very interesting. I have an idea, Nick! Why don't we take Diego to the L.A. Harbor while we investigate the area? asked C.E.

"Diego, you are now officially listed as a foreign terrorist and will be tried in a military court. We will be back in a few minutes for the trip to L.A.," said Nick as C. E. and he walked out the door.

"Did you see the look on his face when you mentioned the dirty bomb?" said C.E.

"Yeah, but the color left his face when he was told we were going to take him to the L.A. harbor. We have a good lead there. I hope we are right!" said Nick.

CHAPTER FIFTY-SEVEN

John A. Fox ran auction sales for philatelic material during the 1950s and 1960s Because of legal processing he was forced to sell his stamp stock to another auction house and this brought to light several counterfeit covers. A specialist in stamps said that the covers and stamps did not originate on the cover and postal markings were counterfeit. The auctioneer at the auction house warned that no warranty of genuineness was given for the items. The original values set for the covers had been set at over $1,000. The covers went for less than $200 at the end of the bidding. Fox was censured in 1966 by the Stamp Dealers Association and expelled from the American Philatelic Society and the American Stamp Dealers Association. He appealed for the removal and was denied in 1967 with the words 'unethical and unbecoming. He continued his auctions until 1987.

GENUINE

FORGERY

Evil counsel travels fast.

— Sophocles

2002 L.A. HARBOR

The meeting room had a bulletin board with photos being tacked to it getting ready for the joint meeting with other units. The photos were of the targeted individuals of their operation. The members of the various units stood around talking when C.E. and Nick walked into the room.

Nick walked up to an individual and said, "C.E. this is Juan from our gang section. He covers all the gangs in the United States and tracks their contacts in Latin America. I know that covers a lot of territory, but Juan and his partner Hector are the best. Hector will be here in a few minutes. So, Juan, why don't we get started and bring C.E. up to date on what we know of this gang's activity with Abdul,"

"Well let's start with the players we know so far. He walked over to the bulletin board and pointed this is Dante. He goes by the moniker 'Big D' and he runs the drugs for several of the cartels. He has to walk a thin line between these groups. He is very careful to remain useful to them all.

"Next, we have Rafael. His moniker is 'Ex-Ray'. I have no idea why. But his job is to send coded messages to the 'coyotes' that smuggle poor victims into the U.S. as slave workers. He works with this guy named Carlos, who goes by the moniker 'Digger'.

"Carlos handles the various tunnels into the U.S. from Mexico to several different locations on this side of the border. We have been watching him for over a year and discovered three of his tunnels. One in California and two in Arizona and each one was discovered by a civilian construction project that by accident opened the tunnel. We started the construction projects so we could keep Carlos in operation. It is better to know the devil you are working with rather than a new guy.

"Finally, there are these two at the end. They are Santiago and Maya who own a storefront for laundering money. They go by Mom and Pop in the neighborhood," said Juan.

"Hold it a minute. What kind of store?" asked C.E.

"It is a small coin and stamp store. Is that important?" asked Juan.

"I think we have just found another link!" said C.E.

"I agree. C.E. this whole thing started with a fire at a print shop and stamp store. It is the best connection we have. Get everything you can on Santiago and Maya," said Nick.

Juan walked over to the door and told the person standing there, "Please go and get Isabella to come to this room and bring all the information she has on the Siesta Coin store!"

"Isabella has been building a case on these two and we are about to pull them in for money laundering for a cartel," said Juan.

"O.K. Why do you want to see me, Juan?' asked Isabella as she entered the room.

"We are interested in the Siesta coin store. We need to know where they have gone in the last few days, who they were with, and if their pattern is different than their normal pattern?" asked C.E.

"Just who the hell are you?" asked Isabella.

"Sorry we are in a rush, and it is my fault, first let me introduce Agent Thomson and C.E. Hall to the Bureau. They are running this operation," said Juan.

"Wow! It's a pleasure to meet the Big Boys!" said Isabelle.

"It is our pleasure. Rarely, do we meet the local with the word pleasure in the introduction," said Nick.

"Don't take her personally. She is the best agent I have in the field, and nothing gets by her," said Hector as he walked into the room.

"Stop the sweet talk, you are a married man, Hector. Now, for your question. No, they only go to the port once a month to pick up coins and stamps. These stamps and coins are sent from Asia by a Japanese shipping company. They sell the coins and stamps to other dealers and buy a lot of products from our local dealers. The money goes to the bank every Friday at 2:30 and comes out at the end of the month to buy more coins and stamps from foreign dealers," said Isabella.

"Has a guy named Abdul been to the store?" asked C.E. and Nick together.

"Yeah, Abdul has been a big customer for the last two months. Why?" asked Isabella.

"We think, or I should say we know, Abdul is a terrorist and has plans to blow up a dirty bomb in the Los Angeles harbor," said Nick.

"You cannot be serious! Are you serious?" asked Isabella.

"That is why this team has been formed and you have just been assigned to this unit. So you have 10 minutes to get ready if you need it," said Nick.

"What about the rest of my group?" asked Isabella.

"Is the stamp and coin store your only investigation?" asked Nick.

"No, it is one of several," replied Isabella.

"Then we just need you. Can they carry on without you?" asked Nick.

"It is a good team. My second is young but very good," said Isabella.

"Now, back to the issue here. Has Abdul had anyone with him when he goes to the store?" asked C.E.

"A couple of times a real thug and once there was a woman and yesterday there was a guy I had not seen before at the store," said Isabella.

Nick placed a photo on the table. "Is this the woman? asked Nick.

"That is her. She stopped everyone on the street when she went to the store," said Hector.

"Why?" asked Nick.

"You're not blind are you, Nick? Look at her," said Hector.

"What about the guy?" asked C.E. showing a photo.

"Yes, he was a gang banger and is about 40 years old with tattoos and missing fingers on one hand. If you want to know more about him, call Mendoza, he knows just about all the career bangers of that age," said Isabella.

"How long will it take to get him in here?" asked Nick

"I just saw him in the kitchen. I'll go and round him up," said Isabella as she walked out of the room.

"This should be interesting," said Juan.

"Why?" asked C.E.

"They were married at one time," said Juan.

"You are so behind the times, Juan. They got remarried a month ago," said Hector.

"What after the blow-up? I did not think they'd even talk anymore," said Juan.

"It was over his mother, who kept interfering and caused the fights. Mendoza finally told his mother to back off and then they made up," said Hector.

"Until about a month ago, I thought I was going to have to transfer one of them," said Juan.

"Here is the man of the hour now," said Isabella.

"What is this all about? I remember you — it is Nick, isn't it? We worked that case for Central America when I was undercover as a health care worker," said Mendoza.

"I believe you were called Filipe and were stone deaf. YOU were very good. I did believe you were deaf. Good to see you again with the right name and that you can now hear," said Nick.

"Wow! Don't you go and tell me that they have come to take over our case for the glory?" said Mendoza.

"No, we have not. We want to include you in a bigger case, but first, what can you tell us about a 40-year-old gang member with missing fingers on one hand?" asked Nick.

"That is most likely Xavier Martinez. He now goes by the name "the fuse" and is the only one in his age group that is still around this area. The others that age are locked up or dead," said Mendoza.

"What is his specialty for the gang?" asked C.E.

"Who are you?" asked Mendoza.

"Sorry, we are in a bit of a hurry. I am sorry. Once more this bright fellow is C.E. Hall. We are looking into a possible terrorist plot in L.A. harbor," said Juan.

"Sorry, I did not mean to be rude," said Mendoza.

"No apology necessary," said C.E.

"A terrorist plot! Then this is a bigger case than drugs and money laundering. We have been keeping a close watch on Xavier for the last few months. His activity within the gang has increased.

"He took a trip to Mexico last month and we lost him down there. He was gone for two weeks before we picked him back up. We have a record of him from assaulted when he was a teenager and then later for breaking. He was playing with Cherry Bombs as a kid and blew his fingers off one hand. Recently, there are rumors he learned the bomb trade while locked up and that is when the nickname the fuse popped up," said Mendoza.

"I think he is another link to Abdul," said Nick.

"Abdul, that is the guy that Xavier went to Mexico with last month," said Mendoza.

"Perfect, collect everything we have on Xavier and meet back here in one hour," said Juan.

"Abdul was in Iran last month. I need to contact another agency and see if they can provide any information," said Nick.

CHAPTER FIFTY-EIGHT

Englehardt Fohl sold forgeries and counterfeit stamps that were from dozens of different countries. His activities came to light as early as 1871 when an Italian stamp dealer discovered the stamps, he purchased from a magazine advertisement were forgeries. He notified the magazine of the forgeries. It was not until 1898 that the real extent of Fohl's activities was known when the printing company he used went bankrupt. Among the company assets were several forgeries printed for Englehardt. He had never sold the stamps inside Germany and avoided prosecution by shipping the counterfeits outside Germany to other countries that were then sold to individual collectors. A few of these forgeries were of excellent quality.

GENUINE

FORGERY

Pleasure, a most mighty lure to evil.

— Plato

2002 IRANIAN SPY

The head nuclear manager on the team was Professor Hormoz and he was all set to go on the trip to the conference on nuclear studies as a guest. He would also give a lecture on the topic of nuclear management at the conference in Pakistan. Once he was done with the lecture he would slip into India and never return to Iran.

Abdul had allowed Hormoz to set his plan in place for his retirement for his part in the plot to harm the West. The plan was not sanctioned by the government and Hormoz had orchestrated the direction of the path of traitors with evidence pointing to only one person. He was smiling to himself, for in hours he would be safe and out of the country.

The plan was so simple. After the lecture, he would be met outside the lecture hall and taken across the border to India as a businessman from Turkey. Ten hours later he would be on his way to a new life. He continued smiling to himself as he imagined what was happening at the courthouse a few miles away.

At the High Court House, most people walked around the area unless one was required to enter. Today the parents of a spy were permitted to be present in a courtroom to watch the trial and the sentencing of their daughter. Lawyers were at their tables and there were few other observers to the proceeding.

"Where is Cyra now?" asked Lavi in Rachel the earpiece.

"They have her in the holding room and are just about ready to bring her into the courtroom," responded Rachel in a low voice.

"Good! Is Aryana ready to give her new information to the court as soon as Cyra enters the room?" asked Rachel.

"Yes, she has the paperwork and documents connecting the manager Hormoz with Abdul," said Yosef.

"If this goes the way we planned it, the honorable Professor Hormoz will be missing his trip to India," said Lavi.

"They are bringing in Cyra now. 'Oh, my god! Look at what they've done. They have beaten her pretty badly. She can barely walk on her own.

I want to punish that pig Hormoz myself," said Rachel. Ruth gasps at the site of Cyra's face.

"Let me know when Aryana enters the room. Are Daniel and Ruth in place?" asked Lavi.

"Yes, they are here and looked like very concerned parents for their daughter. They came in from Pakistan this morning as the Khans, the grieved parents of Cyra, and they were allowed to come to the court which was a surprise. These things are usually done behind closed doors. I think the government wants to make this a show trial for there is a camera and crew in the back of the courtroom.

"That may work more in our favor for our plan. This looked like a slam dunk case and now it may turn into a major embarrassment to the government. They are filming and they will want to avoid the humiliation. Hold on, the court is about ready to start and Aryana just walked in," said Rachel.

Aryana entered the room and walked over to the lawyer for Cyra talked to him for a minute and handed him some papers. Then she went over and sat down. Cyra's lawyer stood up and asked the judge for a conference. The judge stood up and called the prosecution lawyer over. Then they all went back into the chambers. Twenty minutes later they walked back into the courtroom.

"New evidence has been discovered that has demonstrated clear evidence that there has been a great mistake made and the defendant Cyra was the victim of an elaborate conspiracy to place the blame on this poor woman. Turn off the cameras and bring the tape to chambers," said the judge.

Ruth now broke down and fell to the floor crying as Daniel helped her up onto the bench.

"Who is this couple and why are they here in my courtroom?" demanded the judge.

"They are the parents of the young woman from Pakistan, your honor. We were told that since this was a trial of foreign workers, we were to allow the parents of the worker to witness the trial," said the prosecutor.

"Well, there will be no trial and get this poor woman some medical care and turn her over to her parents right now. I want this manager,

Professor Hormoz, arrested and in this court within the hour," said the judge.

In his chambers, he had called and notified the higher-ups about the new situation and evidence. He was told to end the case and get the woman out of the country today.

Thirty minutes later, Cyra and her parents walked out of the building with two medical persons. As she was being placed into the ambulance, they watched Professor Hormoz being dragged into the building.

He was screaming that this was all a big mistake. "I am innocent, I am innocent, why is this happening to me?" He was hit in the head by one of the guards and told to shut up. He had wet himself as he was dragged through the doors.

Once the family was in the ambulance, Lavi turned to the group in the back. "How are you Cyra?"

"I am fine, I was lucky they only beat me. It could have been much worse. What happens now?" asked Cyra.

"You and the team return to Israel by way of Pakistan and then India for the flight home. You need to play the part of a badly hurt and abused woman until we are on the plane to Israel," said Lavi.

"That will not be hard. I think they broke a few ribs and I lost a tooth or two from a punch when I was arrested at the lab," said Cyra.

"We will be home by tomorrow and we will debrief you then. Until then lay back and take it easy," said Lavi.

"Just one thing. What will happen to Aryana?" asked Cyra.

"She is now the manager of the program. When she tried to warn Elena that she was close to being exposed, it worked for the affair with the Russian. Hormoz had reported Aryana was a good religious person and helped expose a possible breach in security with the whore at the site.

"He was wrong once more, and his timing was off. Aryana trying to help Elena came at the right time in the end. I do not know all the details, but Aryana was asked that night for information from another Russian technician at the site about the location of Elena's home. Elena's father was murdered that night and Elena is not at the family home. The mother said the husband was killed in an honor killing by another father. The mother was beaten and tied up until her other daughters found her and she gave the alarm. The community is in a social uproar demanding answers. Our best guess is that the grandfather set the whole operation in motion," said Lavi.

"How?" asked Cyra.

"First, a Russian tech guy asked for Aryana Cyra's home. That set off an investigation by us into who the Russians were at the site. It seems that this Pyotr fellow that Elena was involved with is the grandson of an important Russian Oligarch, who is also an important member of the Russian 'mob'. Then we learned that he and his grandson were in Turkey the night Elena disappeared. We took the small threats we had pieced together and guessed she was possibly taken to Turkey and then we lost her. She was not with the Russians when they returned to Russia and neither was Pyotr," said Lavi.

"I am happy for Elena. Her father was a brute according to Elena," said Cyra.

"He is no longer a brute. The story is all over Iran's human telegram system that the father of an abused young boy killed Elena's father in an honor killing. It now appears that her father was a major leader in their security force and fortunately for us, he is no longer a problem we will have to deal with later. We think the Russians rescued Elena and left a message on the body and that papers found in a hidden drawer at the home have spread a wider investigation net by Iranian security. There were hints about the loyalty of her father, his other two brothers, and their father. These hints are now exposed with photographs of many leaders and the local Imam," said Rachel.

"Was it the traditional Russian message?" asked Cyra.

"Yes, and that was too good for that evil man. I have seen the file on him, his father, and his brothers. They were completely evil." said Rachel as they approached the Pakistan border. The border crossing from Iran was easy and quick for the government did not want the family in Iran any longer than necessary.

CHAPTER FIFTY-NINE

Georges Foure is one of the great master forgers like S. Allen Taylor, Francois Fournier, and Jean de Sperati; yet most philatelists will not recognize the name. Georges and H.G. Schilling were able to produce fraudulent and bogus stamps for several years. Schilling's was an engraver in Prussia, who provided the facilities and equipment for their venture. The full extent of Foure's activities was exposed in 1896 and he fled Germany to Paris and deserted his family. He continued his behavior without much success — dying destitute in 1902. He is one of the most notorious forgers to be known today. The stamps he sold were his creations and many of his fraudulent productions were sold at high prices in 1927 auctions.

GENUINE

FORGERY

Life is neither good or evil, but only a place for good and evil.

— Marcus Aurelius

2002 Debriefing between Agencies

At an office in Washington D.C., a clerk handed a packet to the agent and said, "This is a summary report on the Mossad. It is a short review of the Mossad and its ability as a security agency. This review is to be taken with the understanding that this agency is very reliable."

"Yes, and what am I to do with it?"

"The report is to be given to agent Nick Thomson before his conversation with the Mossad agent, who just returned from Iran to Mossad HQ. That meeting is within the hour."

The report was delivered to Nick.

The Mossad of Israel is one of the best intelligence services in the world. In 1960 they were able to kidnap and smuggle the mastermind of the Final Solution, Adolph Eichmann, out of Argentina for trial in Israel for the mass murder of six million Jews and some five million others in the Nazi death camps during World War II.

This operation was made possible by a tip-off by a stamp dealer, who had overheard another dealer mention he had a stamp he believed that Eichmann would like. That set in motion the plan to find the individual and bring one of the biggest Nazi murders to justice. Eichmann was captured and was packed into a suitcase and sent to Israel.

Those opposed to the Mossad have accused it of target killings of hundreds of people who were conducting terror against the State of Israel. There are allegations of mysterious deaths or outright accusations of assassinations over the years. The 1972 attack on Israeli athletes at the Munich Olympics by a terrorist group set in motion the search for the individuals who conducted and planned the attack.

Three of the terrorists were captured by the West German government and then released three weeks later. The release was an exchange for the crew of a Lufthansa jet that had been hijacked.

The State of Israel under Golda Meir set in motion a planned targeted assassination unit to deal with the individuals that killed the Israeli athletes. By October 1972 the first terrorist killed was Wael Zwaiter, who was shot in a Roman hotel lobby. Another was killed in December

Those terrorist participants were hunted down over the next years in what was called Operation Wrath of God (Operation Bayonet) and another one was killed when Mossad agents placed a bomb in his home. More killings followed until 1973 when the Mossad agents misidentified their target and killed an innocent man in Lillehammer, Norway. The five-man assassination team was tried and convicted of murder. The international uproar had Golda Meir suspend the targeted assassination hit squads. Then in 1979, they were allowed to remove the last member of the terrorist group, who was killed in a car bomb in Lebanon.

The state of Israel is surrounded by enemies and at times seems to conduct operations that are viewed by many outsiders as terrorist actions. It is a nation under siege by those around it.

The nation of Iran seems to be the loudest caller for the destruction of the Israeli State. The Mossad network within Iran has the main objective of keeping a watch on the nuclear program. The Iranians believe a nuclear bomb will provide them with the power to remove Israel from the face of the Earth.

Iraq and Iran were both moving to be the leaders in the Middle East and to relive their past glory. Then Iraq invaded Iran in 1980 and that war lasted until they had an uneasy peace in 1988. The United States supported Iraq in that war.

Iran and Iraq then set about trying to build their rockets and develop nuclear weapons. The U.S. saw Iraq as a balance of power in the Middle East.

Then Iraq invaded Kuwait and the Western powers under the leadership of the United States entered the war supporting Kuwait and forcing the Iraq army to collapse.

Saddam Hussein was allowed to stay in power in part to be a controlling balance against Iran's growing power in the Middle East.

This is the background for the conversation with Mossad agent Cyra.

The Director of Mossad entered the conference room, looked around and saw Cyra. "Cyra the Americans are interested in Abdul and the people he had with him at the site. They want to know if any material was taken out of the facility," said the Director.

"They did not take any active materials, but a few days before my arrest I think Abdul and another guy, that I did not know, were talking about a shipment of waste that would be sent to someplace in Southern California. The name of the ship was the *Maru,*" said Cyra.

"Anything else?" asked Lavi.

"No, I can say that Abdul and the other guy were happy with the news that the shipment was on its way. The other guy looked somewhat like an Arab but spoke in a broken form of Spanish. He was short and was missing a finger or two on his right hand, I think. I could see tattoos on his arms and neck," said Cyra.

"What do you mean broken Spanish?" asked Lavi.

"Not Catalan or Basque dialects, if I were to guess, I say it was one of those South American dialects in Spanish, maybe Mexican. I cannot be sure," said Cyra.

"O.K. did you see the containers that were shipped?" asked Lavi.

"No, but they were most likely not that large. The waste at the program was recorded and any large amount would be noticed. Abdul had first come to the operation about two months ago. He talked with Professor Hormoz in private all the time," said Cyra.

"We are set up for you to talk with the agent in charge in the United States in a few minutes. Then I want to bring him up to date about what we know about Abdul. They have reason to believe that Abdul and his group are planning a plot for a dirty bomb to be set off someplace in California or the American west coast."

"Wait a minute. The guy with the missing fingers or finger kept saying the word Pedro. I thought it was another guy at the time. But is San Pedro by L.A.?" asked Cyra.

"This information adds another piece to the American puzzle. You better come with me to the communication room," said Lavi.

CHAPTER SIXTY

R.P.H. Wolle was convicted of counterfeiting and changing one-dollar bills into five-dollar bills and served a term in a Missouri penitentiary from 1900 to 1903. While in prison it was believed that he continued his fraudulent stamp business. This was his second term in prison for he had a prior conviction for swindling stamp dealers. Then in 1904 after his release, he commenced his business and was arrested once more and sentenced to another four years for stamp fraud.

1ˢᵀ U.S. POSTAGE STAMPS 1847   **FORGERY**

To do nothing evil is good; to wish nothing evil is better.
— Claudius

2002 Things Start to Come Together

"Agent Nick Thomson, I am sorry to jump ahead of the scheduled meeting time, but I think we have another piece of your puzzle that cannot wait," said Lavi.

"It is not a problem we were just setting up for a meeting with our team down the hall. What do you have?" asked Nick.

"This young woman is one of our agents who just came back from Iran, and she will give you what we think may be linked to your case," said Lavi.

"Hello, Agent Thomson. I was in Iran working in a top security lab developing weapons. The individual you call Abdul came several times to the lab and had meetings with the lead scientist. The last time he came was with a man missing a finger or two that spoke in broken Spanish. They were off to the side when I overheard a conversation about a shipment." said Cyra.

"What about the shipment?" asked Nick.

"Just a day before the conversation I began to notice that small amounts of our waste was missing in the reports. I brought it up to the head scientist in the lab and he just brushed it off. The next day I was arrested as a spy. I will not go into the details of my escape but let me give you the information that may be connected to your investigation," said Cyra as she went on to explain what she overheard.

"I want to thank you both for the information and I am sure we need to get on this right now. Thank you for the cooperation and information," said Nick.

"Good luck Agent Thomson," said Lavi as the connection was shut down.

The team was gathered in the conference room when Nick walked in, "Alright everybody I just ended a conference call with a Mossad agent that just returned from Iran. She gave us the name of the ship that was bringing the material into the United States. The SS *Maru* is scheduled to be in port in two days and to be unloaded that day at 9 a.m. at L.A. harbor. The ship picked up three containers in Iran. The Mossad agent also gave some information on who Abdul was with him in Iran and that was our man, Xavier Martinez. This is a pretty solid connection to our investigation."

"Was Mossad working the same case?" asked Isabelle.

"I do not know. I am surprised I got what information I did from them. They run a tight-lipped organization. I think the nuclear aspect opened the door to allow the flow of limited information to us," said Nick.

"So, how do we handle the situation?" asked C.E.

"Well, thanks to the investigation that Juan and Hector have been building on the L.A. Harbor and drugs trade, we know that Abdul has been meeting with the guy that schedules the unloading from the ships. That guy will be interviewed by us tonight at his home. Juan, what can you tell us about the contact between Abdul and the guy in the harbor?" asked Nick.

"The guy's name is Adel. He was born in Iran and came to this country during the Iraq-Iran war in the 1980s. We can find no other connection between him and Abdul besides the monthly visits that have led to an envelope being passed to Adel. Adel has a family, but we have found no connection with the drug trade with any member of the family. If I were to guess, Adel is taking money for favors at the port." said Juan. "O.K., Then C.E. and I shall visit Adel tonight and we will meet again in the morning say at 7 a.m. to formulate a plan for this operation," said Nick.

That night Adel opened his door to two men in suits holding what looked like bibles.

"Good evening may w…," said one of the men before he was cut off.

"No! I do not want whatever you are selling or preaching. I am a Muslim," said Adel.

"Sorry, Adel, we are not soliciting anything. May we come in or perhaps you prefer to come down to the FBI building downtown," said the taller of the two agents.

"What! Who are you?" asked Adel.

"My name is Agent Nick Thomson, and this man is C.E. Hall and we need to interview you on what is happening at the harbor."

"The harbor? I just control the schedule for the unloading of the ships. I do not know anything else!" said Adel.

"Then just let us ask you a few questions and we will leave," said C.E.

"Alright, come in. I hope this will not take long. I must pick up my wife and family at her sister's house in an hour," said Adel.

"This should not take too long. Let's get right to the point! Adel, what are your plans with Abdul? asked Nick

"I do not know anyone called Abdul!" said Adel.

"We know you do, Adel! Now what are the plans?" asked Nick.

"I do not know anyone named Abdul!" Adel repeated almost crying.

"Adel I am going to ask you one more time before I place you in custody and take you downtown for lying to federal agents and possible acts of treason. What is your business with Abdul?" said Nick.

"TREASON! I am a naturalized American! I love this country! I do not know any Abdul!" Now he was crying, "I am a good American! I have nothing to do with terrorists!"

"I warned you!" said Nick.

"Please wait, I am telling the truth I do not know anybody named Abdul. Maybe he has another name. What does he look like? Do you have a photo? I want to help you, please! Please!"

"O.K. here is a photo of him," said C.E.

"That is Ashkan. He and I have a deal. I see that his cargo container is passed through the inspection process first that is all. It is coins and stamps along with some antiques that he sells to what he calls greedy Americans and laughs," said Adel with a worried look on his face. "I know nothing else."

"Do you take money for this service Adel?" asked C.E.

"Yes, a small amount each time. Everything is still checked and nothing illegal is passed through. I just put his stuff first in line. That is all. I swear," said Adel.

"Have you met with him recently? What did he want? asked Nick.

"He came to my office yesterday morning and then this afternoon. He said three containers were coming in and that they were very valuable coins and stamps. He was worried that they would be hijacked. He would like to personally watch the unloading and loading. I told him that the rules did not allow that. He then said he would be with the trucks that picked up the loads. I said that was acceptable."

"What are the numbers of the containers?" asked Nick.

"They are in sequence from 009765 to 67. The ship came in late this afternoon and Ashkan or Abdul as you call him came to the port and he wanted to go on the ship."

"Hold on a minute you said the ship came in this afternoon?" said Nick.

"Yes, about 3:30."

"When did Abdul show up? And what did he want?" asked C.E.

"Like I said he wanted to go on the ship. We never do this. But Ashkan insisted."

"So, I am guessing you let him on the ship for a small fee," said Nick.

"He offered a small amount, so I walked around with him to find his containers. He was only worried about one container the #009766 container and he walked around it with a Giger counter. I asked him why he was doing that.

He said it was just for precaution that the stamps and coins in that container were coming from Chernobyl and he had worried buyers. So, he said he would personally check them. That is all I know. It is just coins, stamps, and a few items of art," said Adel.

"You should rethink your interpretation of greed, Adel?" said C.E.

"What do you mean?" asked Adel.

"Did you not take money for small favors?" said Nick.

"Yes, it is a custom in the Islamic culture. It helps bind individuals together," said Adel.

"You have been here long enough to know that hidden fees are not acceptable," said Nick.

"I had no idea he may be a terrorist. This country has been good to me and my family. I would do nothing to hurt it," said Adel.

"Then I would suggest you stop taking money for small favors," said C.E.

"Yes! Yes, you are right!"

"O.K. Adel that is all for now. We are going to leave, and you will not say a word of our visit tonight to anyone. Is that understood? You go to work and act as if nothing happened tonight," said Nick.

"Yes, yes, I had no idea! Please believe me!" said Adel.

"Do as we say Adel and all will be fine. If you break your word, we will come back and arrest you for conspiracy and terrorist activities against the United States of America," said Nick.

"Terrorist! I love this country! I just take a little money for placing a container first in line. I am not a terrorist! *'Istighfar'* Allah please protect me from evil! What is happening!" cried Adel.

"Everything will be good, Adel, if you remember what was said here," said Nick as they walked away from the door.

"That guy is really worried. Do you think he will be able to hold it together?" asked C.E.

"He'll think about it all night and then he will do what we told him. He is just a poor sap caught up in something bigger than his life. He will more than likely stay in his office tomorrow and stay out of our way," said Nick.

"C.E. we better call everyone and get them into the office. That ship coming in early has disrupted our plans. We need this operation ready to go before that ship is unloaded," said Nick.

In the house, Adel had never been so afraid, and he still was. He looked down and saw he needed to change his clothes. Now, he was worried that they would make good on the threat to arrest him as a terrorist. He would never tell anyone of the late-night visit. He was glad that his wife and kids were visiting her sister. He told himself that he would just stay in the office and let the agents deal with this Abdul or Ashkan whatever name the person called himself.

CONFERENCE ROOM 4 A.M.

"Juan, we have 4 hours to finish the setup and then take down the shipment. The ship came in early and will unload today. We will need all of your people and maybe more if they can be spared. We are almost certain that Abdul is bringing in the material for a dirt bomb for Xavier to build. The problem is we do not know how much material. But the container is number 009766," said Nick.

"We are lucky, Abdul will show up to watch over the shipment," said C.E.

"After I got the information last night, I met with the team here and developed a plan for the takedown. Once the right container is placed on the truck we will move," said Juan.

"Wait, there are three containers.," said an agent.

"Yes,"

"What if they unload all three containers and wait? Will we stop the convoy inside of the port or outside the gates?" asked an agent.

"We stay with the plan. If they load one truck at a time and that truck leaves, we will take each truck outside the port. Right now we are only worried about container 009766," said Nick.

"Everyone, are we on the same page?" asked Nick.

"Yes,"

"O.K. everyone, let's be careful out there. Let's go catch some evil people," said Juan.

The teams headed for the location points.

At 9:30 a.m. Nick got a call from the gate that Abdul had arrived in one of three trucks.

"Keep an eye on him. I do not want to lose him in the chaos that I am sure will break out," said Nick.

"Juan, how is the view from up on the crane?" asked C.E.

"I can see the whole port from up here! It is high and has a great view. Did I tell you guys that I hate heights? I never want to make this climb to get up here again. This thing sways a lot with the wind. Hold on, the unloading has started. The first container is picked up and I am reading the number. It is the 009765 container and is already heading for the trucks. Abdul is out and telling the first driver something. The driver is shaking his head, yes."

"Keep us informed of every movement," said Nick.

"The first truck is loaded and is moving and headed out of the yard. Abdul must have told him not to wait."

"Is Abdul leaving?" asked Nick.

"No, he is walking to the second truck."

"That's O.K. We have a team to follow the first truck and stop it when we move here," said Nick.

"It looks like the #009766 will be the last container. Yeah, that's right the #009767 is headed for a truck bed now and Abdul is telling him to leave."

"Somebody tell me if the second truck follows the first truck. That would make the takedown easier," said Nick.

"The second truck just turned and is following the path of the first truck," said the man at the gate.

"The last truck is just about loaded up. Nobody moves until we get the word that Abdul is in the truck cab and the truck is starting to move. Everyone checks in with an acknowledgment," said Nick.

Everyone checked in.

"Alright everyone Abdul is in the cab and it is starting to move," called Juan.

"Everyone move in now!" said Nick.

The last truck driver was suddenly shocked as a forklift pulled out from a row of containers in front of the truck blocking its movement. The driver tried to back up just as another forklift blocked the back. The driver and Abdul jumped out of the vehicle with guns in their hands.

"This is the FBI. Place your guns on the ground, raise your hands and lay face down on the ground."

That command was met with the driver firing at the front forklift driver. At that point, the truck driver was hit in the chest by a sniper and Abdul was hit in the leg and hit the ground, losing the pistol that he was holding. Nick walked up to Abdul, picked up the gun, and looked over at C.E., who shook his head and said, "The driver was dead."

Nick looked down at Abdul and said, "Abdul you are under arrest for attempting to commit an act of terrorism on the territory of the United States."

Abdul was crying like a baby and holding his leg yelling, "I need medical help. I am bleeding to death. Get me a doctor. Get me a doctor now!"

Later the other two containers, number 009765 and number 009767, were found to hold artifacts that had been stolen from sites around Syria, Iran, and Iraq. They were worth a small fortune plus, there were a large number of counterfeit antique coins.

Container #009766 held items stolen from India and also held five containers of used nuclear waste hidden inside antique Indian and Iranian cabinets.

C.E. and Nick were congratulated for a job well done by the leadership. Then told to sign a statement that they would never discuss the current events with anyone. C.E. was asked to become a paid consultant on call. He accepted the offer.

LATER THAT DAY.

"Well Nick, it is nice to be a hero even if nobody knows about it," said C.E.

"The important people know, and they will remember C.E. We were very lucky on several things. You linked it all to that fire in a printing shop and then with the coin store connection. I'll see you tomorrow and C.E. Then you can tell me why you go by the name C.E.?"

"Hey, you read my file. Use your skills as an investigator for the answers for I will never tell. I am going home and take the next week off," said C.E.

"What? Not so fast pal, we are not done with this operation. We still have people to collect in this little plot. This first part was the easy part. The hard part has to still be done. We just rounded up the thugs now we go after the white-collar bad guys that need to be collected and charged for conspiracy and co-terrorist. You are familiar with some of them, and we still need you," said Nick.

"Yeah, if they are the bankers, you are right. I just hope this time they cannot lawyer out of the charges. O.K . Nick, I'll see you tomorrow bright and early and ready to go," said C.E. as he turned to leave.

CHAPTER SIXTY-ONE

Samuel C. Upham was a dealer in patent medicines, stationery, and newspapers. In 1862 he became an early forger of Confederate stamps. He claimed that it was a patriotic duty to devalue the assets of the Confederacy. He advertised the stamps and currency at half the face value in an advertisement in a local paper. There may have also been the motivation to separate collectors from their money. He had newsboys and stationery stores selling them as curiosities.

The good man is free, even if he is a slave. The evil man is a slave, even if he is a king.

— Saint Augustine

THE SECOND PHASE – FINANCIAL

"C.E. come in and meet the other part of our team. While we were working doing all the hard work, these people were sitting in an office working on the soft work of looking at numbers, taking breaks, and eating catered meals," said Nick.

"Yeah, you did the hard work. We only had to use our brains as you, a bunch of gorillas were chasing everyday criminals," said the tallest of the three other people in the room.

"This is a touchy group C.E. and everyone this is our newest consultant, a fire investigator. The tall guy here is Mathew the lead finance guy, and the ugly one is Moses sitting there behind the computer, our top analysis on the Irish and Middle East connections. Finally, we have Kirk Thorne who is on loan from a sister agency. He is also a finance genius," said Nick.

C.E. went around and shook hands with the three men.

"Let's not spread the genius idea around too much; it might hurt the feelings of those in the field that have limited cranial capacity. Besides, I like fieldwork and if you keep up that kind of talk, I will be at a desk forever," said Kirk and they all laughed.

"I have heard rumors about a fire investigator who helped break up an organization that went back to the 1920's or 1930's. Would you be that fire investigator C.E. Hall?" asked Mathew.

"Yes, I just played a small part. I stumble into it and please call me C.E — all my friends do," said C.E.

"That works for me and the rest of us here. We are not that formal," said Moses.

"Now that the introductions are over, let's coordinate this next part of the operation. The threat of the dirty bomb has been terminated as of yesterday. Now we need to close down the route of the finance connections that Abdul had set up before they have time to transfer the money all around the globe and we lose it," said Nick.

"Just then the door opened, and Juan walked into the room. Sorry, I am late. My supervisor had to check in with his boss to see if I was permitted to be assigned to this operation. He is a good boss, but like all paper pushers he likes everything to be on paper," said Juan.

Introductions were made once more, and Juan was introduced as the specialist on gangs.

"Before we get into the finance aspect of this operation, Juan, please give us a little history of the L.A. gangs," said Nick.

"It is very simple. Once you put people together, you will have gangs or groups joining together to form some kind of an advantage. It happens in national and local politics and social activities. Most are upright and help the community and a small percentage turn into criminal activities.

"There have always been criminal gangs in every culture. Up until the beginning of the Twentieth Century, the criminal gang structure in the U.S. had been based on the same gang system from the old countries of Europe and Asia. There were Irish gangs, German gangs, Dutch gangs, and even Chinese gangs called Tongs. Then those old gangs were merged into the Sicilian-style gang families during the early 20th Century.

"Local gangs were being left on the fringe of the gang wars. The Italians were spreading their reach. The New York City Five Points gang sent Al Capone to Chicago to set up shop under Johnny Torrio and the Italians on the Southside of Chicago.

"The Northside gang in Chicago was run by the Irishman Dean O'Banion, who ran his gang out of a flower shop. When Prohibition started the two groups, the Irish and Italians, formed an alliance under Torrio who took a share of everyone's profits. That alliance failed when a large number of Italian gang members were arrested and O'Banion was not charged.

"The bad blood started gang wars and Torrio was permitted to take out O'Banion. He was shot inside his flower shop on November 10, 1924. Then the gangs went to war in high gear.

"The Northside gang under Hymie Weiss, Bugs Moran, and Vincent Drucci planned to revenge the killing of O'Banion. They ambushed Al Capone in early January 1925, but Al was able to escape.

"Then on January 24, 1925, Johnny Torrio and his wife were ambushed and Torrio was shot several times. He was able to survive the attack and after he recovered he went to Italy and gave control of the gang to Al Capone.

"Hymie Weiss now went to war with Capone. In 1926 Weiss sent 8 to 10 cars loads of men for a drive-by hit on the headquarters of Al Capone at the Hawthorne Hotel. It was reported that the first car fired a Thomson submachine gun at the hotel that did not break any windows or do any damage. The story was that it was blanked to warn the innocence at the hotel.

"Then came the rest of the convoy of cars loaded with men and more Thomson's machine guns and shotguns. One car stopped and a man got out, ran up to the hotel, and emptied his Thomson into the hotel. It was reported that he fired some 100 rounds, then stood up and walked back to the car, got in, and drove away with the convoy. Some claimed there were over a thousand spent carriages on the ground in front of the hotel. Capone paid for the medical care of the injured and nobody died in the attack. It was reported that Capone had asked for a truce.

"Then Hymie Weiss was assassinated on October 11, 1926, and within months George 'Bugs' Moran took over the Northside gang. The two groups had been at it for years.

"Then on February 14, 1929, at the S.M.C. Cartage Company, two men dressed as police officers entered the building with two other men in overcoats. They lined the men inside up against the wall and opened fire with submachine guns and shotguns. George "Bugs" Moran had just driven up to the garage when the police entered the building, and he thought it was a raid and he drove off.

"Chicago and New York gang shootings were always in the news. The big stories were used to catch the public interest to sell papers. Then the Great Depression hit, and the news was the economy. FDR entered office and he ended prohibition that ended a lot of criminal trade in booze. The gangs began to move or expand into other trades.

"It was during this time that the youth gangs began to develop a new pattern of gangs like a family and not an organization. On the west coast during the Great War and the 1920's the city of Los Angeles had an increase in their Mexican community with refugees from the civil war down in Mexico and the demand for farm labor. Many came to this country for promises of better wages in California and western states. Many parents went to work in the cities and left their kids at home alone. To deal with these young kids of these working-class families in L.A. the Catholic church began to form church youth clubs for the new immigrants to socialize and have safe entertainment.

"When the Great Depression hit in 1929, the funds for the youth groups vanished. However, the youth groups continued to meet and they morphed into gangs, one of these was called the 'White Fence' Gang. This early gang structure became a modern pattern for all other young gangs in the country whether they were based on nationality or ethnic groups. The gang was replacing a broken family structure that was missing or lacking for mothers and fathers were working long hours to live and manage a family.

"The new gangs formed followed the structure of the White Fence Gang. It was the largest gang for many years in the LA County area. Others in the gang split off to form their gang and followed the same structure.

"The Great Depression centralized and consolidated these older traditional gangs and the young gangs. Today, there has been a return to the ethnic groups gang but for the most part, they follow the same structure. They are becoming more ruthless and violent with the expansion of the Central American network of gangs entering the states. These gangs have become international business partners in some respects with the economic funds to buy power. By going after their money and cutting into their supply line the gangs will lose their influence," said Juan.

"What do you mean they can buy power?" asked C.E.

"For these gangs violence and money are the path to power. An example is the Mexican Cartels. If money does not work, the threat of actual brutal violence will convince people to go along. Their reach can go deep into the government and down into the prison system. Many of the soldiers in the gang get arrested and serve life sentences. They can be bribed to do favors in prison.

"Just for example, a hit (killing) on another prisoner the gang will provide money for the member's family on the outside. Money can buy political candidates to influence laws and law enforcement. The drug cartels in Mexico are reported to control many politicians. Then there is the threat of violence against the families or the actual murder of family members. The violence also keeps the soldiers in line. The same happens in big cities in the United States. Al Capone controlled several political officials in Chicago before the government convicted him on taxes."

"So, how do we break the connection with the terrorist," asked Mathew.

"That is what I am saying you may never end the connection. Remove the head of the organization and someone below is waiting to step in and take control. The only thing you can do is break the connection once you find one. Evil is like talent; it rises to the top. You can hurt them, but these people are most often one step ahead of the laws and their enforcement. We are lucky in this case that we know the source of the traffic and the individuals like Abdul and Diego," said Juan

"What do you mean one step ahead of us?" asked C.E.

"The first car thief in LA. was chased by a sheriff on horseback. Better yet, let me give you an example of drug traffic during the 1970's. People started using PCP 'Angel Dust' (a tranquilizer for large animals) to get high. They would take their cigarettes, dip them into liquid Angel Dust and then smoke it.

"We caught on to the fact that cigarettes that had liquid stains on them were a sign of drug use. That was a game changer, but not for long. They started to dip thread into the liquid and string it through the cigarette leaving a tiny end of a string at the end of the cigarette. Once they light up there is no telltale stain. That is just one example of the street-smart guys staying ahead of crime prevention.

"Another example is carrying a loaded gun. The street-smart guys started giving the gun to an underage youth and an adult would carry the bullets to get around the loaded weapon charge or carrying a weapon. These guys may not pass a college exam, but their leaders are smart. That's about it."

"I have one question and it is why this discussion on gangs?" asked C.E.

"The individuals we are focused on now are the same individuals we have been looking at for laundering money for gangs. So the two cases have been folded into one case," said Juan.

"O.K. Kirk you're up, what can you tell us about the white-collar banking part of these criminal schemes?" asked Nick.

"In this case, there are two major players involved. One a German banking family named Steiner and the other a U.S. banker named Moody," said Kirk.

"Wait a minute, the German bankers are they Fritz and William and are the Americans Charles and Rudy?" asked C.E.

"Yes, they are fathers and sons that have small banks here and there," said Kirk.

"Well, I know these bankers and they were tied to the case I worked before with the FBI. I thought they were out of business and if not locked up. They were players in that radical organization that had ties to the Nazi organization I helped break up," said C.E.

"Yes! That is another reason we wanted you in this case C.E. for your knowledge of these bankers. We suspected they were involved, but had no proof until Kirk did some digging into the records," said Nick.

"Why are these people still allowed to do business?" asked C.E.

"The American bankers paid for excellent lawyers who claimed their clients did not know about the criminal activities of the organization. No paper trail would connect them to the organization. Any money trail was lost in the global market. They claimed to be bankers and had no other ties to the organization," said Nick.

"I remember that the German Steiner was listed in the album with an identification with a Nazi party number and the date he came into the United States."

"Yes, and he was extradited to Germany and the only charge against him was he was a member of the Nazi party. He renounced that party and was allowed to continue normal life in Germany and his son stayed in the United States.

"As for the Moody's, they had powerful contacts in government and good lawyers. The government could not make a solid connection to the organization. It seems that both bankers were just the money guys, and we had no actual proof of any wrongdoing. The case was dismissed. We have kept an eye on them and not until now did we have any solid link to their bad behavior. That is thanks to Kirk and his special skills," said Nick.

"What is that connection?" asked C.E.

"There was a grower in California that was also connected to the same organization. We have traced some funds through him and his bankers. It reached into the old Soviet Union, Germany, Spain, and Switzerland. These guys are bad."

"Let's take these guys down this time. They belong in prison cells," said C.E.

"We will not be able to do that here, so get your traveling kits. We are off to Mexico in one hour. Moses, you will stand by here with your team and be ready to move once we get the time established," said Nick.

CHAPTER SIXTY-TWO

According to Miguel Segui, his reproductions were marked as 'facsimile' from Barcelona, Spain. He claimed that he never sold any of his stamp reproductions as genuine. The stamps were sold in a dozen different places, and he defended himself by saying others were unethical, but he could not be held responsible for their actions. He used the old stand-by specious defense as other forgers had since the beginning of philately. Admitting his stamps were like a maker of artificial diamonds.

GENUINE   **FORGERY**

He who busies himself with things other than improvement of his own self becomes perplexed in darkness and entangled in ruin. His evil spirits immerse him deep in vices and make his bad actions seem handsome.

— Ali ibn Abi Talib

MEXICO - MONEY LAUNDERING 2002

The plane landed in Mexico and the team went to a safe house, where they were met by Captain Alejandro.

"Greetings my friends. It is good to see you again and it is a pleasure to work with you once more," said the captain.

The introductions were made and then they sat down to go over the plans. "Shall we get started on the joint operation? Kirk, this is your part of the show so bring us up to speed," said Nick.

"First, let me give a little background on banking. Banking today is mostly done by wire transfers and there are many ways it is done. So, when one has a deposit to make, they take the money to a bank and deposit it into an account. That account can then transfer the money to any other bank in the world. When large deposits are moved, they are monitored and reported.

"Any suspicious activity (SAR) is reported when they are over a certain amount. That is intended to make the laundering of the money harder for the criminals when they deposit large sums of money from their various schemes such as embezzlement, smuggling, drugs, arms sales, and prostitution that need to be laundered to cover up the criminal activity. This laundering activity will work best when the banks are involved in the action," said Kirk.

"Can you explain this laundering to me? I am new to this and hope the others are not as ill-informed on the economics of banking as I am," said C.E.

"No, that is a good point. I sometimes get into the topic and lose most of the non-economists in the room. So, here is a summary of the banking underworld. Let's say you have lots of cash from your illegal activity and you need to clean it. The best way is to mix the dirty money with clean money that is from a legitimate business. Then take the money to the bank and deposit it into an account. Then have the bank transfer the money to another bank. The more the money is transferred the more difficult it is to trace.

"This first step is called 'placement' of the funds. That comes by the separating of the funds, which is called 'layering' which is done by the transferring of the funds. The final stage is the 'integration' where the money returns as legitimate funds. The key to success is burying the trail of the funds internationally. This is done with the use of anonymous Shell Companies and money transfers into one or more banks (in or out of the country) then wired back to the original bank. Which brings me to the current operation.

"We have three banks involved, one American, one German, and one here in Mexico. The U.S. bank is run by Rudy Moody and his father who is a retired partner. Then there is the German bank connection in Mexico with the Beltran Bank run by David Beltran, whose family has a long history of connection to the German banker. The German bank is owned by William Steiner who took over from his father, Fritz, who stepped down last year. These three banks were the main movers of Diego's laundering money setup and we were just about to raid their offices until this Abdul guy popped up in the picture." said Kirk.

"In a few minutes, we will have a teleconference with our counterpart in Germany, Agent Volkmann Oldenburg, and with Agent Moses in the United States. Volkmann and his group will raid the Steiner bank in Germany and Moses will raid the Moody bank, while we here will raid the Beltran bank collecting all their records," said Nick.

"Why the coordination on the raid?" asked C.E.

"We need all the bank records and any delay at one bank allows the other banks to issue a warning to the others. Records will be dumped for everything electronically recorded making our job that much harder."

All eyes turned to the screen on the wall. "Hello, is this the right place?" asked agent Moses.

"There you are, Moses always on time. Is your team ready?" asked Nick.

"Yes, and ready to go," replied Moses.

Just then another new face appeared on the screen. "Guten tag, my friends in policing," said Agent Volkmann.

"Good day to you, Agent Volkmann. How are things on your end of this operation?" asked Nick.

"We are ready to move. All we need is a time and place to start the action."

"The same here," said Moses.

"Alright then, since we are in different time zones, let us have H-hour in one hour from now. Will that fit into everyone's schedule?" asked Nick.

"That will make it 10 am New York business time in the U.S. and that will be one hour before German banks close at 4 p.m.," said Kirk.

"Everyone on board with that time frame?" asked Nick.

"Yes," said Moses and Volkmann.

"All right, I want Officer Volkmann to go through the basic plan he outlined on how the banks will be raided just to keep everything current," said Nick.

"To help prevent any notifications being sent out to the banks involved, a part of each team will enter the banks as customers and be stationed around the main room so they will be able to enter all the areas of the bank that have computers. Then once the raid starts, they will rush to the computer stations. All cell phones will be collected to prevent any calls to other individuals who are targets of the raid. Is this agreeable with everyone," asked Volkmann.

All the members of the groups replied with a "Yes."

"The last part of the operation will be that there will be officers stationed by each exit to prevent anyone from leaving the building or the banking area," said Agent Volkmann.

"Good, now before we close are there any other questions?" asked Nick.

"I have one point to be clarified, what about the individuals on the warrants that are not in the banks at the time of the raid?" asked C.E.

"Good point," said Volkmann. Here in Germany, we have all the listed individuals being followed by a team of two individuals since last night. The instructions are to quietly place the individuals in custody if it looks like they are leaving their perspective city and they will be taken into custody at the time of the raid on the bank," said Volkmann.

"You said city. Why?" asked C.E.

"There are three branches of the Steiner Banking institution here in Germany. They are in Berlin, Leipzig, and Munich and they will all be raided at the same time. This is a major operation for us."

"Is that the same in the U.S. and Mexico?" asked C.E.

"We are set to hit the Moody's banks in New York, Chicago, and two branches in Delaware," said Moses.

"We only have one bank in Mexico City. That bank has connections in several other Latin American countries that we are watching. If this raid goes as planned, the link to those other banks will not be interrupted and we will have the connections to a large international banking network," said Alejandro.

"If I may suggest when your people are looking through the paperwork, watch for any reference to stamps. This whole operation began with a stamp. The stamps will most likely be listed as collateral on loans," said C.E.

"Good point, any mention of stamps in the record is to be collected and shared for review. As C.E. said, this whole thing was started around a fire in a printing shop and the death of a stamp dealer who had valuable stamp forgeries," said Nick.

"Are we talking about any particular stamps?" asked Alejandro.

"Good point! We had stamps from several different nations. So look for any government postage stamps," said C.E.

"Are there any other questions or points to be covered? If not, then that is it, and good luck to everyone," said Nick.

The connection was broken, and all the teams went to their staging areas for the raid.

At the appointed time, Agent Volkmann had men and women go into the banks to their assigned places ten minutes before the raid's set time so they would be ready to stop all work on the computers the moment the rest of the team came in with warrants.

Then two minutes before four o'clock the bank doors opened, and the police moved into the bank. The members inside went quickly into the offices of their assigned office. The workers and the occupants in the office were told to step away from the desk and to step outside where their phones were taken. The whole operation took less than five minutes.

At the same time, the banks in Mexico and America were entered and all links outside the banks were closed down. Plus, all cell phones were taken from everyone in the building to ensure there was no communication about the raid. The bank doors were closed and secured within six minutes. There was no sign that the raid had taken place. A rumor was circulated that a bomb scare was the reason for the closure.

A congratulation for a job well done was sent out to all teams. Teams of agents started going through the records. The individual banking members were placed in custody to keep the raid out of the news. The civilians were instructed that they were not to talk about what happened in the bank or they would face charges.

Later that day Nick said, "C.E. we will leave Kirk and Mathew here to go through the files, while you and I return to the States for the next phase of the operation on the Iranian connection."

"Do you think that may be the difficult part?" asked C.E.

"Well, we will be limited in how much we can do, but they have an outside business we can look at."

CHAPTER SIXTY-THREE

Madame Joseph Possibly a pseudonym for a group) was a supplier of forged stamps and over 400 cancellation tools. The forgeries were produced between the Great War and up to 1949. Many of the cancellations and stamps are valued at a higher price than the originals. The collection of the paraphilia was purchased by a stamp dealer and is now in the Royal Philatelic Society in London.

GENUINE

FORGERIES OVERPRINTS

We are victims of evil customs. It is a crime against humanity that our women are shut up within the four walls of the houses as prisoners. There is no sanction anywhere for the deplorable condition in which our women have to live.

— Muhammad Ali Jinnah

IRAN – PHASE THREE 2002

"**M**oses, what have you uncovered in the bank files?" asked Nick. "There is a nice money trail that leads back to several Iranian senior officials through Abdul. The funds seem to have been transferred to Diego and a Chinese business firm. I have not completed the audit of all the files, but the links are there. The best thing I discovered is some of these senior officials are setting up individual bank accounts in various countries that have strict banking rules," said Moses.

"You mean they are hiding money from the Iranian and the Chinese governments?" asked C.E.

"That would be my guess and it could also mean they are skimming funds for personal use. If that is the case, we can use that as leverage," said Moses.

"How are they getting the money?" asked C.E.

"I am not sure how right now, but I think it may have something to do with the stamps that C.E. has been looking into," said Moses.

"The stamps?" asked Nick.

"It appears that C.E. was right about the stamps. In the files there is a lot of money being loaned out with the stamps as collateral," said Moses.

"Is there a way of tracing those transactions?" asked Nick.

"There is a connection between all three banks and the Chinese company and a group in Iran. I cannot tell if the Iran group is a bank or a business group. It will take some time. This is like tracing illicit art sales. Not impossible, but difficult," said Moses.

"So, how do we interrupt the Iranian connection to Abdul's organization?" asked C.E.

"Pretty much what we have been doing. Increase the existing restrictions on oil and chemical movements, procurement operations, and travel activities of senior-level government and business officials. Plus, follow and freeze their funds to Hizballah and other extreme Islamic groups when those funds go through normal banking channels. This is a simple explanation. I know C.E. this is all more complex than I have said, but you get the idea," said Moses.

"I see, but how will that help?" asked C.E.

"The pressure will force them to move the money and then we will track those funds. It will take time," said Moses.

"I would like to know more on the stamps," said C.E.

"That is the interesting part for there has been a lot of activity on stamps in the files of the three banks. The stamps have been used as collateral for loans in other independent banks around the world. The funds have been used to buy land and small industrial companies in the U.S.A., France, Germany, and England. These companies all have a connection to technology and strategic industries, and the stamps were bought through various shell companies. I have turned those files over to Homeland Security for review," said Moses.

"Why stamps?" asked Nick.

"I may be jumping in too soon here, but I think if we check on the Hong Kong stamp market, we will see an increase in rare stamps being used in loan collateral in the last year. China and its new wealth have people trying to collect the past and stamps are part of that past. I have a friend who takes Chinese stamp albums to Hong Kong twice a year to sell and they pay for the trip and give him a handsome profit in return. Many of the buyers come from China mainland. Stamps are as good as land right now in Hong Kong," said C.E.

"Should we flood the market with these phony stamps," asked Nick.

"Are you kidding? That would ruin the market which is already in a period of change. What we need to do is expose the forgeries by issuing a warning that the stamps we know may be counterfeit and should be checked for authenticity. We can describe the errors in the stamps to the public and dealers. Then those that were used as collateral will be exposed and criminal action can be taken. The forgeries will still be sold to collectors, but not at high prices." said C.E.

"I was kidding about flooding the market, but you make a good point. I'll pass the idea up the chain of command.

"They might be able to link it to other parts of operations that have links between the senior officials that are setting up private funds," said Nick.

"This will cause some disruption with the loans once the collateral is proven false. We might be able to do this quietly at first to prevent a panic in the stamp and banking market," said Moses.

CHAPTER SIXTY-FOUR

Michel Zarwski was an accomplished producer of forgeries by taking inexpensive stamps and turning them into high-value stamps. There were many questions put forward about his reputation in the stamp world. To answer these questions in his own words he published a book to show his positive contributions to philately in France. Then, Herman Herst, Jr visited Zarwski and published the book in the English language. That edition went through three printings with the last two dropping Zarwski's name as a co-author.

GENUINE   **FORGERY**

Throughout history, it has been the inaction of those who could have acted; the indifference of those who should have known better; the silence of the voice of justice when it mattered most; that has made it possible for evil to triumph.

— Haile Selassie

THE HOME OF DAVUD DABIRI, IRAN

The Iranian use of surnames did not become popular until after 1919 much like the surnames in Turkey. Iranian surnames became more or less based on the region where one lived or the occupation one was doing at the time. Later other surnames were added to families.

At the home of Davud (David) Dabiri a small group was meeting to discuss the current situation after the disappearance of Abdul.

"What have you heard of Abdul?" asked Davud.

"Our security people think he and his son are in the custody of the Americans. That has not been confirmed," said Ziba.

"What makes the security people think that the two are in the custody of the Americans?" asked Davud.

"What is our exposure?" asked Dana.

"I do not know. The bad news is that the banks Abdul was working with have all been raided by the security agencies of those countries. They will be able to trace the records of our transactions and accounts with those bank's records. Plus, the funds there have been frozen," said Navid.

"Navid, you have not lived up to your name. I am afraid," said Davud.

"What do you mean?" asked Navid.

"Your name!" said Davud.

"What about my name?" asked Navid.

"What does it mean?" asked Davud.

"Oh, I see you are making a joke and a poor one considering the time," said Navid.

"What is he talking about?" asked Ziba.

"My name means 'Good News' and I just delivered bad news."

"We need to come up with a plan to turn this into a 'Sting' operation on Abdul and his operation. We planned to show he was working with the West and the Jews. The private accounts were part of our trap for Abdul and his partners. We had set accounts up to convince Abdul we agreed to enter his plan to blackmail Western nation's leaders. When the money was collected, it would be used for Islam and the downfall of Western society.

We will need a paper trail of our intention, which was to trap others in the government who were working with Abdul like the family of Fardin.

This may work to our benefit and help remove some of those bastards that oppose us," said Davud.

"I'll build a paper trail without using the internet. Our reasoning will be we had a real fear of leaks. We did not know who was working on the same page as Abdul," said Ziba.

"Whatever we do, it must be done in the next 12 hours and be set in place by then. The direction must always be pointed to others. May I suggest that we point the evidence towards General Hashem? He is the one that others will take the evidence as real for the views he has on the West. Many already suspect him and all we need to do is sow more of the evil seeds. He will react as he always does forcibly and arrogantly, which will draw more attention to himself. Then we can leak other little items to Ehsan," said Davud.

"That dolt Ehsan will take anything and build a claim that he has information and evidence to prove treason. He has been used by members of the council to attack the liberal members. Everyone knows he is a fibber," said Navid.

"He was a favorite of the Ayatollah Khomeini and after the revolution, he was part of the victors who removed any opposition to the Ayatollah. Ehsan was young at the time and he and others of the vanguard of the revolution removed more than 8,000 individuals that were accused of being counterrevolutionaries. They made other religions subservient to Shi'a and Sunni. Only three seats out of the 270 seats in parliament are for the non-Islamic minority.

"These minority religions — the Jews, Christians, and Zoroastrians — must have a Muslim principle. By 1990 the government shifted its attention to birth control in schools. Mandatory classes were required for newlywed couples. The subsidies for large families were cut and the government opened birth control clinics. We have cut the birth rate to half of what it was 20 years ago. Even with the government now encouraging more births, the rate remains the same at two births per family. That change came in part because of the war.

"The Iraq-Iran war cost so many young lives. Ehsan was behind the use of all the young boys as young as 14 who were sent into combat to be cut down like trees. None of the Ehsan relatives participated in war combat zones. He did use the war to stir up more anti-American hate," said Navid.

"Be careful Navid. Those words may cost you and your family," said Ziba.

"Isn't that the reason why our group was formed? We wanted to undermine the government and use people like those idiots Ehsan and Abdul.

"This government has pushed *Gharbzadegi* (detoxification) to wipe out Western culture in Iranian society. They want to return to the old religious ways by force if necessary. This has not been completely successful for Western culture influence remains despite the government's efforts to remove it. Over half of our university students in art still chose Western artists as their role models. Western music is still listened to in the homes of Iran.

"Today the government's hate of the Jews and the Americans has them pushing for a nuclear project that will most likely end in a conflict at best with just Israel and at worst with the Western world," said Navid.

"You are right Navid, but we need to focus on the present and how to save our organization from exposure to Abdul and the hardliners here in Iran," said Davud.

"We should have never entered into the operation with Abdul. What were we thinking?" said Ziba.

"The hope was Abdul would get exposed and bring down this government. I admit I was wrong, but now we are in it, and we need to act fast," said Davud.

"I'll have the paperwork trail set up that will make it seem we were attempting to trap the members of Abdul's group in a corruption and anti-government network," said Ziba.

"Good, we have a plan and will meet back here in six hours and go over the plan and details. Now I must go to my wife," said Davud.

Walking outside the home of Davud, Dana turned to Ziba and asked, "Why is Davud so intent on removing the Fardin brothers?"

"That family is evil and joined the group to collect information to blackmail others in power within the government. The death of Fardin has given Davud a chance to rid the organization of individuals that are blood suckers and not true believers in our cause. Davud will not miss Abdul for he was a ruthless taskmaster with no human compassion," said Ziba.

"Then why did Davud allow Abdul into the organization?" asked Dana.

"Davud is a good religious Islamic man that has his conflicts with good and evil. He hates this government," said Ziba.

"I do not understand what you are saying. What conflict?" said Dana.

"Well, let's say you want to change things or prevent certain things and you have a choice on how to accomplish the change. One choice is the expedient way with questionable individuals like the Fardin brothers and Abdul. The other choice is with moral individuals who will not see that the end justifies the methods used to obtain the desired results. Davud has been experiencing a moral dilemma on how he had made his choices. Now, he has welcomed the opportunity to remove part of those bad choices. He has wanted an Islamic world of the past within a modern world," said Ziba.

"I see you have been thinking about this for a long time," said Dana.

"Not really, Davud came to me just before all this happened and was worried that he had lost his moral compass. He was questioning the killing of innocent in the cause. Now I think with this opportunity with Abdul he will move away from the radicals and their Machiavelli methods to save the Islamic world," said Ziba.

"I am glad we have had this little talk for I have also questioned the morality of what we have done at times," said Dana.

"Dana, evil is always wanting for an opportunity to present itself to the world."

CHAPTER SIXTY-FIVE

Rainer Blum was arrested and sentenced to four years probation for philatelic fraud in a case that was bigger than the Madame Joseph case and the Dieter Kruger case. At the time of the Blum case, the agents collected over 600 cancellation devices and some 50 different counterfeit stamps. It is unknown how much damage was done to the philatelic market. The German Philatelic Society published a guide on the forgeries and cancellation marks. Plus, some 41 experts' names were forged to verify the stamps. The case ended in 2006.

GENUINE

FORGERY
OVERPRINT

If money is the root of all evil, then China's manipulation of its currency, the yuan, is the tap root of everything wrong with the U.S.-China trade relationship.

— Peter Navarro

CHINA - PHASE FOUR OF PLAN

"Mayor Bo, what do you have to report on Abdul?" asked Leader He.

"It seems that Abdul failed in his plan to set off a dirty bomb in the L.A. Harbor. It is believed he and his son are now in the custody of the Americans," said Mayor Bo.

"If that is the case, what can come back to us?" asked Party member Ying.

"We have a very limited exposure. There is a connection with the one engineer we sent to North Korea to work on their nuclear project," said Mayor Bo.

"Then have him recalled now and when he returns have him lost in one of the re-education camps. Now what else?" asked Leader He.

"One other thing is the stamps. It appears Abdul was not being straight with us. The stamps are forgeries, and we have a good deal of money invested with them and most of it is in the banks in Hong Kong," said Mayor Bo.

"How did this happen? Did we have the stamps verified by experts?" asked Leader He.

"It appears the expert was in on the deal with Abdul and his Mexican Cartel. The stamp forgery business seems to have many stamp dealers involved in the illegal trade. I will plan to correct this error with our special unit." said Mayor Bo.

"Well, that is a boat that we may not want to rock right now. We will have to take the loss for the time being. Hong Kong right now is a delicate issue with the 'One Country Two System'. Over time that policy will not last, and Hong Kong will be a complete part of China once again. Time is on our side, and we will slowly take steps to undermine their political and economic institutions. I believe that Hong Kong will be under one system within the next 20 years," said Party member Ying.

"What should our response be if the Americans try to connect us to Abdul?" asked Mayor Bo.

"The best thing to do is deny everything. They have no money trail to tie us to Abdul for we did not take any money. The only money sent from us was for humanitarian causes and those old, valued stamps we used as collateral. The only real link is the engineer and our part in helping a neighboring nation. We can blame that on radical Muslims for the theft of nuclear waste.

"Besides, the Americans want the Chinese market to open for their products. Those that we cannot induce for the rewards of our market profit, we will win with brides and 'blackmail'. The greed of some of the American political families will overshadow their national interest. Political policy will bend to that of their greed. No! We will not have much of a problem over this small act of terrorism by Abdul," said leader He.

"What about the stamps?" asked Ying.

"I have begun collecting the stamps to remove them from any collections," said leader He.

"On a different subject, our people in the American Universities are slowly working in research positions. The policy of pulling the agents out after a few years will impede the continuation of their research in areas that we have been giving a high priority. There are two agents in high clearance positions and three more that are in line to work on American projects of national defense. Should I pull them out or allow them to stay?" asked Mayor Bo.

"Leave them and assign teams to watch them for any sign of turning. In fact, why not set up special units in a major city in America to watch the Chinese community there? Living in that open society can turn heads," said Party member Ying.

"Good idea and very well, I'll see that it is done," said Mayor Bo.

"How is the I.T. project going?" asked leader He.

"The foreign communication companies are doing a great job building our telecommunication network. We have had to spin off other companies in our communication companies. The foreign companies have agreed to follow our culturally specific conditions to gain access to our market. Today there is only about ten percent of our population with a cell phone, but that is changing rapidly. The fact that the Western world has allowed us to be a 'transition economy' has been a good economic benefit," said Party member Ying

"That is true, but this new hand-held technology is a double-edged sword. We need to find a way to control it. The increased ability to communicate will allow people to form collective action and give them the ability to mobilize fast. As these devices improve, their speed will increase. We need to control this information network within the country. If not, another demonstration like Tiananmen Square will have a verbal and photographic view of information out there to embarrass the leadership," said Leader He.

"I have a plan that will allow censorship to be in fewer and fewer hands. Then we can control those hands. Give people power and they will try to hold onto it. The West thinks military weapons make powerful nations. That is true in the short term, but communication and control information is a far better weapon. Once we are tied into the world communications networks, our path to be the next world leader will be a lot easier," said Party member Ying.

"Alright, that is all for now, keep me updated. I will need to report our progress," said Leader He.

As Ying and Bo walked out of the room. He picked up the phone. "We need to meet."

CHAPTER SIXTY-SIX

Clive Feigenbaum was a colorful character in the Great British stamp world. Then in 1970 he was expelled from the Philatelic Traders Society. That did not stop him. In 1971 he was charged with dishonesty in handling stamps only to be cleared of charges on the 'judges' direction. Then in 1984 he applied to be readmitted to the Society and leading stamp dealers threatened to resign if he was readmitted. He withdrew his application.

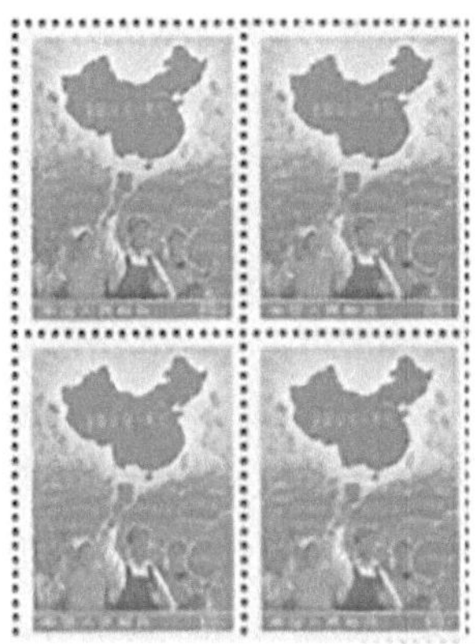

"Everywhere China is Red"

It is a man's own mind, not his enemy or foe, that lures him to evil ways.

— Buddha

HONG KONG 2002

In 1984 the British government agreed to hand over the government of Hong Kong to the Chinese mainland government. The Chinese agreed to allow the people of Hong Kong to have a high degree of autonomy. By 1997 Hong Kong became a Special Administrative Region of China. Then in 1998, the first legislative election was held under Chinese rule and the policy of 'One Country, Two Systems' was formed.

By 2002 Hong Kong banking was the 11th largest bank system of external assets and 7th in foreign exchange trading. The Gross Domestic Product (GPD) of Hong Kong was taking off in real terms by 2002.

Over the years from 1998, the Hong Kong constitution had been re-interpreted and civil liberties were slowly being reduced. Chief Executive Tung Chee-Hwa won a second five-year term without a public vote. Tung then appointed 14 Ministers to run the Civil Service instead of career civil servants. He also shook up the government by appointing new Cabinet members. The interpretation of the law that defined who had the right to live in Hong Kong in 1999 was a Constitutional Crisis. Journalists complained that freedom of expression was deteriorating.

The religious group Falun Gong had its foreign members deported. The group was outlawed on the mainland, but still allowed in Hong Kong. The group was being watched and placed under some government measures to control them. The group's activities were monitored.

Twelve members of Falun Gong were being prosecuted and convicted of obstruction and assault on police officers. A new law called Article #23 was proposed that made any contact with any foreign organizations acts of sedition against the central government of China.

Demonstrations were being planned. Hong Kong was changing, and people were taking caution on what and how to say anything that could be seen by the government as disloyal.

Business owners had to watch who they did business with in any investments in foreign trade. The mainland government was slowly removing the existing policy of One Country, Two Systems.

Mr. Lei was the owner of one of the largest stamp stores on the Kowloon peninsula in the Ho Mong Kok Shopping Centre. He was sitting at his desk and looked up from the stamps he was inspecting to see a banker come through the door. He knew the banker only through his wife's family.

"Good afternoon Mr. Cheng, I didn't know you had an interest in stamps," said Mr. Lei.

"I don't, you are right, but I have a very delicate question you may answer with some desecration," said Mr. Cheng nervously.

"I can assure you that our business information does not and will not leave this office. Most people do not know the value of stamps. Some are very rare and have a great value. So, how may I help you?" asked Mr. Lei.

"My bank took a 1968 stamp as collateral for a loan and now it seems the buyer has defaulted, and I am afraid that stamp is worthless," said Mr. Cheng.

"May I see the stamp in question?" asked Mr. Lei.

Mr. Cheng produced a block of four stamps that were made in 1968 to celebrate the cultural revolution in China. The stamp is known as 'Everywhere China is Red'.

"Oh, my!" said Mr. Lei.

"What is it? The bad news?" asked Mr. Cheng.

"Yes and no," said Mr. Lei.

"What do you mean? I cannot have bad news on this. The bank would be out a huge amount of money," said Mr. Cheng.

"Well, you have a very rare stamp, and this one has very fine details. This is, as you said, a 1968 rare issue stamp. The problem is with Taiwan on the engraving. It has always been considered part of the People's Republic of China. The saying, 'Everywhere China is Red' failed to express that idea on the stamp," said Mr. Lei.

"How? The stamp is beautiful and the young person holding the *Little Red* book makes no doubt that it is about the Cultural Revolution. How could anyone doubt that?" asked Mr. Cheng.

"You are right. Stamps are little pieces of art and are also seen as propaganda with attention to the smallest detail. A word misspelled, a word missing, an image wrong, or the wrong color used can cause the stamp to be recalled and taken out of circulation. So, look again at the stamp and the Map of China and locate Taiwan. Do you see it?" asked Mr. Lei.

"Yes! I see it!" said Mr. Cheng.

"Describe it to me," said Mr. Lei.

"It is the tiny island of Taiwan to the east of China's mainland. Right here," said Mr. Cheng.

"What color is it?" asked Mr. Lei.

"White," said Mr. Cheng.

"Do you see it now and what I mean?" asked Mr. Lei.

"No! I see a white island. So what I need to know is the value of the stamp," said Mr. Cheng.

"What is the stamp saying?" asked Mr. Lei.

"Everywhere China is Red," said Mr. Cheng.

"Yes and is that island part of China?" asked Mr. Lei.

"Yes, of course it is!" said Mr. Cheng.

"If that is true, what color should the island be?" asked Mr. Lei.

"Oh, no, I see what you mean. Taiwan is part of China and should be red and it is white and not red," said Mr. Cheng.

"Yes, and because of that little missing red color on that small island all the stamps were recalled and removed from circulation. A few did get by the authorities in their attempt to remove the embarrassment to the Party. That one stamp, if real, could be worth close to a million in U.S. dollars today in Hong Kong," said Mr. Lei.

"You said good and bad news. I hope this was the bad news," asked Mr. Cheng.

"I am sorry your stamp is a forgery, although a very good one at that, but still a forgery," said Mr. Lei.

"How?"

"The paper is wrong and is missing the chalk surface that prevents any attempt to alter the stamp," said Mr. Lei.

"Has the stamp any value other than as a copy of the original stamp?" asked Mr. Cheng.

"Some, but nothing near the value of an original stamp. I am sorry to give you such news Mr. Cheng. You should have had the stamp evaluated," said Mr. Lei.

"We had the stamp appraised and were told it was an original 1968.

But that appraiser has left Hong Kong and moved to Iran or Mexico. I cannot remember where! We cannot find him now. The bank will have to eat the cost and I will be responsible. I will most likely lose my position with the bank. Thank you for your time. I must go back to the office now and face the inevitable. Thank you again for your time," said Me. Cheng as he picked up the stamp and left the stamp dealer's office.

When Mr. Cheng reached his office, he was told two individuals were waiting for him. He walked to his office and saw two well-dressed men sitting outside. He almost turned to walk away.

"Mr. Cheng?" said one of the men.

"Yes"

"I am Mr. Zhen and this is Mr. Xue we represent an agency that would like to buy a stamp we believe you have in possession of the bank," said Mr. Zhen

"The bank has only one stamp in our possession, and I am afraid that stamp is a forgery and not worth the value we placed on it. I just came back from a second appraisal," said Mr. Cheng.

"We are aware of the fact that the stamp is a forgery, and we are willing to take the stamp for the value that you loaned at the time," said Mr. Xue.

"Why?" asked Mr. Cheng.

"Let's just say that it would be a financial problem if your bank had a scandal and the stamp market would suffer with the news of a forgery of this magnitude becoming public. The only thing is that once we take the stamp nothing is to be said about the stamp again! You may only say it was purchased by an anonymous buyer." said Mr. Zhen.

"When would you like to make this transaction?" asked Mr. Cheng.

"Now, in this briefcase is the required amount. If you have the stamp available, we will finish this transaction today," said Xue.

"I have the stamp with me, and it will take a moment. I will have a clerk fill out the proper paperwork. I'll be right back," said Mr. Cheng as he walked out of the room and down the hall. He took the stamp out of his pocket and handed it to his secretary and told her to fill out a purchase order for the amount. He waited for her to finish then returned to the room.

"Here is the item in question gentlemen."

"Thank you for your cooperation, Mr. Cheng," said Mr. Xue as he looked over the document. There was no mention of the stamp being a forgery.

Later that night Mr. Cheng could not believe his luck but was worried that this was not the end of that stamp transaction. Two individuals just do not show up with a briefcase full of money and know your business transactions. No those were the mainland government officials and worried. He would never tell anyone of the incident. There was more to this than just a stamp and a loan involved. For now, his bank and he were safe from a huge loss.

Miles away on the mainland a meeting was held.

"Have all the stamps been recovered?" asked Leader He.

"Yes, that is all that is in China," said Mr. Xue

"What about those in other countries?"

"There are only five stamps that we know that are still out. One is in Iran and three are in Mexico with the last one in a private collection in the United States. There is no link to us in any of those stamp dealings. These private purchases were done with banks and stores in Israel and Mexico. Since they are held by private parties, there is little chance they will be on the open stamp market soon," said Mr. Xue

"What about the people we have had to buy the stamps from?" asked Leader He.

"The only individual that knew the stamps were fakes was the bank official in the Hong Kong bank that held their stamps as collateral on a loan. The manager had the stamp reevaluated the day our agents were there and when he returned to the bank the exchanges were made right then on the spot.

The bank was in considerable debt with the stamp. The banker told our agents that it was worthless when they asked about it. They said they understood and that they wanted to keep his bank and the stamp market stable. He was very happy to allow us to take the stamp at the price of the loan," said Mr. Zhen.

"Very good, keep a watch on the banker for the next several months. This is not to get into the public view," said Leader He.

"That will be done. There is little doubt he will mention this to anyone. If the rumor of the bank was loaning that much money on a stamp that was a forgery, it would ruin the bank's reputation and his. No, he will never discuss this with anyone," said Mr. Xue.

"Good, keep me informed."

CHAPTER SIXTY-SEVEN

Louis-Henri Mercier (Henri Goegg) produced very high-quality reproductions, but his business sense was poor, and he went bankrupt. Francois Fournier purchased the Mercier collection. Fournier claimed to have been awarded several philatelic awards; however, the dates show that all the awards were won in fact by Mercier.

GENUINE

FORGERIES

No man is justified in doing evil on the grounds of expediency.

— Theodore Roosevelt

2002 – The Arrest of Bankers

At the staging area, Nick and C.E. were coordinating the operation to take individuals into custody from the Arabic Agricultural Bank.

"Everyone, this is a delicate operation on an international bank. Our raid on the Moody and Stiner banks gave us this lead to this source of funds for terrorists. So everyone you must follow the book to the letter on this operation.

It is now 05:30 and we are set H-hour at 06:30. Moses and C.E. will be with the 'M' team. Daniel and I will be with the "B" team. It seems the Israeli Mossad has an interest and has been given permission to participate in the operation. Moses, will you go over your part of the operation?" asked Nick.

"We have been watching this individual for several weeks and his routine begins at 06:15 every day. That is why we will surprise him before he is dressed. Agents will enter the house from the front door with a warrant for the individual and all papers in the house. All exits will be covered so that nobody leaves during the search and their phones will be confiscated. This is a possible terrorist case so be careful.

"Team "B" will be coordinated with Team "A" and members of "B" will be giving all top officials of the bank subpoenas at the same time members of "A" team will serve the vice president of the bank and he will be taken into custody, then taken to the bank to unlock the bank doors. Once we are in the bank all computers will be shut down until our I.T. guys get there to go over the network.

"We will be looking for links to other banks and that is where the Mossad will enter the picture. They have traced the terrorist funds that are at the heart of these organizations.

"We need to know who is funding the terrorism by tracking the money trail. The Mossad has a connection to the Iranians, and we have one with Mexico. The hope is we can make a solid connection between the two," said Nick.

"At 06:30 the front doorbell of Ali Asfour's house rang and was answered by the maid. She was handed a search warrant, and a stream of men and women entered the house. Upstairs Ali was calling out to the maid. "Who is at the door this time in the morning Alice?" yelled Mr. Asfour.

"Men with a search warrant Mr. Asfour!"

"What? Who are they?"

"There is a dozen of them. They just rushed by me, Mr. Asfour!" Alice yelled.

"Are you Ali Asfour?" asked two men as they raced up the stairs.

"Yes! Who the HELL are you?"

"We are the men from the FBI that have been sent to take you into custody and here is your warrant Mr. Asfour. We will wait for you to get dressed in our presence."

"I am calling my lawyer, NOW!" said Mr. Asfour.

"Sorry sir, that will not be possible until you are at the station. I would suggest you read the warrant," said the lead agent.

"This states that I am suspected of terrorism. This is ridiculous! I am a respected banker in this city and country. I want… No, I demand I call my lawyer!" said Asfour.

"Our instructions are to take you into custody and deliver you down-town after you are allowed to get dressed." The man said as he stepped away and spoke into his radio.

"This is team 'M' reporting that the individual is in our custody and the house is secured," Moses said over the phone.

At another location:

Eric Hoffmann was still in bed when the doorbell rang, and his wife answered it. She was greeted with FBI badges and warrant papers that were given to her as the agents started to walk past her.

"What is this?" she asked.

"I am sorry Mrs. Hoffmann. The papers are a warrant for the arrest of your husband. He is to be taken into custody along with all the papers in the house as per the search warrants for the office here at the house. So, will you please step aside so we may proceed?" asked Nick.

"I'll go and wake up my husband."

"That is not possible, I'm afraid Mrs. Hoffmann. So once again please step aside," said Nick.

"What the devil is going on here?" asked Eric as he walked up to the door.

"Are you Eric Hoffmann?"

"Yes, who the Hell are you?"

"Mr. Eric Hoffmann, we have a warrant to take you into custody. We are to stay by your side until you are delivered to our office. We will go with you so we can get dressed. Mrs. Hoffmann, will you show these men to your husband's office?" said Nick.

"I want to call my lawyer right now!" demanded Eric.

"I am sorry our instructions are to allow no phone calls until you are delivered to the office," said C.E.

"Am I under arrest?" asked Eric.

"No, sir, you are being taken into custody for your protection," said Nick.

"My protection? Why do I need protection?" asked Eric.

"Your bank has been doing business with the cartels in Mexico. Their accounts have been frozen, and they believe you are responsible," said C.E.

"What are you saying?" asked Eric's wife.

"That your husband's bank has been doing major money transactions with Mexican Cartels and a known Middle East terrorist organization. Right now they are not happy with him," said C.E.

"Then what about my family?" asked Eric.

"They are also going to a safe house for their protection," said Nick.

"This cannot be serious!" said Eric's wife. "My husband is a banker, not a criminal. I am not leaving my house."

"Do you want to take a chance on what these groups will do to your kids?" asked Nick.

"They would not hurt my children!"

"They will and have done worse to other families. Do not think they will leave your family alone," said Nick.

"Alright, I'll get dressed. My dear, get the kids. We will have to let this play out. The cartels are animals and will wipe out a whole family to send a message," said Eric.

"Banker "H" is in custody and the house is secured," radioed Nick.

Later outside, "That went well. At first, I thought the wife was going to be a major problem," said C.E.

"I think you were right until you came out with that cartel scare. That was brilliant. Even Eric changed when the cartel revenge was brought up. Did you notice he did not blink at the mention of the cartel?" asked Nick.

"Yeah, he knew who he was doing business with in Mexico," said C.E.

"I am sorry I did not ask if we were to say anything about the cartels. I just wanted that woman to think about her children,' said C.E.

"No, it worked perfectly," said Nick.

CHAPTER SIXTY-EIGHT

Erasmo Oneglia worked with many other forgers. He produced stamp forgeries with fairly good watermarks. He was arrested in 1897 attempting to sell imitations to Stanley Gibbons, Ltd. His stock was confiscated, and he was fined 20 shillings.

He continued the shady trade of imitation with many well-known Italian forgers. He died in 1937 after a long career of creating forgeries.

GENUINE

**GDR PROPAGANDA
NOTE THE HANGMAN'S NOOSE**

The World is a dangerous place to live, not because of the people who are evil, but because of the people who don't do anything about it.

— Albert Eisenstein

BANKING AND STAMP SCAMS 2002

Members of the team were sitting in the conference room and Kirk was explaining banking and money laundering to the group.

"This is a quick and very simple explanation of banking. The scams that can reach into the billions of dollars within major lending institutions that either knowingly or unknowingly can be involved in several different ways. Such as 'Mirror Trading' or 'Structuring' or some other scams that are often pulled off with shell companies.

"'Mirror' trading is a scam done with two transactions being done at the same time. For example, money is deposited in the bank. Then the bank is told at the same time to buy stocks with the funds. While stocks are bought, they are sold at a different location within seconds. It appears that on the face of it, nothing has happened. It is called a wash, and the money was moved and cleaned.

"The 'Structuring' trade is slower and takes time. A large number of small transactions are done in a specific pattern. This is done to avoid setting off triggering alarms of large amounts. This is done with "Shell companies" that are used in most of the scams.

"A Shell company exists mostly only on paper and is a very effective way in the mixing of 'dirty' money with legal money. Today an increase in the sales price of property and legalized online gambling is starting to be used in the money laundering market. That is as brief as I can make it," said Kirk.

"O.K., that is the money aspect of this case. Any questions?" asked Nick.

"What is for lunch?" asked one member as the room broke out in laughter.

"Edward you should cut out the lunches as I was told by your belt," said another member as more laughter broke out.

"O. K. Back to the topic, if we may! Mathew, please give us a short rundown on the world of the Black-Market art world," said Nick.

"This area of the illegal art world became better known after the Second World War. The invading armies carried off many pieces of valuable artwork that had already been stolen by the Nazis before and after they swept through Europe confiscating 20% of the artwork of Europe. Then when the Allied troops retook the territory many of the masterpieces were sent or carried home by soldiers only to turn up years later.

"The provenance of the artwork, that is the ownership, was clouded or even lost. Many of the owners were killed in the camps and that left the descendants of the families to place claims on the artworks. Those claims take time. For example, in 2000 Frans Snyder's painting of *Still Life with Fruit and Game* was returned to the rightful owners. There are still some 30,000 pieces of art that have not been discovered or recovered.

"Some of these pieces are in private collections or stuffed in a basement or attic by a returning G.I. that picked up the art as a souvenir. Once in a while, a lost painting will show up at a garage sale or on the Black Market with stolen art.

"The fact is art theft is a poor return because you need a buyer willing to pay. Many art thieves think they can just advertise the item and have buyers falling over themselves to buy the art. That is when someone talks to too many individuals, and we discover the lost artwork is on the market.

"This year the Amsterdam Van Gogh Museum had two of their paintings stolen and, in a few years, they will show up when someone wants to unload them. To show how long this may be, in 1990 the Boston Museum was hit for a dozen paintings. It happened when two criminals impersonating police officers came in and overpowered the guards. They made off with several works of art that have been valued at six million dollars. There were lots of suspects and stories of the Boston Mafia about the theft. The art is still out there.

"The only real way to make art theft profitable is to have a millionaire ready to buy and there are few of those. Few people collect art as a hobby. This brings me to these little pieces of art called stamps. Our consultant on the subject, C.E., will continue that part of the discussion," said Mathew.

"I will do the best I can for I am not an accredited stamp expert, I am just a collector. So, here goes. Forgeries have been around for a long time and the art of stamp forgery has expanded that activity into other stamp activities. For example, stamps are canceled so they cannot be reused, and some canceled stamps can have more value than the never used stamps.

"The 1936 Nazi German Olympics commemorative stamps had two runs. The first run was done when the German population had little money to spend so the first run of stamps was almost all used. That made the first run of unused stamps more valuable.

"The second run was done when the Germans had more money, so they saved the stamps. This run of those stamps has a higher value if they are canceled. This brings me to Madame Joseph and canceled stamps. She had some 450 canceling tools for fake cancellations. Books have been written on how to identify Madame Joseph's forgeries.

"All countries have at one time, or another used forgeries to wage war and propaganda against their enemies. The American government went into fakes during the Second World War to help ruin the German economy in a program called Operation Cornflakes by the OSS.

"One of the most famous examples of this is a stamp during World War II with Hitler's image decaying into a skull. It is called the 'Hitler Death Skull' stamp with the words 'Ruined Empire' instead of 'German Empire' printed at the bottom of the stamp.

This stamp's existence only came to light when some copies of it were discovered in FDR's collection after his death.

"There are many forgeries of this stamp. Operation Cornflake was carried out in 1945 when American planes dropped 320 mailbags over trains that were damaged in bombing raids. The mailbags contained letters addressed to individuals in Germany with propaganda messages and forged stamps. Some of the letters were gathered up and sent on through the German mail system. The efficiency of the German mail system was still delivering mail and stamps to postal offices as the Russians entered Berlin at the end of the war.

"The Cold War did not stop the practice of foreign governments playing with propaganda in stamps. In the East German Democratic Republic, there appeared a propaganda stamp of the William Pieck 24 pfennigs stamp. It went through the postal service. The image of William had a hangman noose around his neck instead of a traditional western necktie. But let's not let me get sidetracked by my passion.

"So, the simple answer is, if there are only a few stamps of a certain kind in circulation the value is higher. For instance, there is a British Guiana "one cent" stamp that has been the only known stamp of its kind in existence. When another stamp of the British Guiana "one cent" stamps was found, the owner of the first stamp bought the second stamp and then had the second stamp destroyed to keep the value of his stamp high. That owner I believe was John du Pont, who owned the genuine stamp. You might remember he was convicted of murder a few years ago.

"As for the present case: We have many different parties involved from different countries including Iran, China, Mexico, Turkey, and the United States. So, now we are back to Kirk," said C.E.

"O.K. now back to the present as we have gone through the banking and files from the Steiner and Moody homes, we were able to trace the money and a few links to the stamp sales. As for Iran and China, they will be dead ends; although, we have a solid link to one bank in Hong Kong and one here in this country which is the Arabic Agriculture Bank. The Hong Kong bank sold the stamp when the buyer failed on a loan. The buyer was anonymous so that is a dead end. We believe the Chinese government or someone high in the Party bought the stamp to cover up the scandal that had ties to China.

"Turkey it seems was just the clearing house for Mexico and Iran and went through the Arabic Agricultural Bank here. One bit of luck was we found two stamps in Rudy's office. It seems he is a collector. He had one of the Inverted Jenny stamps and one of the 'Whole Country is Red', a Chinese stamp that embarrassed that government," said Kirk.

"That stamp was a forgery of the stamp that China had pulled out of circulation because of the missing red color on the island of Taiwan. He had paperwork for the stamps that said he bought it at an auction in Mexico City last year. The problem is the auction house is no longer in business and the owners are nowhere to be found. The scam went to great care to provide documentation," said C.E.

"We do have a paper trail to Charles Moody and Steiner and less on Rudy. The two will be charged with laundering money for terrorists and Mexican Cartels. The best we can charge Rudy with is receiving stolen goods for we also discovered some artwork that was recently stolen in the Middle East and will be returned there after the trial. Some were found in his home. He seems good for those charges," said Kirk.

"So for now this case against these men is closed and it has been a success. We have closed a terrorist network down and shut down a conduit for money laundering. However, the reason for this meeting is to continue looking at this money trail. Good job everyone," said Nick.

CHAPTER SIXTY-NINE

Angelo Panelli began his occupation in the shady stamp world while he was a Tomato grower in Italy. His first stamp contracts were written on the reverse side of 'Wheats Leaf Tomatoes' labels. Soon he was producing his counterfeit stamps and was convicted in 1927 for counterfeiting and served seven months. He continued his trade and became a clearing house for other well-known forgers.

GENUINE

FORGERY

Hell is paved with good intentions.

— Samuel Johnson

CLOSURE 2002

"You know Nick if I ever go into criminal activity I'll do it as a banker. These guys are guilty of stealing hundreds of millions of dollars, and they are forced to pay what sounds like a huge fine. The millions they are going to pay is a drop in the bucket for them. The five-year sentence will most likely be served in a nice white-collar prison and those two bankers will not serve the whole time, because of their age. It makes me wonder why I try," said C.E.

"To tell the truth I feel the same way many days. Most bankers are good honest individuals and very few step over to the other side. I wonder what could happen to this country if we stopped battling evil. These bad guys can buy very good lawyers that poke holes into our case so that they can claim the system is unfair. Justice for these lawyers is following the procedures. Justice is blind except to procedures. It may feel at times that it is unfair, but if we did not have checks on the government's power, then what would we have?" asked Nick.

"It is just that Rudy is as guilty as his father and Werner and yet he walks away a free man again with his millions. We did not have or failed to use the evidence to convict him, and we cannot convict on our personal belief of his guilt.

If you remember right, many at the trial of O. J. Simpson did not believe that O. J. was guilty. The fact was that the government lawyers and police did a poor job and failed to make a good case filled with errors by the officers and attorneys. Yet, they became celebrities and were viewed as experts from O.J.'s defense team including the lead detective and prosecuting attorneys. That case generated over 50 books on the trial within five years.

Yet, today most people today think O. J. did commit those murders. That trial will become as famous as the Sacco and Vanzetti trial or the Lindbergh kidnapping trial. What those trials had in common was they were public show trials and had poor defense attorneys or poor prosecution attorneys." said C.E.

"C.E. you and I know that these trials we are about to set in motion will most likely never make the evening news for more than one night or two. But we will know they will have been tried and hopefully end in conviction. We will know that we have stopped evil once more," said Nick.

"I know you are right we broke up an international plot to blow up the L.A. Harbor with a dirty bomb and took down a major world banking criminal organization. I just do not like loose ends."

"That is what makes you a good investigator and remember you are a member of this team as a consultant. Go home and get some rest, my friend."

"I would say the same to you Nick, but I saw the case on your desk. So good luck."

"See you notice things others miss and I must be more careful with reports and paperwork when you are around. I'll see you C.E."

C.E. got home and Chief Franklin was sitting on his porch. "Agent Nick Thomson told me you were on your way home, and you should be here by seven, so I came over to have a glass of wine with you and hear all about your adventure."

"If you don't mind, there is someone I must call first," said C.E.

"Not at all, but she'll be here in about ten minutes. I think she is a little upset that you did not call every day. I'm just guessing!"

"Did she say that? I tried to explain I was going between here, New York, Chicago, and Mexico. I am lucky, I did not have to go to Hong Kong."

"She said you told her you were too busy to talk or call every day," said the Chief.

"I did not say that C.E. and Chief Franklin. You are trying to stir the pot. I think the Chief has a crush on me and wants to break us up," said Elaine as she walked up.

"Do not start that rumor. My wife has a temper and besides she tells me I am too ugly for anyone, but her. Now tell us all about your adventure and case," said Elaine.

"I would, but I had to sign a national security document and all I can say about the case is that there is always an opportunity for evil out there."

CHAPTER SEVENTY

R. Wiering was given permission from postal authorities to reprint Imperial German stamps of Alsace and Lorraine in 1870 after he contributed 7,000 Marks to the German Postal employee's fund. The reprinting ran 1,000 sheets of the stamps or 150,000 stamps. They are not identified as forgeries today, but are technically designated 'Official Imitations'. Many still refer to them as forgeries and there are many still in circulation.

GENUINE

FORGERY

As human beings we have the most extraordinary capacity for evil. We can perpetrate some of the most horrendous atrocities.

— Desmond Tutu

2002 - BACK HOME

"**C**. E. it is nice to have you home. We all missed you more this time for some reason while you were on this little adventure of yours. I think it was because it was for the FBI," said Elaine.

"I'll second that C.E., you seem to get into the most interesting adventures for a guy with no real talent," said Chief Franklin.

"Elaine, I missed you also, but Chief most of my adventures come from you. That is if you think about it. This recent adventure started with your fire at the print shop. I must say that after this little episode, I am a firm believer in one thing and that is evil will take every opportunity to work its way back into our life," said C.E.

"What do you mean?" asked Elaine.

"Well, remember the case I had recently with the Nazi stamp album. I cannot tell you about this case, but some of the characters in that case popped up once more. Here is a little history of evil. During and after World War II the Allied governments started to fall out between Eastern Europe around the Soviet Union on one side with Western Europe and the United States on the other. The Soviet Union had been a partner with Germany until 1941 when Germany invaded Russia. The West supplied the Soviets with war materials that allowed the Soviet army to stay in the fight. The war ended with the Soviets expanding their control from Moscow.

"Both the West and Eastern powers rushed to collect the Nazi scientific knowledge. The Soviet Union began the rounding up of Nazi scientists and families under a relocation process that did collect some 6,000 individuals with specialized knowledge in rockets and other areas of new technology.

"The United States for its part relocated some 1,500 Nazi scientists in an operation called Overcast and renamed it later as Operation Paperclip which was approved by President Truman in September 1946. There were some 15 other operations like this to bring Nazis to the West for various reasons. The Nazis were running to any place they could to hide their past.

"By 1946 there were two main 'Ratlines' to bring Nazis to the West. The first was from Germany to Spain. The second was from Germany to Rome to Genoa then on to South America. Many of these former Nazis were important in rocket science and went on to win awards for their work for the U.S. Government, such as Wernher von Braun who was the best of the Nazi *SS* rocket scientists.

"Today he is listed as a German American Aerospace engineer. Many of these German Nazis just blended into American society. Only years later a few of the lower-level members were called out to be German Nazi war criminals involved in the Holocaust. They were exposed and went through the courts for extradition. Recently, one of these Nazis was identified and living in Queens, New York. It will take years before his case works its way through the legal system and he is deported. There were over a thousand low-level Nazis allowed to enter this country after the war.

"Many of these Nazis were used by agencies in the United States to undermine the Soviets in Eastern Europe. Most of those individuals trained as spies for the West were picked up by the KGB as soon as they entered the other side of the Iron Curtin. The simple reason was the Western intelligence network was filled with Soviet agents and some of these were in high positions in the British intelligence agency.

"At the same time Stalin and the Soviet Union were using American and Allied POWs as bargaining chips to force the Allied powers to repatriate (in other words to force) Soviet POWs back to the Soviet Union. Many of these individuals were forced to return at gunpoint and were executed as soon as they set foot back on Soviet land. The lucky ones were sent to the Gulags.

"The West had reports and solid evidence that there were some 1.5 million American POWs (Prisoners of War) that were liberated from German prisoners of war camps by the Red Army as it moved into Germany in 1945. Then between March and April, some 500,000 of these Allied POWs disappeared from the records and the American and Western European administrations decided against the use of force to recover these Allied POWs to ensure the Soviets's help against the Japanese Army in Asia. It was believed that 20,000 Allied POWs were held as hostages by the Soviet Union at the end of the war.

"Many of the returning POWs were told not to discuss the issue for national security. In at least one nation, the returning men were required (forced) to sign a document on State Secrets. If they mentioned the POWs left in the Soviet Union that would be grounds to have the individual sent to prison," said C.E.

"Why are you telling us this C.E.," asked the Chief.

"Well, I cannot tell you about what I worked on with the FBI, but I can say that once you think you stopped evil it pops up once more in a different suit. When anyone steps off the moral path it becomes a very slippery slope. That step may seem the right thing to do at the time. It's just that once off the path it is hard to get back on the right path.

"Many Arabs leaders sided with the Nazis during World War II in the hope for their independence. What they did achieve was the idea of a leadership that was based on the principle of "Might Makes Right" which led to conflict between the Arab nations and the new nation of Israel in the first of many wars between the two groups.

"After the first Arab-Israel war, evil worked its way into everyday life in the form of hate. The surrounding Arab nations allowed the Palestinian war refugees to relocate to their territory and kept them in refugee camps. They did not try to assimilate them into their nation. Instead, they used the camps to preach hate and the next war. Those camps soon became breeding camps for hate after years of preaching hate against the state of Israel. That hate grew into stronger hate of the Western powers for supporting the Jews and for some Western-looking leadership in the Arab world.

"King Hussein of Jordan had to fight the Terrorist group called 'Black September' located in his country in 1970 to hold on to power. You might remember that group from the attack on the Israel team at the Olympics. The nations around Israel and the refugee camps were, and are still, a source of a breeding ground for terrorists in many different forms. The most notable is the PLO.

"The history of Egypt during and after World War II is a mixed bag of war and diplomacy. Gamal Abdel Nasser was a supporter of the Nazis during the war. Later he would grab power in a coup and rally the Arab nations against Israel in wars that the Arabs would lose.

"After Nasser's death, Anwar Sadat took power and continued the fight. Then in 1978 saw a complete change; he signed an agreement to work with Israel at Camp David. Three leaders President Jimmy Carter, Menachem Begin, and Anwar Sadat took the step toward cooperation. That agreement made it look like peace was possible in the Middle East.

"That did not happen for extremists in Sadat's military resented this and he was assassinated by his security team and the Army for the simple act of peace. Radicalism was spreading and becoming stronger through the spread of the idea of terrorism. State-sponsored terrorism reached into the Western nations.

"One of these sponsors was Muammar al-Qaddafi of Libya. He took power and funded and provided training areas for various terrorist groups and their campaign of bombings around the world. A bomb at a West Berlin discotheque killed and wounded many American soldiers. In retaliation, President Ronald Reagan set Operation El Dorado Canyon into play with 68 American Air Force and Naval aircraft to strike targets in Libya. Muammar Qadhafi was visibly shaken when 37 people were killed and 93 injured in the raid. Only one American plane was lost killing both men onboard.

"Qaddafi did not get the message and was involved in the downing of the commercial plane over Lockerbie in Great Britain in 1988. After years of investigation, the plot was traced to two Libyan Intelligence operators. The two plotters were placed on trial with Abdel Basset Ali al-Megrahi given life in 2001 and Lamem Khalifa Fhimah was acquitted the same year.

"Arab dictators were building their political and physical power in the world by playing the two sides in the Cold War against each other. The fundamentalists in Islam reacted to the Western culture expanding in their moral lives being threatened by western culture and took steps to cast the modern West as the devil. In Iran, the Iranians revolted and threw Mohammad Reza Shah Pahlavi out of power led by the radical fundamentalist Ayatollah Ruhollah Khomeini.

"The nation was taking a step back into the past away from the modern world using the Americans as an example, when the Shah of Iran came to America for cancer treatment the Iranians occupied the American Embassy and held the male members of the staff hostages for 444 days from 1979 to 1980. The Iranians were in disarray.

"Saddam Hussein in Iraq with his Ba'ath party saw Iran in a weakened state and saw an opportunity to start a war between Iraq and Iran from 1980 to 1988. The United States had stopped supplying Iran with weapons and spare parts that weakened their military force.

"The United States began supplying Iraq with weapons to use against the Iranians that had been armed by the United States. That war was a modern war with Medieval tactics and saw children used as weapons.

"One could say that Arab expression about my brother's enemy is my enemy or something like that. Anytime we go to war in the Middle East we are most likely facing weapons made right here at home.

"When the Soviet Union invaded Afghanistan in 1979 the U.S. sent weapons to the Mujahideen and called them freedom fighter. The term Freedom fighters sounds much better than insurrectionist. Freedom makes a good image for the evening news.

"In Nicaragua, the dictator Somoza was thrown out of power and the communist Sandinista took power. The United States backed the unhappy members of the Somoza Nicaragua Army who began calling themselves the Contra's.

"The President at the time renamed them "Freedom Fighters" to win financial support from Congress for weapons for the fight against the communist leaders in Nicaragua. Later, there was the Iran-Contra Scandal of weapons and drugs nobody in the administration seemed to know about except one Lt. Colonel who admitted he lied to Congress.

"This takes me to drug trafficking through Panama and Manuel Noriega, who worked with the CIA on many operations in Latin America. We removed Noriega from office with an invasion in 1989.

"The American Latin American policy was falling apart. We supported Great Britain in the Falkland Islands war against the Argentina government in 1982. That did not win us any support in Latin America. Then the Island of Grenada turned to the communist leadership, and we invaded the small island with the full might of the American military forces to save American medical students.

"There was also a plan to remove the elected president of Chile Salvador Allende with the help of the CIA and ITT. This was another mark against the American image in Latin America.

"We also made attempts under two administrations to remove Fidel Castro in Cuba before the Bay of Pigs invasion. I have not even started on the Far East and that mess in southeast Asia of Vietnam, Cambodia, and Laos."

"That's a great history lesson C.E., but what is your point?" asked the Chief.

"I guess it is we have stepped off the moral path and allowed evil to slip in between our values and our consciousness," said C.E.

"How do you fight evil, if not by their rules?" asked the Chief.

"The first thing would be not letting evil take control of our actions. We seem to feel today that Niccolò Machiavelli's interpretation that 'the end justifies the means' or the Russian nihilist Sergey Nechayev who said, '…if a goal is morally important enough, any method of getting it is acceptable.' Behaving without a conscious or without laws is to step off the moral path," said C.E.

"At times C.E. one needs to work with evil. Winston Churchill who strongly opposed the Soviet Union took that position to help Stalin during World War II. If I remember right, he said, 'If Hitler invaded Hell, I would make at least a favorable reference to the Devil in the House of Commons' and that was even after Stalin's agreement with Hitler to take half of Poland and then he began a war with Finland," said the Chief.

"You make a good point, Chief Franklin, war and politics make strange bedfellows," said Elaine.

"I did not mean to start a philosophical discussion on the nature of evil or right and wrong. It was just that evil is part of our human nature, and we need to control it and not let it lose with our passion to win at all costs. Because the one side use torture is not a reason for the other side to use it," said C.E.

"Then what is torture? Is it a mental or physical torture or both? Are there many levels of torture?" asked the Chief.

"More good questions. However, it is late. We can discuss this another day," said Elaine.

"You are right it is late. I must say one last thing. When I was in the Marine Corps we had to shave every day in camp and the field. Shaving in the field was not always in the best conditions. When I complained one day to an old sergeant about shaving, his answer to me was that we were shaving to remind ourselves we were still humans and not animals and should act accordingly. This last case I was on tells me that the evil of the Twentieth Century did not stop with the Twenty-first Century" said C.E.

CHAPTER SEVENTY-ONE

George Zechmeyer claimed to have the oldest stamp business in Germany which he opened in 1864 around the city of Nuremberg. He sold stamps that were duplications of stamps and were not intended to deceive. Yet, they are considered some of the earliest philatelic forgeries. There were so many in circulation that there are still many in well-known collections. At one time he sent forgeries to a London dealer and asked for an equal number in return. This action had him placed on the *Philatelical Journal* blacklist. This did not hurt his business for he expanded to a branch in Paris. His packets became known as the 'Zechmeyer Mixture'.

In 1877 he purchased all the remaining Bavarian stamps and stationery after the conversion of the Bavarian currency to the German Imperial currency in 1876. At his death, it was said he earned a well-deserved reputation and a respected memory.

GENUINE   **FORGERY**

The battleline between good and evil runs through the heart of every man.

— Aleksandr Solzhenitsyn

2002 China Office of Mayor Bo

"Where is the nuclear engineer we had in North Korea?" asked Leader He.

"That individual is on his way to the re-education camp in Xinjiang Province with the Uighur criminals and terrorists," said Mayor Bo.

"What orders were given to the camp officials about his treatment?" asked Leader He.

"That he is not to have communication with anyone, not even the guards until he is inside the camp," replied Mayor Bo.

"Why is that?" asked Party member Ying.

"We do not want any connection with the operation in Iran and North Korea to connect us to the dirty bomb episode on the west coast of America. The engineer worked in both places and had a working knowledge of the complete operation. He has no close family members and will just disappear into the camp system," said Mayor Bo.

"Good, now what is happening with our network in the American Universities?" asked Leader He.

"The network is expanding with every student sent to America having a family that can be used to pressure the students to report any information we demand. Our effort to move their industrial production off the American continent is in full swing to our advantage.

"Their middle class is shrinking with the loss of industrial workers. Soon there will be just low-level workers and the elite capitalist and their system will collapse," said party member Ying.

"The Americans are very resourceful and always seem to come out of bad times better than they were before. So, what are you basing this belief of yours on? If I may ask?" said Leader He.

"I have anticipated that question and have asked Professor Zhang to explain the history of republics and their fall," said Mayor Bo.

"You honor me, I am not a historian in the common sense. I study history with anthropology, psychology, and sociology. First what I am saying here today is just theory and not an absolute defendant.

"The world has functioned from the beginning of time and was based around the family unit. That unit to survive joined with other families to form a group. Those groups then formed into tribes and then tribes became a nation.

"The new nation had to control these tribes and that was done by religion and the power of an elite group of individuals. The society was divided into two basic groups: the powerful aristocrats and peasants. That system worked until the Greeks developed the idea of citizenship in their city-states. The idea of citizenship made a person connected to a nation and that implied a duty to the nation over the family and tribe.

"In time, the city of Rome came along and expanded the idea of the citizen in their republic and empire. Laws were written for citizens in civil laws and non-citizens had a system of common laws. But let me move ahead to get to my point faster.

"The Greeks and Romans set into play an intellectual revolution in thought that reshaped the Western world into what is today referred to as the Renaissance and the Age of Enlightenment. These new intellectual ideas of political thinking led to the American Revolution.

"Which brings me back to the idea of the citizen. Republics work when the various groups of tribes are broken up and they become identified as citizens of something larger than the tribe. These new republics will then collapse when the new or the old tribes begin to struggle for power within the new nation. That happened to the republic of Rome which became an Empire and the same happened to other large republics over time. The idea of republics worked only in small nations.

"The American Revolution shifted away from the idea that republics could only work in small nations. James Madison turned that idea upside down in his *Federalist #10*. He said the larger the republic the better. It would be so large that no one faction could ever gain control of the complete political system. Notice, I said factions and not party. The idea of belonging to a political party to these early Americans was abhorrent to the leaders of the American Revolution.

"The recent notion of the Western idea of globalism has begun to put pressure on Western nations with mass migration. African immigrants to England are demanding that African foods be provided in the school system. The Islam immigrants in France have neighborhoods that the French police are reluctant to enter alone. The Germans invited thousands of Turks into their workforce and then resented their presence.

"Massive immigration disrupted the homogenous nature of the nations. The anthropology definition of a Nation is composed of homogeneous people with the same language and customs. Therefore, the United States is a republic and not in the real sense a nation for it is a mixture of nations. The importance and success of the American system was that they developed a strong middle class.

"America is the one country that was able to make citizenship a goal, thanks to the idea of the middle class or as they say the 'common man'. Its history is not always favorable, but it did allow individuals to work their way up the social ladder.

"By 1820 General Andrew Jackson had risen from 12-year-old nobody to the President of that nation. He believed in the common man and pushed the old elite aside for the common man. Just look at those who became national leaders in that nation from low social and economic positions. A few have done it through military success, but many more from within a political party system.

"That system today is in danger for many of the new elite have returned to the idea of tribalism with ethnic identity over citizenship. The Americans have a great ability to self-evaluate their history and that self-evaluation may be the cause of their downfall.

"The power struggle between the tribes and ethnic groups is becoming stronger with the focus in their educational system highlighting the negative American history rather than the positive American values," said Professor Zhang.

"You sound as if you are an admirer of the American capitalists, professor!" said leader He.

"On the contrary, as with Alexis de Tocqueville, I see an institution that is an illusion of good government. Tocqueville said, 'The American Republic will endure until the day Congress discovers that it can bribe the public with public money.' He also, said of the American politics there were men of principle but no party with principles. That 'everyone feels the evil, but no one has the courage or energy enough to seek the cure.' He was speaking of slavery in the new Nation.

"Tocqueville saw the American system with a clear eye. It had advantages and weaknesses, but democracy was not an advantage. The weakness in their expanding rights increased the rule of the mob and servitude. No,

America allows too much freedom that draws away from the progress of the nation," said Professor Zhang.

"I agree with your description of the American professor. Thank you for your analysis," said Leader He.

"Then we agreed to recommend that we continue as we are and let the Americans self-destruct in their ethnic and tribal conflicts, while we continue to build our military and economic power base. We will surpass the Americans shortly," said Mayor Bo.

"Now let us go and have a nice meal," said Leader He.

CHAPTER SEVENTY-TWO

Operation Corn Flakes in 1945 was part of the Allied psychological warfare of the OSS that planned to drop some 320 German mailbags containing over 96,000 letters into the wreckage of mail trains. The idea was that the German public would not read the pamphlets that were being dropped all over Germany and that letters and postcards with stamps would have a better chance of being noticed by the German citizens.

GENUINE　　**PROPAGANDA**

If evil be spoken of you and it be true, correct yourself, if it be a lie, laugh at it.

— Epictetus

2002 AT HOME

"Elaine, it is good to be home. This case was exhausting both mentally and physically. As I said, I had to sign documents that required me never to talk about what happened. I can say there are bad people out there waiting for their chance. Alexander Hamilton said 'Give all the power to the many, they will oppress the few. Give all the power to the few, they will oppress the many.' That can be said of the whole world," said C.E.

"Well, it's over now you can relax, and we can enjoy our time together."

"We can enjoy our time together, but the world out there is a mess," said C.E. as he waved his arm.

"What do you mean?"

"This case has gotten into my head. Is evil a part of our nature just waiting to come out? I am not talking about bad actions. We all make those at different times. I accept that, but evil is something else," said C.E.

"What is the difference between bad and evil and are they not both the same thing?" asked Elaine.

"I do not think so. Bad is an act or repeated acts like a thief wanting something others have. Evil is working all the time trying to divide and conquer for power over others.

"After the American Civil War, the small farmers allied to have collective support from the larger enterprises, like the railroads for one. That Alliance later turned into the Populist political party. It tried to unite the farmers into a solid political block that challenged the controlling Democratic party in the South and West.

"Southern democrats resented the Republican party and Reconstruction laws. They opposed the federal government's rules on the Freedmen with the intimidation of voters and the use of terror. In time the "Mississippi Plan" became the general rule in Southern politics with the slogan 'by the vote and violence if necessary' that was the work of different terrorist groups within the democratic party. Most think it was the KKK, but that was crushed during Reconstruction and only reborn in 1914.

"The Populist party was upsetting this political resurrection of the Old South by having black and white farmers working together. The southern Democratic 'redeemers' found the key to removing the cooperation between the small black farmers and the small white farmers with the program of 'Share Cropping'. It divided the two groups easily by pitting one group off the other by renting the land. The owner of the farmland controlled who held the land it leased. The removal from the land of one group to another group caused resentment between the groups that still exist today. That system worked in dividing the farmers. That turned Populists against each other.

"A good example is Thomas E. Watson. He was a Populist leader in Georgia and advocated for black equality and racial unity in the 1890's. Then by 1904, he did a complete turnaround on blacks and even started attacking the Catholic Church in his publications. He pushed anti-Semitism sentiment in the Leo Frank case and pushed the public into a mob action that ended with the lynched Leo. If Thomas was not a member of these early thugs, he supported the democratic party organizations and Jim Crow laws. I would call that a radical change in attitude.

"By 1890 the Democratic Party had complete control in the lower states and was called the 'Solid South' with a voting bloc that was needed for anyone to win a presidential election. That was done in this country through political influence and intimidation. Just imagine what could and has been done in a nation with total military power," said C.E.

"Don't all nations have military power, and some do take power by force, but not here in America," said Elaine.

"Yes, but what if the population is in agreement with the military to take power?" asked C.E.

"You mean the whole nation?" asked Elaine.

"Yes. Did you ever watch the German film called The *Triumph of the Will* in a history class?" asked C.E.

"No, why?"

"It was a propaganda film done by the Nazi party in the 1930s. There was one section in that film that should have warned the world of what was coming in 1939. The film was filled with mass military units marching and showing off their military might.

"The one part of the film I remember is of Hitler at a stadium filled with the Hitler Youth. He gave a speech and at the end, he drove around the stadium with the 100,000 youth screaming and yelling. Then within a matter of just seconds the whole stadium began to stand at attention saluting and started to sing the same song in unison. Can you imagine that happening in a stadium in this country filled with youth?" asked C.E.

"No,"

"That one scene was a warning to the rest of the world. The Nazis were organized for world conquest."

"You are overthinking this C.E. We have a democratic republic with civilian control over the military."

"The scene is repeated in the present day in Moscow, North Korea, Iran, and China to just list the big players in seeking world power. This mass military display of uniformity in mass. They all reminded me of the scene in *Triumph of the Will*.

"The Chinese have shown they are willing to invade other nations and their re-education camps are just another name for concentration camps. They go back at least to the Cultural Revolution with their youth attacking the old and punishing anything that they did not believe. The Chinese government used the youth then for its advantage.

"Then during the June Fourth movement that gathered at Tiananmen Square after the death of Hu Yaobang the Chinese military and police were ruthless in putting it down. All who watched it on T.V. remembers the 'tank man' with his shopping bags standing in front of all those tanks," said C.E.

"Why all this concern C.E.?" asked Elaine.

"I guess the idea that the country is moving towards a more socialist society. The Nazis were called the National Socialist German Workers Party which represent the German middle class and farmers against the Communist industrial workers' parties. Men walked around the cities with arms in the air in a Nazi salute and other working men paraded in groups with arms in a raised fist salute of communism. If the two groups meet, there is a battle in the street.

"The Nazis and socialists both claimed to be democratic. Yet the only thing they have in common is the word socialism. Everyone talks about equality, Yet each has a different interpretation of the meaning of the word equality. Americans see democracy and equality as a means of extending individual freedom. The socialists on the other hand see equality as for the good of the community," said C.E.

"This country has the U.S. Constitution and the Bill of Rights C.E.

The founding fathers set the government on a solid foundation," said Elaine.

"I am sorry, but the founding fathers knew that three things were important for this new government to work. One was an educated citizenry and the second was a free press with a strong middle class. Our middle class is now shrinking with globalization and the nation's industry moving offshore taking many blue and white-collar jobs. The press is becoming a race for headlines without research. News is not reported, it is discussed with what are called experts and panels.

"The youth today have more distractions than in the past. The new technology and social media platforms influence the public mind. Plato said 'If you do not take an interest in the affairs of your government, then you are doomed to live under the rule of fools.' I hope we are not heading in that direction," said C.E.

"I must say you came home with a philosophical frame of mind. Now let's change the subject. How about taking me to dinner and thinking and talking about other things," said Elaine.

"That is a great idea. Just you and me. I am sorry I just have to clear my head. I feel better now. Thank you for listening."

"C.E. thank you for talking to me. Holding in these thoughts is bad and talking about them brings the thoughts to the light and eases the tension they cause."

"You are so wise and that is why I love you," said C.E.

"C.E. that is the first time you have said that to me and I have loved you since the first day I saw you."

FORGERS

This is a list of some of the best-known individuals in the area of Forgers and fakes.

1.	Jean-Baptiste Phillipe Constant Moens	— 1880's Belgian
2.	George A. Hussey	— 1860's American
3.	James A. Petrie	— 1890's – American
4.	Giovanni Patroni	— 1870's American
5.	Jean De Sperati	— 1880's Italian
6.	Francois Fournier	— 1900 Switzerland
7.	Louis Dumonteuil d'Olivera	— 1890's French
8.	Edward Stanley Gibbons	— 1870's English
9.	Andre Frodel	— 1950's Polish
10.	Adrien Champion	— 1880's Switzerland
11.	James M. Chute	— 1880's American
12.	James A. Croy	— 1980's American
13.	Lucian Smeets	— 1910's Belgian
14.	Peter Winter	— 1850's German
15.	Doctor Bernard Assmus	— 1890's French
16.	Alfred Baguet	— 1920' French
17.	Alfred Benjamin	— 1880's English
18.	Chauncey L. Young	— 1910's American
19.	Albert J. Rabinowitz	— 1940's American
20.	Leon Armanak Hadenkian	— 1930's Egyptian
21.	Robert Haisman	— 1980's America

22. David Cohn   — 1880's German
23. Josef Riesa   — 1860's Mexican
24. Kotaro Wada   — 1890's Japan
25. Joseph Britton   — 1890's American
26. H.E. Macintosh   — 1930's American
27. Robert Steinberg   — 1960's Switzerland
28. Manuel Rivadeneira &   — 1890's Bolivia
     Emilia Rivadeneira de Heguy

29. Kamigata   — 1900' Japan
30. Doctor Hugo Hahn   — 1910's Chile
31. A. Saatjian   — 1900's France
32. James Mc Donald Field   — 1940's American
33. Henry C. Needham   — 1920 American
34. Lieutenant Colonel Charles Mottes   — 1880's Austrian
35. William B. Peters   — 1890's American
36. Enrique Gainsborg   — 1890's Bolivian
37. Oswald Schroeder   — 1890's German
38. Salama   — 1890's English
39. A. Scott   — 1870' English
40. Anton Victor Winter   — 1980's German
41. David Allan Gee   — 1960's Australian
42. H. Kuroiwa   — 1900's Korean
43. H. da Luz   — 1950's Portuguese
44. Charles A. Lyford   — 1870's American
45. John Stewart Lowden   — 1900's English
46. Brewster Cox Kenyon   — 1890's American
47. Raoul Ch. de Thuin   — 1920's Belgian
48. Warren T. Thomson   — 1890's American
49. Placido Ramon de Torres   — 1850's Spanish
50. Harold Treherne   — 1900's English
51. Geza Tarjan   — 1920's Hungarian
52. S. Allan Taylor   — 1860's American
53. Philip Spiro   — 1860's German

54. Hazzonpotas — 1920's Bulgarian
55. Harry C. Heindel — 1960's American
56. Sigmund Friedl — 1870 Austrian
57. John A. Fox — 1960's American
58. Englehardt Fohl — 1890's German
59. Georges Foure & H.G. Schilling — 1890's French
60. R.P.H. Wolle — 1900 American
61. Samuel C. Upham — 1860's American
62. Miguel Segui — 1900 Spain
63. Madame Joseph — 1940's English
64. Michel Zarwski — 1940's French
65. Rainer Blum — 2000's German
66. Clive Feigenbaum — 1960's English
67. Louis-Henri Mercier — 1890's Switzerland
68. Erasmo Oneglia — 1890's Italy
69. Angelo Panelli — 1930's Italy
70. R. Wiering — 1870's Germany
71. George Zechmeyer — 1870's German
72. George K Jeffryes — 1890's German

www.ingramcontent.com/pod-product-compliance
Lightning Source LLC
Chambersburg PA
CBHW021231190726
48289CB00005B/1263